AND TROUBLE FOLLOWED

MICHAEL T. TUSA JR.

AND TROUBLE FOLLOWED
Michael T. Tusa Jr.
Red High Top Press

ISBN: 978-1-7321933-6-9 (paperback)
         978-1-7321933-7-6 (ebook)

In memory of my father.

*One is astonished in the study of history at the recurrence of
the idea that evil must be forgotten, distorted, skimmed over.
The difficulty, of course, with this philosophy is that
history loses its value as an incentive and example; it paints
perfect men and noble nations, but it does not tell the truth.*

—W.E.B. Du Bois, *Black Reconstruction*, 1935.

CHAPTER 1.

"Now what do we do?" Dalton asked, nervously kicking the toe of his boot into the dirt in front of him as the others watched. The four men stood impatiently, in an imperfect circle, freshly changed into their new civilian clothes and standing outside the Taylor Army Barracks in Louisville, Kentucky. The wooden barracks, built in 1864 and named for former President Zachary Taylor, had been an induction center for black Union troops during the war and became barracks for both black and white troops after the war.

Dalton was tall and wiry, taller than the other three, with brown blonde wavy hair that fell to his shoulders and stuck out from under his new cowboy hat. He had an olive complexion, inherited no doubt from his mother who was part Cherokee. There was a hardness in his taut jaw line and a cold distance in his deep set brown eyes, as if he had already witnessed too much, darker things that were forged in life's unexpected fires and hard to forget. He wore a Colt Model 1848 Dragoon holstered low on his right hip and tied down.

The other men standing with him were unarmed. They all moved, hands in their pockets, uncomfortable with the potential emotion of the moment.

"What ya mean?" Emmet, who was called 'Midnight' because of his coal black skin, asked. It was a nickname given to him by older slaves on the plantation when he was a child and it had stuck. Midnight was wearing new dungarees, a new wool shirt, and a Union soldier's Kepi cap. He fidgeted and scratched periodically from the irritation of the rough cloth against his skin. He was muscular and compact, with the beginnings of a beard. He was the most inquisitive and had been the prankster in the group, the one most likely to make a joke in a difficult situation. Perhaps it was a learned characteristic, a moral deflection, he had developed as protective armor during his years growing up as a slave.

"I was a soldier and damn good at it. We all were. Now who will we be with the war long over and our enlistments done?" Dalton explained.

Midnight pursed his lips together and ran his hand over the stubble on his chin. It was a question that they had each been thinking about privately once they heard that Lee had surrendered to Grant in April, 1865 and the war was over. Who are you when you are no longer the soldier you were required to be? What becomes of the survival instincts which were a necessity in war? You are not who you were before the war, impossible to go back to a more innocent time, forget what you have experienced, and be that exact person again. It's uncharted. Each man knew, at least in a general way, that he didn't come out of the war the same man he was when he went in. And now bonds built up between them over the years through the harshness of shared battlefield conditions, their anchors in still evolving self definitions, were about to be broken free and each would go his separate way, without the others as a reference point or to depend upon.

It had taken awhile for them to get mustered out of the Union Army. Their original discharge date was delayed by Lincoln's assassination in '65, days after Lee's surrender, when they each felt the need to re-enlist, and then there was their assigned duty in the South to support the early Reconstruction efforts after the war, the last few months spent in the 3rd Military District. And now, in the latter part of 1868, after many years together, day in and day out, facing every soldierly hardship and enduring incalculable loss, they were about to part company for good.

"I don't know. But for me I'm done with soldiering. I hope I never have to handle a gun again. I think that God has another plan for me. Perhaps it's time that I try to heal some souls instead of being involved in taking them," Harrison replied.

His friends standing next to him, and others in their unit, called him 'Reverend' because of his open spirituality. He felt it was important to be a witness for the Lord and so he was forthright in expressing his beliefs. But those religious beliefs did not stop him from being a good soldier. Over time, during the war, he preferred to doctor to those who were wounded, but he was unafraid of combat, often saying that if the Lord wanted him He could take him at anytime. He had the upright look of a pious man, ramrod straight back, pale white skin, almost Victorian in his bearing, and straight jet black hair. Though prior to the war he may have been inclined to be more dogmatic in his religious beliefs, reflecting an inability to break from his upbringing, he had come to realize in moments of self-reflection and after the carnage he had witnessed, that religious dogmatism about the Lord's wishes was for those living in fear and grasping for certitude as solace. Once he had that realization, and jettisoned what he called the 'inculcated need for certainty,' he felt a childhood heaviness lifted from him and told the others that he felt reborn.

"Me too. Hopes I never has to shoot no one again," Shadrach said.

Shadrach was the shortest of the four men but unquestionably the strongest. He was named after the Hebrew man who survived being thrown into the fire in the Book of Daniel. He was barrel-chested with a granite chiseled chin, and calloused hands. He could outwork, out lift, and outlast any of the others in any physical endeavor, but he was even tempered with a quiet integrity, unless riled by what he perceived as an injustice. And, equally important, in an army where masculinity was prized and where he was often questioned by white officers because he was a former slave, he could fight. He was a natural born fighter, fluid in his movements, with tremendous power in both hands as Dalton, who sparred with him on occasion, learned the hard way. In bare knuckles contests Shadrach, who could seamlessly switch his stance from a dominant right to southpaw, was easily the troop champion winning all of his bouts against his white counterparts. He was a runaway slave who had escaped from the Brentwood plantation in Alabama in January '63 after the Emancipation Proclamation was issued by President Lincoln.

President Lincoln had initially rejected the idea of emancipation. Instead, he supported colonization and remuneration, that is sending former slaves to Liberia, Haiti, or to Central America, and paying slave owners for their loss. But in September, 1862, after the Battle of Antietam which repelled Confederate troops from Union territory, he changed course and gave the Confederate states until January 1, 1863 to end their rebellion. In the carefully worded Proclamation Lincoln wrote that if the Confederate states did not do so he promised to free: "all persons held as slaves within any state, or designated part of a state, [in which] the people …[are]… in rebellion against the United States…." As written it only applied to those states in rebellion and not to the other states, so called

4

border states, where slavery also existed. This oddity in the Proclamation prompted the *London Spectator* to write, critically, that: "The principle is not that a human being cannot own another, but that he cannot own him unless he is loyal to the United States." The Confederacy did not lay down its arms and Lincoln then followed through and issued the Emancipation Proclamation. The Proclamation was a dramatic increase in presidential authority by Lincoln, based on his war powers, and in doing so Lincoln called on the emerging outline of presidential power, still very much in dispute, that had been articulated by Thomas Jefferson and Andrew Jackson.

Jefferson Davis, the president of the Confederacy, called the Proclamation, "the most execrable measure recorded in the history of the guilty man." Disdain for the Proclamation was not, however, limited to the South. The New York Daily News, for example, lamented that, as a result of the Proclamation, "we shall find negroes among us thicker than blackberries." General Brinton McClellan, who had been General in Chief of the Union Army for a little over 4 months, and was also in charge of the Army of the Potomac, strenuously opposed the Proclamation which he saw as changing the war's aim from preserving the Union to one of eliminating slavery, which he did not favor. He privately referred to Lincoln as a "gorilla" and would run unsuccessfully against him for president in 1864 on a platform that would have preserved slavery.

For his part, Shadrach, unaware of the criticism of the Proclamation, had joined the Union Army in 1863, several months after Frederick Douglass' article, *Men of Color, to Arms*, had urged slaves to enlist in it. Douglass, a runaway slave himself, was a tireless recruiter for the Union Army once blacks were allowed to serve and had written powerfully: "Once let the black man get upon his person the brass letters, U.S.; let him get an eagle on his button, and a musket on his shoulder and bullets in his pocket, and there is no power on earth which can deny that he has earned his right to citizenship."

Shadrach heard Douglass' call to arms and felt that enlisting was his moral duty to fight against the evil of slavery, an evil he knew first hand. At the time he fled the Brentwood plantation in Alabama over 435,000 people, or nearly 45% of Alabama's population, were slaves and without rights.

At the start of the Civil War Alabama was one of 5 states that had over 400,000 slaves. The other states with more than 400,000 slaves were South Carolina, Mississippi, Georgia, and Virginia. Virginia had the highest concentration of slaves with 491,000. A total of 18 states, out of the 33 which then existed, had slaves at the start of the war in 1860. All combined there were nearly 4,000,000 slaves spread across those 18 states.

Eventually, along with Shadrach and Midnight, there were over 180,000 black men, more than half of them former slaves, who joined the Union Army after Congress passed legislation, in 1862, which allowed blacks to serve. President Lincoln defended the controversial decision to enlist blacks, in part, by writing: "The slightest knowledge of arithmetic will prove to any man that the rebel armies cannot be destroyed with Democratic strategy. It would sacrifice all the white men of the North to do it."

The War Department then issued General Order 143 in May, 1863 which set up the Bureau of Colored Troops to oversee all aspects of their recruitment and training. Their pay, regardless of rank, was set at $10 per month with a $3 clothing charge, while a white private's pay started at $13 per month. As a result of the disparity the 54th Massachusetts all black Infantry refused to accept their pay for an entire year until they were paid like white troops from Massachusetts. It wasn't until

March, 1865, with continued lobbying by Douglass, Thaddeus Stevens, and others, that Congress approved retroactive pay for all black soldiers to equal what white soldiers had received. Ultimately there were 154 black regiments in the Union Army, of which 140 were infantry, and their contributions helped the Union win the war.

The recruitment of black soldiers, however, was not universally welcomed by all Union generals. General Sherman, for example, issued Special Field Order No. 16 which forbid the enlistment of any black soldiers into his army. For those black regiments that did fight dangerous conditions existed.

The mortality rate for black soldiers in the Union Army was approximately 20% which was significantly higher than that of white soldiers. Indeed an estimated 37,000 black men died fighting for the Union Army. Some were purposely executed or mutilated by Confederate soldiers at the Battle of Olustee, the Battle of Poison Springs, the Battle of the Crater, and at Fort Pillow.

If captured by the Confederacy, black soldiers like Shadrach and Midnight were also at grave risk. Jefferson Davis, the President of the Confederacy, had, in December 1862, decreed that black prisoners of war would either be enslaved or executed, as determined by the government of the southern state in which they were captured. Nevertheless many former slaves and free black men served bravely in the Union Army and Union Navy with 32 of them receiving the recently authorized Congressional Medal of Honor for their actions during the war.

"What about you, Shadrach? Where are you going to go?" Dalton asked.

"I'm gonna go back to Alabama and see if I can find any of my family members," Shadrach replied, absentmindedly mimicking Dalton and kicking at the dirt in front of him.

"You think that's wise? A former slave who ran away and became a

Union soldier going back to the Deep South, back to Alabama?" Dalton asked, as he leaned the palm of his right hand on the top of his pistol.

"Not all Alabama be bad. Lots a Unionists in North Alabama who was against secession. Remember da 1st Alabama Cavalry Regiment? We met 'em. Dey was from North Alabama and was against slavery. Dey fought for da Union," Shadrach said.

"You're talking about 2,000 people in that regiment, out of all the people in Alabama?" Dalton replied, unconvinced.

"That's the regiment that went with General Sherman all the way to Savannah. Before that they were in lots of battles, including Atlanta and Bentonville. Their former Colonel, George Wilson, just got elected to Congress this past summer," Reverend said, reflecting what he had learned.

"Go north wit' me. It be safer," Midnight said.

"I gots to try and find my mother and sisters. Dey might gonna need some help. I'm hopin' Reconstruction troops be still down dere, maybe dat'll help. But I know it's dangerous and dat's why I need to go get dem," Shadrach replied.

Reverend wasn't surprised by Shadrach's desire to return to Alabama and help. If there was a man with a bigger heart and a more developed sense of fair play, despite what he had endured as a slave, or perhaps because of it, he often said that he hadn't met him.

"But you don't even know if they are still there," Dalton said, concerned for Shadrach and trying to argue him out of going.

"Dat's why I need to go, to find dem wherever dey might be," Shadrach replied, aware of his friend's concern but resolute in what he needed to do.

"Alabama, like most of the Confederacy, is still under martial law, I think. Alabama was in the 3rd Military District, you guys know that, that's who we were under these last few years while we were stationed in Georgia," Reverend said.

"Dat's true. General Meade was in charge, but he left. Maybe things be a'right where Shadrach's goin'," Midnight said hopefully.

"You know there ain't troops everywhere, especially in small towns, and Alabama did its best to delay and obstruct Reconstruction," Dalton said to Shadrach.

"Dey say da 3rd was da most violent district durin' our time dere," Midnight said.

"I gots to go," Shadrach replied.

"Just thinking more on this, but the military rule is probably over there, or lessened. Alabama ratified the 14th Amendment and a new state constitution. It was finally readmitted to the Union this past summer. I just remembered that. You might ought to check on that," Reverend said.

"Dat's right. Da new governor, Smith I think his name be, couldn't take office 'til Alabama ratified da 14th," Midnight said.

"Just 'cause they finally ratified the 14th Amendment don't mean nothing. Mississippi, Texas, and Virginia are still refusing to ratify and haven't been admitted back into the Union. The South has been passing those Black Codes since the war ended to contradict the 14th and restrict the rights of former slaves and freedmen," Dalton replied.

The Black Codes were laws passed by southern states in the immediate aftermath of the Civil War while Reconstruction was being overseen with leniency by President Johnson. Some were eventually declared invalid by Union Military governors but remained enforced locally. Similar Black Codes also existed in some northern states. The laws were part of a pattern designed to restrict the freedom of blacks and to replace the Slave Codes that had existed prior to the war.

A principal aspect of the Black Codes was the expansive new laws on vagrancy and other minor and vaguely defined offenses like "mischief," "neglecting a job," "swearing," "insulting gestures," or "handling money carelessly," allowing for the indiscriminate arrest and conviction of freedmen and former slaves for alleged violations. The Mississippi Black Code, for example, required "all free negroes and mulattoes over the age of eighteen" to carry written proof of employment or they were "deemed vagrants." The Black Codes also set curfews for all blacks and were precursors to the Jim Crow laws passed in the South toward the latter part of the century. As Edmund Rhett Jr., editor of the *Charleston Mercury*, wrote at the time, the Black Codes were designed to keep blacks "as near to the condition of slavery as possible, and as far from the condition of the white man as practicable."

"Don't know nothin' 'bout dem Black Codes," Shadrach said.

"Republicans took over Reconstruction from President Johnson last year, in '67. I think things are getting much more difficult for the South. I know the Union Army is now back in charge in many places," Reverend said.

"That's because the South won't comply and give freed slaves their rights," Dalton replied, looking directly at Shadrach who stood by quietly without responding.

In fact, once Reconstruction was controlled by the Republican Congress, through the Reconstruction Acts, federal troops remained stationed in various parts of the South, mainly large cities, until the compromise arising out of the contested 1876 presidential election. In a contest ripe with fraud in Louisiana, Florida, and South Carolina, southern Democrats acceded to Republican Rutherford B. Hayes being named president instead of Democrat Samuel J. Tilden who had won the popular vote. In exchange Republicans and Hayes agreed to withdraw all federal troops from the areas where they remained in the South, ending Reconstruction. Blacks, who had supported the Republicans and had been enfranchised as a result, were left without protection by the federal government and eventually were disenfranchised by the Democrats who again took over in the southern states.

"Reverend, ya think dat people's hearts in da South be changed 'bout slavery now dat da war be ova for awhile?" Midnight asked.

"Midnight, the Lord can work miracles. Let's pray this will be one. We surely need it," Reverend replied. Reverend was not naive, but while some men lost their faith by what they witnessed on battlefields he remained hopeful and his faith remained strong.

"Reverend, a miracle would have been to end slavery before the war ever started, before we were all shooting at each other. You saw when we were stationed in the South these past few years that those people are still angry and their small minded anger is going to be visited on those freed slaves. Trust me," Dalton opined.

"You are too pessimistic. We need to be more hopeful for the future. We should stop holding up force of arms for admiration in this country, turn 'swords into plowshares,' and hold up Christian ethics, loving our neighbor and our enemy, instead," Reverend chided Dalton, in a variation of a conversation that they had had many times before.

"I don't know 'bout no big miracles like you talkin' 'bout but I'm glad to have been friends wit' each of ya and maybe in dis time here, wit' slavery and da war and all da upset, dat's my own miracle," Midnight said. Reverend smiled, touched by the sentiment.

"It's a good start to the change that's needed. A small start can always lead to big changes," Reverend said optimistically.

"I like dat idea. We is each a miracle for da others," Shadrach replied, warming to Midnight's comment and smiling like Reverend as he spoke. The men fell silent for a moment as a group of white soldiers walked past.

"Dalton, where are you going to go?" Reverend then asked.

Dalton had been the highest ranking member of the group. He had not attended any military schools to learn how to lead men in combat but rose through the ranks because he was a fearless soldier, deadly accurate with either a pistol or rifle, and as an admirer of Thaddeus Stevens, treated all the men in his squad equal. Indeed, despite the North's espoused position on slavery, they were aware of only one other Union Army unit, the 103rd Pennsylvania Volunteer Infantry, that was integrated with black and white soldiers. There was also the unique First Indian Home Guard, composed of white, black, and Indian soldiers, that battled Confederate troops in 1862. But in their infantry unit the only two black soldiers were Midnight and Shadrach. Most units, infantry, artillery, and cavalry, with black soldiers were led, with varying degrees of reluctance, by white officers. In other units blacks did the laboring work, building fortifications and earthworks, freeing white soldiers to fight. These four had been in one of the few integrated infantry units that had evolved as such due to a high number of desertions and battle-field casualties from a whites only unit at the start of the war to one with Midnight and Shadrach.

Although it is estimated that over 2.1 million men were mobilized for the Union Army during the war, 25% of whom were foreign born, desertions among the ranks were high. In 1861 and 1862 there were an in excess of 180,000 desertions. In the following two years, 1863-1864, the desertions totaled approximately another 150,000.

"I've got no family. My maw and paw passed when I was a kid. So there is no place that's really home. The army and you guys was the clos-est thing I ever had to family. Might go to the Montana territory and the mountains. I don't know," Dalton replied, sounding purposely unsure.

"I know what ya thinkin' 'bout doin'," Midnight said, looking hard at his friend.

"What's that?" Dalton asked, knowing that Midnight knew him well as only two soldiers who fought together, and shared each other's most intimate thoughts, know one another.

"Ya gonna rent dat dere gun out," Midnight replied, pointing at the dragoon on Dalton's hip.

The other men knew that was a possibility with Dalton. He was that good and fast with a gun. While they were all bothered to some extent by the killing they had witnessed and participated in during the war, Dalton seemed to have been impervious to it. He never showed any outward signs that it bothered him even when he was briefly assigned duty as a sniper. He was always the first one in front of a charge and he seemed, if it wasn't too impolite to say, to enjoy the emotional high of the battlefield where men tested themselves. In moments of doubt during battles the other men relied on his apparent courage to reassure and bolster themselves.

"Don't do that Dalton, please. You are bound to meet a bad end that way," Reverend cautioned.

Reverend, unlike Dalton, had often taken the time to pray for those killed on both sides after a battle. He insisted on tending to the wounded Confederate soldiers who were captured and prayed over those that were dying. When some Union soldiers in their unit first saw Reverend tending to a wounded Confederate soldier and objected, Dalton came to his defense, stepping in front of the soldiers and without saying a word, by the strength of his battlefield reputation, convincing them to walk away and let Reverend minister as he saw fit.

"We'll see," Dalton replied to avoid the issue.

"Guys, you know I'm going to go home to Boston to officially start my ministry. And I'd be mighty proud to have each of you come with me and be part of my congregation. That includes you Dalton," Reverend volunteered. This was something Reverend had spoken about more frequently as the time for their discharge approached.

"Reverend, I'll be an absentee member of your church. I ain't never had much use for the Lord in my life. Folks dying, soldiers slaughtered, people owning slaves, my folks taken from me early, don't seem like much to recommend Him, but I know it means a lot to you and I admire that in you. Always have," Dalton said.

"Was ya parents ever religious?" Midnight asked Dalton.

"My maw was a bit. I seem to recall she prayed a lot when things were tough and we had a bad crop. The old man never opened the good book, though he did throw it at me once when I was misbehaving," Dalton said, recalling a history that he had not dwelled on too deeply.

"Well, Reverend, ya can count Midnight and I as proud members of ya congregation, though da white folks in it might not be too happy 'bout dat," Shadrach said, laughing slightly and expressing what they all knew.

"You three are my first members, absentee or otherwise. And my church will welcome all, no matter skin color 'cause we are all equal in the eyes of the Lord," Reverend said.

"What's gonna be da name of da church?" Midnight asked. Dalton and Shadrach both looked at Reverend.

"I been thinking about that for awhile. Remember when we were outside Petersburg in late '64?" Reverend asked.

"Damn bloody battle. Really a siege. Lost more than a few men there when we joined up with General Burnside's 9th," Dalton replied, recalling the series of battles around Petersburg that lasted nearly 9 months, from June, 1864 to April, 1865.

"Dat's where ya was wounded," Midnight recalled to Dalton, who nodded in agreement before they all returned their gaze to Reverend.

Petersburg, Virginia, was approximately 24 miles from Richmond. At

14

the beginning of the Civil War it was the second largest city in Virginia. It had a large population of free blacks that lived on Pocahontas Island on the north shore of the Appomattox River, though about 89% of blacks in Virginia at the outset of the war were slaves. Many blacks in Petersburg were required to work on behalf of the Confederacy to fortify the town during the war. It was a critical supply route for the Confederacy and the junction spot for 5 different rail lines. The Union battle for Petersburg, in which both General Lee and General Grant were involved, was part of Grant's Overland campaign and was the predicate to capturing Richmond and forcing General Lee to come out and defend it. Grant had moved the campaign to Petersburg after Lee had bloodied Grant's troops badly at the Battle of Cold Harbor. Casualties at Petersburg were extremely heavy, with Union losses exceeding 40,000. When General Lee finally gave up defending both Petersburg and Richmond it led directly to his surrender at Appomattox in April '65.

"The morning after one of the battles ended I got up early. Most everyone was still asleep in trenches, exhausted, except for the night watch. And I walked around thinking, trying to make sense of all I had seen in that battle. As the sun was just about to come up I saw each of you sleeping next to one another and I knelt down by you and said a prayer. Now for some reason it seemed to me that old sun stood still for awhile, peeking over the horizon like it didn't want to rise that morning, like it didn't want to come up over the horizon and see what had been done, all the killing," Reverend said, pausing for a moment to regain his balance from the gravity of the memory. "I remember standing there looking and waiting and waiting, wondering what was happening and if it was going to be the great Judgment Day. And then, as if it finally made up its mind, it burst up all of a sudden like one of them Morning Glory flowers just blooming. Something about that sign right then told me that we were all going to make it. I hung on to the sight of that morning sun every day thereafter," Reverend said, choking up a bit over the last few words. The others looked away from him at the ground so as not to embarrass Reverend. Each one, as all soldiers do, had different memories, often bordering on the mystical, that had sustained them during the difficulty of combat.

"So what ya gonna call da church?" Shadrach asked again, redirecting the emotion they each felt by Reverend's story. Reverend cleared his throat.

"I think I'm going to call it the Morning Glory Church," Reverend said.

"I like dat name, Reverend. Keeps a good thought wit' ya when ya thinks of it," Shadrach said supportively.

"Me too," Midnight replied. Silence passed between them as they struggled with the weight of saying goodbye and, perhaps, never seeing each other again.

"Well, how is we all goin' to keep in touch?" Midnight finally asked.

It was a simple enough question, but an unusual request considering the times. War had brought the four of them together, two white men, Dalton and Reverend, and two black men, Midnight and Shadrach. Four men who would otherwise never have met but were now bound to each other in ways each would be hard pressed to explain to others. But despite emancipation and the end of slavery, true friendships across racial lines were rare and, even in the supposed enlightened North, discouraged. These four, however, had grown close over their experiences in battle, where bullets knew no skin color and where, at least for them, camaraderie held character more important than prejudice. Dalton, a sergeant, had saved Midnight and Shadrach at one time or another from the open hostility of white officers, or from attempts to have them only do the menial or laboring work in the unit. He knew both were fine soldiers and evinced an unusual color blindness to his friendships, despite periodic warnings about his close association with both from his white superior officers. And Midnight had raced across an open field and braved cannon and musket fire to pull Dalton to safety behind a fallen tree after he was wounded in the leg and knocked down at Petersburg. Reverend had patched him up while Midnight and Shadrach stood near them both and returned fire against the advancing Confederate troops. Dalton still walked with a slight limp, but he always credited Midnight with saving his life.

"Let's all keep in touch through da Reverend," Shadrach then said, "since he da only one knows for sure where he gonna be."

"Yes, send any letters or telegrams to me in care of the Hymels, my future in laws, in Boston and let me know where I can reach each of you, once you settle somewhere, and I'll let each of you know where the others are," Reverend replied.

"I ain't much for writing, but I'll try," Dalton said. The men fell quiet again.

"I'd like to say a brief blessing before we depart," Reverend then said.

Reverend, Shadrach, and Midnight bowed their heads. Dalton held his hands in front of him and looked at his three friends.

"As the good book says, 'A friend loves at all times, and a brother is born for adversity.' To each of you, my brothers, may God bless and keep you safe in your travels," Reverend prayed. With nothing else left to say, but much still left unsaid that might never be said, they said their goodbyes, mounted their horses and headed in different directions for their long journeys ahead.

CHAPTER 2.

Dalton had used some of his final army pay to buy his travel supplies, which included beef jerky, coffee, flour, salt, sugar, and bullets for his Colt Dragoon revolver. He also bought a tan duster, a new black leather California Slim Jim gunbelt for his dragoon, and a Springfield rifle, scabbard, and ammunition. He pulled his new 'Boss of the Plains' cowboy hat down low against the rising sun and headed his horse, a fine paint 16 hands high which the army had given him, in a westerly direction, unsure of exactly where he would end up but looking forward to some time alone on the trail to decompress and think about his future. There was a part of him, a wounded childhood dream that had never left him, that had always wanted to disappear into the mountains in the Montana territory where he heard a man could get lost and not see another human being for weeks or months at a time. But there was another part of him, perhaps driven by ego, that wanted to make a reputation with his gun, to continue in some sense to be a soldier.

He knew that there was talk of some possible range wars out West over grazing and water rights between ranchers and free grazers, as well as some disputes in the Midwest between miners and mine owners. Maybe he could latch on somewhere using his gun and get paid for it. It was dangerous but he really didn't have any other skills besides soldiering and his proficiency with a gun. He couldn't see being a cowhand or working long periods on a trail drive. And he felt too restless to try and settle down for good somewhere and homestead. Besides, he was alone. He didn't mind being alone, though there was always that difficult link back to his childhood after his parents died when he had led a hard scrabbled existence in and out of trouble for several years. The army had given him structure and a purpose. He would have stayed in the army and re-enlisted again, perhaps made it a career, but when he inquired about it he learned that it meant going out West to fight Indians.

There had been a lull in the ongoing Indian wars during the Civil War. The Confederacy had quickly signed treaties with the Choctaw and Chickasaw tribes shortly after the war began. Some of these tribes, including the Cherokee and Chickasaw, had African slaves. In fact, the Cherokees had nearly 4,000 slaves at the start of the Civil War. Perhaps hoping to gain something in return, and sharing the South's disdain of the federal government, there were Indian regiments that fought on behalf of the Confederacy. These included members of the Choctaw, Cherokee, Chickasaw, Catawba, Creek, Osage, and Seminole tribes. It's estimated that nearly 29,000 Native Americans fought in the Civil War, including in such battles as Second Manassas and Antietam. Several chiefs and former chiefs of these tribes, including Cherokee leader Stand Waite, were even named officers in the Confederate Army. Other Native Americans, though in much smaller numbers, served in the Union Army including Lieutenant Colonel Ely S. Parker, of the Seneca tribe, who served as an adjunct to General Grant and wrote the articles of surrender which Robert E. Lee signed.

In February, 1868, after his duties related to the war were over, General Sheridan began his campaign against the Indians. Sheridan referred to it as his "Total War" strategy. Dalton knew that the methods that Sherman and the other Union generals would use to fight the Indians included, among other things, killing off the herds of buffalo, destroying all Indian villages and any stored food supplies, in an attempt to subjugate and starve the Indians into giving up. It was a governmental policy with which Dalton disagreed. So now, with his army service over, he was free to choose what he would do next.

Reverend started on his way back to Boston on his horse, a bay mare that he bought from the army. He had grown up in Boston, the son of an itinerant Protestant minister who was often absent from home while spreading the Word. His parents were there, along with his fiancé, Theresa, who had waited for his return throughout the war and his deployment during Reconstruction. His parents, in particular his father, opposed his enlistment in the Union Army and thought he was wasting his life on what his father preached was immoral, as all wars were immoral. It wasn't that his father favored slavery, or was sympathetic to the South, but rather that he had a streak of Quaker pacifism in his Protestantism. As a result, after some harsh words upon his departure, there was a strain to the relationship between Reverend and his parents that still lingered and there had been little communication between them during the war or thereafter. Reverend was disappointed in himself for some of the unkind things he had said to his father before leaving, things he could not easily reel back in, but he remained resolute in his convictions and time had not made him question his decision to enlist, though he was appalled at the killing and destruction which he had witnessed.

Theresa had written him often during the war. He had kept all of her letters and had re-read them at various times to raise his spirits around early morning campfires, or when he couldn't sleep at night. On occasion he read the letters, or parts, to Shadrach, Midnight, and Dalton. The first thing he was going to do when he got to Boston was set a date for their wedding. There couldn't be much of a honeymoon, he didn't have the money for that, but he knew Theresa would not mind. She was the perfect compliment and would be the perfect minister's wife, more interested in serving the Lord than in pursuing material interests which, he thought, consumed too many women. And then he needed to turn his attention to finding a location to start his own ministry, a ministry he told himself that would be different from the hand to mouth existence his father had struggled to maintain for years. He wasn't sure what locations were available, or how he would pay for it, but he trusted in the Lord to show him the way. And he thought that once he returned to Boston he would reach out again to his parents to try to heal the breach between them.

Midnight rode with Reverend out of Kentucky. The army at the Taylor Barracks had reluctantly given him and Shadrach older mounts that were being retired from service, but only after Dalton had intervened on their behalf with the Quartermaster to get them. Midnight had decided to head north, maybe into Ohio. His family, including his mother and siblings, was scattered. He knew that many of his kin had, like him, taken the Underground Railroad before or during the war, but he had lost track of them, his three brothers and one sister. At least one, a brother, had been captured before the war and returned to his master by bounty hunters seeking rewards under the most recent version of the Fugitive Slave Act.

The Fugitive Slave Act of 1793 was built upon the language contained in the Fugitive Slave Clause, Article IV, Section 2, of the United States Constitution. It is speculated that without the Fugitive Slave Clause, and the possibility of recovering runaway slaves from the Northwest territories and northern states where slavery was prohibited, the South would not have joined the Union. The 1793 Act sought to clarify the Clause and was originally passed in response to the fears raised by the ongoing slave rebellion in Haiti which was being led by Toussaint L'Ouverture. The Act was later revised again in 1850 to address northern attempts to get around it and as part of a larger compromise between the slave states and non-slave states. In proposing the 1850 version Senator James Mason of Virginia said that it was necessary "to provide a more effectual execution" of the Fugitive Slave Clause "of the Constitution of the United States." The 1850 version, for the first time, paid people for capturing and returning runaway slaves and required law enforcement to arrest former slaves. It was finally repealed by Congress, during the war, in 1864.

The 1850 bill was so controversial that 21 of the 60 US senators absented themselves for the vote. It, nevertheless, passed but the senators' behavior prompted the New York Herald to write that the Act "has turned Whigs and Democrats into fugitives and it is difficult to tell whether they or the runaway slaves run fastest from the law."

Abolitionists referred to the law as the "Bloodhound Law," as bounty hunters tended to use dogs to track fleeing slaves. Because of the mandatory nature of the law, requiring the return of former slaves and the imposition of fines on those who did not comply, abolitionists, between 1850 and 1860, ferried many former slaves to Canada, in particular to Southern Ontario. At the time Canada was part of the British Empire which had outlawed slavery and it's judiciary had held, in the *Somerset* case, that once on free soil a slave was forever free. It is estimated that 30,000 slaves fled to Canada with the help of abolitionists and the Underground Railroad. Harriet Tubman, herself an escaped slave, was one of many individuals who helped transport slaves across the border.

Midnight never knew his father, but recalled a story his mother told that his father's people were from the BaKongo tribe and were taken by ship from around Angola. His mother's family was from Nigeria. She was sold once he turned 10 years old as Louisiana, uniquely, did not allow the sale of slave mothers with children under 10 years of age. After she was sold he was left alone on the plantation to raise himself. Unlike Shadrach he felt no need to look for his family members. He wasn't sure why he felt no connection, no attachment, to family; maybe those attachments were forever broken in his mind when he watched through a child's eyes as his mother, reaching for him and calling out his name, was standing tearfully on the auction block in New Orleans at the annual 4th of July celebration and slave auction.

The war, however, was a demarcation for him. He felt that it was a complete break from his past, part of his transformation from slave to soldier to free man. But he didn't fear the change. He had always looked after himself, even when he was working the cotton fields as a youngster, and was still comfortable doing so. He knew that he would need to find a job and wasn't sure how easy that would be. It was a new world, a "startin' ova world" he would say, but he was naturally optimistic.

Shadrach set out on his own for Alabama, in particular to a small town called Elyton, which was named after the Elyton Land Company. He had fled Alabama as a slave, but was returning after being a Union soldier. He wasn't sure if it made a difference.

Elyton was where his mother and both sisters were enslaved on the Walker plantation when he ran away from the Brentwood plantation, some miles away. He had not seen or heard of his mother and sisters in the years since he had run away. He knew there were dangers for him in going back to the South after the war, especially in Alabama, but felt a man was incomplete without his family to ground him and support him.

It was only through family, and immersion in all aspects of family life and obligations, that he believed a man could grow into full manhood. Besides, he thought it necessary to reverse the forceful break-up of families that he had too often witnessed as a slave. He loved his mother and sisters and often during the difficult times of the war recalled his early childhood fondly, despite their hardships, when they were all together. The war only intensified his desire to reunite with them and protect them in this new and uncertain world. Once he found them his plan was to leave Alabama, head west of the Mississippi River, and try to find some land that they could homestead. The 1862 Homestead Act promised 160 acres to those 21 or older, including former slaves, who had not fought against the United States in the war.

The awarding of land to veterans or others by the government under the Homestead Act was not unique. Congress had, at various times, issued Bounty Land Warrants, free land, to veterans for their military service in the American Revolution, the War of 1812, and after the Mexican War. Likewise states had passed similar laws. Virginia granted 300 acres and a slave to veterans of the Revolutionary War. In Georgia, for example, Jefferson Davis' father, Samuel, received 200 acres in Wilkes County for his service in the Revolutionary War.

Shadrach planned to make his claim under the 1862 Homestead Act. He dreamed of eventually marrying and starting a family, and he wanted a big family with lots of children, to be raised free alongside his mother and sisters. He hoped that his dreams of doing so had not been orphaned by the war and Reconstruction.

CHAPTER 3.

Dalton set a hard pace of about 30-35 miles a day on his trek west. He enjoyed days and nights of complete solitude and not seeing anyone. He would camp alone at night next to a fire, under a blanket of stars, and think about his life so far, the unplanned trajectory from living on the street as a youngster to his service in the army. On occasion, for no reason that he could yet identify, he would wake at night shaking, in a cold sweat, from a realistic nightmare of a prior infantry battle with all the cannon smoke and the confusion of men screaming and bullets flying. Death and dying, despite what he had seen, had always been a bland abstraction to him during the war. The dreams were a recent phenomenon and, by invading his nights and forcing its way into his consciousness, made the prospect of dying and the deaths he had witnessed seem more real. He didn't know what to make of it, so he did his best to stuff it back down and hoped it wouldn't continue.

About 125 miles from Louisville, Kentucky, as the sun was setting, he met a group of miners that were coming from Union City, Missouri. Union City was an unincorporated area and the short lived result of the towns of Carthage and Murphysburg being combined. It would eventually be renamed Joplin in 1873.

Missouri, as Dalton knew, was a border state that remained in the Union during the war. It had, however, achieved statehood in 1821 as part of the Missouri Compromise and was admitted as a slave state while Maine was admitted as a free state. When the war started it had nearly 115,000 slaves and an intrastate war erupted between supporters of the Union and so called 'Copperheads' who supported the Confederacy. Over 100,000 soldiers for the Union Army came from Missouri while approximately 30,000 served in opposition with the Confederate Army. Factionalism continued in the state throughout the war and early on it even split into two governments, one Union and one Confederate. The factionalism was so severe that martial law was briefly declared in August 1861 by Union General John C. Fremont and by the end of 1861 the Union Army was largely in charge of the state with the Confederate 'government' living in exile.

As part of that intrastate war Missouri was home to an irregular Confederate guerilla group called the "Bushwhackers" or "Quantrill's Raiders." The group raided Union military posts and small towns. It also attacked individuals and families in Missouri and Kansas. Jessie James and his brother Frank were part of the group. After the war the James-Younger Gang arose out of the remnants of the Bushwhackers.

The miners invited Dalton to camp with them one night outside of the small town of Evansville. They were a loud rough group drinking moonshine, watered down bourbon, and telling ribald stories about saloon girls most of the night. But they offered Dalton some beans, some coffee, some biscuits, and a spot to sleep around their campfire. They said that they had left Union City, Missouri, because it had become too lawless. Several had families that they were headed back home to see, others were going to look for work elsewhere. Dalton listened attentively as they talked about the lead and zinc mines where they had worked, the long hours, the physicality of the job, and the inherent dangers of working in the mine shafts.

"We lost men every few weeks to cave-ins. I barely made it out last time it happened," one of them said.

The men told Dalton that they had worked in the mines at Ash Grove, Pierson Creek, and Phelps, towns in and around Union City. But they kept returning in their conversations to the lawlessness of Union City and the growing conflict between the miners and the mine owners.

"The sheriff came over from Carthage when the towns were combined. He was appointed by the mayor and is trying to keep order, but it's just too much for one man," the one called Road Dog said.

"Especially after that young deputy he had was killed. Nice kid just trying to do his job. But that was the final straw for me. I knew it was time to leave," Bones, another miner, replied.

"Does the sheriff have any other deputies?" Dalton asked.

"No. No one wants that job. Trust me. That'd be suicide, especially with that new gun man in town," Bones said.

"A professional?" Dalton asked.

"Yeah, hired by the mine owners to intimidate us," Bones said.

"Well, he scared me into leaving," another man quickly volunteered.

"I was in the war. I can handle a gun, but I can't compete with a professional gun man," Road Dog said, as an aside.

"The miners need to do something or the mine owners are just going to pick them off one at a time," Bones said.

"How far is Union City from here?" Dalton asked, when the miners went silent.

"We've been on the road about two weeks. But we have wagons

slowing us down. And we lost a few days due to bad weather. Just depends on how fast you want to travel," Bones said.

"You thinking about going?" Road Dog asked.

"Might go check it out," Dalton replied, with a practiced look of disinterest.

"I see you have a fancy new holster that's tied down. You a gun man?" Bones asked Dalton, as the other men crowded in closer and listened.

"Not really," Dalton replied.

"I'm guessing you ain't got that gun and holster just for show," Bones said, before taking a long swig of liquid courage on a moonshine jug and then passing it to the next man.

"Just got out of the army. Trying to figure out where to go and what to do next," Dalton replied, a bit evasive.

"Well, I don't recommend it, but if you go, stop by and see Sheriff Wilson. He's a good man. Just outnumbered," Road Dog replied.

"If I go I'll do that," Dalton said. The conversation then returned briefly to the men's families, stories of their youth, and more stories of the mines told and retold.

After some time passed Dalton got up and went and checked on his horse. A wolf howled in the far off distance and Dalton paused to listen to the lonesome howl; a single wolf, sounding forlorn in the night air, looking for a mate or, perhaps, for a pack to join. A minute later, and further away, Dalton heard another wolf answer and he smiled.

Dalton came back to where the men were gathered and spread out his bedroll. The talk around the campfire was slowly dying down as some men fell asleep. He unbuckled his gunbelt, put it next to him and laid down with his saddle as a pillow. He pulled his blanket up over him, to ward against the crisp air, and tilted his hat over his eyes and hoped for an uninterrupted night of sleep.

Dalton woke up at the first glimmer of light the next morning and moved around the camp site silently, an innate ability learned as a scavenging youngster and honed further during his days as a Union sniper. The campfire was smoldering as men snored and squirmed in the cold twilight of the dawn. He felt a surge of excitement as he rolled up his canvas bedroll, put on his gunbelt, and saddled his horse, while the miners slept off the effects of the moonshine. He had decided. He would head to Union City, Missouri, and get there as quickly as he could.

CHAPTER 4.

Reverend and Midnight rode together into Columbus, Ohio, in the late afternoon looking to spend the night. They had been riding for seven days. There was a light snow falling. Columbus was a big town compared to those that they had previously passed through and they hoped to find lodging and to get a good meal. The state government was quartered there along with an active railroad depot. It had been a major staging area for Union troops during the war as well as a training camp for Ohio volunteers.

Like several states that had been aligned with the Union, Ohio was politically divided with southern Ohio sympathetic to the Confederacy. Nevertheless, the state was a major supplier of soldiers and officers to the Union Army, including General Ulysses S. Grant, General Philip Sheridan, and General William Sherman.

Columbus, Ohio, included Camp Chase, one of two sites in the state which were used as prisons for captured Confederate soldiers. The camp had closed after the war, but at the time Midnight and Reverend arrived, the remains of over 2,200 Confederate soldiers, formerly prisoners, were buried in a two acre plot named Camp Chase Cemetery. Many in the prison had died of smallpox and other diseases because of the overcrowding. Rumors had begun circulating around town shortly after the end of the war about a female ghost dressed in all gray and carrying a white handkerchief, called the 'Lady in Gray,' who it was alleged haunted the cemetery looking for her lost Confederate love.

In addition to numerous men in business suits, working for the government and moving hurriedly down the streets, there were lots of men, some missing an arm or leg, still wearing the dark blue shell jackets of the Union troops from Ohio. Other former Union soldiers in town wore their gray or red wool overshirts.

"It's hard to tell that the war is over here," Reverend said to Midnight, as they rode slowly down the city's main street side by side on their horses.

"Looks like dey is all former Union soldiers. Some look like da uniforms dat was in Ohio's 23rd Regiment dat fought wit' us," Midnight replied, to Reverend's agreement.

The 23rd Regiment was active from 1861 to 1865 and fought in numerous engagements, including the Battle of Antietam. Rutherford B. Hayes, future president, was a member of the 23rd Regiment, Ohio Volunteer Infantry. Despite having no prior military experience he started in the Regiment as a Major, was promoted to Colonel, and eventually to Brigadier General. He was elected to Congress for the first time while he was still serving in the Union Army. William McKinley, the future 25th president, also served in the Regiment achieving the rank of Major.

Men milling around on the sides of the street, many former soldiers, with nothing to do and nowhere to go, looked with jaundiced eyes at Reverend and Midnight. It was still an unusual sight, a white man and a black man riding freely together. Midnight exchanged glances with several of those standing on the street, a soldier's practice borne of habit to detect possible danger, while Reverend, appearing unconcerned, just looked straight ahead. Reverend saw a small crowd gathered near the end of the street in front of an ornate building that looked like a church and haltered his horse in that direction with Midnight riding at his side.

"What's going on here?" Reverend, who remained seated on his horse, asked a man who was standing at the back of the crowd watching the end of the ceremony.

"It's the dedication of St. Mary's. A new Catholic church. The ground breaking was in '66 but thankfully there's enough completed now to open it for weekly mass," the man said politely.

"Let's see if someone can direct us to a lodging," Reverend said to Midnight.

Reverend and Midnight dismounted and then tethered their horses to a nearby hitching post. Reverend made his way to the front of the crowd with Midnight following close behind and approached the man who had been conducting the dedication ceremony.

"Excuse me, sir. My name is Harrison and this is my friend Emmet. We are former Union soldiers traveling together and I was wondering if you could recommend a boarding house for the night. Nothing fancy," Reverend said. The man, who was wearing vestment robes, looked at Reverend and then at Midnight.

"Not sure there is any place that will let you both bed down together. Things are segregated here, at least as to housing. My name is Bishop Rosecrans. I'm the new bishop. Relatively new anyway. Come with me," the bishop said, somewhat formally. The bishop then immediately walked toward a red haired priest with a ruddy and freckled complexion who was speaking to several people as Reverend and Midnight followed.

"Father, excuse me. This is…I'm sorry, gentlemen, I have forgotten your names," Bishop Rosecrans said, turning to Reverend and Midnight. Reverend and Midnight introduced themselves to the priest and both shook his hand.

"These men are looking for a place to spend the night. Is there any place you could recommend?" Bishop Rosecrans said to the priest.

"Nothin' fancy," Midnight echoed.

"I see. I can't recommend any place in town for both of you if you want to stay together. Actually, I'm not sure if there are many rooms available anywhere right now. The town is pretty crowded as you probably noticed. But I tell you what, you are both welcome to stay the night with me in my new quarters here at the rear of the church. I'm Father Sprecht," he said.

"If you are sure we would not be imposing," Reverend said.

"Not at all. I'd appreciate the company and the church always welcomes travelers. You two will be our first," Father Sprecht replied.

"Father, that's very generous. It looks like we are interrupting you from talking to other folks. Sorry about that. How about we go get a bite to eat and come back and talk to you when we are finished. Can you suggest a place?" Reverend asked Father Sprecht.

"That's Fine. Try Rosie's Cafe just up the street for something to eat. Food is good and there won't be any trouble there," Father Sprecht replied, pointing down the street in the direction of the cafe.

The men shook hands again and Reverend and Midnight departed. They walked past several other diners and bars until they came to a glass storefront with a painted wooden sign overhead that read "Rosie's Cafe: All are Welcome." Midnight stood and looked up trying to mouth the words on the sign. Reverend read the words out loud.

"Let's see if dat be true," Midnight said to Reverend, as they entered the crowded cafe.

CHAPTER 5.

Dalton heard yelling, mad crazy yelling, indecipherable orders being barked out that were hard for him to understand above the constant din of musket and carbine fire. He ran past a screaming Confederate soldier who was bleeding from the stump of his knee, where the bottom portion of his leg should have been. Blood drained quickly out the soldier's leg. He stood and watched as the soldier turned a deadly pale and gasped his last breath. Another Confederate soldier charged toward Dalton with his bayonet out in front. Dalton pulled his revolver and shot him in the head at close range. Blood splattered on Dalton's uniform as the soldier fell at his feet. He saw Shadrach out of the corner of his eye, rifle in hand, moving forward on his right, along with other members of their unit. Somewhere in the smoke to his left, but out of his line of sight, were Midnight and Reverend. Dalton moved ahead and shot another rebel soldier who fell across his path.

And then his right leg, near his hip, suddenly felt like it was on fire. He fell. He tried to get up but could not stand and fell back down. A gray coat approached and stood above to bayonet him and then the soldier's face contorted in pain. The soldier dropped his rifle falling face forward next to him from the bayonet Midnight had driven into his back.

"Can ya stand?" he heard Midnight say, above the sound of gunfire, as Midnight shouldered his rifle and reached out his hand.

A bugle sounded in the distance but Dalton couldn't tell whose it was, whether Confederate or Union, whether for a charge or retreat. Men were running in all directions, the organized chaos and cacophony of battle. Dalton managed to get up on one leg by grabbing Midnight's hand and pulling himself up. His right leg seemed useless. Confederate cannon fire hit the ground nearby knocking both of them down from the percussive blast and partially covering them with the dirt and grass that it kicked up.

Midnight jumped back up, helped Dalton to his feet, and then led him toward a downed oak tree. Dalton slipped over and behind the tree trunk, falling hard on his right shoulder and found Shadrach and Reverend there. He finally looked down and saw his leg wound and the blood soaking through his pants below the hip. Reverend took out his knife and ripped Dalton's pants' leg open where he had been hit and began to try to clean the wound. He felt a jolt from the sting of some liquid, probably bourbon, that Reverend had poured on the wound. Reverend shoved a stick in his mouth to bite down on, which he spit out, and then, after pouring the same liquid on his knife, Reverend tried to dig out the shrapnel which was visible.

"Dey is comin' back at us," he heard Shadrach say, as Shadrach and Midnight began firing to pin down the advancing Confederate soldiers, while other Union soldiers seemed to be in retreat, leaving the four of them on an island alone. Dalton tried to sit up so he could help return fire but Reverend pushed him back down.

"Stay still. I need to clean this out and stop the bleeding or you might bleed to death," Reverend said. Dalton reluctantly complied.

"Gettin' close," Midnight yelled out. Shadrach was reloading as Midnight then stood up, exposing himself, and directed fire at specific Confederate soldiers leading the advance.

"I'm out," Midnight yelled, sitting down to reload his rifle and revolver.

Shadrach then stood to continue firing. A cannon ball whizzed by overhead toward the Confederate troops. A bugle sounded and Union soldiers leading a charge rushed past the four of them. Midnight and Shadrach then left the refuge of the fallen tree to advance with the other Union soldiers while Reverend tended to Dalton.

And then Dalton woke up. He sat up quickly, startled by what he had just relived. It was another dream, another nightmare. He was breathing heavy, his heart beating hard and unnatural against his chest. He wiped his face with his hand and realized that he was sweating, despite the cold weather. He breathed out and watched the cloud of his breath crystallize and then gradually dissipate. His awareness of the present came back to him slowly, in bruised uncertainty, as the edges of the battlefield nightmare receded. He stared blankly into the orange glow of the last embers of the fire which he was sleeping next to, alone on his way to Union City. His senses were heightened as he anxiously waited for his heartbeat to slow, for his mind to regain its focus on the here and now and for his breathing to return to normal. He stood up and instinctively grabbed his gunbelt and put it on. He remained awake, restless, the rest of the night, pacing and adding wood to the fire, worried that if he fell back asleep the nightmare would return.

In the morning, at daybreak, there was a chattering of small birds that took flight from nearby trees disturbed by the saddling of his horse. He watched with envy as they took flight together.

CHAPTER 6.

Shadrach took his time traveling south toward Alabama. Although he didn't admit it to his friends he was nervous about returning, unprotected, to an area where he had experienced so much harm. The further south he went the more anxious he became by what he saw.

When he arrived in Chattanooga he saw the lingering effects of the war and of the recent historic flood. As he rode through town he also saw numerous former Confederate soldiers, some on makeshift crutches, loitering about in their tattered Army of Tennessee uniforms with bitter eyes that stared at him, a free black man, in puzzlement and contempt. There were still some Union soldiers in town but Tennessee, which had been readmitted to the Union in July 1866 after ratifying the 14th Amendment, had been excluded from the Reconstruction Acts and, therefore, had not been part of any of the Military Districts, districts set up by the Republican Congress over most of the South.

The people in Chattanooga kept their distance from him, as if trying to avoid something they felt was contagious. It looked to Shadrach like a powder keg with a fuse that had not yet been lit, but with many people waiting for just the right moment when someone would ignite it. There was a hollowed look in the faces of the few people he met. They had experienced a deep unexpected loss that they were grieving, did not yet understand, and, as a result, were still denying.

They had lost the war. Tennessee had declared its secession from the Union in June 1861, only after the war had begun, and then in 1867, two years after the war's end, nature had inflicted a further insult, or perhaps a cleansing of sorts, with a four day rainstorm of biblical proportions that flooded the entire town of Chattanooga. As a result the nearby Tennessee River, the largest tributary of the Ohio River, had crested 58 feet above its normal level. The town had 4-8 feet of water throughout it for several days once the rains stopped. The actual death toll from the flooding remained unknown.

Shadrach left Chattanooga and made his way to Chickamauga, the location of the 1863 battle. It was not a battle in which he had fought but he knew of it, had heard soldiers talk about the bloody fight and the high losses suffered by the Union.

Although it was considered a Confederate victory by the Army of Tennessee, which was led by General Braxton Bragg, over the Army of the Cumberland, led by General William Rosencrans, both sides had suffered significant casualties. The Union dead was over 1,600, with another 9,700 wounded and almost 5,000 captured or missing. The Confederates had over 2,300 killed and over 14,000 wounded.

Shadrach was drawn to the site and he walked the grounds, walked past others who also wandered the grounds in cauterized disbelief. He sat awhile alone at the North Chickamauga creek which flowed into the Tennessee River. Then he walked to Horseshoe Ridge, which ran east to west with high peaks and low valleys, lingering and lost in the sorting out of his own emerging memories of the battles he had fought in during the war, the grim poetry of men in war, things he had not previously had time to dwell upon. Here many men had died. He hoped it was a sacrifice that would change things for the better, but he wasn't sure. He decided to walk back and spend the night camped out along the creek, to honor in a simple way by his presence and his silent reflection, those who had fallen here.

After Chattanooga and Chickamauga, and what he saw there in the faces that stared suspiciously at him, Shadrach decided to avoid staying in towns at night when he traveled, feeling that it was safer to stay away and still feeling, despite his freedom, that he was an outsider in the South and that he didn't belong. He preferred to camp outside of the towns by himself in forested areas where he could hear any approaching trouble.

On occasion, on the outskirts of a town, he would stumble onto a bullet riddled and bloated body of a black man hanging from a tree. Some of those who had been hung had parts of their bodies cut off while others had also been set on fire. It repulsed him and only served to heighten his sense of danger.

He met groups of former slaves in the countryside who had huddled together in their disorientation. While the white folks in town had been distant, the former slaves in the countryside were frightened and confused. Freedom was a nice word but the former slaves knew intuitively what some of their white northern supporters did not, that the evil behind slavery, the mindset that blacks were inferior and mere property, would not just disappear.

Slave masters and plantation owners, deprived of the economic engine of slavery, did not suddenly become friends and neighbors, willing to lend a helping hand, to their former slaves. The Black Codes were just the beginning. There was going to be a reckoning for the financial and perceived cultural loss that the South had suffered and somehow the former slaves instinctively knew that, whatever its shape, whatever name it was given to hide its true intent, they would bear the weight of that reckoning. So they lived an apprehensive existence trying to start their lives anew while waiting for the next hammer blow, which they knew was coming, to fall and trying to be sure that they did nothing to precipitate it. This was not freedom Shadrach thought as he listened to their muddled tales of survival. The institution of slavery may have been gone but they were still being beaten down and deformed by the indoctrinated fear, the broken chord of their families, and the pained memory of the overseer's whip.

Shadrach was treated royally by the former slaves that he met, a sullen people wanting in some way to share momentarily in his sense of freedom while being unsure of their own. They wanted to hear his stories about running away, about the war, about his soldiering, and about what he thought the Union victory and the changing Reconstruction would mean for them. They looked to him for reassurance, to know if the old spirituals about 'a great day a coming' might be true after all and asked about the towns he had seen and if it was true that things were better in the North. When he mentioned that he had served in an integrated army unit they were doubtful. When he told them about his close friendship with Reverend and Dalton, some of the former slaves treated this as a humorous myth too far-fetched to be believed.

Shadrach told them he was headed to Elyton to try to find his family members. One older former slave, a mechanic, told him that he had been lent to the Walker plantation in Elyton to pay off a debt his master owed to Mr. Walker. He seemed to recall meeting Shadrach's mother during the month he had worked there. But he said that was maybe five or six years ago. He didn't know if she was still there.

And they were inquisitive, wanting to know about the wider world, the world that they had long been excluded from.

"Is it true dat dere is a new law says in da government dat we is all citizens now?" one of them asked.

"Sure is," Shadrach replied.

"We was property but now we is citizens?" the person asked.

"Dat's right," Shadrach answered.

"And dere ain't no mo' slavery?" another questioned.

"Not s 'pose to be," Shadrach said.

"How can dat be?" one asked.

"Dey say da war changed da governments and dere relations some kinda way. Da Union one, dat is called da federal one in Washington, gonna now be stronger, mo' involved ova da state ones 'bout da t'ings dat da states can do," Shadrach replied.

"What dat mean?" someone asked.

"Federal gonna increase its role. Passed dem constitutional amendments, dat new Civil Rights law, t'ing's da states now has to comply wit' for us to be free," Shadrach explained.

The Civil Rights Act of 1866 provided that all male persons born in the United States, "without distinction of race or color, or previous condition of slavery or involuntary servitude," were now citizens. President Johnson vetoed the legislation claiming that "no such system as that contemplated by the details of this bill has ever been proposed or adopted." Congress overrode his veto. It was the first time the Federal government preempted the states on what constituted citizenship. In particular, it was done to make it clear that slaves were now citizens and not chattel.

In light of legal concerns raised by many about the constitutionality of the Civil Rights Act, and to be certain that citizenship changes could not be challenged in the future, the 14th Amendment which confirmed citizenship for former slaves was proposed and then later ratified in July

1868. Many southern politicians objected to the Civil Rights Act and the 14th Amendment as examples of improper federal interference and overreach into traditional state issues.

"Heard a white man say dat freedom be when da government just leaves da people alone. Dat sound good but if government do dat we black folks ain't gonna have no protection, no kinda freedom," someone offered.

"Maybe we just need it for a little bit, a little while, da protection dat is, so dat folks can get on dere feet," Shadrach replied.

"And dey say we might can vote?" another asked.

"Da Reconstruction Act requires it of da former Confederacy. Some of our folks voted last year, in '67. I heard tell dat freedmen was even elected to da governments in Louisiana and Florida," Shadrach replied.

In fact during the Reconstruction period 16 black men served in Congress and it is estimated that approximately 600 were elected to serve in state legislatures in the former Confederacy. However, in 1868, unbeknownst to Shadrach, the Georgia state legislature, in its ongoing battle with Reconstruction, voted to expel all elected black members (2 senators and 25 representatives) from government. At the same time northern states like Minnesota, Michigan, and Ohio, between 1865 and 1868, rejected proposed laws which would have granted suffrage to black men.

"Mr. Frederick Douglass say dat 'slavery is not abolished until da black man has da vote.' I was told 'bout dat," another man said, proudly quoting Douglass to the approval of others.

"Ain't no way dey gonna let us vote. Ya'll gonna see," another man interjected.

"But I be told it's happenin' now," Shadrach said.

"Dey gonna figure somehow to take it away," the man replied.

"Well, I'm votin'. As citizens it be a duty," someone said.

"Yeah, and dey gonna kill ya if ya try," the man said.

"Da Union League is helpin' people learn 'bout dere rights, includin' 'bout da votin'," Shadrach said.

Union Leagues were originally created in the North in 1861 to support the war effort and the policies of President Lincoln. The Leagues sprung up throughout the South after the war, and were tied to the Republican Party, to educate former slaves about their rights and obligations as new citizens and to teach them about the system of government. In Alabama, Macon County in particular, a former slave named James Alston was the principal organizer and, like all Union Leagues, he helped register freedmen to vote once they were able to do so.

The 15th Amendment granting black men the right to vote was passed by Congress in February, 1869 after General Grant became president. It was ratified a year later in February 1870 and thereby overrode any state laws which barred black men from voting. After Reconstruction ended, however, southern Democrats used various means, violent, semi-legal, and/or fraudulent, to intimidate and suppress blacks from voting. By the late 1800s southern states had passed various forms of legislation, including poll taxes and literacy tests, that for all intents and purposes disenfranchised black voters. In defending such actions the *Charlotte Observer* wrote that it represented, "the struggle of the white people of North Carolina to rid themselves of the dangers of the rule of Negroes and the lower class of whites." These practices, restricting voting rights, were upheld by the Supreme Court in the 1898 case of *Williams v. Mississippi*. It wasn't until the Voting Rights Act of 1965, passed during President Lyndon Johnson's administration, that the federal government passed legislation to address the disenfranchisement of black citizens by the states.

"Is we better off goin' somewhere in da North? What ya think?" several of the former slaves asked.

"Maybe so. Time gonna tell if dis here Reconstruction t'ing gonna make a difference. I'm hopin' so," Shadrach replied.

"We heard dat dere be a slave lady, like us, a Miss Truth, speakin' to white folks up North 'bout us slaves being equal and free. Is dat true?" one of the women asked, while the rest listened attentively.

"Yeah, her name be Sojourner Truth. Dat's da name she took afta bein' a slave herse'f. She speaks to lots of white folks as part of her ministry. She was an abolitionist and even met wit' President Lincoln at da White House. Don't know much more den dat," Shadrach said. He had learned of her during the war from Reverend who had heard her speak at an abolitionist meeting. The former slaves found this astonishing that a former slave could speak, would be allowed to speak freely, to groups of white folks and had met former President Lincoln.

"Jesus mustta touched her soul," the woman said.

In fact Miss Truth was born into slavery in New York as Isabella Baumfree. She later escaped with her infant daughter and took the name Sojourner Truth when she felt that God had called her to minister and testify. She also successfully sued her former master to get her son out of slavery and returned to her. Once Congress voted to allow blacks to enlist she actively helped recruit former slaves and freedmen for the Union Army.

"Is we gonna git land? Heard tell 'bout we gittin' 40 acres from da government?" a man asked.

"Dey said dat was so and Freedmen's Bureau was doin' it. Even General Sherman give some land 'long da coast for us slaves, but den President Johnson said no and stopped it," Shadrach replied.

General Sherman had issued Special Field Order No. 15 on January

16, 1865, while President Lincoln was alive, which was designed to provide approximately 400,000 acres of land along the Georgia-South Carolina coast, in 40 acre plots along with a mule, to freedmen, hence the origin of the old saying of '40 acres and a mule.' This resulted in thousands of freedmen being provided land. Property used to support the South's rebellion had also been confiscated under the First Confiscation Act of 1861, during Lincoln's administration. Both attempts were short lived, however, as President Johnson essentially revoked Sherman's order. President Johnson, who had been a slave owner and a strong advocate of state's rights, but an equally strong opponent of secession, also undermined the enforcement of the Confiscation Act.

"Well wit' out property how we s 'pose to be free?" one asked. Shadrach didn't have an answer.

The freed slaves wanted to own property because inherent in the American idea of freedom at that time, which, despite their tortured distance from it, they had imbibed, was the notion that freedom was founded on economic independence. And economic independence, as they had witnessed, required property ownership. Without property ownership they knew from experience that they could be subjugated or made subservient by others who had it, but with it they had the possibility of economic success and could refute the false stigma of their inferiority.

In May, 1865, a month after Lincoln's assassination, Johnson began to reverse property confiscation policies and laid the groundwork for undermining Reconstruction, as envisioned by Congress, when he issued his "Proclamation of Amnesty and Reconstruction." The Proclamation granted to "all persons who have directly or indirectly participated in the existing rebellion, except as hereafter excepted, amnesty and pardon, *with restoration of all rights of property*, except as to slaves...." The only condition to obtaining this amnesty was the taking of a loyalty oath to defend the United States Constitution and the United States. For those specifically excluded under the terms of the Proclamation, like Confederate officers and officials, they could still apply to Johnson directly for a pardon. By the latter part of 1867 Johnson had issued over 13,500 individual pardons, including to former Confederate governmental officials like Alexander Stephens, Confederate Vice President, and John Reagan, Confederate Postmaster General, much to the growing dismay of Republicans in Congress. In December, 1868, immediately prior to leaving office, Johnson issued a general amnesty which pardoned all persons, including former Confederate President Jefferson Davis, who had been part of the South's rebellion.

Immediately after his Amnesty Proclamation Johnson also began to unilaterally appoint governors in Alabama, Georgia, South Carolina, Mississippi, Florida, and Texas. In Alabama he appointed Lewis E. Parsons as provisional governor. Parsons was well known as opposing the right of blacks to vote. In South Carolina he appointed Benjamin F. Perry, a former judge in the Confederacy. These actions, taken together with his Amnesty Proclamation and his issuing of pardons, led directly to Congress passing four different Reconstruction Acts between February 1867 and March 1868 and taking over Reconstruction from the president. Johnson vetoed the first three Reconstruction Acts but each of his vetoes were overridden. He simply ignored the fourth Act.

In response to Johnson's ongoing actions to undermine Reconstruction, Charles Sumner expressed the sentiments of many of his Republican colleagues when he wrote that: "The suffering at the South is great, through the misconduct of the president. His course has kept the rebel spirit alive, and depressed the loyal, white and black."

"Heard 'bout President Johnson be impeached. What do dat mean?" one of the former slaves asked.

"Yeah, dey tried to remove him but didn't have 'nuff votes. Don't matter as General Grant be da next president. He be runnin' on da sayin' of 'Let us have Peace,'" Shadrach replied.

The House of Representatives had in fact voted 126 to 47 to impeach Johnson. The impeachment vote in the Senate occurred on May 16, 1868. Johnson was found not guilty on any of the 11 Articles of Impeachment, including Article 10 which said he had brought contempt on Congress, when seven Republicans broke rank and voted to acquit him. Allegations of bribery to get him to vote against impeachment followed at least one Republican senator, Edmund Ross of Kansas.

Grant won the November 1868 election with 214 out of 294 electoral college votes and 58% of the popular vote. Three states, Virginia, Texas, and Mississippi, did not cast votes in the election because they had not yet met the conditions to be restored to the Union. Johnson, who had grown to dislike Grant and who seems to have never forgotten an insult, real or imagined, refused to participate in Grant's inauguration.

"I neva did like dat President Johnson," one of them said.

"He neva like us neither. My ol' massa used to repeat sometin' Johnson say 'bout us, dat we was 'splay-footed, bandy-shanked, hump-backed, thick-lipped, flat-nosed and wooley headed.' I heard dat too many a time to forgets it," an older man recited, shaking his head wearily.

Indeed Johnson's views on race and slavery were consistent with his southern roots. He routinely opposed abolitionists in his public speeches and in a speech while a congressman described blacks as "an inferior type of man" and "inferior to the white man in point of intellect." In 1859 he had even gone so far as to claim that the portion of the Declaration of Independence, which declared all men to be equal, did not apply to blacks. Ultimately, in late 1863, he publicly embraced Lincoln's emancipation of slaves, though he still made it clear that he favored a "white man's government." When the 14th Amendment was proposed, guaranteeing citizenship to blacks, he actively lobbied against it which led to the resignation of three of his cabinet members.

There were many rumors, heard through the grapevine telegraph, that the men wanted to pass on to Shadrach, to warn him, including that local sheriffs in Alabama, upset with the Confederacy's loss of the war and the end of slavery, were using the Black Codes to routinely arrest former slaves and force them to work on the plantations, railroads, sawmills, or in the mines. The former slaves didn't know anything first hand but had heard it being passed on by other former slaves who had spent a night or two with them before heading north.

"Dey gonna have to do sometin' 'cause we was da onliest workers," a man said, by way of explanation.

"It be a confusin' time for us but also for dem dat was massas. We was all harnessed together like two plow mules but now we is separate. Got to each pull on our own," one of them said.

"Ya wrong. We was da onliest mules," another insisted.

"We free now. Dey can't make us work for nobody we don't wants to work for," Shadrach replied to their stories.

"Yeah, dey wants us to sign dem labor contracts, but I don't trust 'em. It be just like slavery, but wit' a contract," a man said in response.

"Do ya know how we can gets some work?" another asked.

"Freedmen's Bureau is s 'pose to be helpin' wit' dat. Best check wit' it," Shadrach said.

Shadrach spent an extra day at the camp of the former slaves at their insistence. They shared their meager meals with him and tried to convince him not to go to Elyton and, instead, to lead them further north. He politely declined, and the next day he said goodbye and got back on his horse and headed to Elyton to try to find his mother and sisters.

CHAPTER 7.

On the last leg of his journey to Union City Dalton met other miners and families in covered wagons that had recently left town. Each told a different story but with a common thread, it was getting too dangerous to stay. Shootings were random and it wasn't safe for women and children. Still, despite the warnings, Dalton kept riding towards Union City, riding towards the possibility of trouble.

Sometimes when he was in the saddle for long hours his mind wandered and he asked himself why. Why was he running towards possible danger? He didn't have any stock answers, but the one that kept rolling around until it gained slight purchase was the innate need to continue to prove himself and to seek approval from others as a result. Maybe that's why he was always in front during battlefield charges. And though he wasn't sure he wondered if that bravado concealed something else, a feeling of self doubt about having been left alone in the world, without family. When that thought crossed his mind he would think about his deceased parents and then he would think about Reverend, Midnight, and Shadrach. He might have to accept that it was as close as he would ever get to having a family again.

It was an early evening after many long windy days in the saddle and cold snowy nights around campfires when Dalton finally arrived in Union City. He passed the train station, several saloons, heard piano playing in one and what sounded like a barroom brawl in another. He saw men, who were intoxicated, walking and stumbling in the street and drunks laying in alleys. The sound of gunfire echoed every few minutes as several men were celebrating their inebriation by firing their guns into the air.

At some point he reached the middle of town and saw the jail and the sheriff's office. He rode up, dismounted, and tied his horse off. He pulled his Springfield rifle out of the scabbard on his saddle and holding it in one hand stepped onto the wooden walkway in front of the sheriff's office. There was light coming through the window in the office so he opened the door without knocking and stepped inside. He found the sheriff, a tall lean man in his late 40s with a neatly trimmed beard, a full head of salt and pepper hair, sitting behind his desk and pointing an 1860 Army Model Colt revolver at him.

"What's your business here? Be damn quick about it," the sheriff said.

"Are you Sheriff Wilson?" Dalton asked. If the gun being pointed at him bothered him Dalton did not show it and took a step toward the sheriff.

"Yes, who are you?"

"Name is Dalton Bonnett. I understand you may need a deputy." The sheriff looked at Dalton, sizing him up, but kept the gun on him.

"What makes you think I need a deputy?"

"I heard from some miners I passed on the way to town that the last one got killed and thought you might need some help. I got out of the

Union Army a few weeks ago and I'm looking for a job." The sheriff put the gun back in his holster and then stood up.

"Have you been a deputy before?" Sheriff Wilson asked.

"No. Just a soldier in the Union Army. A sergeant," Dalton said.

"How long were you in the army?" Sheriff Wilson asked.

"Too long. Saw combat and then stayed on for awhile, eventually in Georgia under the military district with Reconstruction," Dalton replied.

"Any good with a gun?" Sheriff Wilson asked.

"Not too bad. Was a sniper on occasion," Dalton replied.

"I can't be too careful," Sheriff Wilson said, having decided that Dalton was not a threat, as he extended his hand. Dalton set the Springfield rifle down leaning it against a chair and shook the sheriff's hand. Both men sat down and Sheriff Wilson began detailing the duties he expected to be performed by his deputy as Dalton listened. He then turned his attention to the problems he faced in town.

"It's pretty wild here at night. I came over from Carthage where I was the sheriff," Sheriff Wilson said, matter of fact.

"I've heard it's rough. Are they organized in any way? The folks causing the trouble," Dalton asked.

The sheriff explained that there was constant conflict between the mine owners, who had hired gunmen, and the miners. The miners had the advantage in numbers but they were outgunned by the paid gunmen that the mine owners brought in on occasion and he was caught in the middle. The miners also fought among themselves. It was hard for him to know whom to trust, Sheriff Wilson said.

"It's a bit of a hornet's nest and I've been unable to find another deputy," Sheriff Wilson concluded.

"What happened to your prior deputy?" Dalton asked, telling the sheriff that he had been told about the deputy's death, but he didn't know the details. The sheriff leaned back in his chair before answering.

"Good young fellow. Would have developed into a fine sheriff one day. Left behind a wife and baby. I don't know who shot him and no one's talking to me about it. He was shot in the back shortly after this new gun, Batiste, came to town. Batiste went to work for a fellow named Hawkins, the biggest mine owner, who heads up the mine owners association," Sheriff Wilson said. "Hawkins had another gun man working for him, before Batiste, who left town in a hurry when he learned that I discovered a wanted poster on him. Anyway the miners say this Batiste was a sniper in the Confederacy. Don't know if that's true or not, but he's cold blooded. My deputy had confronted him and drew on him while Batiste was pistol whipping one of the miners. Made Batiste back off. My guess is Batiste killed him in retaliation but I can't prove it and Batiste denies it. I'm not looking forward to the day I have to tangle with him. Not sure I could beat him on the draw straight up," Sheriff Wilson concluded.

"You think that will happen?" Dalton asked.

"It's inevitable. Hawkins wants the law out of the way, or to replace me with his own man, so he can force the miners to do as he wants. He wasn't happy when I came over from Carthage at the mayor's request, so he got the town council to hem me in by limiting me to one deputy, claiming the town can't afford more," Sheriff Wilson said.

"Sounds like this fellow Hawkins is a problem," Dalton said.

"Yeah. But he generally keeps his hands clean. He lets others do the dirty work for him," Sheriff Wilson replied.

"But he's hiring gunfighters," Dalton said.

"That's not illegal in itself. He always claims it's for his personal protection or to protect his property. If they aren't wanted by the law there is not much I can do about it," the sheriff said.

They talked for awhile longer. Dalton told Sheriff Wilson about his time in the army and the different places where he saw battle.

"You sure you want to do this? It's dangerous here," Sheriff Wilson asked.

"I think so. Nothing better to do," Dalton replied, seemingly nonchalant about the possible dangers.

"You might regret it. In fact I know you will. Killing never leaves a man if he has a conscience. I expect you know that already from the war. Anyway, pay is $15 a month, little sleep, and all the grief you can handle," Sheriff Wilson said smiling.

"Just what I need. I'm used to little sleep and lots of grief," Dalton replied, also smiling.

Sheriff Wilson eventually swore Dalton in as his deputy and gave him a badge and told him the stable where he could put his horse up. There was a cot for him at the jail to sleep on which Sheriff Wilson offered. Dalton left the office, went to his horse and gathered the rest of his gear and brought it into the jail.

Dalton then walked his horse down to Scully's stables. On the way back to the jail he noticed a bearded man standing in the dim light of an overhead oil lamp on the wooden walkway directly across from the sheriff's office. He was wearing a shiny black leather vest and black leather chaps with an ivory handled set of Colts in his holster, an outfit Dalton thought was purposely designed to draw attention to him. When he walked back into the jail he described the man to Sheriff Wilson.

"That would be Batiste. Be careful. He probably saw you leave my office or saw your badge and now knows you are here working for me. He's been shadowing me the last week or so. My guess is you'll be seeing more of him," Sheriff Wilson said.

"And he'll be seeing more of me," Dalton replied. The sheriff laughed at Dalton's response.

"I'll say one thing for you. You don't lack in confidence," Sheriff Wilson said.

CHAPTER 8.

Reverend and Midnight walked into Rosie's Cafe. They were tired, cold, and hungry. The restaurant was loud with conversation and the sound of utensils hitting metal plates, but there was a small two person table near the back wall that was empty. A young caramel colored waitress named Emmalene waved them over to sit before removing some empty plates and then wiping the table down. Reverend noticed that as they approached the table Midnight looked Emmalene over trying, unsuccessfully, not to be obvious. As they sat down she quickly told them what was on the limited menu and then took their order of steak, potatoes, and coffee.

When she walked away from their table Midnight's gaze followed her and then fell upon a very large man with whom she was speaking that was seated on a bar stool in the corner of the restaurant. He had a double barrel shotgun laying across his lap. Once Emmalene stepped away from the man Midnight noticed that the man continually scanned the crowded room looking at the patrons. Reverend saw the man as well.

"Dat's a really big man. Might be da biggest dat I is ever seen," Midnight said, with a mix of fear and admiration in his voice.

"Probably there to make sure there's no trouble," Reverend replied, continuing to look in the same direction.

"He'll get none from me. I'm not sure even Shadrach could whup him," Midnight said, with a slight laugh. Reverend leaned his head back and closed his eyes for a minute or so.

"I am really tired. Those last few miles just about wore me out," Reverend said.

"We been a long time in da saddle for old foot soldiers like us and be runnin' on what dey call dat adrenaline so long wit' da army dat we got to learn how to slow down. Might be a tirin' t'ing at first," Midnight replied. Reverend agreed.

At some point Emmalene brought their meals and coffee. Midnight asked her about the big man with the shotgun.

"That is Mr. Alfrick. He and his wife are the owners. They are both German. We have lots of German immigrants living in town now. Many are exiles from the failed 1848 European revolutions. They are referred to as the Forty Eighters," Emmalene said, in an almost too perfect grammar, but with a disinterested tone.

"Revolution? What dat be 'bout?" Midnight asked, missing the subtle note of hurried disapproval in Emmalene's voice.

"There was political upheaval in various European nations that year, including in the states of the German Confederation, but ultimately it was not successful, at least not politically. So many people fled and came to the United States," Emmalene recited, as Midnight looked at her and Reverend listened.

"I was just a young boy back den, in dat '48. At least I think so. Like most us former slaves I don't rightly know my birth date," Midnight said.

"I was born that year. I believe it is important to understand history so that you can understand people. Too many people ignore history at their peril," Emmalene replied.

"Dat Mr. Alfrick fella, how tall is he? Wonder what he weigh?" Midnight said, trying to redirect and continue his conversation with Emmalene.

"I'm certain that I would not know. You must realize that it would be very impolite to ask such questions of him," she replied, in a clear rebuke of Midnight.

"Emmalene, has there been a fire in town recently? I smelled lots of smoke as we rode into town," Reverend asked.

"Yes. Unfortunately the Asylum, the one for Central Ohio, burned down several days ago. They are not sure of the cause of the fire and are still trying to find places for the displaced people," Emmalene replied, more formally.

"Were any former soldiers there?" Reverend asked.

"I don't know the exact numbers but there were some former soldiers, both Union and Confederate, that were housed there. People, I assume, that never properly recovered from their experiences in the war," Emmalene said.

"We was both in da war. Union side," Midnight proudly said, pointing at himself and then at Reverend, and again trying to engage Emmalene.

"Well, give you a big gold star," Emmalene said, and then she walked off to check on another table.

"Man, she has got some attitude toward you," Reverend said.

"Asylum? What dat?" Midnight asked, ignoring Emmalene's remark.

"Probably folks that are crazy or gone mad to get them off the street and maybe get them some help. Hard to know how to cure such an injury of the mind like that. It ain't like putting a poultice on an open wound," Reverend replied.

"Guess dere be former soldiers like dat. We saw some in da war go crazy. Remember dat youngsta, Private Judice? Couldn't get him to stop screamin' at Petersburg. I guess we is all affected by da war in some way or anutta. It's kinda cold out. Hope dat dey has enough places for such folks to stay out da weather," Midnight said.

"There is so much need in this world," Reverend quietly lamented.

A few minutes later Emmalene returned to their table to refill the coffee in their cups. Midnight thought it best not to say anything else to Emmalene.

Reverend and Midnight engaged in some further small talk, finished their meal, paid their bill, and then left. It was dark and a light snow was falling when they stepped outside. They retrieved their horses and walked the horses to a nearby stable, paid the stable man, unloaded their gear and unsaddled their horses.

"Dey been run pretty hard dese last few days. Prob'ly need a good salt lick, some oats, and rub dem down," Midnight told the stable man. Reverend and Midnight then went back to the church to find Father Sprecht. He showed them to his room which had two single beds, a bookshelf filled with books, a desk and two chairs.

"I'm afraid one of you will have to sleep on the floor between the beds," Father Sprecht said, apologetically.

"Not a problem. We've been sleeping on the ground for years in the army. We just appreciate the hospitality," Reverend replied.

The three of them sat down and Reverend told Father Sprecht about his plans to start a ministry once he returned to Boston. Reverend explained that he had been raised Protestant, that his father was a Protestant minister, and that he was partial to the Protestants prior to the war, but had learned from his battle experiences that the Lord didn't pay any attention to the denominations men made up to separate themselves, to try to claim superior access to the truth, so he wasn't going to either.

"We are so vain in setting up different denominations, or condemning those that differ from our own, and then using those to separate us. I mean it's the same God for all, wouldn't you agree?" Reverend said, hoping his opinion did not offend Father Sprecht.

"I do agree. But the war still colors everything here. In a very real sense, for most folks, the war is not over and won't be over for a long time," Father Sprecht said, unfazed by Reverend's comments or, perhaps, seeking to change the direction of the conversation.

"We saw lots of folks still in their military uniforms when we rode into town," Reverend replied.

"Yes, that's the outward sign of their displacement, of their inability to move forward, but there's more to it than that. There's a spiritual confusion that was created by the war as well," Father Sprecht said

"What ya mean 'bout da war colorin' t'ings?" Midnight asked, sitting on the floor between the two beds.

"There is vengeance in the eyes of many who can't seem to make the transition back to civilian life. And everybody here, whether in the war or not, has lost someone or knows a family that has. The war pitted neighbors against neighbors," Father Sprecht said. "Ohio had Union supporters and it had Confederate supporters. We now live in a world created by the polarizing consequences of the war. It was a collective trauma that has had spiritual and emotional effects, as I learned when visiting with former soldiers at the asylum, or those Confederate soldiers that were imprisoned here at Camp Chase," Father Sprecht concluded.

"Dey say dat lots of peoples be killed in da war. Peoples on both sides. We know'd some of dem and sad to say killed more den a few," Midnight said.

The early estimates were that approximately 620,000 soldiers died in the war. Of this number it was thought that approximately 360,000 were Union soldiers and about 258,000 were Confederate soldiers. In addition over 475,000 individuals were wounded. Virginia and North Carolina had the largest number of military casualties for the Confederacy while New York had the most for the Union. More recent scholarship has suggested the actual death toll of soldiers and civilians was between 750,000 and 850,000.

"Father, that's where the Lord comes in, don't you think? To do the healing of the trauma I mean," Reverend said. Father Sprecht agreed, but said it was going to take time, a long time, and it wouldn't be easy.

"This war was as much a theological war as a war over slavery or secession and those of us in the ministries need to address that fact when we minister to folks suffering about the war and before a healing can take place. We need to talk openly about the sin of slavery, but also about the role theology played in promoting it. If we bury it, if we don't face religion's role in this war, I am afraid for the future," Father Sprecht said.

"A theological war? How so?" Reverend asked, as Midnight listened, intrigued by what Father Sprecht had said.

"We must remember the effect slavery had on churches. The General Assembly of the Presbyterian Church passed a resolution describing slavery as 'kindly and benevolent.' Several churches split over the issue of slavery. The Methodist Episcopal Church split in 1844 over the South's support of slavery. The Southern Baptists, which supported slavery, broke off from the Northern Baptists. And while the Union was preserved the churches that split have not reunited. So the idea that churches and their theology, or what passed for it, were unaffected by slavery is absurd," Father Sprecht explained.

"All of that's true," Reverend managed to say in response as he thought about what Father Sprecht had said.

It was not until 1939 that the Methodist Episcopal Church, South reunited with the Methodist Episcopal Church. In 1995 the Southern Baptists, who never reunited with the parent church, finally adopted a resolution apologizing for its past embrace of slavery, white supremacy, and segregation.

"Southern ministers, white southern ministers, sought to support the institution of slavery with biblical references. You know the so-called Curse of Canaan about Noah's son Ham and the curse on Ham that they claimed proved that the darkened race was ordained for slavery by God. They cited Genesis and the line that said Ham was to be 'a servant of servants…to his brethren.' As a result hostility to the black race became spiritualized," Father Sprecht said, as Reverend and Midnight continued to listen. "Southern ministers like Reverend Thornton Stringfellow and Fred Ross were promoters of slavery. As a result they contended that slavery was the natural order of man as set forth by God. They let the political views of the congregation, and their own prejudices, infect and subvert the teachings of Jesus and they lost the war and the biblical argument. That damaged theology for all of us. It damaged the comfort theology might have otherwise offered to folks on both sides after the war," Father Sprecht said. Reverend nodded in slow agreement.

"Never thought about it that way, about how it might undermine believers. But you're right. I recall those justifications being put forth at the outset of the war," Reverend said, before yawning.

"Stringfellow was the one that cited Exodus and Paul's letters to claim that slavery was established by God and Ross even wrote a book entitled, *Slavery Ordained by God*. This gave religious sanction to all those slave owners and legitimacy to slavery as the economic basis of the Confederacy. Of course politicians picked up on it. Jefferson Davis, while still a senator, often cited the Bible and said slavery was 'the decree of God,'" Father Sprecht said.

"I'm guessing that slave owners were also the biggest contributors to the southern churches," Reverend replied.

"That's correct. The churches were dominated by local landed whites, plantation owners, and had long preached a class system telling slaves to be subservient to their masters. Imagine though what would have been the effect if southern ministers had united and instead preached that slavery was a sin, or was against God's will, if they had challenged those plantation owners and class assumptions. That would have been a powerful statement. Of course we will never know, but I think it might have made a difference," Father Sprecht said.

"Don't seem right dat a man would use da Bible dat dey say is da word of God to enslave anutta man, but I remember hearin' da white preacher, C.C. Jones, dat come to da plantation where I was at sayin' sometin' 'bout it. He quoted da Bible saying dat 'servants obey in all t'ings ya massa.' He told us slaves dat dis is where we was s 'pose to be, but I didn't neva believe him," Midnight said.

"It's not right," Father Sprecht said, "but many cited scripture for their own purposes and many did so, either naively or with ill intent."

"Reverend, he always told us soldiers dat God be color blind and didn't see no race. We is all his chil'ren," Midnight said to Father Sprecht, as Reverend yawned again.

"Well, that's certainly something I agree with," Father Sprecht said.

"Why do ya t'ink dere was a difference between da churches on slavery? Same Bible, right?" Midnight asked.

"It's a good question. Setting aside the financial considerations, the southern churches tended to read the Bible literally claiming it was inerrant, at least where and when it suited their purpose, and cited specific examples of slavery from antiquity in the Bible. The northern churches generally recognized that the Bible is not inerrant and focused more on the underlying principles set forth in the Bible, principles like love and forgiveness, which resulted in the rejection of slavery," Father Sprecht said.

"Maybe now dat da war be ova da southern churches change dere views. What ya t'ink?" Midnight asked.

"Unfortunately, they are now rewriting their history, creating a mythological southern culture, instead of admitting the sin of slavery. The same ministers now claim that the South lost the war as part of God's plan, because the South was not religious enough. It's an old refrain," Father Sprecht said.

"Dat just seem like dey is tryin' to 'splain away what dey did. Ain't never gonna admit no wrong, I guess," Midnight replied.

"Too often organized religion fails to find fault in itself when it errs and then blames its failings on its' believers for not being religious enough. It writes the history to vindicate itself. That's not unique to the South," Father Sprecht said. "Others in the South," Father Sprecht continued, "like Edward Alfred Pollard, are writing books about the so called 'lost cause,' reframing the war as a battle for states' rights and having nothing to do with slavery. It will be their new narrative, one that will continue to blossom with the South's defeat."

"Dat remind me of sometin'. Dere was a old slave on da plantation when I was a boy dat dey called Uriah. He used to tell us lots of African sayin's when we was in da field workin'. He had a bunch of dem. I remember one dat went like dis: 'Until da lions become da history writers da hunters will always be da heroes.' Guess we need some lions to write da history," Midnight said, happy with his ability to recall the proverb.

"Good point. And one more thing. Northerners who supported the war run the risk of claiming they have the market cornered on virtue. That by fighting the South they somehow have proven they are above prejudice and sinfulness. Not so. In fact de Tocqueville made note of this in his book, *Democracy in America,* when he wrote that, 'the prejudice of race appears to be stronger in the states that have abolished slavery than in those where it still exists,'" Father Sprecht said.

"Dat's interestin'," Midnight replied.

Midnight then asked Father Sprecht about the church and the town as Reverend slowly drifted in and out of sleep seated on one of the beds but leaning his back against the wall behind the bed. Father Sprecht told Midnight about the ongoing church construction and the years it had taken to finally get the church open. He told him about his hope for a future steeple, the influx of many German and Irish immigrants to town, and his dreams for the role of the church in the larger community.

"We must minister to the entire community. We have freedmen, former slaves, who are being discriminated against. We also have a growing Irish community here who are Catholic and fled Ireland during the potato famine of the 1840s, some of whom were members of the Fenian Brotherhood, and are being harassed, as there is a strong anti-Catholic sentiment here. They all need guidance and I'm only one man. I am going to need some help. Not sure yet where I'll get it," Father Sprecht said.

"Fenian Brotherhood? What dat?" Midnight asked.

"That was a group of various Irish militias seeking independence for Ireland. The group held a rally in New York and some say 100,000 people turned out. They actually raided British targets in parts of Canada in '66. Their plan was to capture Canada and exchange it for Ireland's freedom. Of course, it didn't succeed," Father Sprecht replied.

"Didn't know 'bout dat or 'bout da Catholics bein' harassed, but I can sure 'nuff identify wit' folks dat's bein' mistreated. How 'bout da church here? Is it in danger?"

"I sure hope not," Father Sprecht replied.

Anti-immigrant and anti-Catholic sentiments ran high at various times throughout the 1800s. In 1831 St Mary's Catholic Church in New York City was burned by Protestants. In 1844 there were mobs that attacked Irish-Americans and destroyed Catholic churches in Philadelphia in the so called Bible Riots. In 1854 riots in Bath, Maine, and along the coast resulted in, among other things, the tarring and feathering of a priest named Father John Bapst. In 1849 and thereafter several secret societies were formed to harass and oppose immigrants and Catholics. The Rough and Readies, the Black Snakes, and the Order of the Star Spangled Banner were just a few. Finally, in 1855 these groups joined together to form the Know Nothing Party. It was anti-immigrant and anti-Catholic and during its existence was sometimes called the Native American Party or the American Party. Violence broke out in Baltimore in 1856, which at the time was named "Mob-Town," when Know Nothing supporters, known as the Blood Tubs and Rip Raps, fought groups affiliated with the Democrats. The Know Nothing Party even managed to field a presidential candidate, Millard Fillmore, in the 1856 presidential election. He received 21.5% of the popular vote but finished third. It was, however, a short lived party, dissolving in 1860.

"So what ya need here at da church, another priest?" Midnight asked.

"No. I need a cook. I need a handy man to help with some building projects. I need someone to clean up, run errands, and help me deliver our church bulletin. Those types of things so I can focus more directly on the ministry," Father Sprecht said.

Reverend started to snore so Midnight gently woke him and told him to go ahead and lay down on the bed. Reverend nodded his head, did as Midnight suggested, and repositioned himself on the bed.

"We been ridin' all day. We talk more in da mornin'," Midnight said to Father Sprecht. Midnight then rolled his bedroll out on the floor and pulled a blanket over himself as Father Sprecht lay down in the other bed for the night and turned down the oil lamp on the table against the wall.

CHAPTER 9.

Shadrach rode until he came to the town of Fort Payne, in north-eastern Alabama. He had not been traveling as fast as he had anticipated. Fort Payne had its own history of suffering that included Willstown, a nearby Cherokee village, where Sequoyah, a Native American who in 1821 created the Cherokee alphabet, had lived years before. More importantly it was the site of the beginning of the Trail of Tears from which local Cherokee Indians, in light of Congress passing the Indian Removal Act of 1830, were forced to march with other tribes to the Oklahoma territory west of the Mississippi river, leaving behind their ancestral homelands and the only lives which they had ever known. The forced march from the Southeastern states to the Oklahoma territory, which lasted until 1841, included approximately 60,000-70,000 Native Americans from the Seminole, Chickasaw, Creek, Cherokee, and Choctaw nations.

Prior to the forced march Fort Payne was used to imprison local Cherokees. Many died at the fort or during the march to federal lands from disease and starvation. Overall nearly 20,000 Indians died on the various forced marches required by the government. Shadrach was not familiar with the details of this history but, in a sense, he was working his way back down his own people's trail of tears to try to find his mother and sisters.

After the Civil War former slaves also migrated to the Oklahoma territory and set up all black towns. The migration was spurred by the need to escape persecution and to come together for mutual protection. It is estimated that between 1865 and 1920 at least 50 towns were set up by former slaves throughout the Oklahoma territory. This included, among others, the towns of Boley, Taft, Langston, Brooksville, Lima, Vernon, and Tullahassee. This migration to the Oklahoma territory was also necessitated by the laws of several northern states like Illinois, Ohio, and Missouri which prohibited or restricted blacks from settling there. Oklahoma became a state in 1907 and shortly thereafter its' legislature began to adopt laws that mandated racial segregation.

Fort Payne was used briefly by Union troops during the war. The town was sparsely populated and, other than minor skirmishes between the Union and Confederate forces, had not been the site of any significant battles. Shadrach walked his horse for awhile in the surrounding woods until he came upon another encampment of former slaves. They were clustered around two clapboard tenement shacks and were trying to scrape out their survival with some chickens and a few crops that they were growing.

Shadrach spent an hour or so talking with them while young children, oblivious to how the new world that they were living in would dictate their lives, ran around barefoot in ragged clothes in a game of tag that appeared to have no real rules. He asked if anyone knew his mother or sisters, but no one did. He then asked if they knew of the Walker plantation in Elyton and one of the men spoke up.

"I knows it. I was on da Arcola Plantation. Before da war Mr. Walker, he used to deliver his cotton dere in Elyton. I believe he was run off by da Union troops durin' da war but once dey left he returned. I'm thinkin' he was back dere when da war ended, but ain't for sure. Dat's when we all left. It be not too far by da Red Mountains, da ones wit' all dat red dust," the man said.

The Red Mountains divided Jones Valley from Shades Valley. It was part of the ridge and valley region of the Appalachian Mountains and got its name from the red hematite iron ore which was visible in its rock face.

"But ya don't wants to be goin' down dere. Nothin' good can come down dere," he advised, surprised that Shadrach was even considering it.

"Reconstruction still goin' on. Union soldiers still in da towns. Should be alright," Shadrach said.

"Not down dere. And dem riders in da Klan dat been ridin' lately be down dere. Dey da ones be scarin' da people wit' fire an doin' all da lynchin'," the man said.

Shadrach had heard of the formation of the Ku Klux Klan and about some of its tactics, including the recent assassination of Arkansas Congressman James Hinds who had advocated for the rights of former slaves. There were other organizations that had formed after the war claiming to protect white rights in the South like the Knights of the White Camellia, the White League, the Regulators in Kentucky, and the Constitutional Guard, though none attained the eventual notoriety of the Klan. Shadrach was also aware, however, of the changes Alabama and other Confederate states were required to make in order to rejoin the Union while it was governed by the military district.

"Alabama had to adopt a new constitution afta da war to comply wit' Reconstruction and dey had to adopt da 13th and 14th Amendments, da ones dat s'pose to be protectin' us. So I got to t'ink dat t'ings be alright down dere," Shadrach said, something he held onto in the hope of blunting his fears.

"Don't know nothin' bout no constitution or 'mendments. Dat be 'bout government. But dat don't change people in dere hearts dat hate, an da men doin' da lynchin' be hatin' us. Dey don't want us free. Ya go down dere ya gonna get ya se'f hurt," the man said.

"I 'preciate ya concern but I need to find my mother and sisters. Dey was at da Walker plantation last I knew," Shadrach said, ignoring the warning.

"May not be dere no more. Some stayed wit da massas but most a us left once da war ended. Ya just don't know. Might a headed up North," the man said, trying to dissuade Shadrach from going. It didn't work. Shadrach thanked him and then mounted his horse and continued slowly and uneasily on his journey to Elyton.

CHAPTER 10.

The next morning, after a night of sleep which was interrupted by sporadic gunfire and a recurrent dream in which he was a sniper trying to avoid capture by the Confederacy, Dalton sat up on his cot and wiped the sleep from his eyes. Sheriff Wilson was already awake and had a pot of cowboy coffee, where the grinds are put directly into the water and heated, on top of the wood burning stove. He poured Dalton a cup.

"What's on the agenda for today?" Dalton asked, before sipping the black coffee and wiping some grinds off his lips.

"I guess we need to walk the town and be seen by folks. I try to do that every morning and night. See what damage, if any, was done last night. But first let me buy my new deputy some breakfast," Sheriff Wilson said.

"I could use it. Been eating hard tack and trail stuff for too long," Dalton replied.

Dalton pulled on his boots, stood up, and then buckled on his gunbelt. He checked the chambers of the dragoon and stuck it back in his holster. He slipped on his duster to protect against the cold and placed his cowboy hat snug on his head. After finishing their coffee he and Sheriff Wilson stepped out of the office and into the street.

"We can get a bite to eat at the Miners' Kitchen. It's inexpensive and run by a former miner. Besides food I'm sure, whether we want to or not, we will get to hear the latest complaints from Mack, the owner," Sheriff Wilson said, in a discouraging tone as they walked down the street. A slight breeze with heavy snow flurries swirled and Dalton felt the chill of the winter air on his face. He pulled the collar on his duster up around his neck. It was early, the sun barely over the horizon, and the street was mostly empty.

The Miners' Kitchen had a dozen tables and there were only a handful of miners inside, half awake, many recovering from their night out drinking and others catching a quick bite to eat before heading to their shift at one of the mines. The sheriff and Dalton walked in and sat down at a table. Mack, a tall thin man with bushy eyebrows and a similarly unkempt beard, wearing a stained white kitchen apron, immediately came over to talk to them.

"Batiste was in here last night threatening my customers," Mack said to the sheriff.

"Mack, this is Dalton my new deputy," Sheriff Wilson said.

"Sheriff, did you hear what I just said about Batiste?" Mack asked, running his hand nervously across his forehead and ignoring Dalton and the introduction.

"Yes, I heard you. I was introducing you to my new deputy," the sheriff said, referring back to Dalton and annoyed that Mack had accosted him as soon as he sat down.

"Nice to meet you," Mack said, glancing at Dalton but immediately turning back to Sheriff Wilson and waiting for an answer.

"What precisely did he do?" Dalton asked.

"Well, he stood outside the place with his hands on his guns trying to intimidate people from coming in and every so often he stepped into the place and stared at people who were inside, like he was letting them know he was taking notice of who was in here," Mack said.

"What do you want me to do about that?" Sheriff Wilson asked, his annoyance with Mack showing.

"He's a hired gun working for Hawkins. You know that. Can't you run him out of town?" Mack asked.

"Would have to have a reason, a legal reason, to do so and I ain't found no wanted posters on him," Sheriff Wilson said.

"You know he shot your deputy in the back," Mack replied.

"Mack, I can't prove it. I can't arrest someone without proof. You bring me the evidence and I'll jail him," the sheriff said.

"The miners are scared to talk. I don't know if they know anything but they're afraid that if one of them fingers Batiste it will be their death," Mack said.

"That doesn't help me. I need a witness," Sheriff Wilson replied, rehashing a discussion he had had with Mack immediately after the deputy was killed.

"Sheriff, you know what he is doing to me. Hawkins wants this place. He wants me out of business 'cause I support the miners and that's why Batiste is hanging out in front," Mack said. Mack looked at the sheriff waiting for a response.

"Mack, I hear you but unless you have information I can use to arrest Batiste, let us eat. We'd like to order breakfast," Sheriff Wilson said instead and then proceeded to tell Mack the breakfast order for Dalton and himself. Mack walked away frustrated by the sheriff's response.

"Is that true? What he said about this fellow Hawkins?" Dalton asked.

"Probably. Hawkins is definitely trying to squeeze the miners and

Hawkins might well want this place. He is that type. One of those businessmen that wants to own everything, poisoned by power or the idea of it. Never satisfied with what he has. I'm not smart enough to know if that's greed or ambition. When is owning enough stuff enough?" Sheriff Wilson said.

"I can't answer that question. I came from nothing. Both my folks passed when I was young and I ain't never had the money itch like some folks," Dalton said.

Mack finally brought their breakfast out, but it was clear from his silence when he delivered their meals that he was not pleased with Sheriff Wilson. After eating and paying for their meal the sheriff and Dalton left the Miners' Kitchen, without speaking further to Mack, and began walking the streets to check on the rest of the town. As they turned a corner the sheriff saw Hawkins and Batiste, at a distance, walking toward them.

"Here we go," Sheriff Wilson said quietly to Dalton.

"Sheriff! Sheriff!" Hawkins immediately yelled out, waving his hand above his head to get the sheriff's attention and quickening his pace.

Mr. Hawkins was a roly-poly shaped man with slicked down black hair, a waxed mustache, and a penchant for three piece suits and expensive cigars. He wore a new gray wool overcoat, black leather gloves, and a black Stetson hat to protect against the cold. Dalton and Sheriff Wilson stopped and waited for Hawkins and Batiste to approach. Dalton recognized Batiste as the one who had watched him the night before when he left the stable. The four men eventually stood within arms' length of each other.

"Sheriff, we hear that the miners are considering going on strike. Now we can't have that. Mining is important to the economy of this town. This town can continue to grow and prosper, but not if there is

74

a strike. We mine owners have contracts to fill so I'm telling you the mine owners expect you to break up any strike that might occur and arrest the organizers," Hawkins said, while fingering the chain on his gold pocket watch.

"And why would they be striking?" Dalton asked, before the sheriff could reply. Hawkins looked at Dalton disdainfully for having the temerity to speak directly to him. Batiste absentmindedly stroked his pointy beard while keeping his eyes on Dalton.

"This is my new deputy, Dalton," Sheriff Wilson said.

"Batiste told me you had another one. Hope he lasts longer than the last one. Well I certainly don't know why they would want to strike. That's irrelevant, Deputy. What's important is assuring that the mining operations are not interrupted," Hawkins said.

"Could it be that the miners are tired of being squeezed by you and the other mine owners? And by the way, what's your interest in the Miners' Kitchen?" Dalton pressed, tilting his cowboy hat back as he spoke. Hawkins seemed startled by Dalton's aggressive questioning.

"I don't know what you are talking about. Be careful with your accusations," Hawkins finally said.

Batiste moved his gun hands closer to his ivory handled guns and stepped back a half pace from Dalton. If the intent was to intimidate Dalton it didn't work. Dalton casually brushed back his duster and instinctively moved his right hand closer to his dragoon.

"You don't want to bow up with me Reb, least not while I'm facing you," Dalton said. Sheriff Wilson feared Batiste would draw his gun, but Hawkins put his hand on Batiste's shoulder.

"Not now. Not now," Hawkins said, as he looked directly at Sheriff Wilson. He gently pushed Batiste aside and they turned away as Dalton stood his ground.

"You need to have a talk with your deputy. I wouldn't want to bet money on him lasting long with that attitude of his," Hawkins said, over his shoulder, as he and Batiste walked away.

"Goodness, you trying to get killed on your first day on the job?" Sheriff Wilson said seriously to Dalton, after Hawkins and Batiste were half a block away.

"Not likely going to happen. Just feeling him out in case we do clash," Dalton replied.

"You certainly aren't one for taking things slow," the sheriff then said. Dalton smiled.

"Never have been," he replied.

CHAPTER 11.

Reverend woke after sleeping soundly all night. It was his first night sleeping under a roof since he and Midnight had left Louisville together. When he looked around he saw that he was alone in the room. It was mid-morning. Midnight and Father Sprecht were gone. He sat up in bed, put on his boots, and slowly made his way into the main area of the church. Father Sprecht and Midnight were walking down the center aisle putting hymnals on the pews in preparation for the next mass.

"Sorry, I slept late," Reverend said as he approached.

"You must have needed it," Father Sprecht replied, walking toward Reverend.

"I did. I think we'll get breakfast and then get back to traveling. I can't thank you enough for giving us a place to stay. I have not slept that well in a good while," Reverend said to Father Sprecht as Midnight walked up.

"Thanks for helping," Father Sprecht said to Midnight.

"You ready for breakfast?" Reverend asked Midnight. Midnight looked at Father Sprecht before answering. Father Sprecht nodded his head in appreciation for Midnight's help.

"Sure," Midnight said.

Reverend and Midnight then left the church to return to Rosie's Cafe. Upon entering Emmalene again waved them to a table. They sat down and ordered breakfast.

"Midnight, I'm looking forward to us getting back on the road. I'm anxious to get to Boston," Reverend said.

"Reverend, I'm gonna stay here. I spoke wit' Father Sprecht 'bout it dis mornin'," Midnight replied.

"Really? You sure?" Reverend asked.

"Father Sprecht, he needs some help at da church and he offered me a job, so I'm gonna stay. I be runnin' errands and stuff. I think I'll enjoy it," Midnight said.

"I'll miss your company, but I'm happy for you. Father Sprecht seems to be a good man," Reverend said, as Emmalene set down their plates of food and cups of coffee.

"Miss, ya gonna be seein' much more of me, dat's for sure," Midnight blurted out to Emmalene.

"Excuse me? Who are you?" Emmalene said, furrowing her brow, putting her hands on her hips, immediately dismissing Midnight's attempted flirtation and dampening his enthusiasm.

"I be Emmet. My friends call me Midnight. I meant to say I be workin' at da church wit' Father Sprecht so I be here for breakfast more and dat's why ya be seein' me more often," Midnight said, feeling properly chastised, but hoping he had corrected any misimpression.

"You and every other dim wit in town," she said, stepping away from the table as Midnight's eyes followed her.

"Subtle Midnight. Got to be more subtle," Reverend said, laughing gently after Emmalene had left the table.

"I be out of practice wit' da ladies, but she sure is a mighty pretty one," Midnight said, laughing along with Reverend at his chastisement, but keeping his eyes on Emmalene.

"You sure you staying for the job and not for that gal?" Reverend teased.

"Might be both," Midnight said, smiling sheepishly in response. "But don't seem like she be much interested in me. Maybe she got herself a beau already," Midnight said. They began to eat their breakfast in silence.

"I wonder where Dalton and Shadrach are in their travels right now," Reverend then said.

"I worry 'bout Dalton. He a fast draw but dat be dangerous. And Shadrach goin' down South be dangerous too, but we each got to do what be best for us. Ain't no massa or army officer to tell us what to do no more. Dat's what I call freedom, but it be a bit frightnin'," Midnight said. Reverend lifted his cup of coffee and finished it.

"Yes, it is. It can be scary to be torn from the familiar. This war has made me think about it a lot. I've learned that freedom means different things to different people. Is it a right or a privilege? Some folks think it means setting aside your individual desires for the common good. Other folks think it's an individual thing and private, to do as you please. I guess sometimes it can be a bit of both," Reverend offered philosophically.

"Reverend, I thought a lot 'bout freedom ova da years myse'f, 'specially when I was on da plantation, and I ain't got no one thought on it 'cept I t'ink to be truly free ya got to be free of da fear and hate, cause if ya bitter 'bout t'ings it just kinda blinds ya," Midnight replied.

"Can't disagree with that," Reverend said, as he wrapped up a biscuit in a napkin to take with him and then pushed his empty plate away.

"You be headin' to Boston I 'spect now," Midnight replied and then sipped the last of his coffee.

"Yes, I need to get back home. I can't wait to see Theresa and start our life together," Reverend said, as he and Midnight stood up after putting money on the table to pay their bill.

"I be seein' you," Midnight said to Emmalene, who was waiting on another table, as he walked by her. She looked up at him as if they had never met and she didn't know who he was.

"You better be careful with that one. I don't think she suffers much foolishness," Reverend said, as they stepped out of Rosie's Cafe.

"I gots to come up wit' a betta plan. She gonna be a tough one," Midnight replied.

Midnight and Reverend went back to the church and Reverend retrieved his belongings. He again thanked Father Sprecht for his hospitality and then he and Midnight walked over to the stable. Reverend saddled his horse, tied his bedroll on, and, stuffing the biscuit in it, secured his satchel bag behind his saddle.

"I guess dis be it," Midnight said, extending his hand. Reverend shook it firmly.

"Take care of yourself, my friend," Reverend said and then turned from Midnight and mounted his horse.

"If you needs to reach me Father Sprecht know where I be," Midnight said. Reverend nodded his head and slowly rode his horse away as Midnight watched. "Dere go a good man and a good friend," Midnight said to himself. He then headed back to the church.

CHAPTER 12.

Shadrach finally made his way into Elyton, Alabama. It was situated near the head of Valley Creek. Initially known as 'Frog Level' it was an approximately 2,500 acre area originally given by Congress to the American Asylum for the Instruction of the Deaf and Dumb. The Asylum sent down Mr. Elyton to inspect the land and after doing so he concluded that the land was useless. He sold it shortly thereafter and the town, now called Elyton, was incorporated in 1820. It was one of three farm towns in the general area and had been the county seat of Jefferson County since 1821.

Jefferson County was one of the largest producers of coal for the Confederacy during the Civil War. Coal was used by both armies to fuel locomotives and steamships and to make iron and steel which was used in the manufacturing of cannons. The county also had Howard College, later renamed Samford, which, during the war, was converted into a military hospital for the Confederacy.

There had always been talk of combining Elyton with the other two small farm towns in the county, but in late 1868, when Shadrach arrived, it hadn't happened. Several years later it would occur and be renamed Birmingham. The town's population was about 1,000. The beginning of the Alabama-Chattanooga Railroad to Elyton would be started in 1870, but no railroad connecting Elyton to the larger outside world existed there yet.

When Shadrach rode into town down Broad Street, in the center of town, he looked to see if there were any Union soldiers on the street but did not see any. He dismounted and tethered his horse to a hitching post outside of Murphy's, the only dry goods store in town.

"What you want, boy?" an overweight white man, standing behind the counter, immediately shouted out as soon as Shadrach entered the store.

"Excuse me sir, can ya tell me where da Walker plantation be?" Shadrach asked, his head down and his speech subservient, not making eye contact with the man. As soon as he did this he realized that he was acting docile like he was required to do as a slave in the presence of a white man. Despite his freedom, and his years as a soldier, some habits, tied to the oppressive years on the plantation, were hard to break.

"Who are you and what's your business with that plantation?" the white man asked, still confrontational, and moving stoop shouldered from behind the counter toward Shadrach.

"My name be Shadrach and I be lookin' for my mother and sisters. Last I knew dey was sold to Mr. Walker at da Walker plantation 'bout ten years ago," Shadrach said, regaining his sense of self and lifting his head up.

The man seemed to be considering his response when another white man walked in behind Shadrach. Shadrach could sense that the man was standing directly behind him and moving closer.

"Jefferson, this boy says that he is looking for his momma," the white man, who was the store owner and named Walt, said sarcastically to the other white man.

"Nigger, is that your horse outside? It's got a Union Army brand. Who'd you steal him from?" Jefferson said, while he remained standing behind Shadrach.

Shadrach slowly turned around and looked at Jefferson. He was tall, unnaturally thin with a hawk shaped nose, pale drawn skin, and a bony jaw line. He was poorly dressed in stained blue overalls that were slightly too large and a long sleeve wool shirt that was threadbare at the elbows. There was enmity in his eyes and fear etched in the corners of his mouth. Shadrach immediately recognized him, despite the passage of years and the toll that the war had taken on Jefferson, as one of the overseers on the Brentwood plantation that he had run away from in '63.

"I remember you," Jefferson suddenly said, his lips trembling as he pointed a wrinkled finger at Shadrach. "You a runaway slave."

"I'm not a slave. I be a man. A free man," Shadrach said, turning his shoulders to face Jefferson directly. Shadrach looked Jefferson in the eyes. It startled Jefferson who reflexively reached for a whip on his hip that was no longer there. Shadrach then promptly walked past Jefferson to head to his horse and leave before anything escalated.

"Where you think you goin', boy?" Jefferson said, as Shadrach stepped onto the porch in front of the store.

Shadrach heard Jefferson spit something in his direction, but he did not turn back or respond. He untethered his horse, mounted it, and quickly rode off as Jefferson took a step out of the store and watched Shadrach ride away.

"I remember him well. He was trouble on the plantation and you can bet he is here now for more trouble. Why else would a runaway slave come back to Alabama?" Jefferson said to Walt, after he stepped back into the dry goods store.

"Probably right. What do you need today? Are you here to settle up your bill?" Walt asked Jefferson. "It's way overdue."

"Ain't got no money at present. Still can't find me no job. The war ruined everything. Damn Union Army destroyed the furnaces, the mines, blew up railroad track up North Alabama way, and messed up the plantation lands that was growing crops," Jefferson replied.

"Talbot opened one of the old mines back up. Mine is always lookin' for workers," Walt then said.

"I ain't workin' in that mine for no amount of money. That ain't work for no white man, unless he needs a guard or a whippin' boss," Jefferson replied.

"What about the railroad? They might need help fixing the rails. They say railroads gonna be big business now," Walt said.

"I don't know. I hear they ain't paying regular and they got those China men working on it. I ain't workin' 'long side them," Jefferson replied.

"You could work out a share wage with one of the plantation owners. Work a deal like that with someone," Walt said.

"That's what slaves are doing. And you know them land owners cheat 'em. Charge 'em for everything. That ain't for me," Jefferson replied.

"Listen, I sympathize, but you got to pay your bill. No more credit," Walt said.

"Walt, it ain't my fault we lost the war. And dere ain't no more work for an overseer. That's the problem. Damn Union did this to me and mine. They shoulda left us alone. We wasn't hurtin' nobody and with no slaves I don't know what will become of us," Jefferson replied.

"The Freedmen's Bureau is giving out food to folks, if you need some," Walt offered. Jefferson sneered at the thought.

"I ain't accepting nothing from them," Jefferson said.

"Might have to, if you ain't got no money," Walt replied.

The Freedmen's Bureau was established by Congress in 1865 and was headed in Alabama by Union General Wager Swayne. Its function was to find employment for former slaves, set up hospitals and schools, and provide food and clothing to those in need. Originally it had control of over 850,000 acres of land, abandoned or confiscated from Confederate supporters, and began a program to allocate the land to former slaves. Most of the property was seized pursuant to the Second Confiscation Act of 1862 passed under President Lincoln. President Johnson in his ongoing fight with Republicans in Congress reversed the process, as he did with other attempts to allocate land to former slaves, and ordered that the confiscated lands be returned to their prior owners thereby evicting the former slaves who had been apportioned some of the land.

The Bureau issued food rations to both blacks and whites. During its existence it issued 21 million rations, with approximately 15 ½ million going to blacks and 5 ½ million going to whites. In Alabama alone in 1866 it provided approximately 800,000 rations to more than 33,000 people. Congress passed legislation to extend the life of the Bureau but President Johnson vetoed the legislation and there were insufficient votes to override his veto. As a result the Bureau shut down its food operations at the end of 1868 and ended all of its efforts in Alabama in 1870.

"Maybe check with the sheriff or some of the other Klan folks and see if they know of something for you. I don't know what else to suggest," Walt said. Jefferson nodded his head, stuck his hands in the pockets of his overalls, and, frustrated with the inexplicable upending of the hierarchy of his world, walked out the store.

Shadrach headed to the outskirts of town looking for any settlement of former slaves where he could get some information and directions. Not too far off the main road he saw several men working a small patch of ground near former slave quarters and rode towards them.

"Hey dere. I be lookin' for da Walker plantation," Shadrach said, as he rode up on the two men with hoes in their hands working the hard ground. A woman and several children sat on the dilapidated porch of the nearest house watching the men work.

"That be 'bout 2 mile toward da Red mountains. Got a new owner. Northern man dat bought it," one of the men, thin but muscular, volunteered.

"Mr. Walker don't own it no more?" Shadrach asked.

"No, heard tell he sold it to a northern man, don't know his name," the man replied again. Shadrach got off his horse, introduced himself and told them he was looking for his mother and sisters.

"My mother's name be Betsey and my sisters be Cecilia and Clotilde. Last I know dey was all at da Walker plantation but dat was a few years ago, back in '63," he said. One of the men leaned on his hoe and scratched his head.

"I don't know no Betsey, but dere be a Miss Cecilia dat I hear people talk 'bout dat be workin' in da saloon. Heard 'bout her. I think she used to work at da Walker place. Not sure. Don't know if dat be ya sister. Dey say dat she a light skin," the man said.

"Yeah, she is. Which saloon?" Shadrach asked.

"Let's see.... Da one dey named afta one of da slave ships...da Wanderer," he said.

"What she be doin' workin' dere?" Shadrach asked.

"Well, I don't rightly know. But don't matter none 'cause ya can't be goin' in dere. We ain't allowed. Only white folks can," the man said.

Shadrach was puzzled that his sister would work in such a place. Maybe it was someone else, but at some point he might have to check and see. He thanked the men and headed off in the direction of the Walker plantation.

CHAPTER 13.

Dalton walked the town alone one morning and talked with a few miners who sought him out to complain about the working conditions in the mine. It wasn't just the low wages, it was the dangerous conditions inside the mines and the long hours. The mines were unsafe and despite the miners' complaints they felt that the owners cared nothing about worker safety, pushing the men beyond their endurance.

"It's hard to get ahead. If you break a tool they charge you for it. If you don't make your quota they cut your pay. If you complain about anything they cut down your hours," one miner told him.

The miners were in fact considering going on strike to demand a couple of changes. Dalton also learned more about Batiste and the incident where he pistol whipped that miner, who had since left town beaten up badly.

"Billy was just minding his business when Batiste tried to get him into a gunfight. But Billy was too smart. He knew how fast Batiste was so he dropped his gunbelt in front of everyone so Batiste would be shooting an unarmed man. Batiste called him a coward and Billy raised his fists," a miner named Johnson said. "They started to fight and Billy was holding his own but then Batiste hit him with the butt of his gun. Once Billy went down Batiste started putting the boot to him and that's when that young deputy showed up. He came up behind Batiste, stuck his gun in Batiste's ribs and made him stop and leave. Two nights later the deputy was found in the alley with a bullet in his back. No one saw what happened, at least no one says they did. Batiste did it but the sheriff can't prove it. You can't play around with a man like Batiste," Johnson concluded, with several other miners gathered around and agreeing with his recitation. Dalton listened and then asked a few questions.

"Sheriff Wilson said that Batiste was a sniper in the Confederacy. Is that true?" Dalton asked.

"Yeah. We got some miners here that were in the Confederacy and one of them recognized him. Said he worked alone a lot as a sniper. They say he's the one that shot a Union soldier near Fort Sumter from over 1,300 yards away in '64. Might just be a rumor," Johnson said.

"Must have been using a Whitworth rifle," Dalton said.

"Maybe so," Johnson replied, "but they say those rifles are only accurate for about 800 yards. Not sure how it could be over 1,300 yards."

"He might have used a stand for the rifle. But I remember that story. That shot was illegal. It was during a ceasefire," Dalton said.

"Anyway, that won't help him in a gunfight. Anyone seen him draw?" Dalton asked. The men all spoke at once and talked about seeing Batiste shoot a miner named Lou who had tried to draw against him.

"Billy saw that too. Lou's gun didn't even clear his holster when he was shot," Johnson then said.

"Hey look," one of the miners said and the group turned as one to see Batiste walking toward them.

The miners, fearing a gunfight, moved a few feet away from Dalton. Dalton thought about what to do. He unbuckled his gunbelt and handed it to the miner named Johnson.

"Hold this," Dalton said.

Batiste looked at him puzzled, but continued to walk towards the group. When he got to within ten feet, and as the miners continued to back away, Dalton called him out.

"I understand you don't know how to bare knuckle fight and had to pistol whip a fellow named Billy that was beating your ass," Dalton said, surprising the miners and Batiste with his comment. Batiste, who was only an inch or two shorter than Dalton, but about the same weight, took a few more steps forward and stopped 2 to 3 feet away from Dalton and glanced at the miners who were all watching him to see what he would do.

"That's a lie. I beat that boy fair. Weren't no pistol whipping involved," Batiste replied, with a slight grin, staring at the miners and daring any of them to contradict him. "Anyone that says otherwise is a liar and is going to have to answer to me," he said, raising his hand to point a finger at the group of miners.

"I say otherwise and I'm standing right here waiting for that answer," Dalton said, squaring his shoulders the way Shadrach had taught him before throwing a punch. A couple of the miners laughed. It was clear they were laughing at Batiste.

"Any time you are ready, Deputy," Batiste said, the word 'deputy' dripping with sarcasm.

"Drop the gunbelt if you are man enough. I wouldn't want to get accidentally pistol whipped like the last fellow," Dalton said. Batiste stood silent for a few seconds, looked at the miners again, and then slowly unbuckled his gunbelt.

"This is going to be easy," Batiste said confidently.

He lowered his gunbelt to the ground and then immediately tried to throw a punch hoping to catch Dalton off guard. Dalton ducked back from the punch and then, as Shadrach had taught him, he immediately dropped his right shoulder down. Batiste was still leaning forward, overextended and off balance after throwing his abortive punch when Dalton threw a powerful right uppercut with all his might that caught Batiste right under the chin. Batiste's feet came slightly off the ground from the force of the punch. He wobbled, his equilibrium having temporarily abandoned him, and crumbled to the ground, his legs tangled unnaturally beneath him, unconscious. It was a one punch knockout. The miners couldn't believe it and whooped and hollered in excitement. Dalton flexed the fingers on his hand, the one that he had punched Batiste with, to make sure none were broken.

"Did you see that punch?" one of the miners said.

"I missed it. Too fast," another said.

"What an uppercut!" another exclaimed.

Johnson handed Dalton his gunbelt back and several miners slapped Dalton on the back to congratulate him as he buckled the gunbelt back on. Batiste lay sprawled in the middle of the street as a small crowd that eventually included Hawkins came running into the street to see what the hollering was about. Dalton, thinking of Shadrach, walked back toward the sheriff's office as Batiste, having had a miner pour the remnants of a warm beer on him, slowly awoke from the punch and tried, initially unsuccessful, to sit up. Hawkins helped him to his feet as the miners dispersed, laughing and talking, leaving Batiste's gunbelt on the street next to him, which Hawkins also retrieved.

Dalton entered the sheriff's office grinning and walked over and plopped himself down on his cot.

"You look mighty proud of yourself. What's up?" Sheriff Wilson said, seated behind his desk. Dalton smiled and then told him what happened.

"One punch, huh. Where did you learn to do that?" Sheriff Wilson asked, shaking his head in disbelief.

"I use to spar with a buddy that was the troop bare knuckle champ. He taught me how to throw that punch," Dalton said, relaxing on his cot.

"You are full of surprises. You got to teach me that move one day," Sheriff Wilson said.

Several minutes later Hawkins and another mine owner burst into the sheriff's office.

"I want this man arrested for an unprovoked assault on my employee, Batiste," Hawkins said, gesturing at Dalton, who along with the sheriff had stood up when Hawkins entered the jail.

"Batiste threw the first punch and I simply defended myself. Pretty well I might add," Dalton said, casually.

"That's a lie. He sucker punched Batiste when he wasn't looking," Hawkins said, as the other mine owner shook his head in agreement.

"There are a dozen miners who will back me up. You weren't even there," Dalton said dismissively to Hawkins. Hawkins looked at Sheriff Wilson.

"Were you there? Did you witness it?" Sheriff Wilson asked. Hawkins did not reply to the questions.

"So that's the way it's going to be. Well, Sheriff I can't control what Batiste may do if this man is not arrested. He has the right to defend himself," Hawkins threatened, continuing to ignore the sheriff's question.

"You mean you don't want to control what he does," Dalton corrected.

"Sounds like it was self defense to me. I don't see that there is any basis to arrest Dalton," Sheriff Wilson finally said.

"We will get no satisfaction here," Hawkins said in a huff to the other mine owner and then they left slamming the door to the sheriff's office behind them.

"It's going to happen now. You embarrassed him. Batiste ain't gonna let this pass, but I'm expecting you knew that before you threw that punch. I hope you're ready," Sheriff Wilson said.

"I'm ready and it won't be in an alley like your deputy got it. It will be on my terms not his," Dalton said, sitting back down again.

CHAPTER 14.

"Emmet, can you deliver these church bulletins to Rosie's Cafe for me? Mr. Alrick said that he would set them out on the counter for people to pick up. And when you come back let's talk about a few more things you can help me with," Father Sprecht said.

"Father, ya can call me Midnight. It be what da men on da plantation called me when I was a youngsta. We used lots of nicknames back den instead of da names dat we was given by dem dat owned us," Midnight said. Father Sprecht was not comfortable with the name but said that he would try to remember to do so.

Father Sprecht handed Midnight a stack of folded bulletins to deliver and as soon as he had them in his hands Midnight left the church for Rosie's Cafe. Midnight entered the restaurant, which was not crowded. Mr. Alrick was seated in his usual chair in the corner near the front door with the shotgun across his lap. He asked Mr. Alrick where he wanted the bulletins to be put.

"Give those to Emmalene. She knows where to put them," Mr. Alrick said. Midnight turned and saw Emmalene standing behind the counter with her hands on her hips glaring at him. He walked toward her uneasy in light of how she had previously responded to him.

"Dese be da bulletins from da church. Mr. Alrick said to give dese to ya to put dem out," Midnight said, holding out the bulletins to Emmalene. Instead of taking the bulletins from him she folded her arms in response.

"I know what those are," she snapped at him. Midnight cleared his throat and set the bulletins down on the counter.

"Ya gonna come to church services dis Sunday? Da services be listed in da bulletin," Midnight asked, undeterred and gesturing to the bulletins.

"Yes," Emmalene replied.

"Well, uhm…I be mighty proud to escort ya," Midnight said, screwing up his courage to ask her.

"What makes you think that I want to go to church and be seen in public escorted by you?" she replied, keeping her arms folded, tapping her foot, and waiting for his reply. Midnight shifted his weight impatiently from one foot to the other having absorbed her scolding.

"I'm a grown man, tough as dey come. I don't take to no such comments. I ain't done nothin' to deserve it from ya. If ya don't wants to go wit' me just say so. Dere ain't no cause for bein' mean 'bout it," Midnight said, frustrated by her treatment and finally letting it show.

"Even the toughest men with the hardest exteriors have a scared child underneath," Emmalene replied.

"I don't know nothin' 'bout dat," Midnight said, confused by her comment.

"And I am an educated woman who can read and write. I speak proper English and I read to learn just like Ms. Harriet Tubman has suggested. I can only be with a man who understands and supports me and who also supports women's rights," Emmalene said.

"What ya mean, women's rights?" Midnight asked. Emmalene pinched her lips together and disapproval flared in her eyes. Midnight thought about just walking away.

"The right of women to equality, to be treated equal before the law and in a relationship. The right for women to vote and to hold public office. That is what I mean by women's rights," Emmalene answered.

"How is dat gonna ever happen? Who gonna agree to sometin' like dat?" Midnight asked, smiling a bit too much in amusement at what she had said.

"I would not expect someone like you to know or to understand, but we have our own leaders and our own writers and it will happen someday. The first convention on Women's suffrage was in 1848 in Seneca Falls, New York, and Mr. Frederick Douglass attended. He is a supporter and also spoke about universal suffrage at the Equal Rights Association in 1866. Did you know that?" Emmalene asked, not really expecting an answer. Midnight didn't reply but rather looked away at the ground. "Have you heard of Mary Wollstonecraft?" Emmalene then asked, leaning toward him.

"No, can't say dat I has," Midnight replied, his previous smile having been removed with a more defensive look.

"I didn't think so. She wrote a book entitled, *A Vindication of the Rights of Women*," Emmalene said.

"But I know "bout Mr. Douglass, everybody do," Midnight quickly added.

"Did you know that Elizabeth Stanton and Susan Anthony formed the Women's National Loyal League in 1863 to petition Congress to pass the 13th Amendment outlawing slavery? They presented a petition with almost 400,000 signatures on it. Women did that because our causes are linked," Emmalene recited.

"Dat's good to know, but I was fightin' back den for our folks to be free. Didn't know nothin' 'bout what doze ladies was doin'," Midnight managed to reply, still looking away from Emmalene. Emmalene reached underneath the counter and pulled out a printed paper.

"Here, educate yourself. This is *The Agitator* by Mary Livermore. It is a paper that advocates for women's rights. Read it and maybe you will learn something," Emmalene said, thrusting it into Midnight's chest. Midnight took the paper from her, turned, and then he began to walk away, unsure what else he could say, unfamiliar as he was with the issues she had raised.

"Thank you, sir," he said politely as he approached Mr. Alrick, but as he got to the open door to leave Emmalene hollered at him.

"What time?"

Midnight stopped and, though he might have thought better of it, walked back over to her. She remained standing in a posture that suggested she would reprimand him at any minute for the slightest mistake.

"Ya is a mighty difficult one to figger. How 'bout 'goin wit me to da 9:30 one. I meet ya in da front of da church," Midnight said and again turned to leave.

"No. If you are escorting me to church you will act like a gentlemen, if that's even possible, and walk with me from my place," Emmalene said. Midnight turned back to face her and shook his head. He couldn't get anything right.

"Where dat be?" Midnight asked reluctantly.

"I reside at the Baldwin House which is on Mound Street, in the south end of town. And another thing, you need to speak properly if you are going to speak to me," Emmalene said.

"I see ya, I mean you, at 9:15," Midnight said and then, without waiting for a further reply or additional criticism, he walked away holding the copy of *The Agitator* and left the restaurant.

CHAPTER 15.

Shadrach continued on his way toward the Walker plantation to find his mother and sisters. He thought he would look there first before trying to see if the woman at the saloon was his sister. As he rode along he met more people on the road, or in the woods, who were trying to start their lives anew. When he arrived at the plantation he saw a large Antebellum style house that was set back from the road. A white man with dark curly hair, a thick gray mustache and beard, in work clothes, was seated on a rocking chair on the front porch. He introduced himself to Shadrach as Mr. Blanchfield.

Mr. Blanchfield was cordial but initially distant, unsure of who Shadrach was and what he wanted. After they spoke for a few minutes, and Shadrach advised that he was looking for his family members, Mr. Blanchfield invited Shadrach to get off his horse and join him on the porch. He asked Shadrach if he wanted any water to drink. Shadrach accepted and appreciated the kindness. He explained to Shadrach that he was a transplant from Pennsylvania and had bought the plantation from Mr. Walker.

"I haven't had time to change the name of the plantation. Probably wouldn't matter anyway as folks in these parts would still call it the Walker plantation. They don't think too much of a northerner like me and I can't say I blame them considering some of the abuses of Reconstruction I've heard about. Corruption in the Reconstruction governments seems rampant. But I paid Walker a fair price for this place which was pretty run down," Mr. Blanchfield said.

Shadrach reciprocated telling Mr. Blanchfield that he had run away as a slave and, until recently, had been a private in the Union Army and served for awhile in Georgia during Reconstruction. Mr. Blanchfield revealed that he came from a family of abolitionists and had also served in the Union Army as a Lieutenant Colonel in the 1st Pennsylvania Cavalry. He had fought at the Second Battle of Bull Run and at Gettysburg.

"Doze was some real battles," Shadrach replied.

"I served under Colonel Bayard, then Colonel Jones, and then Colonel Taylor. We had lots of casualties," Mr. Blanchfield said.

"Gettysburg, dey say was da turnin' point in da war," Shadrach said.

"Probably so. That was May of '63 as I recall. Lee and his Army of Northern Virginia had won at Chancellorsville and decided to invade the North. It was the bloodiest three day battle I ever was in. Most casualties in the war. I think there was over 50,000 killed or wounded. It haunts me to this day when I think about the men we lost," Mr. Blanchfield responded.

"It was later dat year, in '63, dat President Lincoln gave dat Gettysburg address. I 'member hearin' 'bout it from one of da officers. He said doze dat died 'shall not have died in vain,'" Shadrach said, reciting what he recalled. Mr. Blanchfield said that he remembered reading the address and certainly hoped that Lincoln was right.

When asked Mr. Blanchfield said that he did not know Shadrach's mother or sisters.

"Most of the men and women that were working here, I should say enslaved here, when the Union Army ran Walker off for awhile, are gone. I bought it late last year when cotton prices were down and the bad weather had damaged production. My plan is to get it fully operational again," Mr. Blanchfield said. He then told Shadrach that he was welcome to ask the men he had recently hired if they knew his mother or sisters.

"They are over by the bunkhouse and all worked here or at other plantations nearby prior to the war. I worked with the Freedmen's Bureau to hire them on a contract basis," Mr. Blanchfield said.

After the war the Freedmen's Bureau worked to have labor contracts used for the employment of former slaves. It was thought this would allow more freedom for the former slaves who could contract out their labor on terms that they saw fit, but it met with limited success as many plantation owners and other southern businesses sought to impose contract provisions, similar to slavery, that gave them complete control over the lives of the former slaves.

Shadrach thanked Mr. Blanchfield and then walked over to a newly built bunkhouse where three men sat in the shade of a large pecan tree. One man was seated upright but the other two were laying down in the grass. It appeared that they were taking a break from clearing significant overgrowth from land nearby, which, once cleared and tilled, was to be used for growing crops.

Shadrach introduced himself and told them who he was looking for. All three were former slaves and the oldest one with white hair, who was seated, told Shadrach that he had worked briefly on the plantation when it was owned by Mr. Walker. The old man, who looked to be in his seventies, but in remarkably good physical shape, told Shadrach that he knew his mother, Betsey.

"She worked in da house here mosly as a cook," he said, while the other two men continued to lay in the grass.

"Dat's right. Do ya know where I can find her?" Shadrach asked.

"Best I know she be buried ova by da ol' quarters," he said without emotion. Shadrach was not certain he heard right.

"She dead?" he asked. He wasn't sure what he had expected, but the idea that his mother was dead was not something that he had allowed to cross his mind.

"Got hers'ef shot by Union soldier and never recovered. Ain't had no real doctor. Conjure man tried to help wit some herbs and charms, but it weren't no good. Mr. Walker had her buried by da others. But I 'member her, she was a nice woman," the old man said in a voice weary with recollection.

"Union soldier?" Shadrach asked in disbelief.

"Dey overrun da place and she was tryin' to protect da house from da lootin'. Soldier dat was lootin' shot her," Rory replied. Shadrach was puzzled that she died in such a way.

"Protectin' da house?"

"Dey was gonna loot it. Heard tell dat happened utta places too. She was da one runnin' da house so maybe felt she had to," Rory suggested.

Although a large number of slaves fled the South during and after the war, others remained on the plantations where they had been enslaved and loyal to their former owners. While the Union army was seen as a liberator by many there were numerous abuses, from murder to rape to theft, by Union soldiers. Indeed some believe that there were so called "Black Flag" operations where Union soldiers purposely looted and vandalized Southern civilians. It was so endemic within

General Sherman's troops that such soldiers were given the nickname of "Bummers."

"Ya sure it was her?" Shadrach asked, hoping there was some mistake.

"Can't be sure a nothin' in dis here world, but she was named Betsey, worked in da big house," he replied.

"Can ya show me where she be buried?" Shadrach asked. The old man stayed seated, turned at the waist, and just pointed.

"Back dere a ways. Dere be da graves," he said. Shadrach took note of the direction in which the man pointed.

"What 'bout my sisters?" Shadrach then asked.

"I heard Cecilia be sold at some point, but don't know when," he said.

"Do ya know where she was sent?"

"Sure don't. Might be afta I was sent over to anutta place to work by Mr. Walker. I wasn't here when da war ended," he said.

"Ya know anything 'bout da women dat dey say work in dat saloon, da Wanderer, in town?" Shadrach asked.

"No. Dey say dere is some dat works upstairs. Dat's been dat way a long time, but don't know no more. We can't be in dere ya know," he said.

"What's ya name?" Shadrach asked.

"White folks call me Rory. Dat's da name dey give me when dey bought me, but I was born wit da name of Seydou. I'm from da Ivory Coast. My father give me my name. Dey kidnap me from my home and put me on a ship when I was seven wit' others from my tribe," he said, with a nostalgic glint in his old eyes. "I be preferrin' my original name now dat I ain't no mo' a slave. It ain't much but it be all I got of where I be from to honor my family," he concluded.

Shadrach thanked him and walked back to his horse, saddled up, and, thinking of his mother, rode in the direction that he had been pointed to, until he came to a partial clearing in a valley between two hills with some broken and rotten wooden fencing around part of it.

"Dis must be it," he said aloud.

There were three dozen or so raised mounds of dirt bunched in rows within the fencing. Shadrach got off his horse. He stood and looked at the different mounds of dirt. There were weeds, tall grass, small seedlings that had sprouted, and vines running over the graves which had not been tended. Several rotting tree limbs from an overhanging oak tree had fallen into the graveyard. The limbs crumbled when Shadrach lifted each to move them off the grounds. There were no markers of any type, other than a few large broken rocks at the head of each mound of dirt, so there was no way for him to know which grave, if any, was his mother's. Maybe this fellow, Seydou, was simply wrong. He had no choice now. He would have to go back to town to see if the woman in the saloon was, in fact, his sister, Cecilia. If she was, he hoped, she would know about his mother and his other sister.

CHAPTER 16.

The Union City mine owners, through Mr. Hawkins, requested an urgent meeting with Sheriff Wilson. Word about a possible miners' strike was spreading around town and the mine owners wanted to press Sheriff Wilson with their thoughts on how he should handle it. Although he was not specifically invited, Sheriff Wilson asked Dalton to come to the meeting with him.

"You might as well see what we're up against," Sheriff Wilson said.

The meeting was held in a suite in the Hawkins Hotel, which was owned by Mr. Hawkins. All of the mine owners, dressed in their business suits, were there when Sheriff Wilson and Dalton walked into the room. The mine owners were seated and several were sipping on glasses of whiskey. Mr. Hawkins remained standing, periodically puffing on a cigar. The local bank president, Mr. Daigre, who had lost his left arm as a colonel in the war, was also present. His bank was the one used by the mine owners and by other business owners in town. Dalton looked around the room but did not see Batiste. After some brief pleasantries the meeting began.

"Sheriff, we are certain that the miners are planning to strike though we don't know exactly when. We have been able to determine who the ring leaders are and want you to arrest them now so that this strike won't occur," Hawkins said, on behalf of those present.

"On what charge?" Sheriff Wilson asked.

"Disturbing the peace," Mr. Walsh, a mine owner, promptly offered. He had been the town Constable several years earlier before getting into the mining business.

"But they haven't done that yet," Sheriff Wilson replied, as Dalton sat quietly watching and listening.

"Sheriff, the miners have no right to strike, no legal right, and you can use any means necessary to assure that no strike occurs and disrupts the mining operations," Hawkins said, to the grumbling approval of the other mine owners.

"Yeah, you can think up a crime to charge them with after you arrest them. No one cares about that, just arrest them to derail the strike," Mr. Gloop, a balding mine owner with a high pitched voice, offered. Mr. Gloop had inherited his mining rights from his deceased father.

"I'm sure we can make it worth your while if you cooperate on this," Mr. Walsh interjected, before lifting his glass of whiskey.

"Settle down, boys," Hawkins said to Walsh, Gloop, and the other mine owners who were present and had begun to talk among themselves.

The right of workers to strike was not protected until 1935 when federal legislation entitled the National Labor Relations Act was passed. Under Section 7 of the Act it provides that "employees shall have the right…to engage in other concerted activities for the purpose of collective bargaining or other mutual aid or protection." Under that law strikes are generally considered protected "concerted activity."

"Have you talked to the miners to find out what their complaints are? Maybe this can be solved peaceably," Sheriff Wilson asked.

"Sheriff, we don't need to do that. We want you to arrest the ring leaders. Now look we have identified them as Mack, the owner of the Miners' Kitchen, Ralph Day, Dean O'Sullivan, Charles McKinney, and Nuncie Spizale," Hawkins said, flicking the ashes off of the cigar he held between his fingers into an ashtray.

"I'm not going to arrest people without cause," Sheriff Wilson replied firmly. The mine owners again began to all speak over each other.

"Quiet! Sheriff, if you don't arrest them we will be forced to take matters into our own hands. You've met Mr. Batiste. I have some of his associates coming to town as well to assist if we need it in case there is any trouble. We will not be intimidated, nor will we allow the mine operations to stop. You better get right with that," Hawkins threatened smugly, again to the vocal approval of the other mine owners.

"I don't think you understand how important the mining business is to this town. It pays your salary. It generates the revenue for the other businesses here. If there is a strike all of that is jeopardized," Mr. Daigre, the bank president, said in a more reasonable tone. Several mine owners began to speak over each other.

"Alright! Alright!" Hawkins interrupted, waving a hand to again quiet them. "Sheriff, we've made our position to you clear. It's your decision now. You know what you have to do."

"I think we are done here. I'm not arresting anyone just because you tell me to. That's not how I enforce the law," Sheriff Wilson said directly to Hawkins, before abruptly standing up. Dalton stood as well.

"You are making a mistake," Mr. Daigre said. Sheriff Wilson ignored Mr. Daigre's remark and with Dalton in tow he then left the meeting.

"What are we going to do? Any ideas?" Dalton asked, as they walked down the entrance stairs of the hotel.

"I don't know yet. But I'm going to talk to Mack. I doubt he is provoking a strike, but he'll definitely know what's going on with the miners," Sheriff Wilson said.

"Yeah, my guess is he is on the list to get him out of the way so Hawkins can take over the Miners' Kitchen," Dalton said.

"Probably so," Sheriff Wilson said.

"And what about the threat to bring in Batiste's associates? You think he means it?" Dalton asked.

"Got to think about that too. I wish I had more deputies," Sheriff Wilson said. He stood for a moment in the street contemplating his next move. "Let's go talk with the mayor first and see if there is anything else that he can do," Sheriff Wilson then said.

Sheriff Wilson and Dalton went to the mayor's office. They spoke with the mayor but despite his sympathy he made it clear that he could not authorize any other deputies without the approval of the town council.

"You know what they are doing, Mayor," Sheriff Wilson said.

"I do, but I'm already out on a limb by keeping you on. I'm sure they are trying to figure out how to get rid of me, but in the meantime the council simply will not approve any more deputies in the budget and I don't have the authority to appoint any more. You know that," Mayor Adams said.

"I'm not blaming you, Mayor. Just frustrated, that's all," Sheriff Wilson replied.

"I understand. Just do the best you can. No one can blame you if this gets out of control. I'm glad you were able to get Dalton as your new deputy. After what happened to the last one I didn't think anyone would want the job," the mayor said.

Dalton and the sheriff then left the mayor's office and headed to the Miners' Kitchen to speak with Mack and see what, if anything, they could learn about a possible strike. Mack, however, was not forthcoming on details, other than to confirm the miners' dissatisfaction with current working conditions and press the sheriff to do more to protect the miners.

"Sheriff, you just need to run that Batiste fellow out of town. That will solve the problem. He's up to no good and you know it," Mack said.

"Mack, you're not answering my question. I don't want to be blindsided. Are they planning a strike, and if so when?" Sheriff Wilson asked. Mack again ignored the question and instead continued to complain about the mine owners and about Batiste.

"Let's go, Dalton. Can't get any information here," Sheriff Wilson said, looking directly at Mack as he spoke.

The next morning Ralph Day was found dead in his boarding room. He had been beaten badly and pistol whipped. Dalton and the sheriff asked around but no one had seen anything, though suspicions among the miners against Batiste ran high.

CHAPTER 17.

Midnight met Emmalene at the Baldwin house on Sunday and they began to walk together to St. Mary's Church. Emmalene wore a starched white cotton dress with white gloves and a white hat with black embroidery around the brim. Midnight thought that she was beautiful. He was embarrassed by his attire and felt underdressed. He didn't own a suit, so he wore his new frontier clothes which he had cleaned and brushed as best he could.

"Have you read the paper that I gave you on women's rights, *The Agitator*?" Emmalene asked, looking straight ahead as they walked.

"Not yet, but I been thinkin' on da subject. Ain't never heard 'bout such a t'ing before, but it do seem to me dat everyone be created equal like it say in da Declaration of Independence and dat includes women, so maybe dere ought to be sometin' done," Midnight said, hoping that he had spoken correctly about the Declaration of Independence. Emmalene did not respond and continued to look straight ahead as they walked so he was unsure what she thought of his comment.

They entered the church and took seats in the front pew. Midnight noticed that most of the men were wearing suits and the women wore dresses. Father Sprecht thanked the Sunday morning crowd for coming to mass. He then announced a collection, as a plate passed around, to help rebuild the Asylum which had been damaged in the recent fire.

As the service began Emmalene picked up a hymnal and, for the portions of the mass that were not in Latin, followed along with Father Sprecht. Midnight picked up one as well but his ability to read was not good. He had been taught his alphabet as a child by his mother before she was sold off but, as a slave, he had never been allowed any formal schooling. Indeed, prior to 1869, every southern state, except Tennessee, had legislation, called anti-literacy laws, which prohibited the education of slaves and imposed fines, whippings, and/or imprisonment for any violation. Reverend had tried on occasion to help Midnight with his reading during the war and he had proven a quick learner, but there wasn't much opportunity. Emmalene gently took the hymnal from his hand and turned it to the right page and handed it back to him. When she turned a page Midnight would also turn the page in his hymnal so it would appear that he was following the service.

As was the custom, one of the men in church went up to the dais on the altar and then read from a portion of the Gospel of John, which had been selected by Father Sprecht for the mass. When the reading was done Father Sprecht stepped from behind the altar as the man returned to his church pew.

"I'd like to introduce the congregation to my new assistant, Emmet. You will be seeing more of him as he helps me with the day to day operation of the church," Father Sprecht said, gesturing for Midnight to stand and be recognized. Emmalene gave Midnight a slight nudge and he stood up halfway and reluctantly raised his hand in the air.

Father Sprecht then returned to the altar and along with the altar boys prepared for communion. He stepped out from the altar again as those in attendance fell in line to receive communion. Although he was told by his mother that he had been baptized by an itinerant preacher in a stream near the slave quarters, Midnight was not familiar with Catholic services. Emmalene got up to get into the communion line and Midnight followed her and received his first communion.

After communion Father Sprecht cleaned the chalice and set the altar in order. He then bowed his head and offered a concluding prayer. Once the prayer was finished he looked up and smiled widely at the congregation.

"Folks, we are going to change things up a bit in a way I'm sure you will enjoy. Miss Emmalene Davis has agreed to sing a brand new song, *Near the Cross*, for us, which you are welcome to join in, to end our service this morning. The song words are in a handout in the hymnal. The song was written by the mission worker and friend of all Christians, Miss Fanny Crosby. We have received one of the first copies of this song, even before formal publication, and Emmalene has been practicing it. So Emmalene, if you would," Father Sprecht said.

Emmalene stood up and, without a word to Midnight, walked to the front of the church. Midnight did not know what to think when he heard the announcement. He glanced around the church, looked at Emmalene and then at the handout with the words of the song on it. He recognized the first word in the hymn, 'Jesus.'

Emmalene stood to the side of the altar and began to lift her voice, singing a cappella, as Father Sprecht and the altar boys slowly made their way down the middle aisle of the church.

Jesus, keep me near the cross;
There is a precious fountain,
Free to all, a healing stream,
Flows from Calvary's mountain.
In the cross, in the cross,
Be my glory ever
Till my raptured soul shall find
Rest beyond the river

Midnight was stunned by the allure of Emmalene's singing voice. It reminded him briefly of his mother singing to him at night when he was a child and had trouble falling asleep. He glanced down again at the handout and tried his best to mouth the words he heard her singing and to sing along with the others. However, despite his best efforts he was always slightly late and off key in his rendition. When she was finished singing the congregation clapped lightly and slowly dispersed. Midnight walked right up to Emmalene, who was still standing in the front of the church.

"You is a real good singer," he said, gushing over the fact that someone so pretty and with such talent was with him.

"You *are* a good singer," she corrected him.

"Oh, yeah. You are a good singer. Ya know you is so good ya ought to sing in a saloon wit' one of dem dancin' girl saloon shows. I bets you could make lots of money dat way," Midnight said, trying to show his appreciation for her talent and trying his best, though incompletely, to remember to say 'you' and not 'ya.'

"A saloon! You really are a fool!" Emmalene said and immediately walked away from Midnight. He hurried to catch up to her and she stopped and turned to face him. "I will see myself home, Emmet.

112

Goodbye!" she said, before he could speak, and then she left him standing alone in the middle of the church puzzling over what he had done wrong.

CHAPTER 18.

Shadrach spent several days and nights on the outskirts of Elyton watching the rhythm and movement of the people in town hoping that he would see his sister on the street. He saw white men going in and out of the Wanderer each day and night but he never saw her. On one occasion, near nightfall, he watched as a dozen or so men dressed in their different Klan robes, some wearing improvised hoods, entered the saloon and thirty minutes later left on their horses with unlit torches in hand. He knew that they were up to no good.

In 1866, when Shadrach, Reverend, Dalton, and Midnight were hearing rumors about being assigned Reconstruction duty in the South for the army, the Ku Klux Klan was formed. Former Confederate General Nathan Bedford Forrest was the first Klan leader, given the peculiar title of Grand Wizard. There were other odd titles bestowed within the group, like Grand Scribe, Grand Giant, Grand Titan, and such, as if it was a quaint southern college fraternity. General Forrest had his own checkered history in the Confederacy, which included a massacre of 200 black Union troops that had surrendered at the 1864 Battle of Fort Pillow in Tennessee. It was one of the most controversial battles of the Civil War. Eventually, however, even Forrest could no longer tolerate the Klan's reign of violence, which included numerous lynching's, and resigned. Estimates are that between 1868 and 1871 the Klan lynched more than 400 people in southern states. The lynching's continued unabated thereafter. In Alabama alone it's estimated that 340 people were lynched by the Klan between 1877 and 1943.

After the 1892 brutal lynching's of three men in Memphis, Thomas Moss, Calvin McDowell, and Will Stewart, Ida B. Wells began her sustained journalistic campaign against lynching's. Pressure built up in some states which resulted in the eventual outlawing of lynching in North Carolina (1893), Georgia (1893), South Carolina (1895), Kentucky (1895), Ohio (1897), and in Texas (1897). The first anti-lynching bill was introduced in Congress in 1918 but failed to pass. Thereafter such bills were repeatedly introduced, nearly 200 times, but failed to pass both houses of Congress.

Indeed the rampant violence of the Klan throughout the South resulted in the passage by the Republican controlled Congress of the Ku Klux Klan Act of April 1871 which, for the first time usurped the role of the states over criminal matters and designated certain crimes as federal crimes subject to federal penalties. The Act sought to criminalize individuals who "conspire together, or go in disguise…for the…purpose… of depriving any person or class of persons of the equal protection of the law." It was one more instance, along with other examples arising during the Civil War and Reconstruction, of the change in federal and state relations and the expansion of the federal government's authority over traditional state law matters.

General Robert E. Lee had rejected the request of some of his soldiers to continue fighting a guerrilla war against the Union after the surrender to General Grant at Appomattox. Jefferson Davis had also opposed the idea noting that, "guerrillas become brigands and any government is better than that." The Klan, Shadrach thought, was in essence a disreputable guerrilla unit doing what Lee had specifically rejected, except that their victims were not army combatants but former slaves or southern whites who supported the Union or the rights of the recently freed slaves.

From conversations with former slaves in the woods Shadrach had learned that the Wanderer had 4 or 5 bedrooms upstairs. A former slave woman he met told him she had cleaned those rooms before the war, that the owner was very mean, and that there were women who stayed upstairs. Shadrach never saw any of the women leave the saloon so he was not even sure the one who might be his sister worked there. Late one night he went up the stairwell behind the saloon but found the door at the top of the stairs on the second floor bolted shut. One thing was for sure there was going to be no easy way for him to get in and out of the place without being seen.

Nevertheless, from watching, he realized that the bar ran out the last patrons around 2:00 a.m. and the staff then spent some time cleaning up before locking up for the night.

The next night he waited outside of town. A few minutes before closing time he left his horse tied up in the nearby woods and walked, ran, and periodically hid, making his way through town to the saloon. Finally he got there without being seen and he watched from a nearby alley as the last two drunken patrons were run out of the bar. He stepped out of the shadows, looked through the saloon window and saw the outline of a large white man behind the bar, wiping it down and putting up glasses. Several women were picking up empty glasses. However, he couldn't see well enough through the dirty windows to know if any of the women were his sister. He had to enter the bar.

"Boy, what are you doing here?" the large man behind the bar said, as soon as Shadrach stepped into the saloon through the swinging front doors. The man immediately retrieved a heavy wooden club from under the bar and started to move menacingly from behind the bar toward Shadrach as the women looked up to see who had walked in.

"Mr. Jack, wait. It's my brother," one of the taller women, blue eyed with long curly brown hair and light copper colored skin, said. She ran over to Shadrach and hugged him.

"Better be quick about it," Jack, the bartender, said to her.

"You can't stay here," she said.

"OK. I got a campsite off da logging road 'bout a mile down by da stream. Can ya meet me dere tomorrow?" Shadrach asked quietly.

"I try. It ain't easy," she whispered into his ear.

"Cecilia, get him out of here now and get back to work," Jack said, raising his voice and setting the club down on the top of the bar.

"Let'em talk, Jack," another of the women, with a cast iron skin tone, who was named Lizzy, said.

"Watch your mouth, Lizzy. This don't concern you," Jack replied.

"Anyt'ing concern Cecilia concern me. Dat's my girl," Lizzy replied. Jack stared at Lizzy who mumbled something derogatory to herself and then smiled insincerely at him.

"If da owner be here he kill you. Go now. I do my best," Cecilia said, kissing Shadrach on the cheek, as she pushed him out of the swinging doors, thrilled to see him but fearful for his safety.

Jack walked to the front of the bar and closed and locked the exterior doors.

"Don't you be getting no ideas about running," Jack said to Cecilia, after locking the doors.

"Yeah, it be such a great place to work why would we run?" Lizzy said sarcastically causing the other women to laugh.

Shadrach quickly ran away from the saloon, down the alley, and made his way back to his horse. He then rode to his temporary campsite, angry that after everything he had been through as a soldier, now as a free man, there were still places where he was not welcome and had to hide from the potential violence of a white man.

Once the women were finished with their cleaning Jack, who lived upstairs and served as the guard of the women living there, escorted them upstairs making sure that each was locked in their separate bedrooms for the night. Cecilia sat on the edge of her bed and her thoughts returned to Shadrach. She had not allowed herself the luxury of thinking about her family members, or the possibility of reuniting with them, in a long time.

CHAPTER 19.

Reverend finally made his way into Boston, a town that Ralph Waldo Emerson had recently written had "the same meanness and sterility...as one finds in a boot manufacturer's premises." Reverend had been pushing hard covering as many miles every day as possible. He would rise early each morning at daybreak, eat his meager meals in the saddle, and then bed down for the night, often in a cold camp, as it got dark.

He rode down the snow covered city streets that he knew prior to his enlistment when Boston had been the center of the abolitionist movement. One of the country's leading abolitionist newspapers, *The Liberator*, had been published there by William Lloyd Garrison until 1865. The abolition articles in the paper so inflamed opinions in the South that several southern states indicted Garrison for allegedly provoking slave revolts. Georgia even offered a $5,000 reward for his capture and return there for trial and hanging. Bostonians, in highly publicized incidents, had also resisted the return of several slaves under the Fugitive Slave Act.

Despite it being a leading light for abolition, of which Reverend was proud, there had often been open hostility toward abolitionists in town by some of their fellow Bostonians who feared that the movement would prompt a war. Business owners that relied on materials like cotton from the South, materials made available because of slave labor, had also feared the disruption of their businesses if the abolitionists prevailed and slavery ended. Nevertheless the 1780 Constitution of Massachusetts had specifically prohibited slavery within its borders, one of the earliest state constitutions to do so.

The city seemed to Reverend to be changed since the war, or was it, he wondered, his vision of things, his sense of space and distance, that had changed, like an adult returning to find the surprising smallness of his childhood neighborhood. Had his horizons widened or was the town just smaller than the many open fields and places he had raced across in battle that were now somehow an integral part of him? The people on the streets seemed parochial, busier, and yet more individually detached, more somber. He didn't know if that was true or if he was seeing them through a war weary lens.

He was tired, but excited as he rode down a side street to the home of his fiancé and her parents. It was a small unpretentious framed house. He got off his horse in front of the house and tied the reins to the front fence. The sun was over head, though snow lay in heavy patches on the ground, as he walked down the gravel lane to the front door and knocked. The house seemed unchanged since he had last been there many years ago. A minute later Theresa opened the door and fell into his arms in an emotional embrace. Her parents heard her yell when she first saw Reverend and came running from other parts of the house. All four of them embraced. Theresa and her mother were crying.

"We prayed every day for your survival and the Lord has answered our prayers," her mother, Mrs. Hymel, said, as she wiped the tears from her eyes.

"Amen," Mr. Hymel replied, as he absentmindedly pulled on his mustache. Reverend felt a bit light headed, bracing himself against the door frame, and asked if he could sit for a moment.

"Are you alright?" Theresa asked.

"Yes. I…I just haven't eaten much the last few days and…I think it has caught up with me," Reverend said.

"Mother, get some water for him," Mr. Hymel said to his wife, who immediately headed for the kitchen.

"And then you are going to eat something," Mrs. Hymel said, as she walked away.

Mrs. Hymel came back with some water which Reverend drank and then they all made their way into the kitchen so that she could feed Reverend. While the Hymels remained mostly silent, occasionally engaging in small talk, Reverend ate the chicken and potatoes that she heated and served, wiped his plate with a piece of homemade oatmeal bread, and swore that it was the best meal he had ever eaten.

"We read all your letters and I read all the articles in the *Boston Evening Transcript* paper, but now that you are here tell us about the war and Reconstruction. Tell us about what you saw. Was it as bad as they say?" Mr. Hymel, who worked as an administrator in the Port of Boston, asked in rapid fire succession.

"Honey, let him rest a bit. He just got here and he's worn out," Mrs. Hymel replied to her husband.

"It would be hard to know where to start," Reverend said in response. But nevertheless he did so, in measured tones. He told them of the poor field conditions, the chaos and confusion of the battles, the pitiful medical treatment available to soldiers on both sides and the many deaths and injuries which he had witnessed.

"There is nothing romantic or gallant about war and the constant anguish we felt as soldiers over the threat of death. Men are killed or maimed. The only requiem for the dead on the battlefield is the blast of bugles and the percussion of cannons. Why we romanticize it, I'll never understand. Only someone who has never been in battle could do so. What glory is there in killing another human being or in constantly worrying about whether you will be killed? As Hannah said in the Bible, 'not by might shall a man prevail,'" he said.

He told them about men who had bled to death because of inadequate medical care, primitive amputations, and about the men who lost their limbs and then their lives to gangrene. He told them of the selflessness of some soldiers on both sides and about Midnight, Dalton, and Shadrach. He told them about his prayers each night and each morning and about how Theresa's letters had lifted him so often. And then, tired from his journey home and needing to start the process of cleansing his soul of what he saw as his potential sins, of an unnamed heaviness which he carried, he told them a story where his voice broke and that he trembled in telling.

"It was our second engagement with the Rebs. I was still trying to figure out what I was supposed to be doing. We really hadn't had much training. If it weren't for Dalton's leadership we would have been a lost group most of the time. There was cannon fire and lots of smoke as both sides ran across an open field towards each other firing and yelling," Reverend said, occasionally glancing at Theresa as he spoke. "I watched Dalton shoot and kill a man at point blank range. I saw Shadrach slam a Reb to the ground and then, without hesitation, knife him with his bayonet. And then I was knocked down by a Reb I didn't see, but who ran straight into me from the side," Reverend said exhaling hard, his breathing momentarily labored. "As I lay on the ground he tried to stab me with his bayonet. I managed to roll and kick his legs out from underneath him. He fell next to me. It was pure instinct on my part. Before he could get to his feet I shot him in the chest at close range. He lay there bleeding and I tried, in the midst of all that noise and confusion, to comfort him. He told me his name as I held him...James Doyle. Right before he died he asked me to reach into his pocket. I did...a picture... I've carried it ever since," Reverend said, but stopped as his emotions finally took away his voice.

Reverend's hand shook slightly as he pulled a dull and wrinkled black and white photo of a young woman and baby out of his coat pocket and set it on the table. He hung his head down, tears filled his eyes, and he sobbed openly. Theresa stood up and pulled him to her bosom.

"You had no choice, no choice," Mr. Hymel said defensively, as Mrs. Hymel lightly bit down on her lower lip. Reverend sat up straight and wiped his eyes. Theresa sat back down next to him continuing to hold his hand.

"If the Lord wanted to take you at that point He would have," Mrs. Hymel then interjected, appearing positive in her belief.

"All that matters now is that you are here and alive," Theresa said, ignoring the indelible grief displayed in what Reverend had just said.

"From that point on, instead of fighting, I tried to care for all the wounded, no matter which side they were on, and tried to learn as much as I could about treating battlefield wounds, which herbs to use to make a poultice, how to sanitize instruments, how to bind wounds and stop bleeding. It seemed to me there was no more blue or gray, just red from all the blood that I saw," Reverend said, his voice becoming more even.

"There were no doctors to tend the troops?" Mr. Hymel asked.

"Not often. I was fortunate at some point to meet Clara Barton and

Dorothea Dix, both Union nurses. Amazing women who I watched patch up soldiers after one of our battles and from whom I learned much," Reverend said. The table fell quiet for a moment.

The use of women as nurses stirred moral controversy at the time, resulting in a rule that in order to be a nurse for the Union Army the woman had to be over 30 years of age and "plain looking." Clara Barton was known as the "Angel of the Battlefield" for her heroic service during many battlefield engagements. After the war, in 1882, Barton founded the American Red Cross. Dorothea Dix had worked as an advocate for the mentally ill before the war and was instrumental in creating the first asylums for the mentally ill in the country.

"And maybe that's why the Lord let you live. To show you the evil of war, but then use you to help ease the suffering of the wounded," Theresa finally said, trying in her own way to make sense of what Reverend had said.

"It's not a war we asked for," Mr. Hymel said, in a distracted voice, as if he was thinking back over the long years of the war and the toll it had taken on the country.

"What I learned talking with all those soldiers, Confederate and Union, that I was tending, is that we are all the same. They were not any different than me. They had the same hopes, ambitions, and fears," Reverend said.

Reverend's eyes moistened again. The table fell uncomfortably silent reflecting the historical disconnect, the broken bridge of understanding, between those soldiers who expend themselves in combat and the citizens who stay at home. Mrs. Hymel stood up and put her hands on her hips, deciding to change the emotion of the moment in the only way that she knew how.

"Enough of this. I haven't heard anyone ask for my apple pie?" she said.

"I would love a piece," Reverend replied with a faint smile on his face.

CHAPTER 20.

"A nutta busy day," Midnight said happily to Father Sprecht, as the men prepared to go to sleep for the night.

"Yes it was. Thank you for all your help making the deliveries and helping me clean up. I think this arrangement is going to work out fine, don't you?" Father Sprecht asked, as he sat down on his bed and removed his shoes.

"Me too. I really appreciate da work. As soon as I can I promise dat I move to my own place so as not to be a bother to ya. I knows ya would like some privacy sometimes," Midnight said, laying on his bed with his hands behind his head.

"No bother at all and no need to hurry. There's not much housing available out there right now, and what is available is not very good. Besides the rent here is free," Father Sprecht replied, as he stood, pulled back the covers and then got into his bed.

Midnight got out of bed and walked over to the bookcase in the room. He looked at the dozens of books on the shelves that included David Walker's *Appeal to the Colored Citizens of the World* and William Lloyd

Garrison's *Thoughts on African Colonization*. He pulled a copy of one of Frederick Douglass' autobiographies, *My Bondage and My Freedom*, and held it in his hands looking at the front and then at the back cover. There was a picture of Mr. Douglass on the front cover. The book was Douglass' second autobiography and was published in 1855.

"Father, uhm, I was wonderin' if maybe ya could help me wit' some-tin'," Midnight asked, hesitant.

"Sure," Father Sprecht said.

"I be wantin' to read. Maybe da Bible some, to learn more 'bout da stories and da true meanin' of da stories. I also be wantin' to work on my words and such, but I has trouble wit' readin' some of da words. I know my alphabet. My momma taught me dat, but I never had no proper education. Dere weren't no school house on da plantation. Just has trouble sometimes wit' how to say all da words right," Midnight said, placing the book back on the shelf and then returning to lay on his bed.

Father Sprecht was a gentle man. He understood what Midnight was really asking.

"I tell you what. Every night before we go to bed, we'll sit at the desk together and work our way through a part of the Bible. I'll show you about the words, and the proper pronunciations, so that you can read it yourself and we can then discuss the meaning behind the stories. We can start with the New Testament," Father Sprecht said.

"I be greatly appreciatin' it. I has always wanted to learn more 'bout t'ings in an educated way. Seem to me dat if ya has education ya can reason 'bout t'ings and den ya ain't govern by prejudice or da emotion of da moment," Midnight said.

"I couldn't agree more. Then it's settled. We'll start tomorrow night," Father Sprecht said, as he pulled the covers over himself to go to sleep.

"Goodnight, Father," Midnight said, reaching over to turn down the oil lamp between the beds.

"Goodnight, Emmet," Father Sprecht replied, wiggling his body to get comfortable on the bed.

"Imagine dat, me learnin' to read right. I'm a free man, I got me a job, and now I'll learn how to read. Momma would sure be proud if she knew," Midnight then thought to himself, his settled memories of past joys and sorrows flooding into him as he closed his eyes. It was awhile before he fell asleep, excited as he was about this new possibility in his life.

CHAPTER 21.

Cecilia, Lizzy, and the three other women who were imprisoned at the Wanderer were making sure that the chairs were set up around the tables, emptying spittoons, and lightly dusting in anticipation of the bar opening, a task that they were required to perform every morning. Each of the women, like Cecilia, had been sold to the bar owner by their prior owners before or during the war and were then forced into prostitution for the white male clientele of the saloon.

Sexual abuse of female slaves was not uncommon. On occasion, if the sale price was high enough, or if a jealous plantation owner's wife found a female slave too attractive, a female slave was sold into prostitution or as a sex slave. Indeed Longfellow's poem, *The Quadroon Girl*, written in 1842, chronicled the fictional sale of a slave daughter by her plantation owner to be the sex slave of another. The poem, reflective of the practice, ends with:

> *The Slaver led her from the door,*
> *He led her by the hand,*

To be his slave and paramour
In a strange and distant land.

Female slaves were also compelled to breed with male slaves selected by the plantation owners, while others became the unwilling paramours of the plantation owners or their sons. It was one more insidious aspect of the human bondage of slavery and was designed by the slave owners, consciously or not, to demoralize the community of slaves, to emasculate the male slaves, and as a show of their complete power over every aspect of the lives of their slaves.

Jack, the bartender, stepped from a side office into the bar followed directly by Mr. Monroe, the owner of the Wanderer. Mr. Monroe was a balding man with a sallow complexion, bulbous eyes, a noticeable limp, and an uncontrolled twitch of his upper lip, who tended to perspire profusely when he was nervous. He had owned the Wanderer since it opened ten years ago and, for reasons that were unclear, had managed to avoid service in the Confederate Army. Still he was a staunch and vocal defender of the Confederacy, covering his lack of military service with a full throated embrace of the ways of the pre-war South. There were rumors, however, which he vehemently denied, that his family tree included British convicts who were sent to America in the 1600s.

The British Parliament had, in fact, set up the earliest North American colonies as a penal colony. Transportation to the colonies was deemed a legal punishment for certain crimes. It is estimated that nearly 50,000 convicts were sent to the colonies by Britain, with most ending up in the Virginia, Maryland, and Georgia colonies.

Cecilia stiffened her back and eyed Mr. Monroe cautiously as he walked up to her. Lizzy moved closer to Cecilia hoping by her presence to offer some protection.

"Jack told me that your brother came by here last night. That's the one that was a runaway years ago and never got caught, right? He better never step foot in this place again or he'll be carried out dead. You hear me?" Mr. Monroe said to Cecilia, his upper lip trembling as he spoke. Cecilia simply nodded her head in response as she continued to wipe down a table hoping he would step away from her. Mr. Monroe grabbed her by the arm, jerked her toward him, and then slapped her across the face.

"When I speak to you, you will answer me. Now, did you hear me?" Mr. Monroe said, raising his voice angrily for the other women setting up nearby to hear. The women looked up at him with tired fear in their eyes. His temper was well known and each of the women, at one time or another, had been subjected to it.

"Ain't no need for dat, for dat hittin'. She heard ya. We all did," Lizzy said to Mr. Monroe

"One day that smart mouth of yours is gonna get you killed," Mr. Monroe said angrily to Lizzy taking a step toward her.

"Yes, sir," Cecilia quickly said, putting her hand to the side of her face where he had hit her, now reversing roles with Lizzy and hoping to distract Mr. Monroe from hitting Lizzy.

"That's better. I bought you and nothing has changed as a result of the end of the war, least not for you or the other girls here, you understand? This is still the South. It don't matter to me what those jackasses in Washington say or do. This is where you live until I decide otherwise," Mr. Monroe said, turning as he spoke to face all the other women.

"Yes sir," Cecilia and the other women replied in frightened unison.

Mr. Monroe turned back to Cecilia. He ran his hand gently through her long brown hair as the other women watched. Cecilia started to harden herself for what she knew was about to occur.

"All you women hear me. You better not try to leave here. There will be hell to pay if you do and I catch you. I promise you that," Mr. Monroe said, as he continued to hold Cecilia's hair between his fingers and look at her. She met his gaze and forced a quick tenuous smile on her face. "Now get your ass upstairs into your room. I'll be up there shortly," he said to Cecilia. She set down the rag she was using and ascended the stairs up to her room on the second floor.

"Jack, if that brother of hers shows up here again you have my permission to shoot him. Kill him. There'll be no trouble with the law from Sheriff Maddox. I'll see to that," Mr. Monroe said.

"Will do, Mr. Monroe," Jack said.

"Time to go work off some stress and start my day right," Mr. Monroe said, tugging his pants higher up on his bulging waist before walking up the stairs to go to Cecilia's room.

CHAPTER 22.

Dalton dictated a telegram to Reverend in Boston to let him know where he was living and that he was a deputy sheriff. It wasn't much of a telegram but at least it let Reverend know where he was for the time being. As he left the telegraph office he saw a group of miners gathered together further up the street. That was a bit unusual for that time of the morning. They were all facing in the other direction, with their backs toward him. Then, as if fleeing some imminent catastrophe, they quickly dispersed to either side of the street leaving one man alone who was facing another about 20 yards away. The other man was Batiste. It was going to be a gunfight.

Dalton quickened his pace but before he could get much closer a gunshot rang out and the man, who the miners had been standing with, fell to the ground shot dead by Batiste.

The miners gathered back around the dead man as Dalton arrived and knelt down to check his pulse. It was Dean Sullivan, another of the men Hawkins had asked Sheriff Wilson to arrest as a strike leader. Dalton stood up and looked at Batiste who was walking away.

"You ain't gonna do something?" one of the miners said to Dalton.

"It was murder," another miner said, as Sheriff Wilson came on the run, past a grinning Batiste, toward the men.

"Looks like he coaxed him into a gunfight. Shot him right in the heart," Dalton said to Sheriff Wilson when he arrived.

"Dean Sullivan tried to draw on Batiste? I didn't think he even owned a gun," Sheriff Wilson asked the miners.

"Batiste had been riding him all night, calling him a coward and yellow and stuff and kept it up this morning as we left the Miners' Kitchen. Handed him a gun and told him to use it if he knew how," one of the miners said.

Dalton leaned over and picked up the gun near Sullivan's body. It was an older gun that looked to him like it was in slight disrepair. Dalton looked in the chambers and saw that the gun Batiste had given Sullivan was not loaded.

"We told him not to do it, but he got angry and he had been drinking, so he agreed to step out in the street," another miner said, as several miners lifted Sullivan's body to take it to the undertaker.

"Look at this," Dalton said, handing the unloaded gun to Sheriff Wilson.

"Damn. That's murder," Sheriff Wilson replied after examining the chambers. Dalton took the unloaded gun back from the sheriff and tucked it into his belt.

"This has to end," Dalton said to Sheriff Wilson.

"I'll arrest him," Sheriff Wilson said.

"Won't be time for that," Dalton replied, his eyes narrowing in anger with childlike determination.

Sheriff Wilson and Dalton drifted away from the few miners still milling around and walked briskly toward the Hawkins Hotel which

Batiste had entered. Dalton walked into the hotel and then went into the bar off the lobby with Sheriff Wilson following close behind. Batiste was seated at a table with Mr. Hawkins. A bottle of whiskey and two glasses were on the table between them. Mr. Hawkins was filling Batiste's glass and laughing at something Batiste had said. Dalton and Sheriff Wilson approached their table.

As Batiste turned his head in Dalton's direction, and before Sheriff Wilson could say anything, Dalton slammed his right fist into Batiste's left eye knocking him and his chair over onto the ground. Batiste made a slight move for his gun while laying on his back but Dalton already had the dragoon pointing at him, so Batiste slowly moved his hand away from his gun.

"Outside in 5 minutes. You gave the man an unloaded gun. If you don't show we'll know you are a coward," Dalton said loud enough for everyone in the bar to hear him. He then tossed the unloaded gun onto the table knocking over Hawkins' glass of whiskey. And then to make sure he was heard he repeated to those in the bar, "he gave a man an unloaded gun and then shot him. I'm calling him out as a coward."

"I don't believe that," Hawkins said, standing up, frantically wiping the spilled whiskey off his suit pants, and trying to defend Batiste.

"Believe it. It was murder, plain and simple," Sheriff Wilson said, as Batiste managed to sit upright on the ground. Dalton then reared back and kicked Batiste hard in the ribs with the point of his boot doubling Batiste over in pain on the ground.

"Outside!" Dalton repeated and then he left the hotel bar and walked outside. Sheriff Wilson stayed briefly and then hurried to catch up to Dalton.

"Do you know what you are doing? I already lost one deputy," Sheriff Wilson said, walking by Dalton's side.

"I think so," Dalton replied, as they walked to a spot in the street that Dalton picked out to wait for Batiste.

"I could just as easily arrest him," Sheriff Wilson said.

"And you think he is just going to go quietly with you? No, this is the only way. He has to be stopped or he's going to go after the others that Hawkins wants out of the way," Dalton said.

"Are you alright?" Hawkins asked, setting Batiste's chair back up and then helping Batiste up to sit in the chair. "You are going to have some swelling under that eye. Are you alright?" Hawkins asked again. Batiste grunted out an indecipherable reply. He checked his gun but immediately doubled over again from the rib pain where Dalton had kicked him. He grabbed his glass of whiskey and downed it.

"Don't go out there now. Wait. He is baiting you," Hawkins said. Batiste grabbed the bottle of whiskey and took another long swig directly from it. He tried to calm himself.

"That's twice he punched me. It ain't happening again," Batiste said. Hawkins convinced him to sit for a minute. Hawkins then picked up the unloaded gun and looked into the chambers.

"You gave Sullivan an unloaded gun?" Hawkins asked, holding the gun in his hand.

"You don't tell me how to do my job. I got him out of the way like you wanted," Batiste replied, angry at being confronted by Hawkins.

"You're right. You're right. Collect yourself. He has you mad so you'll make a mistake," Hawkins said, setting the gun back down on the table.

Batiste took one more long swig of whiskey and then stood up. He shoved Hawkins hand away when Hawkins tried to steer him back into the chair and headed outside with a small crowd from the bar following him. Word had quickly spread from those who fled the hotel bar and some miners were already on both sides of the street to watch.

"He killed Sullivan," a miner explained to the others who walked up and were asking what was happening.

Dalton was waiting in the middle of the street with his back to the morning sun. Batiste walked out into the street to face Dalton.

"No one calls me a coward and lives to tell about it," Batiste yelled out to Dalton. Dalton did not respond.

"You asked for him. You got him," Sheriff Wilson said before moving away from Dalton to the side of the street.

The two men stood about twenty five yards apart. Batiste flexed the fingers on his gun hand as he stared at Dalton. He then pressed his hand firmly against his ribs where Dalton had kicked him. He looked to his side and saw the miners and others who were watching him. He straightened his back, slowed his breathing, and lowered his hands next to his guns. To Batiste's surprise Dalton started walking quickly toward him closing the distance between them to about 15 yards. The sun shined brightly in Batiste's face. Batiste reached for his gun, but he wasn't fast enough. Dalton shot him dead as Batiste's gun had just cleared his holster.

CHAPTER 23.

"Take the damn hood off, Walt. Everyone knows who you are. Can't mistake your big belly. I can tell you ain't missing too many meals," Mr. Monroe said as Walt, the dry goods store owner, waddled slowly into the Wanderer that night for a meeting.

"I like wearing it. Sewed it myself," Walt replied proudly. He was wearing the hood with his newly designed Klan robes.

"No doubt you'll make someone a good wife," Mr. Monroe said. Several others in attendance were wearing white sheets while still others wore parts of their Confederate soldier uniforms.

Walt sat down at a table next to Sheriff Maddox. Sheriff Maddox, who was the sheriff of Elyton, did not have on a robe or hood. He was a member of the group but, at least at such meetings, didn't feel the need to hide his identity. The sheriff was a non-descript man who carried himself with an air of arrogant mediocrity and pretentiousness, which passed as substance and character in Elyton. He was hard to describe other than with the basics of being 5'8", about 165 pounds, with straight black hair and a high flat forehead. His appearance suggested that he might be a common laborer, not a sheriff. His brutish temperament, however, which was well known, suggested otherwise.

"Hey, Walt," the sheriff said, in a southern Alabama drawl to Walt, who did not respond.

"Gentlemen, let's get started. I want to start by introducing our special guests tonight: Grand Dragon, Thomas R. Jackson, for our realm, Alabama, and Grand Giant, Arthur Macon, over our county," Mr. Monroe said, as both men, wearing misshaped cone hats, stepped forward to stand in front of the crowd of 20 or so men.

Cecilia had cracked open the door to her bedroom upstairs to listen. Neither she or any of the other captive women were allowed downstairs during such meetings. Although the identity of Klan members was supposed to be hidden she recognized most of the voices she heard as local men, several of whom had, over the past few years, paid Monroe to visit her, or the other women, upstairs.

"Thank you, honorable sons of the Confederacy," Grand Dragon Jackson said, producing a mild round of applause from those seated at the tables. "The war may have been lost but we will not lose our southern culture, our way of life. We will never cease to protect the honor of our women from the black hands that we know are forever reaching for them," Grand Dragon Jackson said, again to a smattering of applause. "Congress keeps passing laws to increase federal power over the states. This is a threat to the unfettered liberty we have always enjoyed as white men. It's a threat to state's rights, to government by white men, and to our constitutional right to own slaves. We must do everything in our power to resist it and restore the Constitution," Grand Dragon Jackson said, again to applause.

Southern politicians, like Jefferson Davis, had long argued before secession that the United States Constitution protected the right of states to allow slavery. In particular, he and others referred to the Fugitive Slave clause (Article IV, Section 2, Clause 3), the fact that slaves were counted as 3/5ths of a person for determining representation in Congress (Article I, Section 2), and the provision of taxation for importation of slaves (Article I, Section 9), all of which were referenced in the Constitution, as proof of the peculiar institution's constitutional protection.

"Now the first matter of business is what to do about the northern carpetbaggers and local scalawags in this county, to show them that we will redeem and defend our way of living. Let's send them a message that we will not lay down," Grand Dragon Jackson said.

"We got one that bought the Walker plantation, named Blanchfield. Former Union officer. We hear he hired niggers through the Freedmen's Bureau and is paying regular wages to them," Mr. Monroe immediately offered.

"That has to be addressed. I think he believes he's better than us. Damn Yankee," Walt added loudly, emphasizing the word "Yankee" and quickly surveying the room as he spoke to assure that everyone heard him.

"Are any merchants in town selling goods to him?" Grand Dragon Jackson asked. Several men turned in unison and looked at Walt.

"Sure. Money is money and not all good white folks around here have any right now," Walt replied, suddenly defensive, with his folded hands resting on his stomach. Grand Dragon Jackson didn't seem too happy with Walt's response.

"He knows better than to come into my place. He'll get no service here," Mr. Monroe interjected, as a rebuke to Walt, while looking for approval from Jackson.

"I ain't the only one selling him stuff. The lumber mill sold him lumber and he has a lawyer in town doin' work for him. We have to make a living. We've been hurt enough by the war," Walt replied, as several of those present mumbled disapproval in response.

"Are you accepting those damn greenbacks?" the Grand Dragon Jackson asked Walt.

"Sure," Walt replied again, provoking another round of grumbling from those seated in the bar. "Not everybody's got gold," Walt said, turning again in his chair to look for approval at some of those around him.

Greenbacks were paper currency which the Union issued during the war when banks wanted to charge interest rates between 24% and 36% for loans to the Union. Lincoln refused to borrow on such terms. The currency, which was the first paper currency authorized in America, was in either Demand Notes or United States Notes. Although it was considered as legal tender, the greenbacks were not backed by gold or silver. The Union eventually issued over $300 million worth of greenbacks to help finance the war effort. By the war's end the national debt had skyrocketed to $2.8 billion dollars. It is estimated that the combined expenditures of both governments in the war was $3.3 billion dollars. The South financed the war, at least in its early stages, through tariffs and duties on international trade.

"Alright, enough of that. Who else besides this Blanchfield fellow?" Grand Dragon Jackson asked.

"I see that Charles Hays got elected to the Alabama senate. Damn scalawag! He's now a Republican. We ought to do something about him," Sheriff Maddox said.

"His time will come," Mr. Monroe said.

"Let's focus more locally. We have other groups looking into taking action against those running for office," Grand Giant Macon said.

"We know of at least two local men, scalawags, over in Trussville. They're working with the Freedmen's Bureau and are serving as judges on that Freedmen's court. Been doin' that for a while, despite us warnin' them about it," Jefferson, the former overseer who was standing at the bar, said.

"What's their names?" Grand Dragon Jackson asked.

"One's name Ewell and the other is Anderson. Don't think either of them fought in the war and word is they both took that loyalty oath the Union government has required. I think they were against secession," Jefferson volunteered, happy to be asked and to offer an opinion.

"I know where they live and he's right. They own a dry goods store. Word is they also work for that bureau," Sheriff Maddox said.

"Well, let's take care of them first. What do you think? I can't condone one of our own helping the other side, that's worse than a carpetbagger. We'll deal with Blanchfield later. He ain't going nowhere," Mr. Monroe said, his upper lip twitching after he spoke. It was put to an informal vote and approved.

"I expect you know what to do," Grand Dragon Jackson said to the men, smiling as if he was sharing an intimate secret.

"Burn 'em out," Mr. Monroe promptly replied, to make it clear, as several men nodded their heads in agreement.

"Let's all meet tomorrow night in front of my office," Sheriff Maddox said.

"Be sure to leave something behind so they know it was the Klan that burned them out. We need to create a reputation," Grand Giant Macon said.

Although cross burning would eventually be associated with the Klan it was not part of their terror symbols during or after Reconstruction. The use of the burning cross as a Klan symbol would occur in the early 1900s after a cross burning scene appeared in Thomas W. Dixon Jr. 's 1905 novel entitled, *The Clansman: An Historical Romance of the Ku Klux Klan.* The book was the basis of D.W. Griffith's 1915 silent film, *Birth of* a *Nation*, and, like the movie, glorified the Klan. It was instrumental, along with the influx of a large number of immigrants in the 1890s, to the re-emergence of the Klan in the 1900s. The movie was also premiered at the White House for President Woodrow Wilson and his cabinet. After viewing the film, which casts blacks in an unfavorable light, Wilson reportedly said, "it is all so terribly true."

"We'll let 'em see some of us in our robes and hoods," Jefferson said in response to Macon's request. By the way, can I ask if anyone knows of any jobs that are available? I was an overseer," Jefferson said.

"Save personal business for after the meeting," Mr. Monroe interrupted cutting Jefferson off. Jefferson glanced at Walt who shrugged his shoulders in response.

"White trash," someone leaned over and whispered to the person seated next to them as Jefferson, overhearing the comment, looked around the room to try to determine who said it.

"Have any of the mine furnaces that were destroyed by the Union in this area been restored or reopened?" Grand Dragon Jackson then asked.

"Tannehill got a small cupola furnace going but it can only handle scrap and some pig iron," someone said.

"Thankfully, the Vernon furnace over in Lamar is operating again," Grand Giant Macon announced.

"Mining just resumed in the Red Mountains. Talbot is running the place. It's back fully operational," Sheriff Maddox said.

"Mining is a good way to get the economy around here going again. This county has lots of good ore," Grand Dragon Jackson said.

"I'm helping him get the mine workers," Sheriff Maddox added.

"I bet you are," Grand Dragon Jackson said, with a slight laugh.

Cecilia listened as best she could to all their plans. She didn't know Ewell, Anderson, or Blanchfield, though she had heard them make derogatory remarks about Blanchfield before. She was hoping to hear something that might suggest a good time to try to escape to meet her brother. Her best bet, she decided, was to leave during the morning, when the town was not busy, after Jack had opened up for the day. It would have to be before Mr. Monroe had arrived, and when, perhaps, Jack went to the back storage area to get liquor. She wondered if Lizzy might go with her and planned to talk to her about it. But without a horse it would be difficult to get very far. Still she was determined to try.

Once the meeting downstairs adjourned Sheriff Maddox handed Jack some coins and then went up the stairs to Cecilia's room as he had done after every such meeting. Several other men, including the Grand Dragon, followed him up the stairs to head to Lizzy's and the other women's bedrooms.

"Sure wish I had me some money," Jefferson lamented, as he watched the men walk upstairs.

CHAPTER 24.

Reverend sat uncomfortably at the kitchen table of his parents' house. His mother and father sat at the table with him, physically close but emotionally distant, a metastasized tension lay between them. His reception back home by his parents was cordial, but it was immediately clear to him that, despite the intervening years and his survival in the war, he had not been forgiven for ignoring his father's request not to enlist in the army.

"I'm glad you survived that immoral war, son. But you should never have gone in the first place. You should have stayed here and worked with me in my ministry, as I told you," Reverend's father lectured, intermittently squeezing his lips together in disapproval and adjusting the prince-nez glasses he wore.

His mother sat at the kitchen table with her hands folded in front of her on the tabletop, a dour yet submissive look on her face. Reverend didn't appreciate the continued scolding by his father, nevertheless he thought he would try once more to explain his actions in the hope that he would be understood.

"Father, what was immoral was slavery. My beliefs required me to do what I could about it. Besides, as you must surely realize, if I had not enlisted I would have been drafted," Reverend said. His father listened politely but did not immediately reply.

In 1863 the United States initiated its first military draft, the Civil War Military Draft Act of 1863, also known as the Enrollment Act. The Confederacy had acted first, with a conscription law of its own in 1862, which eventually exempted from service one white male for every 20 slaves on a plantation, resulting in poorer whites, who didn't own slaves, calling it the "Twenty Negro Law." The United States government, under the 1863 Enrollment Act, established draft quotas for each Congressional District. The draft applied to all male citizens between the ages of 20 and 35 and to all unmarried men between the ages of 35 and 45.

Under the Act a person drafted could pay a substitute $300 to go in their place and get out of serving. John D. Rockefeller, Grover Cleveland, J.P. Morgan, Andrew Carnegie, James Mellon, and others who could afford it, paid the sums to substitutes and as a result never served in the Union Army during the Civil War. Others, like John Muir who would later become famous for his exploration of Yosemite, fled to Canada to avoid the draft and only returned after the war. The implementation of the draft in the North was opposed by many and resulted in significant race rioting in places like New York City, Detroit, Chicago, Buffalo, Cincinnati, and Boston.

The July 1863 New York riot lasted 4 days and resulted in approximately 120 deaths and several thousand injured. The property damage estimates exceeded $1,200,000. It started as a protest of the draft with an attack on the Office of the Provost Marshall which oversaw the draft but quickly turned into a race riot with numerous attacks on blacks and the burning of their property, including the Colored Orphans Asylum.

Union troops had to be diverted from battle and sent into the city to restore order.

"There are many injustices in this world. You can't solve them all. You must simply prepare yourself, purify your soul, for the next life, because there are no injustices there and, as I have repeatedly told you, that's the only one that matters," his father finally replied. His mother moved her hands off the table and nervously began to smooth and re-smooth her skirt with her hands.

"I know that's your view, Father. It's not mine. I was 22 years old at the time the war started. And I made my own decision. I supported the abolitionists before the war and once it started I needed to take a stand by enlisting. Silence in the face of evil, in my opinion, is complicity with that evil. In this case, as Emerson wrote, part of that complicity was a 'race living at the expense of race.' I could not sit by quietly and be compliant while the evil of slavery existed, something that should stain all our consciences," Reverend said, as he rehashed the arguments that had led to their harsh break before he left for the war. His father, however, remained emphatic in his views, a stolid pastoral inerrancy and Manichean mindset that had permeated his entire life, unwilling to bend or acknowledge any merit in the views of his son.

"I don't condone slavery, never did, but I'm not responsible for it or its eradication. God metes out punishment in the hereafter for injustice, not me," his father said, in an offhanded but defensive tone.

"By remaining silent you, and everyone else who remained silent were responsible. Not guilty, please understand, but responsible," Reverend said, pushing back to the edge of the widening theological and personal abyss that lay between them. His father's face hardened. His mother looked down, cleared her throat, and fidgeted uneasily in her chair.

"I am not responsible for the sins of others! That's ridiculous," his father replied, his voice rising.

"I don't agree. I believe God calls on us for action, to respond to and be a witness against injustice. Being a Christian is not just about knowing and being able to recite various bible verses, showing up for church services, and waiting for judgment day. We must also act," Reverend said firmly. His father's face hardened again.

"Your 'action,' as you call it, of enlisting to fight against slavery was a futile act. Entirely futile. It merely drug you deeper into sin. Slaves, former slaves, will never be treated as equals. Look what is happening to them now in the South. Lynching's. Black Codes. So your action, this entire war, was an utter failure," his father said.

"Father, you may not agree with me but my actions, like all attempts to make changes for the better of man, even if not immediately successful, are never futile and you seem to be overlooking the fact that the slaves were freed," Reverend replied.

"You can't free people by legislation or proclamation. Freedom comes from spiritual commitment," his father said. "And make no mistake you sinned in that war," his father said, ignoring Reverend's defense of his actions.

"Yes, but some sins are justified," Reverend promptly responded.

"I assume that you killed men in this war. You can't be in a war without killing. That is a violation of the commandments and will condemn your soul for eternity. You added the sin of murder to the sins of slavery. That's the only 'action' I can see," his father lectured, his voice quivering with incipient anger.

"I spent most of my time during the war patching men up," Reverend calmly replied, deflecting the question.

"Did you kill?" his father said, raising his voice again and slamming

147

his hand down on the table, his full throated anger at Reverend, or at Reverend's prior refusal of his counsel, finally coming through.

Reverend looked at him but did not respond, fearful that he would say something to further inflame the situation. It occurred to him that there was nothing he could say that would appease his father or gain his approval.

"We will not solve this today," his mother then said, speaking up for the first time and arbitrating the matter for the moment.

"I agree, Mother," Reverend said, with a hint of antagonism and disappointment in his voice. Reverend's father, slightly red faced, crossed his legs and looked away from him.

"Mother, I am here today to invite you and Father to Theresa and my wedding this Saturday," Reverend then said.

"This Saturday? Who is performing the service?" his father immediately asked, upset with the apparent urgency and, perhaps, with the fact that he was not being asked by Reverend to officiate it.

"So soon? What about inviting your aunts and uncles? Your brother in New York?" his mother asked, a slow distress rising in her voice and etched in the bunched lines suddenly appearing on her forehead.

"We have waited a long time. We want to just go ahead and marry now and get on with our new life together," Reverend replied, a calmness returning to him as the thought of Theresa crossed his mind.

"The only reason you had to wait to marry is because you went to war. Whose fault is that?" his father chimed in, not willing to let go of his anger even with the news of the impending wedding of his son.

His mother stood and left the room visibly upset. Reverend looked across the table at his father who would not meet his gaze. Although there were many things he wished to say to him in reply, he realized the futility of engaging his father in any further discussion. It struck him, almost as an epiphany, that the dogmatism of his father's religious beliefs extended to a concrete certitude in all aspects of his life. He brooked no dissent, never seemed to consider that he may have erred, and Reverend wondered, for the very first time, what deep insecurity or fear was the foundation of that overwhelming inflexible need to believe that he was always right. It was the moment when whatever greatness Reverend's childhood had bestowed upon his father was completely washed away by the realization of an overarching smallness in his father's thinking.

"I'll see you later, Father," Reverend finally said, standing up to leave. "I hope you will both come to the wedding." His father did not reply.

CHAPTER 25.

Shadrach waited for two days at his temporary campsite off the logging road but Cecilia did not appear. He puzzled over what to do next knowing that if he walked back into the saloon he could well be killed. And he had another problem. He was out of food. He had killed a rabbit and a squirrel with some snares two days before but that hadn't lasted long and the forest seemed devoid of game. He had tried fishing in a nearby stream with a tree branch that he had rigged up like a cane pole and some grubs taken from a rotting log as bait, but had no luck. He still had some of his final army pay, but, in light of his experience on his first visit to town, he was not sure if anyone in town would sell him anything, or if they would even take his money.

After another day with no luck catching food and with no visit from his sister he had no choice. He had to go back to town to try again to get supplies. He wished he knew more about the surrounding towns but worried that his reception there might be worse. He decided to go early in the morning to Elyton before too many people were on the street.

There was a light rain that morning which he thought might be helpful in keeping folks inside. He rode into town and was headed again to Murphy's dry goods store. But as he rode onto Broad Street he saw his sister at a distance being dragged down the street by a white man who had her by the hair. The man, Monroe, was dragging her back to the saloon as she struggled to get free.

"I told you, I own you! You ain't never leaving!" Monroe yelled at Cecilia, as two men walked past Monroe and Cecilia unconcerned by what was occurring. Monroe let go of her hair and then slapped her hard across the face knocking her down before grabbing her by the arm to drag her back unwillingly to the saloon.

Shadrach spurred his horse toward them as his sister continued to resist. He jumped from his horse and running full steam ahead, as Monroe turned to face him, tackled Monroe knocking him to the ground. Before Monroe could get to his feet Shadrach punched him twice, bloodied his nose and busted his mouth, knocking a tooth out. Monroe was semi-conscious and rolling on the ground mumbling about his lost tooth and in too much pain to resist further. As a few more people started gathering on the street, watching, Shadrach grabbed his sister, lifted her up on to his horse, which he then jumped on, and headed out of town at a gallop.

"Stop him," Monroe managed to yell to some men on the street as he struggled to stand up. A moment later a shot from a gun whizzed by Shadrach and Cecilia as they approached the edge of town.

Shadrach rode fast through the slight drizzle with Cecilia hugging him around the waist and as soon as he was out of sight of the town he immediately cut off the main road. Over the next hour he backtracked, stopping periodically to drag leafy branches over some of his tracks, and then waded his horse for a long distance through a stream to purposely obscure his tracks. When he finally got to his campsite they dismounted. Cecilia's scalp was bleeding slightly from where her hair had been pulled. Shadrach fetched some water from the nearby stream and did his best to clean the wound.

"Wish Reverend was here. He know 'bout treatin' wounds from da war, but it don't look too bad," he said to his sister.

Once he had finished cleaning her up he and his sister began to try to catch up. She confirmed to him that their mother had died during the war and was buried in the graveyard which he had seen. Cecilia did not know where their other sister was.

"I ain't seen her since da day she was sold early durin' da war to a man from Georgia," she said, a remarkable yet unremarkable thing in those times.

"How did ya end up workin' at dat saloon?" Shadrach asked, as he poured some water on the smoldering fire to put it out completely.

"I was sold right afta we heard ya run away. Da sheriff came by and told Mr. Walker dat ya had run. Don't know how he knew. Mr. Walker, I think he figgered best to sell me so I don't run to meet up with ya. Da sheriff arranged it. Seems da sheriff done dat for other white folks, arrange sales of slaves durin' da war. Da massa dat bought me," she was saying.

"Dere ain't no massas no more," Shadrach quickly interrupted.

"Well, he owned da saloon so he paid Mr. Walker and put me dere and I ain't been able to get away. I was tryin' dis mornin' to get to ya. My friend, Lizzy, she distracted Jack so I could run, but he done caught me. I hate to tell ya what I been doin'," she said, lowering her head.

"Ain't nobody ever gonna hurt ya again as long as I'm 'round. I make sure of dat," Shadrach said, trying to control his anger. "What be da owner of da saloon's name, da man dat be draggin' ya back?" Shadrach asked, as the rain began to briefly come down harder forcing Cecilia and Shadrach to crouch under a lean to he had previously built.

"Dat be Mr. Monroe. He really a mean little man. I worried 'bout Lizzy. He gonna take it out on her now dat I be gone," Cecilia said and then as soon as she said it, "ya don't be crazy and go back at him. He kill ya."

"I just wantin' to know in case I ever runs across him again," Shadrach said, with a slow rising boil in his voice.

"So now what we gonna do? We can't stay here. He bound to tell da sheriff who gonna come lookin' for us," she said, as a lingering moss covered southern dampness hung in the air. The rain began to let up and a slow rolling fog began to blanket the area.

"I know, but I got to get some supplies. I don't even have a gun to shoot no game," Shadrach said.

"White man ain't gonna sell ya no gun and dey might not sell ya food," she said.

The Slave Codes which existed in southern states before and during the war prohibited any slave from owning a gun. When the war ended the same states prohibited former slaves and freedmen from owning guns and justified it on the basis that neither were "citizens" entitled to the Second Amendment's "right to keep and bear arms." In fact in 1866 Alabama, as part of its Black Codes, prohibited "any person to sell, give, or lend fire-arms or ammunition of any description whatsoever" to free blacks or freedmen. Once the 14th Amendment was adopted, making former slaves and freedmen citizens with a constitutional right to bear arms, several southern states responded by either banning the sale of inexpensive guns or selectively imposing very high taxes on the purchase of the guns to further restrict blacks from owning guns.

"What 'bout da man dat bought da Walker plantation? I met him da other day when I was askin' 'bout Momma and he seem alright," Shadrach said.

"I don't know him. I hear he a northerner," she replied. "Maybe we see dis new man and go up to da North, if ya think he be alright," she said.

"I think dat might be what we have to do in da mornin'. Go see him," Shadrach said.

"I be preferrin' to go now. Don't want to wait here any much longer as people gonna come lookin' for us, especially at night when dey send da hooded riders out. Dey catch ya dey gonna lynch ya," his sister said.

"Let's wait till da mornin'. I covered our tracks good. I learned how to do dat in da army. Let's move camp down da stream a ways and set up another lean to. It still be rainin' some and dat gonna wash things out. Be hard to track us as dis fog be settin' in. So shouldn't be no problem. I gonna try fishin' to see if I can gets us some food. I need to eat. Got to set some snares too. And I'll do some more back-trackin' tomorrow so dey can't follow us," Shadrach replied.

"I be nervous 'bout dat, but at least we be together," Cecilia replied. They mounted Shadrach's horse and walked it further down the stream to set up a new camp.

CHAPTER 26.

Hawkins paced back and forth in his office at the hotel. He pulled out his gold pocket watch to check the time. Two of the other mine owners, Walsh and Gloop, were seated on a sofa in the office which was thick with Hawkins's cigar smoke. Hawkins had called them together.

"This is the last of the Cubans I got from New Orleans," Hawkins said, looking at the cigar in his hand as if speaking directly to it. Hawkins then puffed on his cigar as Gloop and Walsh watched him closely.

"What are we going to do about this?" Walsh finally asked, as Hawkins continued to pace the length of the office.

"The sheriff's not cooperating with us and that new deputy he hired is dangerous. You saw what he did to Batiste," Gloop added in his high pitched voice.

"He outsmarted Batiste. Got him angry and off his game," Hawkins said.

"The way I hear it, folks say, he was much faster than Batiste. Much faster," Walsh contradicted.

"That's the way I heard it as well," Gloop added. Hawkins took a long drag on his cigar.

"Forget about Batiste. His type are a dime a dozen," Hawkins said. "Now look, the combination of Carthage and Murphysburg into Union City is going well. This is going to be one big city soon. Bigger than it is now. We need to be in the right position when this happens so we can continue to profit from our current business endeavors. I still want to expand to other areas outside of mining, maybe dry goods or even a diner. I know you both have an interest in owning the stables and the lumber mill. We can start to buy up some of the land between the towns. It will be more valuable over time. And the first step to our expansion is getting the sheriff out of the way," Hawkins said, before taking another long drag on his cigar.

"Agreed. So how are we going to do this?" Walsh asked, glancing at Gloop.

"Got to be careful," Gloop immediately chimed in.

"Gentlemen, I think it's time for our dear Sheriff Wilson to have an accident," Hawkins said. Walsh and Gloop quickly agreed. "The mayor will then have no choice but to pick our man to replace him," Hawkins said, rolling the cigar lightly between his two fingers.

"What about the deputy, that Dalton fellow?" Gloop asked.

"Once our man is in as sheriff he can get rid of him. If not, there are other ways to sideline him. I have sent for some other men. He'll get another chance to prove how fast he is with a gun," Hawkins said.

"I don't get Mayor Adams. Why doesn't he just get rid of Sheriff Wilson like we asked?" Walsh said, not really expecting an answer.

"And we supported him when he ran for mayor. I thought he'd be more practical. Big mistake," Gloop said.

"We'll deal with Adams in next year's election. He's taking his oath to uphold the law too damn serious. It shouldn't be used to restrict businessmen like us. We are the future of this country. But we have to solve the problem with the sheriff first so we can keep these miners in line. Keep our profits high and our expenses low," Hawkins said.

"You got someone in mind to help the sheriff have his 'accident'?" Gloop asked, with a slight laugh.

"Not sure yet, but offering a $50 gold piece ought to get lots of folks interested in the job," Hawkins replied.

"Great, but in the meantime we need some more men good with a gun," Walsh said.

"I told you I'm working on that. They should be here soon. So let's have a glass of good whiskey to toast our future and the sheriff's unfortunate demise," Hawkins said, as he then casually blew a large smoke ring before setting the last of the cigar in an ashtray. He walked over to a stack of boxes and opened the top case and pulled out a bottle of whiskey. "These just came in. Good thing the war has been over for awhile, we can finally get good whiskey that we don't have to water down," Hawkins said, as he opened the bottle and poured glasses for himself, Gloop, and Walsh.

Whiskey had an interesting history in the Civil War. The South quickly prohibited the distilling of bourbon during the war because it needed the corn to feed its troops and the copper, used in stills, to produce cannons. Besides soldiers drinking it whenever they could get their hands on it, and its use as a sort of anesthesia before surgery in the field, it was used as an antiseptic to clean wounds on the battlefields and in hospitals. It also helped finance the Union's war effort. In 1862 Congress, struggling to pay for the rising cost of the war, imposed an excise tax on all whiskey. The tax started at 20 cents a gallon in 1862 but was raised to 70 cents a gallon in 1864 and finally to $1.50 a gallon in

1865. After the war, with all the restrictions removed, several distilleries were launched in the South. In 1866 this included Jack Daniels, who put a portrait of Confederate General Benjamin Franklin Cheatham on its bottles, and Deep Spring distillery, which used a poster of Robert E. Lee to promote its bourbon.

"To Sheriff Wilson and his accident," Walsh said, lifting his glass and laughing. The three men then clinked their glasses together in a conspiratorial toast.

CHAPTER 27.

"Didn't mean to wake you. I'm going to walk the town one more time," Sheriff Wilson said to Dalton, as he opened the jailhouse door.

"What time is it?" Dalton asked, groggy, sitting up on his cot in the jail cell and rubbing the sleep out of his eyes.

"A bit after midnight. It's been pretty quiet for a change," the sheriff said.

"I must have drifted off," Dalton replied. "I'll go with you."

"Well, catch up if you want, but no need. I'm just going to do a quick walk through," Sheriff Wilson said and then left the jail.

Dalton got off the cot, poured some water in the wash bowl and rinsed off his face to wake himself up. Sheriff Wilson began walking the town checking doors to be sure each was locked. There weren't many people on the street. He could hear piano music coming from the Union City bar so he headed in that direction.

Dalton dried his face with a hand towel and then sat down on his cot to pull on his boots.

Sheriff Wilson continued his walk and a half block from the Union City bar he heard what sounded like arguing in an alley between two buildings. He slowly stepped into the dark alley.

"Who's in there? This is the sheriff. Show yourself," he yelled out. The voices went silent so he stepped further into the alley, which was filled on both sides with stacked empty crates and wooden barrels.

Dalton buckled his gunbelt, holstered his dragoon, slipped on his duster, grabbed his cowboy hat, and stepped out into the cold night air onto the porch in front of the sheriff's office.

The sheriff stood still in the darkness of the alley and listened. Hearing nothing he turned to go back out when someone rushed him from behind and struck him in the head. If the intent was to knock him out it didn't work. He had turned slightly at the last moment resulting in a glancing blow on his head. He then saw the flash of a knife blade that just missed his torso. Dazed, he stumbled into the dim light of the street away from his assailants and pulling his pistol managed to fire a shot into the ground as he fell. Dalton heard the shot and saw the sheriff fall. Two men ran out the alley toward him. Dalton fired a shot into the air and scared them off.

Dalton ran toward the sheriff and saw the shadowed figures of the two men at a distance splitting up. Sheriff Wilson was on his hands and knees when Dalton finally got to him. Dalton helped him to his feet. The back of the sheriff's head was bleeding a little.

"Who did it?" Dalton asked.

"I didn't get a good look," the sheriff said.

"I saw two guys run out but I was too far away to see much of them or who they were. But one was pretty tall and the other much shorter," Dalton said, as he and the sheriff walk back towards the jail.

"Do you remember anything about them?" Dalton asked, once they entered the jail and the sheriff had sat down. Dalton checked the back of the sheriff's head. "Looks like you'll have a pretty good lump," Dalton said. The sheriff ran his hand gingerly over the tender spot on his head.

"My head is clearing a bit. When they ran past me I saw one guy's boots. They were like Indian boots, soft brown, maybe buckskin, with tassels. And in the alley someone flashed a knife and tried to stab me. Just missed me. Looks like he cut a fold in my shirt. Didn't see anything else," Sheriff Wilson said, fingering the cut near the waist line of his shirt.

"Well, the two split up, but it looked like one of them, the tall one, ran into the Hawkins Hotel," Dalton said.

"Let's go over and check it out," Sheriff Wilson said, starting to stand up.

"No. You stay here. I'll check it out," Dalton said. Sheriff Wilson reluctantly agreed.

"I'll ask Doc Fierke to come over and look in on you," Dalton said. The sheriff nodded his head.

"If you catch him, arrest him. I want to know who he is and what this is about," Sheriff Wilson said.

"Will do," Dalton replied and then left the jail.

Dalton stopped a miner who was walking down the street and asked him to go find Doc Fierke and send him to the jail. Then Dalton went into the bar in the Hawkins Hotel and scanned the room.

At the end of the bar he saw a tall man wearing an all deerskin outfit, as if he was an Indian scout. His clothes were dirty and worn and he had on the boots with tassels that looked just as the sheriff had described them. The man was not wearing a gun but he had a Bowie knife in a sheath on his leather belt. The bartender had a glass set up in front of the man and was pouring him a drink.

161

"You, at the end of the bar. Come with me. You are under arrest for attacking the sheriff," Dalton said from across the bar.

The men standing at the bar, or seated nearby, looked around and when they realized to whom Dalton was talking moved away from the bar and from in-between Dalton and the tall man. The tall man stood without moving.

"I said get moving toward the jail," Dalton said.

The man downed his drink, set the glass down, and glanced over his shoulder at Dalton while continuing to lean against the bar. He then turned away from the bar to face Dalton and began to raise his hands in the air as if he was going to surrender. Just as quickly he dropped both hands and grabbed the Bowie knife with his right hand to throw it. He didn't get the chance. Dalton drew his gun and shot him dead. The man stumbled, dropped the knife, and fell forward onto a table and chair upending both and crashing some glasses that were on the table onto the ground. Dalton holstered his dragoon.

He checked the tall man for a pulse and found none. Dalton asked several men to carry the body of the tall man to the undertaker as Hawkins, having heard the gunshot, appeared in the bar.

"Hold on. Check his pockets. See if he has any identification on him," Dalton said to the men who were leaning over to pick up the tall man's body.

"What are you doing, coming in here and shooting my customers? This is a respectable hotel. I'm tired of you disrupting my business," Hawkins said, as the bartender set up the table and chair that the tall man had fallen on.

"You know this guy?" Dalton asked, pointing at the tall man still on the floor.

"No. I mean he's a customer that's all," Hawkins said.

"Maybe I can help," a patron, who heard Dalton's question, said, stepping up next to Dalton and Hawkins.

"Who is he?" Dalton asked the patron, who appeared slightly intoxicated.

"I met him an hour or so ago. He told me his name was Rayne. He just got into town yesterday. Said he was here to make some money and met someone here in the hotel about a job. Didn't tell me who the job was for," the patron told Dalton, as Hawkins eyed the patron nervously.

"Look what's in his pocket," one of the men, who was going to help carry the body out, suddenly said. He stood and handed Dalton a new $50 gold piece.

"He don't look like the type to have a $50 gold piece on him. Guess he got paid in advance for his 'job,'" Dalton said, holding the gold piece up and looking directly at Hawkins. "Is this yours?"

"You must be kidding," Hawkins replied.

"Good. Since it's not, I think I'll give this money to the sheriff for his troubles," Dalton replied to Hawkins. "By the way the sheriff is alright," Dalton added, for all those present at the bar to hear. "Now get this piece of trash out of here," he said to the men who had lifted up the man's body.

CHAPTER 28.

Reverend and Theresa walked out of the chapel after their brief wedding ceremony. He wore a suit and tie borrowed from a friend of his father-in-law and Theresa, her long red hair piled in a bun on her head, wore her mother's wedding dress. Her parents and his parents were the only witnesses. They had discussed it and, despite his parents' objections, decided to go forward with the quick wedding. The newlyweds were going to live with Theresa's parents until they could find their own place. Reverend had originally hoped that this would be the start of a rapprochement with his parents, but instead it now appeared it would became just one more point of contention to which he knew his father would repeatedly return.

The next day Reverend and Theresa began looking for a location for his church. In the process of looking they stopped at First Church, a Unitarian Universalist church. The church had a long history, having been founded in 1630 by the original Puritan settlement in Boston. It had initially been organized as the state congregational church of Massachusetts and was provided state financial support until 1833.

Financial support for churches by states, which were referred to as "Nursing Fathers" by Anglicans and Congregationalists, a phrase borrowed from Isaiah 49:23, was not uncommon in the late 1700s and even the early 1800s. Providing such ongoing support had been a contentious issue in the drafting of several state constitutions. In the early 1800s a split developed in the congregational churches which converted First Church of Boston into a Unitarian church and as of 1833 it was no longer affiliated with the state. Its Pastor was Rufus Ellis. He met Reverend and Theresa as they were seated inside of the church quietly talking about their future.

Pastor Ellis introduced himself and explained the church history, some of which Reverend knew from his prior time in Boston. That history included being led at one time by the legendary Pastor Charles Chauncy who had debated Jonathan Edwards and warned Christians about the anti-intellectual strain of Edwards' popular religious revivals.

Reverend told Pastor Ellis that he had recently returned from service in the Union Army, that he and Theresa had just married, and then explained his plans for his own church. The men then talked about their beliefs and found that they had much in common.

As they spoke Pastor Ellis explained the Unitarian approach to spiritual growth and its inclusiveness, which included the idea that every person, regardless of race or creed, has worth and dignity. Reverend was attracted to what he heard, so welcoming and different from the hard shelled and divisive judgments of the religion of his upbringing.

"You should come to one of our services as we are open to all," Pastor Ellis said.

Pastor Ellis and Reverend agreed to meet over the next few days to further discuss their respective beliefs. Pastor Ellis offered to ask around about a possible location for Reverend's church and invited Reverend and

Theresa to come to the First Church's weekly evening discussion classes.

"We call it the 'First Church Lyceum' and we have a wide ranging discussion group every Monday night covering spiritual as well as philosophical ideas. We don't believe that spiritual inquiry or truth should be limited by denominational restrictions. I think you might enjoy it," Pastor Ellis said.

Reverend and Theresa agreed to attend and told Pastor Ellis goodbye. They left the church, uplifted and holding hands, to continue their search for a location of their own. After another hour of walking they stopped at a small diner near Theresa's parents' house to get some coffee and to escape the cold.

"I didn't realize how tired I was. Can't seem to catch up on my sleep and get past this fatigue that seems to be in my bones," Reverend said to Theresa who, in response, reached across the worn wooden tabletop and grabbed his hand.

"I guess it will take time to heal yourself," she said.

"Body and mind," Reverend replied.

"Whatever I can do to help I will," Theresa said. Reverend smiled. He sipped at his coffee, glanced around the busy diner, and then stared vacantly for a few minutes out of one of the diner's windows.

"What are you thinking about?" Theresa asked, a sometimes troubling question women too often ask the men in their lives. Reverend hesitated.

"A couple of things. My need for redemption. How do I make up for the few men I killed? Was it all justified? I tell myself it was," he said, perhaps thinking of his recent conversation with his father. "One of the casualties of war that folks don't talk about much is the deep wound to your conscience. It's a heavy burden to carry and difficult to heal. I haven't figured out how yet," he said, pausing again as Theresa listened. "I also think about my friends. What they might be doing and how they are dealing with their memories of the war, now that it's over and there is so much time to reflect on it. Wish I had them around to talk to about it."

"Tell me more about them," Theresa said.

At this kind gesture Reverend began, slowly at first, to fill in the details of the friendships. The more he spoke the more animated he became, telling every humorous story he could recall, humor having been the antidote to their boredom and fear in the field, though he was only beginning to become aware of the defensive nature and the salutary effect of that humor.

"One time, this is so childish, but it's an example of what we did when we were bored, Midnight made a pot of coffee in the morning for the four of us and, without us knowing, put a dirty sock in the coffee pot. When he asked Dalton how the coffee tasted, Dalton said it 'was a bit earthy,'" Reverend said, laughing hard at the memory.

Theresa was slowly realizing, as the spouse of a returning soldier, that this was part of a process of decompression for Reverend. She would need to remember to encourage him to talk about his friends or about his war experiences, to shed light on the hidden spaces where he had compartmentalized his thoughts and his trauma. She had heard that there were some suicides among returning Union soldiers and others who had become addicted to morphine to mask their physical and emotional pain, but didn't know how pervasive it was. The trauma, she was learning, was significant.

Statistics concerning suicides by Union and Confederate troops were not tracked closely. Still Union Army records reflect at least 391 suicides. The Confederate Army kept no such statistics. As to serious or debilitating injuries it is estimated that approximately 60,000 surgeries during the war were for amputations. In fact Mississippi devoted 20% of its 1866 state budget for the purchase of wooden legs for returning soldiers.

"You know, I've always believed in the power of prayer and I am grateful for all the prayers I received while a soldier, but now having stepped out of the crucible that was the war, I think it's more important to be able to talk about it, to talk about what we saw, and have folks, who were not in the war, just listen," Reverend said, to thank her.

CHAPTER 29.

"Midnight, this is the first Gospel that was written. At least that is what theologians, people who study the Bible, believe. It is believed Mark's Gospel was written around 65-75 AD in Greek. I personally believe that the apostle Mark the Evangelist wrote this Gospel, but others think it was someone else who wrote it and just used Mark's name to sound more authentic. Apparently that was not an uncommon thing to do at that time," Father Sprecht said, by way of introduction. Midnight was attentive. He asked a few questions and then began trying to read. He struggled with his pronunciations.

"Try that part again. Start at the beginning," Father Sprecht said to Midnight. They were sitting up prior to going to bed and working on his reading. Midnight looked at the paragraph again.

"The be...."

"'The beginning,'" Father Sprecht said, patiently.

"I has trouble wit' dat word," Midnight said.

"Have, not has, and sound out the 'th' in with," Father Sprecht said.

"Oh, that's right," Midnight replied.

"That's OK. Sound the word out, be-gin-ning," Father Sprecht said. Midnight repeated it phonetically, syllable by syllable several times.

"'The beginning of the good news' ab…ab…."

"About. Like a-bout," Father Sprecht said.

"'The beginning of the good news about Jesus Christ, the Son of God. It is' writ…writ…."

"Writ-ten," Father Sprecht said.

"'The beginning of the good news about Jesus Christ, the Son of God. It is written in the book of the'…, Father, what dat next word?"

"Prophet, that is someone who prophesizes, makes predictions, about the future," Father Sprecht said. Midnight thought about that meaning.

"I knew a travelin' man, a plantation preacha, dat dey called da prophet when I was real young. He was friendly wit da womens. Too friendly, and be run off by da massa," Midnight said.

"Different kind of prophet. Quite often in the Bible, especially in the Old Testament, the prophet tells the people about the future or about their moral failures. He is usually an outsider speaking truth to power. Christians believe that there were Old Testament prophets who predicted the coming of Jesus, or the one who would make a way for Him. It is in essence history that is being prophesized," Father Sprecht replied.

"Dat's interestin'. And dey say dat Jesus gonna come again and every-tin' will den be alright. Do ya believe dat, Father?" Midnight asked.

"Yes, I do," Father Sprecht said.

"Would a been a good t'ing if Jesus had come back before da war. Woulda saved lots of lives don't ya think?" Midnight replied, trying to pronounce words properly, before returning to his reading.

"I suppose so," Father Sprecht said. "Remember, for pronunciation purposes, to sound out the 'th' in words like the, that, them, they," Father

170

Sprecht again reminded him. Midnight then practiced pronouncing the words with 'th' in them.

"'The beginning of the good news about Jesus Christ, the Son of God. It is written in the book of the prophet' I...," Midnight continued.

"Isaiah. That's a hard one I know," Father Sprecht said.

The men sat next to each other for the next 30 minutes or so before Father Sprecht called it an evening and climbed into his bed. Midnight then propped himself up against a pillow in his bed with Father Sprecht's Bible in his lap and kept reading and re-reading from the Gospel of Mark.

Midnight reached over on the side of the bed and grabbed the notepad and pencil that Father Sprecht had given him to write out words. He took the pencil and he wrote out the words he had difficulty pronouncing:

beginning

about

written

prophet

Isaiah

He repeated each word softly, so as not to disturb Father Sprecht, until he thought he had each one pronounced correctly. He smiled, pleased that he was slowly learning how to read. He then set the Bible aside and picked up *The Agitator*, the paper that Emmalene had given him. He looked at the captions for the different articles and then decided to practice his reading on it. Eventually he fell asleep with his notebook on his chest and the Bible and *The Agitator* by his side.

CHAPTER 30.

Dalton sat with Sheriff Wilson in the sheriff's office continuing to discuss what they should do next to contain the widening conflict between the miners and the mine owners. It was the day after Sheriff Wilson was jumped in the alley and nearly a week since Dalton had shot and killed Batiste. The sheriff was feeling better, just a mild headache, he said.

"Batiste is gone but I don't think that will slow Hawkins and the mine owners down. Those fellows in the alley were not a coincidence. The price on my head must be $50 so there will likely be others sent to do the job. And now the miners may feel emboldened with Batiste out of the way. But hopefully we have a bit of a reprieve with Batiste, and that fellow that jumped me, dead," Sheriff Wilson said, relaxed, with his feet propped up on his desk. Dalton was stretched out on his cot. His cowboy hat was pulled down partially over his eyes, as if he was going to take a nap.

"Who do you think wants you out of the way bad enough to have you killed?" Dalton asked.

"Likely Hawkins, or one of the other mine owners," Sheriff Wilson replied.

"We'll just have to be more careful. Try to always be together. No more walking the street alone at night," Dalton said.

"Nice idea but there's no way we can always be together," Sheriff Wilson replied. "And by the way, I been meaning to discuss this with you. You didn't tell me how fast you were with that dragoon. I saw it with Batiste and you were obviously faster than the fellow with the Bowie knife," Sheriff Wilson said. Dalton remained lying on the cot.

"Didn't know whether I was fast enough or not with Batiste. That's why I punched and kicked him to slow him down," Dalton replied.

"And you stood with your back to the sun. That's what some professional gunfighters I've known do," Sheriff Wilson said. Dalton pushed his cowboy hat back slightly and lifted his head so he could see Sheriff Wilson.

"When I was a kid and my old man was teaching me how to use a gun, he told me that. He also told me not to stand still, but to move quickly toward the other guy, to close the distance before shooting. He made me practice drawing my gun while walking toward a target. He would set up tin cans on a post that I had to walk toward and shoot," Dalton said.

"I never saw that before, like you do it," the sheriff said.

"I think maybe it disrupts the other guy's concentration. He's not sure when I'm going to draw if I walk forward fast like that," Dalton said.

"Was your old man a gunfighter?" the sheriff asked.

"Nah. He was a farmer, not a particularly good one, if my memory of missed meals is correct. But he sometimes did deputy or posse duty when the sheriff needed it. I'm guessing that's where he learned the stuff he told me, though I really don't know much about what he did before he met my Maw. They never talked much about their lives before marrying. After they both passed on and I was living on the street I heard that my Maw may have worked in a saloon and that's where they met. I don't know if that's true or not. Don't much matter to me," Dalton said.

"Do you have any siblings?" Sheriff Wilson asked.

"Nope," Dalton replied.

The door to the sheriff's office opened prompting Dalton to sit up quickly and Sheriff Wilson to take his feet off the desk and put his hand on his gun. It was Jack Ebarb who worked in the telegraph office.

"Sheriff, I think you may want to see this. Two men just rode into town and tied their horses up in front of the Hawkins Hotel," Mr. Ebarb said.

"So what?" Sheriff Wilson asked.

"They both had their holsters tied down like that Batiste fellow. I'm pretty sure they're gunmen and I'm told they went into the hotel to see Mr. Hawkins," Mr. Ebarb said. Sheriff Wilson looked over at Dalton who stood up. Sheriff Wilson stood as well.

"So much for a reprieve," Dalton said.

"Thanks, Jack," the sheriff said. Mr. Ebarb nodded his head, turned, and left the office. Sheriff Wilson grabbed a shotgun off the rack to take with him and tried to hand one to Dalton.

"Don't need it," Dalton said, checking the chambers in his dragoon. The sheriff loaded the shotgun with buckshot.

They left the office and walked down the street to the hotel. When they got to the hotel they paused to look at the horses that were tied up in front. Both horses were Appaloosas. One had a chestnut base coat and the other was bay. Each horse had the white sweat on them of having been run hard and long. There were expensive metal studded saddles on each and new Springfield rifles in black leather scabbards attached to the saddles.

"Looks like they were in a hurry to get here," Dalton said, patting one of the horses on the rump with his hand.

He then walked with the sheriff up the stairs into the hotel lobby and into the bar. Hawkins was seated at a table with two men. All three had half-filled glasses of whiskey in front of them and there was a newly opened bottle on the table, which Hawkins, puffing on his cigar, lifted to top off the glasses. One of the men was tall and lean with a scar across his left cheek. He seemed very calm as he finished rolling a cigarette and placed it in his mouth. The other man was shorter with straight brown hair past his shoulders. The shorter man wore a slouch hat, Confederate Army pants, and a cadet gray jacket with an upright collar, suggesting that he had been an officer. The taller man was dressed neatly in all black with a liberal coating of road dust on his clothes. Both men had their holsters tied down and each man had a 1861 Navy Colt Revolver in their holster. Hawkins looked up as Sheriff Wilson approached with Dalton.

"Sheriff Wilson, glad you dropped by. I'd like you to meet my two new men. This is Rocky Annala," Hawkins said, pointing to the tall man with the scar. "And this is Ray Dumas," Hawkins said, gesturing to the shorter man who looked to be Creole. Dumas nodded his head in response and sipped from his glass of whiskey. Rocky Annala purposely ignored the introduction, striking a match on the bottom of his boot and then cupping his hands to light his rolled cigarette. Sheriff Wilson tilted the shotgun in his hand slightly so that it was pointed indirectly toward the two men.

"Gentlemen, this here is Sheriff Wilson that I told you about and his deputy, Dalton," Hawkins said, grinning like someone who thought he had suddenly obtained the upper hand in a fight.

"Union?" Dumas said in a raspy voice, looking up at Dalton.

"That's right, Reb," Dalton said. Dumas lifted his upper lip in a mock sneer. Rocky Annala just puffed on his cigarette and stared dull-eyed at Dalton without speaking.

"What are you men doing in town, or for Mr. Hawkins?" Sheriff Wilson asked, keeping the shotgun tilted toward the table.

"They are here for my protection. Perfectly legal. After your deputy killed Batiste, these miners are getting cocky. I have to have protection," Hawkins said, continuing to smirk with a countenance that suggested he knew that the sheriff knew that he was lying.

"Tough way to make a living," Dalton said to Dumas.

"Not when you're as good as me," Dumas replied.

"There's always someone faster," Sheriff Wilson added.

"I can't see either of you being much of a concern," Annala said, finally speaking with his eyes fixated on the sheriff.

"Mind if I see your dragoon?" Dumas then said to Dalton before the sheriff could reply to Annala.

"Not at all if you hand me your Colt," Dalton replied, as he began to lift out the dragoon from his holster. Dumas in a very quick movement of his hand pulled his gun out and handed it, gun butt first, to Dalton who simultaneously handed the dragoon to Dumas. Dumas felt the weight of the dragoon in his hand.

"Too heavy for me," Dumas said, spinning it in his hand so the barrel pointed at Dalton before handing it back.

"Faster than Batiste's Colt," Dalton said.

"So I heard. Impressive," Dumas replied, a bit more friendly, as if he was offering a professional courtesy.

"Was he a friend of yours?" Dalton asked, as Sheriff Wilson and Hawkins watched the exchange between the two men with interest.

"Worked together on a few things with General Shelby in Mexico for Emperor Maximillian after the war. Slower than me though," Dumas said.

Napoleon III had invaded Mexico in 1861 after President Benito Juarez imposed a moratorium on loan interest payments to creditors in France, Spain, and Britain. Napoleon III replaced Juarez with Maximillian, an Austrian archduke. After the Confederacy's defeat in 1865 Major General Joseph Shelby and some former Confederate soldiers fled to Mexico to assist Emperor Maximillian who, in exchange, had offered them a chance to establish their own town in Mexico. Although most eventually returned to the United States, Shelby and his most ardent supporters founded Cordoba outside of Veracruz. But in 1867, after Maximillian was caught and executed, Cordoba was overrun by Juaristas forcing Shelby and his followers to flee for good.

"You must have been scared of Batiste. Hawkins here tells me you punched and kicked him before calling him out," Dumas said, continuing to look up casually at Dalton.

"He gave a man an unloaded gun to draw against him. Did Hawkins tell you that part of the story? He's damn lucky I didn't beat him to death. Seemed like such a coward thing to do," Dalton replied. Dumas laughed as Hawkins squirmed in his chair.

"Batiste was always looking for any advantage he could get. That was cowardly. Me, I don't need one. Straight up I'm the best," Dumas said.

"Funny, but your buddy Batiste thought the same thing," Dalton replied, smiling.

"He didn't have 18 kills like me and that don't count the Yankees I killed while I was serving in the war," Dumas said, patting the gun on his side. "And you won't find any wanted posters on me," Dumas then said pointedly to Sheriff Wilson.

"Is there something else we can do for you, Sheriff?" Hawkins asked, in an attempt to end the discussion.

"No. Just wanted to see who rode into town," Sheriff Wilson said.

"Now you know and you can point that shotgun elsewhere unless you want me to wrap it around your head," Annala then said, abruptly, to the sheriff.

"Any time you want to try," Sheriff Wilson said, shifting the shotgun to point it directly at Annala.

"Must be scared to carry a shotgun," Annala replied, with a dry laugh, to the sheriff.

"It kills like a pistol, just a bit messier," Sheriff Wilson replied, as he and Dalton began to slowly back away from the table.

"Be seeing you," Dalton said to Dumas.

"Look forward to it," Dumas replied, lifting his glass of whiskey toward Dalton as he spoke.

The sheriff and Dalton then left the hotel and stepped outside. They stood briefly by Dumas and Annala's horses.

"Dumas was awful quick with that gun in his hand. And 18 men killed, geez," Sheriff Wilson said. Dalton agreed.

"He was. But we can't overlook that Rocky fellow. I seen men like him on both sides in the war. He's already dead inside. Ain't much that will frighten him," Dalton said, as they started to walk to the sheriff's office contemplating what the addition of these two men to the mix meant for the town and for their attempt to maintain order.

"Speaking of the war. Don't mean to be nosy, but last night it seemed like you were fighting with someone in your sleep and calling for more ammunition. I didn't know whether to wake you," Sheriff Wilson said. Dalton looked down as they walked.

"Were you in the war?" Dalton asked.

"No. I've been sheriff for twelve years," Sheriff Wilson replied. "Was the dream about it?"

"Yeah, sometimes it all comes back," Dalton said. He walked a short distance with the sheriff at his side. "I'm learning that the dead, the ones killed on both sides during the war, are like ghosts that get no peace. They have a way of showing up in dreams and exacting their revenge on those of us that survived it," Dalton said, a bit embarrassed.

CHAPTER 31.

Shadrach and his sister rode in the morning toward the Walker plantation to see Mr. Blanchfield. As they rode Shadrach told his sister more about how he escaped to the North, how he ended up enlisting in the Union Army, his war experiences, and his final duties during Reconstruction in Georgia. And he told her about his friendships with Midnight, Dalton, and Reverend.

"Momma was so worried when she heard dat ya had run. We was all talkin' 'bout it," Cecilia said.

"I got whipped again by Jefferson da overseer. Thirty lashes for bein' disrespectful and decided to go dat night. Me and Mingo. Mingo was a driver so it be a surprise dat he run. I think he got caught pretty quick by dem dat was huntin' us for da reward monies, but I made it away. Dem was some dark days runnin' and hidin' but some folks helped me long da way," Shadrach said.

A driver on a plantation was a slave who acted as a foreman over the slave labor gangs and generally had the trust of the plantation owner. Some were just as abusive toward the slaves as white overseers, while others tried to balance their duties to the other slaves. It was a difficult position to be in, caught often between the demands of the slave owner and their personal attachments to the other slaves.

"Ya mentioned ya friends in da army. Where dey be now?" she asked.

"Well, Reverend he probably be in Boston for da church he is startin'. Dalton, who knows. Midnight, I ain't sure. He a independent one. We is supposed to all write Reverend and tell him where we be. I figure I will once we is settled somewhere," Shadrach said, explaining who he was supposed to send a letter or telegram to in order to reach Reverend at Reverend's fiancé's house. "Her name be Theresa Hymel," he said.

"What be Reverend's real name?" she asked.

"Harrison. And Midnight be Emmet," Shadrach told her, as they approached the big house on the Walker plantation.

"Are ya sure 'bout us doin' dis?" she asked, as Shadrach halted his horse. They both sat on the horse at a distance and looked at the house.

"We ain't got no choice. Got to get some more money and some supplies before we can go to da North," Shadrach said, spurring his horse to move forward.

Once they got to the house Shadrach got off his horse and then helped his sister get down before tying his horse to a hitching post in front of the house. He could see the men he had spoken to before that were working in the field. A servant woman came out of the house onto the front porch and asked what Shadrach wanted.

"Would like to talk wit' Mr. Blanchfield to see if he needs any help," Shadrach said. The servant lady nodded and then went back into the house. A minute later Mr. Blanchfield stepped out onto the porch.

"I understand you are looking for work," he said.

"Yes, sir," Shadrach replied. "I used to work on a plantation and knows da work pretty well."

"I could use some kitchen help but I don't need any field hands right now. Can your woman cook?" Mr. Blanchfield asked.

"She be my sister. Her name Cecilia," Shadrach replied.

"Yes sir, I am a good cook. And I know da kitchen here from when Mr. Walker be here and my Momma cooked for him. I was here back den," Cecilia said.

"By the way did you find out about your mother?" Mr. Blanchfield asked, remembering their conversation when Shadrach had visited the place earlier.

"Yes sir. Unfortunately she passed durin' da war and be buried out yonder," Shadrach replied.

"I'm sorry to hear that. Truly sorry. I need to get that graveyard cleaned up, just haven't had the time yet. The workers I hired are trying to get the fields cleared and ready for when we plant, once the weather warms up. This place had been overrun during the war and apparently damaged by Union soldiers. Walker didn't keep it up after that so we are slowly getting things fixed and cleaned up. But it's on my list to clean up," Mr. Blanchfield said.

"Well sir, I ain't meanin' to be pushy, but if ya don't need no field hands right now maybe I could just clean up dat graveyard for ya. I sure like it to be nicer wit' my Momma bein' buried dere," Shadrach said.

"That's not a bad idea. Can you come by tomorrow?" Mr. Blanchfield asked.

"Yes sir. I be here first t'ing in da mornin' if dat's alright," Shadrach replied.

"That's fine. Where are you two staying?" Mr. Blanchfield asked.

"Tell da truth we just be campin' out. My sister she was workin' in town but not in a good place," Shadrach said. Cecilia looked at him concerned about what he had said.

"I don't think much of that town. Your sister can work here in the kitchen and bunk here with the other ladies if she wants," Mr. Blanchfield said to Shadrach.

"We be much obliged for ya takin' her in and givin' her a job. I'll be alright campin' in da woods. As a former soldier I be used to it," Shadrach said.

"Mr. Blanchfield, sir, don't mean to be speakin' outta line but I overheard da hooded men, da ones dat meet at da Wanderer, talkin' in town and dey say dey gonna come here soon, called ya a carpetbagger," Cecilia told him. Mr. Blanchfield stuck his hands in his pockets and exhaled.

"I'm not surprised. Thanks for telling me. I'll tell my men to be on the lookout for trouble. I'm guessing they will try to burn something at night, maybe the new bunkhouse. Lynching and burning seems to be their way," he said. "You can start today, Cecilia, if you wish. The ladies who work here will take care of getting you set up. Just come in when you are ready," Mr. Blanchfield said.

"Mr. Blanchfield, one utta thing, sir. I be needin' a gun to hunt and I expectin' dat dey won't sell me one in town," Shadrach said, thinking he might as well take a chance and ask.

Mr. Blanchfield sighed and looked for a moment like a cornered cat. He knew that some southern states had outlawed former slaves owning guns, but wasn't sure if Alabama was one or if such a law was still on the books, as there had been so many changes with the two versions of Reconstruction, the Presidential one and the Republican one. It was hard to keep up and stay informed.

"I don't think I can do that, as your sister said they are already after me," Mr. Blanchfield said and then, promptly excusing himself, stepped back into the house. Shadrach and his sister stood and spoke.

"I want us to go to da North, but for now ya take dis here job and make some money and I'll see what I can find and den when we have some saved and I get supplies we can go. Maybe in a month. Mr. Blanchfield seem like a nice man so I thinks ya be OK," Shadrach said.

"What 'bout ya?" his sister asked.

"I be back tomorrow for cleanin' up da graveyard. I'll camp somewhere nearby till I find sometin'. I be checkin' in on you regular 'til we go," Shadrach said. Cecilia looked at him and then hugged him.

"It ain't safe in dat town, so don't ya be goin' back dere," she said, hanging on to him and whispering in his ear.

"I has to at some point, but I be fine," Shadrach said, as he pulled away to mount his horse.

He waved as he rode off and Cecilia watched from the porch, then she walked into the house. Once she was out of sight Shadrach rode until he found a spot to set up a new camp. He thought about going to town for supplies but decided to wait until he got paid for cleaning up the graveyard. After that he planned on finding out what jobs the Freedmen's Bureau had available.

CHAPTER 32.

Reverend and Theresa felt like they had worn out the soles of their shoes looking for a location for his church but had not found any place to use. They had attended mass several times at First Church and had enjoyed the service.

"I really like the folks at the church and their attitude toward people," Theresa said to Reverend, as they sat at the kitchen table. Reverend agreed.

"There is something inviting about their inclusiveness, about their belief in the dignity of all men that is uplifting," Reverend replied.

"It's very positive," Theresa said.

That night they stopped back at First Church to participate, for the first time, in the weekly discussion group to which Pastor Ellis had invited them. There were ten other people present at the discussion along with Pastor Ellis. The group covered some New Testament passages, discussed the emerging question, raised by German scholars like Julius Wellhausen, of who were the actual authors of the Pentateuch. Traditionally Moses was considered the author but Pastor Ellis advised that recent German scholarship suggested there were actually several authors and Moses was not one of them. In addition they discussed some tracts from writers like Kierkegaard and John Stuart Mill.

The group moderator, Pastor Ellis, would read a quote, or a passage from one of the philosophers and the group would then discuss it. For Kierkegaard, for example, they discussed his writing that, "The function of prayer is not to influence God, but rather to change the nature of the one who prays" and "Once you label me, you negate me." For John Stuart Mill they discussed his comment that, "A person may cause evil to others not only by his actions but by his inactions and in either case he is justly accountable to them for the injury." Reverend was not familiar with these philosophers, but enjoyed listening and testing his beliefs against their ideas. Theresa sat by his side quietly throughout the discussions.

Pastor Ellis then turned the discussion to an 1859 book by Charles Darwin, *On the Origin of the Species*. Reverend had not heard of the book or its theories. Pastor Ellis did his best to explain the thesis about descent with modifications, noting that while Darwin's book was about the evolution of animal species, some others, like Thomas Huxley, were claiming its applicability to humans as well.

"I don't know about this book. I was not aware of it, but from what I've seen people do to each other, especially during the war, maybe we aren't that far removed from the animals. Maybe it's our vanity that makes us believe otherwise," Reverend said, only partly in jest. Several others voiced their thoughts, pro and con, on the book as Pastor Ellis had explained it and the meeting ended shortly thereafter.

"Reverend, can I speak to you?" Pastor Ellis asked as those in attendance stood up to leave. Reverend and Theresa said goodbye to the other members of the discussion group and then sat back down to hear what Pastor Ellis wanted to talk about.

"Have you found any place for your church?" Pastor Ellis asked.

"We have not had any luck," Reverend replied.

"I thought that might be the case. There is not much empty space out there to rent. So I have a proposal that I'd like you to consider. I'd like to offer you a chance to conduct some brief sermons here. It would have to start off with our regular schedule, but maybe over time we can expand that," Pastor Ellis said.

Theresa looked at Reverend with a wide smile of appreciation.

"That is a very generous offer, Pastor. Let Theresa and I talk about it tonight and I'll let you know first thing tomorrow," Reverend said.

"Of course," Pastor Ellis replied, standing up. Reverend and Theresa told Pastor Ellis goodbye and then left to walk home.

"I know it's not your own church, but maybe it's a good start to that. People can get to hear you and that may help build your own congregation," Theresa said, hopeful that this proposal would lift Reverend's spirits.

"You know sometimes the miracle you ask for is not the one you get. I'm inclined to accept, if it is alright with you," Reverend said, grabbing his wife's hand as they walked home.

"Absolutely. I will support you in every way I can," Theresa said, and then she raised up on her toes and kissed him on the cheek.

CHAPTER 33.

"Shadrach, I'd like to help you today with cleaning up the grave-yard," Mr. Blanchfield said, stepping down from the porch in his overalls and work boots to greet Shadrach when he arrived the next morning. "Let's get some shovels, rakes, and swing blades from the barn. We may need some other tools, but this should give us a good start."

Shadrach agreed and they walked together to the barn, retrieved the tools and then stopped at the new bunkhouse. Mr. Blanchfield called out for Rory, who stepped outside.

"I spoke with him yesterday and I understand that he may know which grave is your mother's, so I've asked him to come along to point it out to us before starting his other work for the day. Thought you would want to know," Mr. Blanchfield said.

"Thank ya, sir," Shadrach replied.

The three men walked through the fields, some areas overgrown and others recently cleared, until they came to the slaves' graveyard. It was set down in a depressed area of the land, in a spot that one could see would easily flood in a hard rain. A raven was perched on one of the broken fence boards around the graveyard as a self appointed guardian and repeatedly cawed its disapproval at their approach. As the raven took flight Rory looked carefully at the mounds of dirt and walked around the perimeter of the graveyard, studying it and looking at the layout from different angles.

"Seem to me it be either dis one or dat one," Rory said, pointing to two mounds in the last row of the three dozen there. "Ya see I t'ink she was one of da last one's buried here durin' da war. I knowed da man dat dug da graves. He was from da Ivory Coast like me. He gone now but I recall he say dey was 'bout out a room. So I'm guessin' it be one of dese two wit da big rocks," he said, again pointing at the last two mounds.

There is some evidence that slaves placed certain rocks at the head of a grave to indicate by the type of rock or its size, whether it was a child's grave or an adult's grave. In addition, recalling African customs, slave graves were often dug east to west with the deceased's head facing west. If the slave master allowed a procession to the gravesite, the slaves sang an old hymn as they walked. One that they sometimes sung was:

When I can read my title
To mansions in the sky
I bid farewell to every fear
And wipe my weeping eyes.

"I'm afraid that's the best we can do," Mr. Blanchfield said to Shadrach.

"I greatly appreciate it, Seydou," Shadrach said, shaking Rory's hand. Rory then left.

"What did you call him?" Mr. Blanchfield asked politely, after Rory was out of hearing distance. Shadrach suddenly felt hesitant though he didn't know why.

"Seydou. Dat be his name in Africa when he was a boy. Rory be his slave name, da name he be givin' by da slave massa," Shadrach finally said.

Slaves were given their names by their owners not by their parents. The slave owner could give them any name they wished. On occasion this consisted of no more than a first name. More often the slave was given the last name of their owner. Once a slave escaped, or after being freed, it was not uncommon for them to choose a new name. Frederick Douglass, for example, was named Fredrick Augustus Washington Bailey by his owner at birth, but after escaping he adopted the last name of 'Douglass,' which he saw in a poem written by Sir Walter Scott entitled "The Lady of the Lake." Phillis Wheatley, the former slave who became a published poet in the 1700s, was given her first name after the slave ship that brought her over at 7 years old, Phillis. Her last name, Wheatley, was the name of her owners.

Mr. Blanchfield did his best to pronounce it. "Say-doo. I didn't know that, or really anything about his history. I'll have to ask him which name he prefers. OK, where do you want to start?" Mr. Blanchfield then asked.

"I'll start on dis end," Shadrach replied, picking up a swing blade and stepping to the north end of the graveyard.

"Alright, I'll start on the other end," Mr. Blanchfield said.

Both men began the arduous task of cutting down the tall grass that had grown in and around the graves. At some point Shadrach grabbed a shovel and dug a small drainage ditch around the perimeter so that any rain water would not pool around the graves. They each knelt and pulled weeds by hand that were on the mounds of dirt and as they did so they discussed their time in the Union Army. Shadrach mentioned the battles he was in with his regiment and Mr. Blanchfield talked about his war experiences. Mr. Blanchfield also explained why he came to the South after the war and his desire to assist in its rebuilding.

"As hard as it is for some people to see right now we're one country and I want that to succeed," Mr. Blanchfield said.

While there were many abuses, by northerners who went South after the war, some former Union soldiers ventured South with noble ambitions. One of the most notable was Albion Tourgee who moved to North Carolina hoping, as he stated at the time, to help "form a better union" between the states. He became a judge, and was later involved in the Supreme Court argument in *Plessy v Ferguson* on behalf of Mr. Plessy, but he was never accepted by his North Carolina brethren and his efforts there met with derision and failure. After leaving the South he wrote a fictional best seller about his time there entitled, *A Fool's Errand: A Novel of the South During Reconstruction.*

After a few hours the burial mounds were more visible, the grounds were clear, and they had pulled down the old fencing and stacked it up away from the graves.

"I need to get some headstones or some markers to designate this as a graveyard and pick up some lumber for new fencing when it becomes available. There's been a shortage, but I was told some will be in soon. I was lucky to get the lumber to build the new bunkhouse a few months back," Mr. Blanchfield said, looking over the cleared graveyard.

"Fencin' would be nice," Shadrach replied.

They picked up their tools and walked back to the barn to put them up. Mr. Blanchfield paid Shadrach, who thanked him and pocketed the money. He had his kitchen staff bring Shadrach a plate of food. Shadrach ate the food and then spoke to his sister.

"He a good man, Mr. Blanchfield. Was in da Union Army like me. Now I knows where Momma be buried," Shadrach said to her. "Listen, do ya know if dere are any dry goods stores other den da one in Elyton? I'm needin' a few supplies," Shadrach asked.

"I don't think so. Used to be one in Trussville but heard tell it got burned out by doze riders. I ain't sure if dat be true or not," Cecilia replied.

"Well, I'll be headin' out to my campsite. It ain't too far. And I got to go to da Freedmen's Bureau tomorrow 'bout gettin' a job," Shadrach said. He didn't want to tell her that he was going to set up a new campsite further away because he had barely escaped detection by some riders with tracking dogs last night.

"Ya be safe and be checkin' back wit' me," Cecilia replied, hugging him.

"I will," Shadrach said, as he got on his horse and then rode off.

CHAPTER 34.

Midnight and Father Sprecht continued to practice Midnight's Bible reading each night. Father Sprecht, at Midnight's request, also pressed him on his grammar and the proper pronunciation of certain words. They focused on one Gospel at a time until Midnight felt he had read it properly and understood it. Father Sprecht would also discuss with him the Old Testament prophecies that he believed were fulfilled by what was written about Jesus in the New Testament. Midnight continued to keep a listing of words in his notebook, words that he had struggled with initially:

Messenger
Wilderness
Proclaiming
Repentance
Garment
Locusts

Father Sprecht was surprised at how quickly Midnight's reading and pronunciation had improved.

"It's a shame that you were denied a formal education. I think you have a real knack for learning, much quicker than any other student I've ever had," Father Sprecht said to Midnight.

"We were denied lots of things when we were considered as property. But I always wanted to learn more, to be more educated," Midnight replied.

Each night after he practiced his reading with Father Sprecht, Midnight would lie in bed and mouth the proper pronunciation of each of the words in his notebook and put them in sentences to be sure he understood the meaning. He would also pick up the copy of *The Agitator* that Emmalene had given him and read and re-read it.

Midnight didn't want to seem too proud but he felt a growing sense of himself as a new person, as he learned how to read and was exposed to new ideas. That seemed fitting to him, a new person to go along with his new freedom.

Midnight continued to run errands for the church including dropping off the weekly bulletins at Rosie's Cafe and handing these to Emmalene or leaving the bulletins on the counter. Sometimes he would grab a meal there, but he also stopped at other diners in town. Emmalene remained cool to him. He would see her at the 9:30 a.m. mass each Sunday where she sang the concluding song in church, though they did not sit together. He was contented with the routine he had established in his life.

"Father, I need to get a proper suit for mass. Do you know where I can get one? I feel bad wearing the same clothes to church each time. I saved some money so I can pay," Midnight said one day when he and Father Sprecht were folding bulletins for delivery.

"Ever been to a tailor before?" Father Sprecht asked.

"No. I ain't never owned a suit before. Never had any prior need," Midnight said with a slight grin.

"I guess not. Silly question. Mr. McCarthy, one of our church members, is a tailor. Let's go talk with him and see what he can do," Father Sprecht said.

CHAPTER 35.

Dalton was sleeping soundly when Sheriff Wilson decided to leave the jail for one final walk around town. He closed the door as quietly as he could so as to not wake Dalton. It was late evening and as he stepped out into the street he could hear voices raised and the occasional gun shot down the street. Now that Dumas and Annala were in town, tensions were rising again. Dumas had already tried to coax several miners into gunfights but the miners had walked away each time. Annala had been hanging out every day in front of the Miners' Kitchen, reprising Batiste's role, staring at people, unnerving Mack the owner and trying to discourage miners from eating there. Sheriff Wilson and Dalton knew it was just a question of time before the lid boiled over.

He stopped in front of the Union City bar where, as usual, he heard some commotion. When he walked in he saw Dumas squaring off with a miner, Nuncie Spizale, for an apparent gunfight with a few dozen miners encircling them both.

Nuncie Spizale was a short muscular man and not a typical miner. He had been educated in his native country of Sicily, had worked on ships in the high seas, claimed to have climbed several mountains, and spoke three languages. In addition he knew how to use a gun. As a younger man he had fought alongside Giuseppe Mazzini and Young Italy, a political movement of Italians under 40 years of age, for the unification of Italy. He also said that he had fought successful duels on several occasions to defend his honor. A gunfight, or at least facing someone in one, would not unnerve him as it might other less experienced miners. He wore his revolver and holster at all times. The revolver was a Pietta Model 1860, black powder. It was unlikely that he was as fast on the draw as Dumas but he had told the other miners, when asked about facing a faster gun, that he only had to be faster once and it seemed that he had decided to take that chance.

"There will be no gunplay in here. Break it up!" Sheriff Wilson announced forcefully, as he entered the bar.

The miners stepped back from him. Spizale reluctantly stepped aside. Dumas, however, frustrated by the sheriff's intervention, stood his ground and then turned to face off with the sheriff.

"And whose gonna stop me?" Dumas asked.

"I will, if necessary," Sheriff Wilson replied.

Dumas quickly pulled out his gun before Sheriff Wilson could even reach for his. He aimed the gun at the sheriff and laughed as the crowd of miners backed further away, bunched up tightly on the sides of the two men, out of the direct line of fire.

"I'm gonna give you a chance to draw, Sheriff. Let's see how fast you really are," Dumas said.

Dumas then holstered his gun and backed up against the bar while facing the sheriff. He raised his right hand, the one he used to draw his gun, chest high in the air, laughing again, and daring Sheriff Wilson to draw on him first. Sheriff Wilson lowered his hand to his side so that he was ready to draw.

While the miners had all moved away from Sheriff Wilson and Dumas, once Dumas had challenged the sheriff, Tony, the bartender, had moved directly behind Dumas. He reached over the bar top and swung an empty whiskey bottle as hard as he could, crashing the hard bottom of it on the top of Dumas' head. Dumas stood for the briefest of moments before falling face first onto the ground.

The miners in the bar then converged on Dumas like a disturbed nest of fire ants and began pummeling Dumas' limp body with punches and kicks. Spizale stepped up, stretched out Dumas's gun hand on the floor, and repeatedly stomped on Dumas' hand with the heel of his boot until Dumas' knuckles were a bloody mess.

"He will a not threaten any of us again," Spizale said, as he stomped down one last time.

Sheriff Wilson moved in to stop the beating, removed Dumas' guns from his holster, and then asked several miners to carry Dumas to the jail.

"Someone get Doc Fierke to come over and check him out," Sheriff Wilson said. As the men lifted Dumas' body to carry him roughly out of the saloon, Spizale threw one final hard punch to the side of Dumas' head raising a cheer from the miners.

Dalton heard the crowd approaching the jail and woke up, quickly grabbing his dragoon. The door to the jail opened and Sheriff Wilson entered in front of the men carrying Dumas' body. The men dragged Dumas into one of the cells and tossed him, half conscious, onto the cot in the cell. Other miners remained outside talking loudly about what had just occurred.

Several minutes later Doc Fierke made his way through the miners and into the jail to check on Dumas. Sheriff Wilson explained to Dalton what had happened as Doc Fierke examined Dumas.

Dumas stirred awake and complained to Doc Fierke, somewhat

incoherently, about his head and hand. After several minutes examining him Doc Fierke stepped out of the cell.

"Probably a concussion. Maybe broken ribs and it looks like someone stomped his gun hand pretty good. Swelling already and probably broken bones in several fingers and in that hand. It will have to be set once the swelling goes down," Doc Fierke said to Sheriff Wilson and Dalton. "He won't be using that hand for a long time. Might never use it again for gunplay. Tell him to come see me when the swelling goes down," Dr. Fierke concluded and then left.

Shortly after Dr. Fierke left, Hawkins, accompanied by Rocky Annala, began pushing his way through the rowdy crowd of uncooperative miners still standing outside the jail.

"You just a lost one of ya men," Spizale mouthed off to Hawkins. Annala shoved Spizale out of the way and into some of the other miners as he and Hawkins moved past the crowd and into the jail.

"What is he charged with?" Hawkins immediately asked Sheriff Wilson, pointing at Dumas who was sitting awkwardly on the cot in the jail cell.

"Nothing," Sheriff Wilson said.

"Then why is he here?" Hawkins demanded, while Annala and Dalton eyed each other like two tom-cats circling for a midnight alley fight.

"Just protecting your investment. The miners were pounding him pretty good. Thought it would be easier for Doc Fierke to examine him in here," Sheriff Wilson said, without further explanation.

"Are you going to charge the miners for this?" Hawkins asked.

"No. He was trying to provoke a gunfight, first with Spizale and then with me. But I expect you knew that," Sheriff Wilson replied.

"Get him out of there," Hawkins said to Annala, who took a step towards the jail cell. Dalton stepped in front of him blocking his path.

"It's OK. They can take him," Sheriff Wilson said to Dalton, who waited a pregnant moment and then stepped aside.

Annala then went into the cell and helped Dumas to his feet before escorting him out of the jail. The crowd of miners jostled Annala and Dumas in front of the jail. Annala managed to walk him out of the crowd toward the Hawkins Hotel, followed by a clearly irritated Hawkins.

Sheriff Wilson closed the door to the jail after Annala, Dumas, and Hawkins had left, leaving only him and Dalton inside. Sheriff Wilson reiterated to Dalton that he was glad Tony had intervened and crashed the bottle onto Dumas's head.

"Well, I'll have to buy Tony a drink. The good news is don't look like Dumas will be causing any trouble with his gun anymore," Dalton said.

"Thank goodness. He was really fast on the draw," Sheriff Wilson said.

"Faster than me?" Dalton asked.

"I'd hate for my life to have to depend on the difference," Sheriff Wilson said. Dalton just nodded in response.

The crowd of miners, led by Nuncie Spizale, slowly disbursed from around the jail returning to the Union City bar to retell and, with the aid of their alcohol consumption and their imaginations, embellish their roles in the events of the evening.

CHAPTER 36.

Shadrach couldn't wait any longer. He had no choice. He decided to ride into Elyton early and go directly to Murphy's dry goods store to get the supplies he needed. It was another cold, damp, and overcast morning with only a few people on the street. He dismounted, tethered his horse, and walked into the store. Walt, the store owner, confronted him as soon as he came through the door.

"You ain't coming in here, boy, and startin' no trouble," Walt said, standing near the register behind the counter.

"I need to get me some supplies, dat's all," Shadrach said, looking directly at him and walking toward the counter.

"How did you get the money to buy supplies?" Walt asked.

"Don't worry I got money. My money. I need some flour, some hard tack, beans, and I want to buy a gun and some bullets," Shadrach said.

"I ain't selling you no gun," Walt said.

"I'll take da utta supplies den," Shadrach said, standing his ground.

"Let me see your money," Walt demanded. Shadrach stepped up

to the counter and fished the money out of his pocket, holding it tight fisted for Walt to see.

"Well, if you got money," Walt said. He reached up on a shelf and grabbed some hard tack out of a tin, placing it on the counter. Then he grabbed a sack to put some flour in and started to scoop flour into the sack as Shadrach stood by patiently.

"This boy causing you problems, Walt?" Sheriff Maddox interrupted, as he stepped into the store from a side door.

"Yeah, he threatened me. I wasn't going to sell him anything...I was...I was just leading him on...hoping you'd show," Walt replied, changing his tune when the sheriff was present, setting aside the sack and picking up the hard tack to return to the tin on the shelf.

"Can't have that, that sounds disrespectful and he might be the one that beat up Monroe. And Monroe was minding his own business, just protecting his property. Boy, I'm placing you under arrest," Sheriff Maddox said, pulling his gun on Shadrach.

"I didn't threaten no one. I'm just lookin' to buy me some supplies and den I be on my way. Gonna leave town," Shadrach said, turning to face the sheriff.

"Sure you were. That's what they all say. Now get moving toward the jail," the sheriff said.

"I ain't goin'. I done nothin' wrong," Shadrach protested.

"I told you to move," the sheriff said, cocking his gun.

"What am I bein' charged wit'?" Shadrach asked.

"Boy, you about to be dead if you don't shut up and start moving toward the jail," the sheriff said.

"What 'bout my horse and saddle?" Shadrach asked.

"Walt, take the horse to the livery," the sheriff said, pushing his gun into Shadrach's back to get him walking out of the store toward the jail.

"What you doing in town, boy? You know Cecilia, that worked at the Wanderer?" Sheriff Maddox asked as they walked.

"I ain't no boy. I'm a man. My name is Shadrach. I came down lookin' for my mother but learn she passed durin' da war," Shadrach replied.

"I don't care what your name is. You and your kind ain't nobody to me, ain't never gonna be nobody," the sheriff said dismissively before shoving Shadrach forward.

Once inside the jail the sheriff made Shadrach empty his pockets. He had $10 on him, part was his remaining military pay and part was from Mr. Blanchfield for clearing the graveyard. He then locked Shadrach in the only cell in the jail.

"This is a lot of money for someone like you. Where did you get all this money, boy? Might have to charge you with stealing," Sheriff Maddox said.

"Where I got it is my business, ain't none of yours. But it ain't stolen," Shadrach said, not wanting to reveal his Union Army service or to get Mr. Blanchfield in any trouble.

"Awful uncooperative for someone in so much trouble," the sheriff replied, before taking a plug of chewing tobacco out of his pocket and cutting off a chunk.

There was a short man with a ruddy complexion, in an ill-fitting blue suit wearing stove pipe boots, with his legs crossed, at a corner desk in the jailhouse and two other larger men holding rifles standing on each side of him. They had watched with interest the interaction between the sheriff and Shadrach.

"What's his fine gonna be, Sheriff?" the man in the blue suit, named Larry Talbot, asked as the first part of a recently orchestrated southern play. The sheriff played his part in the play as Shadrach stood in the cell, confused, and listened.

"Let's see. He's got $10 so the fine will be $30 or 90 days in jail," the sheriff said before getting the chewing tobacco situated between his cheek and gums.

"Hate to see a strong man like that use up town resources for meals and lodging when he could be working and contributing, helping us rebuild the community," Mr. Talbot said. He then offered to pay the fine and, even though Shadrach strenuously objected saying he would rather serve the 90 days in jail, the sheriff said that he would accept payment of the fine.

"How can dere be a fine wit' out a trial and wit' out a chance to defend myse'f? Ya makin' all dis up," Shadrach said, standing with his hands gripping the bars of the cell.

"Shut up, boy. You had a trial. I tried you when we were walking over here. You were disrespectful to Walt. Can't have that. Now this man here," the sheriff said referring to Talbot, "is doing you a big favor. A big favor. You should be grateful to get out of jail."

"Ya must really be dumb if ya think I believe dat," Shadrach said.

"I said shut your mouth! Talbot, he's got a horse at the livery you should go pick up. Might be worth a few dollars," Sheriff Maddox said to Mr. Talbot and then spit out the juice of the chewing tobacco into a spittoon near his desk.

"The $10 is yours, Sheriff. That's your finder's fee," Talbot said, ending the charade and reminding the sheriff of their private arrangement whereby the sheriff was personally paid $10 for each prisoner he handed over to Talbot to work in his mine. The rest of the monies paid by Talbot went into the town coffers.

Other southern sheriffs, with the economic engine of slavery gone, were developing similar arrangements throughout their states. Indeed, the one-time head of the Klan, former General Forrest, had already set up a private prison where black men, who were arrested and convicted of minor charges like vagrancy, were auctioned off as laborers to the highest bidder. Eventually the state of Alabama would get in on the action and lease convicts, overwhelmingly black, to a dummy corporation which paid the state for the labor and then leased the convicts to mine owners, plantations, railroads, and construction companies. It would truly blossom, after Reconstruction ended, with the development of the for-profit prison system throughout Alabama and several other former Confederate states and was used to finance each state's bottom line. In 1883 Alabama gave exclusive rights to lease prisoners to Pratt Coal and Iron Company, the Tennessee Coal and Iron Company and Railroad, and to the Sloss Iron and Steel Company. That year approximately 10 percent of its total revenues came from convict leasing but by 1898, 15 years later, that had increased to 73 percent of Alabama's total revenues. Although statistics are sketchy it's estimated that in 1883, for example, 25 percent of black convicts leased out to such businesses died while on the job.

The sheriff then explained to Shadrach that since Mr. Talbot had paid his fine, Shadrach would have to go with him to work it off. Sheriff Maddox was simply implementing one aspect of this cruel game, which replaced slavery in the South. It was called debt peonage.

"And how long ya say I gotta work to pay it off?" Shadrach asked.

"That's entirely up to Mr. Talbot," Sheriff Maddox said.

Shadrach was released from the cell and the two men with rifles took him over to the blacksmith shop.

"Why we goin' to da blacksmiths? What dat's got to do wit' workin'?" Shadrach asked, slowing down. The men didn't respond and simply pushed him forward.

"Got another one for you," one of the men with the rifle said to the smithy when they arrived. The smithy got his tools and, without speaking, began to put leg irons and chains around Shadrach's ankles while the two men kept their rifles aimed at him.

"What kinda job shackles men?" Shadrach asked, already sensing what was happening but not fully believing it.

"Can't have you runnin' off," one of the guards replied.

The two men then led the shackled Shadrach away to a horse drawn wagon where another black man was shackled and already sitting in the wagon. Shadrach got into the wagon and the two men with rifles climbed in as well to sit across from Shadrach and the other man.

"Where we goin'?" Shadrach asked.

"To work in the mine," one of Talbot's men said.

"What mine?" the other man asked.

"The one just opened in Red Mountain," the man said.

"How long I'm gonna be dere?" the other man in leg irons asked. Mr. Talbot climbed into the front of the wagon and snapped the reins so the horses would move forward.

"Boy, Mr. Talbot just bought you. You're his property now and you ain't likely to ever come out of that mine alive," the man with the rifle replied.

CHAPTER 37.

Reverend met with Pastor Ellis and told him that he would be greatly honored to give some sermons at the church as he built up his following for his own church. Pastor Ellis was pleased. He told Reverend that the church normally did not hold services on Tuesday night so he was free to use it that night, but in order to help him out he suggested that Reverend first give a few sermons as part of the regular Sunday service so people in the congregation would get to know him. Reverend agreed and eventually on a Sunday he gave a short sermon on the idea that he had heard from Father Sprecht when he and Midnight spent the night at St. Mary's Church. He spoke about the Civil War as a theological crisis.

> I was a Union soldier. I saw firsthand the destruction caused by the war to people and to property. But I also witnessed in the run up to it, and while it ensued, something equally malevolent, the destruction and undermining of people's religious beliefs. What do I mean by that? Most of us who are Christians use the

same Bible, the King James version. Yet there were very different theological interpretations and uses given to the same words in the Bible by folks on each side of the slavery issue, and by ministers who should have known better. Many southern ministers looked for ways to justify slavery with a biblical basis, a literal reading, to sanction this most unnatural arrangement. I believe they promoted a political agenda instead of a theological one, which even led to splits in certain denominations. They sought to soothe the conscience of their slave holding members, who were often their biggest financial supporters, by using the words of the Bible, instead of afflicting them in their comfort and making them confront their evil. How can that be? How can it be that people would use biblical scripture to support enslaving other human beings? This is something we must discuss. The Bible that we love so much is subject to interpretation and, as a result, it is also subject to misinterpretation and can be used for evil instead of good.

My larger point then is that the war was not just a military crisis, it was a theological one as well, and we must acknowledge and examine it as such if we are to heal this nation and if religion is to play a part in that healing. If we don't address it I fear religion will lose credibility for many and the fault lines that have arisen within churches, within congregations, and between people, because of slavery and issues of race, will harden and continue to expand.

Reverend spoke for about 10 minutes. He admitted that he had no solutions to the problem he was raising, other than speaking openly about it and asking those in attendance to do the same. The sermon was different and the congregation seemed attentive and appreciative. When he finished his sermon he returned to his seat next to Theresa in a church pew.

"Reverend Harrison will be conducting Tuesday night services here at the church for all who might be interested. I think he brings a very unique perspective to the ministry and I encourage you to attend when you have time," Pastor Ellis told those assembled in the church.

At the conclusion of the mass several people introduced themselves to Reverend and Theresa and told him they enjoyed his sermon and promised to attend his Tuesday night services. After the final person left Reverend thanked Pastor Ellis again and he and Theresa left the church to walk home.

"I think we have found a home here. I cannot wait to start building my ministry and reaching out to those in need," Reverend said. Theresa leaned into him and held his arm supportively as they walked toward home.

"That was a unique sermon, very thought provoking. I never thought about the war that way. You have such a different perspective on things and I think your views have changed since the war," Theresa said.

"They have, in many ways. I don't think one can go through what I've seen, what all of us saw in the war, and not be changed by it," Reverend replied. He squeezed Theresa's arm affectionately. "Whether one was in the war or not, in this life we have two choices when confronted with new circumstances. We can just harden our existing opinions, existing prejudices, and build a wall of denial around them to protect our ignorance or we can change and open ourselves up, open up our hearts and minds, to other perspectives, to a larger world. One way is bound up in insecurity, while the other requires a deeper reflection," he said.

"That makes sense," she replied.

"As far as the sermon, I've been thinking about that idea since Father Sprecht first mentioned it to me when Midnight and I stayed at his church that night. Not sure I have it all figured out yet, especially how to repair it," Reverend concluded.

"Well, the folks here seemed to like it," Theresa said.

CHAPTER 38.

"Rocky Annala is in the street in front of the bar calling you out, Sheriff," Johnson, one of the miners, told Sheriff Wilson as he stood in the doorway of the jailhouse. The sheriff was sorting wanted posters and doing paperwork at his desk in the jailhouse. Dalton was not at the jail having gone to get something to eat.

"I knew this day was coming," Sheriff Wilson said quietly.

"Should I go find Dalton?" Johnson asked.

"I can fight my own battles," Sheriff Wilson said. "I'll be out there in a minute. He can wait." Johnson stepped out of the jailhouse, but in a moment stepped back in.

"He ain't alone," Johnson said.

"What do you mean?" Sheriff Wilson asked.

"There is another guy next to him. I can't see who it is, maybe Dumas," Johnson said.

Sheriff Wilson straightened out the last of some papers, stood up, tied down his holster so it would not slip up in case he had to draw his gun, and then grabbed a double barrel shotgun out of the gun cabinet and loaded it with buck shot. He walked from behind his desk and exited the jail.

Johnson was right. There were two men standing side by side in the street across from the Miners' Kitchen with the sun at their back. Sheriff Wilson couldn't immediately tell if it was Dumas but doubted it as he had not been seen around town, presumably because his hand was still busted up. Indeed the rumor was that Dumas had left town in the middle of the night after Doc Fierke had put a splint on his hand. Sheriff Wilson walked out into the street.

"I thought you'd be too chicken!" Annala yelled. Sheriff Wilson was about 40 yards away but he continued to walk towards Annala and the other man, without replying.

"Hurry up! I want a drink," Annala hollered to try to further goad Sheriff Wilson. The other man with Annala seemed to laugh. As the sheriff got closer it was clear that the other man wasn't Dumas. Sheriff Wilson didn't recognize him.

When Sheriff Wilson got to within about 20 yards he stopped. The two men stepped away from each other so that any shotgun blast would not hit both of them.

"Any time you are ready, Sheriff," Annala said.

"Annala!" Dalton yelled out, descending the steps in front of the Miners' Kitchen where he had been eating. Dalton was to his right. As Annala turned to face Dalton, Sheriff Wilson moved to his right so he was lined up directly with the other man standing in the street.

Dalton walked down the last step toward Annala as the sheriff, duplicating what he had learned from Dalton, walked to close the distance between himself and the other gunman. The sheriff dropped the shotgun as he walked. When Dalton got to about 15 yards from Annala, he drew his dragoon and shot Annala dead. Annala managed to get his gun from his holster and fire it, but it hit the dirt in front of Dalton.

The echo of Dalton and Annala's gunfire reverberated as both Sheriff Wilson and the other man drew their guns. They shot at about the same time, but Sheriff Wilson was more accurate. The other man fell to his knees and then fell over face first into the dirt. Sheriff Wilson was grazed on the top of his left shoulder. He walked over to the man lying in the street who he had shot while Dalton checked Annala's pulse to confirm that he was dead.

"Who are you, son?" Sheriff Wilson said, squatting down next to the dying man, turning him over, and seeing that he was young. The young man never spoke. His head then rolled to the side. He was dead. There were two notches on his gun, suggesting he had killed before. In checking his pockets for identification, the sheriff found another $50 gold piece as Dalton stepped up next to him.

"I guess someone still wants me dead. How's Annala?" the sheriff said.

"Dead. You need to get the doc to look at that shoulder. Looks like the bullet just creased it," Dalton said, inspecting Sheriff Wilson's shoulder.

"I will but we got one more person to visit. It's risky, 'cause we don't have the evidence, but I'm tired of playing nice," Sheriff Wilson said. He stood and, with Dalton and a group of miners following, went into the Hawkins Hotel. Mr. Hawkins was seated at a table in the bar talking to Mr. Gloop.

"You're under arrest," Sheriff Wilson said to Hawkins.

"I was wondering when you were going to get around to that," Dalton said.

"For what? I have committed no crime," Hawkins said.

"For conspiracy to commit murder. For sending others to do your dirty work. And you better start offering more than a $50 gold piece for my head, though I do like the money. Now get up," Sheriff Wilson said, holding up the gold piece for Hawkins to see and then pocketing the money.

"That's a lie. I have not offered money to anyone to harm you. You have no proof of that," Hawkins protested. Dalton grabbed him by the arm and pulled him out of the chair.

"It will be my pleasure to lock you up," Dalton said, forcefully escorting Hawkins out of the bar and into the street, with the sheriff walking in front of him.

"Who is that laying in the street?" Hawkins asked, turning to see a crowd of men where Annala and the young man still lay.

"Your hired gun, Annala, and the poor kid you enticed with a $50 gold piece," Dalton replied.

"I did no such thing. I want to see the judge. I demand to see the judge! This is outrageous," Hawkins said, as they approached the jail.

"As soon as Circuit Judge Wagner gets here we'll have your trial. Should be in a few days. In the meantime stay quiet," Sheriff Wilson said.

They entered the jail and locked Hawkins in a cell. Dalton then walked with the sheriff out of the jail toward Doc Fierke's office.

"The judge will probably release Hawkins unless we can find some proof that he's offering the $50," Sheriff Wilson said, frustrated by the fact.

"Might be hard to prove since we've killed the only ones who knew where they got the money. But we can ask around. At least he can't offer any money to folks while he is in jail," Dalton replied, as they entered Doc Fierke's office.

"Doc, need to get patched up," Sheriff Wilson said.

Doc Fierke had the sheriff remove his shirt to examine him. Dalton immediately noticed older healed gunshot wounds on the sheriff's shoulder and back. Doc Fierke cleaned the new wound on his left shoulder, put two stitches in it, and covered it with a bandage.

"This is the fifth time I've had to patch you up from a gunshot wound. You're like a darn cat. You must have nine lives," Doc Fierke said, helping the sheriff gingerly lace his arm through the sleeves of his shirt.

"Just lucky I guess," Sheriff Wilson replied, as he buttoned up his shirt.

"You won't listen to me but my advice is to take it easy for a few days and let this wound completely heal. Come back in a few days and I'll change the bandage for you," Doc Fierke said closing his medical bag.

"Doc, you have been patching me up for years. First in Carthage and now here. I never follow your advice and I'm still alive. I'm afraid if I start doing what you tell me to do it may be the end of me," Sheriff Wilson joked. "So what do I owe you?"

"Get out of here! Get out of here!" Doc Fierke grumbled, waving his hand dismissively at the sheriff. Sheriff Wilson laughed. He and Dalton then left Doc Fierke's office to return to the jail.

"Man, you must have nine lives like Doc Fierke said. Or were they all bad shots?" Dalton said in jest.

"I'm not as fast as you but, as you know, to face a man and kill him takes a certain amount of nerve that I guess I have in abundance. I'm also pretty damn accurate," Sheriff Wilson said.

"I saw that," Dalton replied.

CHAPTER 39.

Before Shadrach could enter the mine he was shackled to another man, named Gabriel. Gabriel had also been arrested in Elyton by Sheriff Maddox. Gabriel's upper body was muscular, but he limped badly on his right leg. The leg was slightly atrophied, good enough to stand on but not as strong as his other leg. It was one of the reasons he hadn't left the South after the war, too injured to run or walk long distances.

"Everyone here be arrested by da sheriff," Gabriel said to Shadrach, once he was inside the mine and he and Gabriel began to work.

"What was ya arrested for?" Shadrach asked.

"Dey say vagrancy, whatever dat be. Most us here be arrested for it. Been here best I can tell 'bout two months," Gabriel said.

"When did all dis start?" Shadrach asked.

"'Bout a week afta Talbot reopened da mine. Dey just tryin' to figure anutta way to keep us as slaves. I'm bettin' it also happenin' elsewhere in Alabama," Gabriel replied.

"Some folks warned me 'bout it on my way down here. Just didn't believe 'em," Shadrach said. "What happen to ya leg?" Shadrach then asked.

"I got caught afta I ran away da second time so dey cut my heel to keep me from runnin' again. But I cans still work. Was a field hand b'fore da war," Gabriel replied.

Slaves who ran away repeatedly, like Gabriel, would sometimes have their Achilles tendon cut by their owners. It would not affect their ability to work in the fields but would hobble them and eliminate their ability to run. It was also a way to discourage others who might be considering running.

There was red dust in the mine that covered everything including the 20 men, all black, who were imprisoned there. The two men with rifles, who had transported Shadrach, were part of the six man team that ran herd over the prisoners, pushing, always pushing them to do more and assuring that none escaped. The meanest of the men who oversaw the prisoners was a former Confederate soldier named Roscoe. He was also in charge of all the other guards. During the war he had been a guard at the notorious Camp Sumter in Andersonville, Georgia, where Union prisoners were starved and beaten. There were nearly 45,000 Union soldiers imprisoned there through the course of the war and almost 30% had died. The commander of the prison, Henry Wirz, who was born in Switzerland, was charged with war crimes after the war, one of only two men so charged, and executed. Wirz was offered clemency if he would implicate Jefferson Davis in the crimes, but refused.

Roscoe was a big man with a dark red beard standing six feet tall and weighing about 240 pounds. He carried his rifle, a revolver in his holster, and a 7 ½ pound leather bull whip tacked to his gunbelt, which he often used capriciously on the backs of men who he thought were slacking. He was sadistic, with a violent timbre in his voice, and seemed to believe that excessive brutality was the singular proof of one's manhood. Often when a wound was opened on a man's back with the whip Roscoe would stop to dip the end of his whip in sand or, if he had some, in salt or sugar before continuing the whipping.

"What's da story on dat Roscoe? He look like a mean one," Shadrach asked Gabriel eyeing Roscoe as he walked near some other prisoners.

"He dangerous. Don't wanna mess wit' him, ya gotta treat him like ya handlin' dat barbwire," Gabriel replied.

Shadrach quickly learned that no one had ever been set free. No one had ever succeeded in working off the money that had been put up for their release from Sheriff Maddox's jail. It was a scam, just another form of slavery and economic exploitation with the recently enacted Black Codes providing a patina of legality. The prisoners got barely enough to eat and often what they did get was barely edible, one more way to keep the cost of operating the mine low and the profits high.

Shadrach got to know a few of the other men imprisoned besides Gabriel. At night when the men were allowed to sleep for six hours they had the chance to talk, but usually most were too tired. There was Skinny, who was all of 5 feet tall and couldn't have weighed more than 100 pounds. He had been a carpenter as a slave, was of light skin, what people called a mulatto at the time, and had a quick smile that suggested he knew more than he was willing to reveal. There was Rat, who Skinny was shackled to, a short squatty man who had been branded on his right cheek upon being recaptured after running away as a slave. He had whiskers that started at the corners of his mouth and seemed to prefer digging with his hands.

Slave owners sometimes branded recaptured slaves, like Rat, who had run away to make it clear to everyone that they were runaways. The branding was done with a hot branding iron, just as it was done with livestock, and could be placed on the slaves shoulders, palms, or cheek.

There was also a man there named Toussaint. He had been a free black man prior to his arrest by Sheriff Maddox. His parents were both slaves in Kentucky but were granted manumission by the terms of the will of their owner upon his untimely death.

Manumission was one vehicle by which slave owners could grant slaves their freedom. George Washington did this in his will, granting freedom to his slaves upon his death. Another method, less common, was for the slave, or someone on behalf of the slave, to buy their freedom. Joseph Rainey's slave parents bought his and their freedom and he went on to serve in the South Carolina Senate and later as the first black man to be elected to the United States House of Representatives. Frederick Douglass had his freedom purchased by friends in England for the sum of 150 pounds sterling, roughly $1,000.

The oldest man working in the mine, who was shackled but not to anyone else, was a very dark skinned bald headed man, with a mournful countenance, who had been a brick maker and bricklayer as a slave. He was named Levi and his back and arms were covered in scars. He was also the largest by far at almost 7 feet tall. He never spoke and kept to himself doing his work. At night he slept away from the other prisoners. While Roscoe harassed and whipped other prisoners he and the rest of the guards generally steered clear of Levi, which prompted rumors among the other prisoners, who also kept their distance from Levi, not sure of his loyalties.

The prisoners were classified by the guards and by Mr. Talbot as 1st class, 2nd class, 3rd class, and 4th class, based on how much they produced each day. Levi was the only prisoner that the guards ever referred to as a 1st class prisoner. The guards periodically referred to Levi and his level of production when trying to motivate the other prisoners to work harder.

On two occasions, during Shadrach's first few weeks in the mine, men died and the other prisoners were required by the guards to carry the bodies out of the mine. Those who died were buried in a newly dug common grave outside the mine with no marker. Within a day or two other men arrested in Elyton or in one of the surrounding towns were brought to the mine ostensibly to work off their debt to Talbot and to replace those who had died.

On occasion the prisoners would see the mine owner, Mr. Talbot, at a distance when they were hauling stuff out of the mine and he was sitting in a rocking chair with a drink on the front porch of the big house that overlooked the mine. But mostly they stayed in the mine, deprived for long stretches of time from even seeing the sun and often unable to tell the difference between daytime and nighttime, their circadian rhythms upended and gradually reset by the start and end of each work day.

"Ya sure no one ever been let go?" Shadrach asked Gabriel again one evening.

"Ya must be kiddin'. Dey gonna work us till we die an den bury us outside wit' da others. Dat's da onliest future we got. Ain't no one ever gonna know 'bout us or 'bout us bein' in dis here mine. We ain't nuttin' to nobody," Gabriel said, as they lay down covered with red dust to try to sleep for the night.

Six hours later Roscoe was on top of them swinging the whip and hitting a few of the men to get them up and to start working. Lamps were lit and the men slowly got to their feet in the dark gloom of the early morning.

"I am a free man! A free man! You must let me go!" Toussaint protested to Roscoe.

"Ain't no such thing as a free nigger. Get back to work!" Roscoe yelled.

"I was more free than you will ever be!" Toussaint replied as the other prisoners watched, surprised that he was taking the chance of talking back to Roscoe.

"See how you like this, free man," Roscoe said and then he unfurled his whip and struck Toussaint, who held his ground.

"You are the slave, not me!" Toussaint said.

Roscoe became enraged by the comment and hit Toussaint with the whip again and then stepped up to him and cracked Toussaint in the ribs with his rifle butt. Once Toussaint was on the ground Roscoe crashed the rifle butt onto Toussaint's head as Toussaint tried to cover up. He would have continued beating Toussaint but one of the other guards, named Collins, pulled him off.

"Get moving!" Roscoe boomed out to the rest of the prisoners before lashing out at Rat, hitting him in the calf with the tip of the whip. The prisoners went to pick up their tools and started working. Roscoe walked the line behind them as two other guards stood with rifles watching. Toussaint struggled to get to his feet, blood dripping from his forehead.

Shadrach and Gabriel began to work their section of the mine near Rat and Skinny. Rat rubbed at the open cut on his calf.

"We put some water and a mud poultice on it tonight so it ain't get no infection. Afta dat we check on Toussaint," Skinny told him. Rat nodded in agreement.

Shortly after the work day started Levi lifted a very large boulder that had been freed. Roscoe and the other guards stepped back and watched as Levi carried the boulder that had to weigh 200 pounds. He dropped it into the mine cart and it filled the entire cart. Levi returned to his pick-axe without saying a word.

"Dey is scared of dat man," Shadrach said to Gabriel about Levi, as he watched the guards' reaction.

"Hell, I scared of him too," Gabriel replied.

Shadrach and Gabriel lifted an odd shaped boulder together to bring to the mine cart. Once they dropped it in Roscoe lashed out at Shadrach with the bull whip catching him across the shoulder. It would have caught his face but Shadrach had lifted his arm at the last minute and deflected it.

"What dat for?" Shadrach demanded turning to face Roscoe, as Gabriel tried unsuccessfully to pull him away.

"Don't get smart with me boy or I'll break you in half. Sheriff and Mr. Talbot can always find me another to take your place," Roscoe said, and raised his arm and brought the whip down on Shadrach again as Shadrach and Gabriel then ambled back to their section of the mine.

That night, after another eighteen hour day, the men lay about exhausted with several wheezing and coughing from the dust. Skinny and Rat sat with Toussaint and listened to his stories of being free as they cleaned off the dried blood from his head.

"Anyone ever try to escape?" Shadrach asked Gabriel, who was sprawled out on his back next to him.

"Yeah. Two tried one night. Dey was shackled together, fella dey called Doot and 'nother named Sylvester. Dat Roscoe shot 'em both dead a couple yards past da mine and den he made us all see da bodies. Ya can't run wit' dese here chains on," Gabriel said. Shadrach pulled at the chains binding them together.

"We could maybe use da pick-axe to break da chain, or one of da welds on da links," Shadrach replied.

"Evens if ya could, how ya gonna get pass da guards settin' outside wit' dem rifles? Stop talkin' nonsense and get some sleep. Ya just wastin' energy wit' dat talk. Mornin' gonna be here b'fore ya know it," Gabriel said.

"What 'bout dat Levi? Maybe he could help," Shadrach said.

"He don't talk to no one. I done tried. He musta been some trouble as a slave. Heard one of da guards talkin' 'bout it. Ya seen da scars on his arms and back. Best to stay away from him," Gabriel replied, before closing his eyes. Shadrach sat awake for awhile, checking and recheck-ing the links in his chains and trying to pry one open with his pick axe, to no avail.

CHAPTER 40.

Reverend spoke on several Tuesday nights at First Church, putting together his own mass. There was a small but regular crowd that was now attending his services, including Theresa's parents. His own parents had not attended, though he had invited them. As a staunch Protestant his father had made it immediately known to Reverend that he felt the Unitarians were heretics and atheists destined for eternal damnation.

"You have strayed too far for me to save," his father said, rendering his harshest judgment yet on Reverend. When Theresa, angered by the comment, offered to speak to his father, Reverend told her he appreciated it but it was no use.

"He won't hear anything you say," Reverend had replied.

Reverend and Theresa had decided to put off looking for their own church for the time being as they felt so welcomed by the First Church congregation. Pastor Ellis was impressed with Reverend's Tuesday night sermons and the one he had delivered that first Sunday, so he asked Reverend to speak again at one of the Sunday services.

Reverend spent several days working on his sermon. He entitled the sermon: "What's to become of us?" Using portions of the various gospels Reverend laid out how Jesus had reached out, without judgment or condemnation, to those in the communities he visited that were marginalized: the poor, the sick, the prostitutes, the criminals, and how he healed and uplifted folks from all walks of life.

We are facing an issue in this young country. How will we deal with our less fortunate brethren? How will we deal with our Negro brothers? Former slaves? Immigrants from other countries that are fleeing persecution or famine and coming here for their freedom? Those poor individuals with mental troubles locked up in asylums? Too often, way too often, I hear people dehumanize one of those groups of people, talking about them in negative ways as if they were somehow less than human. We must recognize that when we do this, when we strip a person or a group of their humanity, we are not revealing anything about them but rather we are revealing something about ourselves. By passing judgment on others we are unwittingly passing judgment on ourselves.

And how much harm comes to people who are mistreated in such a manner? What lingering effects, internalized effects across generations, will there be because former slaves were ripped from their families, denied an education, forced to be reliant on a plantation owner, and treated by many in this country as less than human? I suggest to you that, as the Bible verses I have cited make clear, Jesus would have embraced all of these folks because we are all God's children. And we should model our behavior on His whenever we are dealing with any of God's children.

Religion, our religion, is not just about our individual relations
with God. It is also about our moral, social, and ethical relationships with each other. It is about how we treat one another.

Reverend then told the congregation about Dalton, about Midnight
who he called Emmet, and about Shadrach.

In war I learned that these men were my brothers no different
than if we were all born from the same mother. And indeed in
a way we were since the Bible says we are all descendants of
Adam and Eve.

In the Book of Malachi it is written: "Have we not all one Father?
Hath not one God created us? Why do we deal treacherously,
every man against his brother, by profaning the covenant of our
fathers?" So if we believe that to be true, if we believe that we
all have a common origin, it means that we are all one family,
all His children, brothers and sisters, regardless of our place of
birth, the color of our skin, or our station in life. How arrogant
is it to think that we are somehow better, or superior, than our
brothers and sisters. On what basis can a Christian claim such
superiority over others? None that I know of.

The notion, however, that all men and women, regardless of color,
were related, even as a theological concept, was not universally shared
in the 1800s. Indeed the so called "American school of physical anthro-
pology," which included Harvard scholar Louis Agassiz and anthro-
pologist Josiah Clark Nott, proposed the doctrine of polygenesis, the
idea that the human races were distinct, with unequal attributes,

and separate with no common ancestor. Nott, who had co-authored a book on the subject entitled, *Types of Mankind,* was a slave owner and defended slavery by claiming "the Negro achieves his greatest perfection, physical and moral, and also greatest longevity, in a state of slavery." Agassiz , who wrote numerous articles promoting polygenesis, opposed slavery, but supported the theory of polygenesis by claiming that the Book of Genesis, the creation stories in the Bible, referred only to the white race.

Then Reverend concluded his sermon by telling them about the life of the Confederate soldier that he took, how it occurred, and the guilt that he carried ever since.

I have sworn to the Almighty that I shall never lift a hand to harm another human being. I will spend my time in this world trying to save souls and trying to better understand my fellow man. If I want others to understand me, to understand my struggles, I must make the effort to understand them. Trying to understand others is a critical element of our moral duty that breaks us out of a self-centered world. It's only when we see other people as different, as somehow not like us, that hatred arises out of our insecurity and fear.

When he finished speaking he returned to sit with Theresa until the service had ended.

CHAPTER 41.

The regular 9:30 Sunday Service at St. Mary's started and Midnight was seated in the first row in a neatly fitting gray suit which Mr. McCarthy, the tailor, had made and sold him. It was an important day for Midnight and he wanted to look his best. He was a bit nervous, but also excited. It was a day to reflect back on the journey from his days as a slave, his difficult escape from the plantation, and his military service. He thought about his mother and tried to hold a childhood image of her in his mind to calm himself, something he had often done during the war immediately before a battle. Despite the fact that he had not sought out his family members after the war, this was a day when he wished they could all be present. Emmalene was also in church, in the front row, but on the opposite side of the church from Midnight. When she had entered the church she walked past him without speaking.

Father Sprecht gave the opening remarks welcoming people. He then turned to the rituals of the mass and when it came time for the reading of the Gospel he smiled widely in anticipation.

"Today's reading of the Gospel will be by Emmet, or as his friends call him, Midnight," Father Sprecht said.

Midnight stood and made his way into the center aisle and then over to the lectern to read as Emmalene leaned forward in her church pew and watched him walk past her. He stood behind it, opened the Bible on the lectern to the right page, and cleared his throat. He glanced over at Father Sprecht who was looking at him from behind the altar and nodded his head to indicate that Midnight should proceed.

"Today's reading be..is from the Gospel of Mark:

The beginning of the good news about Jesus Christ, the Son of God. It is written in the book of the prophet Isaiah: Look, I am going to send my messenger before you; he will prepare your way. A voice cries in the wilderness: Prepare a way for the Lord, make his paths straight. And so it was that John the Baptist appeared in the wilderness, proclaiming a baptism of repentance for the forgiveness of sin....

Midnight finished reading the entire excerpt without an error. "Thank you," he said, closing the Bible, and then, his back straight and beaming inside, he returned to his seat in the church pew. As he walked to it he thought he saw Emmalene out the corner of his eye staring at him with her mouth open in disbelief. Father Sprecht continued with the rest of the mass and then, as usual, when the service was ending Emmalene sang a concluding song.

When Emmalene finished singing Midnight made his way to the center aisle with the other church members in attendance. Several church members shook his hand. He ended up standing briefly next to Emmalene as the congregation moved slowly to exit the church.

"That was a very nice reading, Brother Emmet," she said to him in a perfunctory manner, looking straight ahead, as if his reading of the Gospel was nothing particularly special to her.

"Thank you, Sister Emmalene," Midnight said. "I almost forgot. I wanted to let you know that I finally read the copy of *The Agitator* that you gave me. Very interesting subject matter. Mary Livermore, the editor, makes some compelling arguments for women's rights. I understand that she was also an abolitionist, so she has my respect. Now please excuse me," he said, purposely haughty in his speech, and then he stepped past her without looking back. As he did so her eyes followed him carefully.

The Agitator merged in 1870 with the newly published *Woman's Journal*, for which Mary Livermore became co-editor. It continued to be published under one name or another until June, 1931 and advocated for women's rights. Ms. Livermore was a frequent public speaker on women's suffrage and wrote numerous books on the subject. She died in 1905 and, in recognition of her contribution to the fight for women's suffrage, a World War Two battleship was named in her honor in 1943, the *SS Mary A. Livermore*. The battleship was damaged by a Japanese Kamikaze pilot in Operation Ten-Go in May, 1945.

CHAPTER 42.

"Mr. Blanchfield, sir, I'm sorry to bother ya wit' my troubles but I'm worried 'bout my brother, Shadrach. I'm guessin' he headed to town, but I ain't heard from him in a few weeks. I'm thinkin' he might be in some kinda trouble," Cecilia said. Mr. Blanchfield was seated on the front porch and Cecilia had walked out of the house to speak to him.

"You may be right. The town would not be a safe place for him to be. What do you want me to do?" Mr. Blanchfield asked.

"Well, sir, if ya goes to town soon maybe ya could ask 'bout for him. See if anyone knows anythin' or if dey has seen him," Cecilia said, not meeting his eyes.

"Cecilia, look at me. You are a good worker and I enjoyed getting to know Shadrach when we worked on the graveyard. I wish I had hired him. I've got to go to town tomorrow. I'll ask around for you," he said, though, as usual, he worried about provoking those in town. However, he had gotten to know Shadrach by working with him that day and felt it was the least he could do.

"Thank ya, sir," she replied.

"Do you want to go with me?" he asked.

"Sir, dat be a bad idea. I..uh…well, Shadrach, he rescue me from workin' at da Wanderer and, well, my ol' massa, Mr. Monroe, he don't know where I be," she said. Mr. Blanchfield nodded his head. He had heard rumors about the women being held at the Wanderer and didn't realize Cecilia had been one. He had still not figured out the tangle of relationships between former slaves and their former masters.

"I see. You stay put. You're safe here for now. I'll see what I can find out," he said.

"Thank you, sir," she replied, and then left the porch to return to her cooking duties. Later he told Cecilia that, in light of what she told him about Shadrach rescuing her from the Wanderer, if the sheriff or Mr. Monroe ever came looking for her she was to hide in the cellar.

The next morning Mr. Blanchfield hitched one of his horses to his carriage and headed into town alone. He stopped at Murphy's dry goods store to pick up some supplies and without much prodding, while loading the supplies into his carriage, learned from Walt that a man fitting Shadrach's description had been arrested by the sheriff.

"Probably sent him to work it off with that fellow, Talbot. Sheriff arrested another one that day as well. Serves him right. He was in here looking for supplies but like all his kind was pretty uppity, like he was entitled to something. Said he had money on him, but I doubt it," Walt said.

Mr. Blanchfield listened without comment and then went to visit his lawyer in town on legal matters related to the property adjacent to the Walker plantation which he was seeking to buy. He eventually asked about the arrangement between Mr. Talbot and the sheriff. The lawyer explained in detail exactly what Sheriff Maddox and Mr. Talbot were doing.

"It's called debt peonage," the lawyer said.

"Is there anything that can be done to stop it?" Mr. Blanchfield asked.

"It's illegal. Congress passed a law last year outlawing it called the Anti-Peonage Act of 1867. It applies to all the states and territories, but ain't nobody here in Alabama going to challenge what they are doing and if I was you, Mr. Blanchfield, I'd stay quiet about it. They're trying to get that mine producing again which would be a good thing economically for this area and they need workers. So Talbot pays the fines to the sheriff on behalf of the prisoner, kind of like a surety, and the prisoner has to work for him," the lawyer said, sanitizing the process with his surety analogy and appearing unconcerned about the impact on those individuals imprisoned in the mine.

Mr. Blanchfield then stopped at the telegraph office to see if there were any messages for him. The telegraph operator, Mr. LaFleur, was an anomaly among the citizens in Elyton. He was originally from North Alabama and was one of the few folks in town friendly to Mr. Blanchfield. The two men often discussed privately their disdain for the attitudes exhibited by the sheriff toward former slaves. Mr. LaFleur didn't recall Shadrach, when Mr. Blanchfield asked, but told him he saw men being taken to the smithy to have leg irons put on and then hauled off by Talbot and his guards.

"They was taking them to the mine. Seems like it happens every couple of weeks. They use those Black Codes to arrest them," he told Mr. Blanchfield.

"Thanks, Mr. LaFleur," Mr. Blanchfield said.

"I don't cotton with the sheriff or Talbot. Never have. What they is doing is criminal and I wish someone could stop them but there ain't nothing I can do about it. If I did object I'm sure they'd come after me," Mr. LaFleur replied.

When he was done, and had as much information as he could gather, Mr. Blanchfield went down to the jail. Town folks were not fond of Mr. Blanchfield and he knew it. They saw him as an interloper trying to make money off Reconstruction and disliked him because of his Union Army service. And there were rumors in town, true as it turned out, that he treated his workers, former slaves, well. He had built them a new bunkhouse, and paid them a decent wage, which infuriated some of the other local landowners who had no such intentions. So he decided on a tact that would hopefully give a cover story to his inquiries without putting Cecilia at risk.

"Sheriff, I'm looking for someone that I understand you arrested a few weeks ago," Mr. Blanchfield said upon entering the jail.

The sheriff was cleaning and oiling one of his rifles as he sat behind his desk. His feelings toward Mr. Blanchfield were such that he didn't respond to Mr. Blanchfield's question. Larry Talbot, the mine owner, was seated in the jail as well.

"Who are you looking for?" Talbot asked.

"A young fellow named Shadrach," Mr. Blanchfield said, and then described Shadrach's physical appearance to the sheriff and Talbot.

"What's your business with him?" the sheriff then asked.

"He was supposed to start working for me a few weeks back and didn't show up. Actually he worked one day for me and after telling me he was coming to town to pick up supplies he never showed up again," Mr. Blanchfield lied.

"Can't tell with niggers. He could be anywhere," the sheriff said with an easy condescension.

"Well you arrested him. Where did he go when you released him?" Mr. Blanchfield asked, realizing that he was purposely getting the run around.

"Oh, that boy is working for me now in the mine. He's not a good worker, real lazy. Probably best he didn't show up back at your place," Talbot said, smiling insincerely after he spoke.

"I'd like to speak with him and find out why he didn't show up at my place. Can that be arranged?" Mr. Blanchfield said to Talbot, knowing this was not likely to happen.

"Now that ain't possible. See he is working for Mr. Talbot who was kind enough to pay his fine and he has to work it off," the sheriff said.

"What crime did he commit?" Mr. Blanchfield asked, already knowing the answer from the conversation with his lawyer.

"Does it matter, Blanchfield? Does it really matter?" Talbot asked with a snicker, as he eyed the sheriff. Sheriff Maddox set his rifle down and sat up straight in his chair looking at Mr. Blanchfield with obvious contempt.

"I don't have to answer to you, Blanchfield. In fact, just so you know, I don't like you and your carpet-bagging types coming down here and trying to pick at the bones we were left with after the war. So don't come in here asking me to chase down someone who didn't show up for work. This is Alabama and we do things our own way. My way," the sheriff said, picking up the rifle again and returning his attention to cleaning it. Mr. Blanchfield glanced at Talbot and then he quietly left the jail.

"Damn, Blanchfield. I hear he's trying to buy more land. I say it's about time he gets a little retribution. We need to make things uncomfortable for him," the sheriff said to Talbot.

"The rumor is he is buying the land to build a schoolhouse for former slaves to use. That's what his lawyer told me. We can't have that. Let's get the Klan boys to do something. They'll have some fun with it," Talbot said.

"We were going to do something to him last time we all met but went after some scalawags over in Trussville instead. Burned them out for helping that Bureau," Sheriff Maddox replied.

"Yeah, I missed that meeting. Blanchfield built a new bunkhouse for his niggers. Bought the lumber here in town. Sure would be a shame if that bunkhouse happened to catch fire," Talbot said, as he stood and then walked over to the sheriff's desk.

"Now that sounds like a good idea. Best one I heard today," Sheriff Maddox said, setting his rifle down again before standing up as Talbot reached over to shake his hand.

In the meantime Mr. Blanchfield had gotten in his carriage and was on his way back to the Walker plantation. When he returned home, he unloaded the dry goods from his carriage and then spoke to Cecilia.

"Cecilia, looks like they arrested your brother and then had him placed in the mine. Talbot runs the recently opened mine in Red Mountain. The sheriff arrests folks, Talbot supposedly pays the fine and then forces them to work for him. It's called debt peonage," Mr. Blanchfield said to her. "It's despicable and illegal. I'd like to help more but there isn't anything further I can do without putting myself at risk," he said.

"I thank ya for what ya done," Cecilia said.

But a few hours later Cecilia had an idea and spoke to Mr. Blanchfield about it. He seemed to hesitate a bit.

"I would greatly appreciate it. I'd do it myself but I can't go back into town," Cecilia said.

"Let me think about it," Mr. Blanchfield replied to buy time, though he was not inclined to do what she asked. He still thought it best to continue to try to avoid a direct confrontation with the sheriff or to do anything that might get back to the sheriff and provoke a dangerous response.

The next day, however, after dark, a half dozen Klan riders appeared at the Walker Plantation and tossed burning torches onto the roof of the new bunkhouse where the workers were sleeping. They also ran their horses through the garden plots near the bunkhouse that Mr. Blanchfield had allowed the workers to use to grow their own crops. Blanchfield managed to get off a few shots in the air forcing the riders to flee before they could set anything else on fire.

In light of Cecilia's prior warning Blanchfield had many buckets of water already filled and ready by his well in case of just such a fire. The other workers, including Cecilia and the kitchen staff, along with Mr. Blanchfield, quickly hauled the buckets of water and then refilled these allowing them to put the fire out in time to save the exterior walls, but the roof, where the fire was started, had collapsed. The men worked through the night into the morning hauling out the burnt timbers, damaged shingles, wet bedding, and then sweeping the water out of the bunkhouse so it could all dry out.

Exhausted from fighting the fire, from helping with the all night clean up, and from the ongoing open hostility toward him by those in town, Mr. Blanchfield drove his largest wagon into town the next day with Seydou to pick up lumber and roof shingles to rebuild. He had no intention of being run off and wanted to make that clear to the sheriff and to others in town. Fortunately the small mill in Elyton was willing to sell to him, though at a slightly inflated price, and had enough of the material he needed to rebuild the roof, along with some fence boards he could use to start fencing the former slaves' graveyard. The sheriff and Talbot stepped out of the jailhouse into the street and watched as Mr. Blanchfield and Seydou loaded up his wagon.

"Bastard is going to rebuild," Talbot said to the sheriff.

"We heard about the fire, Blanchfield! Wonder how that happened?

Second fire in the last few months! Had one over in Trussville as well!" Sheriff Maddox yelled out, to Talbot's obvious amusement.

Seydou looked angrily in their direction and jumped down from the wagon to face the sheriff and Talbot. He had seen several of the riders up close and told Mr. Blanchfield he was certain the lead rider that night was Sheriff Maddox.

"What you looking at, boy?" Sheriff Maddox said, taking a few menacing steps in Seydou's direction.

"Don't say anything. Just help me load the wagon," Mr. Blanchfield said. Seydou reluctantly complied and turned away from facing the sheriff.

"You better look away, boy," the sheriff said. "He's too old for the mine or I'd arrest his ass," the sheriff then said to Talbot.

Mr. Blanchfield was going to have to figure out how to navigate in such a belligerent town. He now knew, however, that just staying quiet wasn't going to do it. They would attack him regardless. It was a hatred and a mindset which he did not understand. And despite doing his best to avoid trouble, it grated on him, a former Union officer, to just sit by and take their abuse without doing something to respond. He didn't have the men or the resources to fight the whole town. And the sheriff, his principle nemesis, was the only recognized law in town. So while in town, after the wagon was loaded, Mr. Blanchfield decided he would do the favor that Cecilia had asked of him.

CHAPTER 43.

Roscoe was in a particularly bad mood. Even the other guards were keeping their distance from him as he growled and repeatedly cursed the prisoners. He used the whip on Skinny and then on Rat for no apparent reason before moving on to use it against Gabriel. He struck each man once or twice, as he screamed obscenities at them. When he raised the whip on Shadrach and flung it down, Shadrach, who had watched him strike the others, was in no mood to be compliant. He grabbed the end of it and held tight as Roscoe tried to pull it back from him. Though Roscoe was much bigger than Shadrach he underestimated Shadrach's strength. Shadrach wrapped the end of the whip around his hand and Roscoe could not pull the whip away from Shadrach or pull Shadrach off his feet. Indeed when Shadrach pulled back on the whip Roscoe almost fell forward.

As the other prisoners watched, Roscoe straightened up and tugged back on the whip handle. Shadrach refused to let go. One of the other guards stepped up next to Shadrach and crashed the butt of his rifle on the side of Shadrach's head. Shadrach fell to the ground dazed and in doing so released the whip. Roscoe then coiled the whip and angrily brought it down repeatedly onto Shadrach's back and head until Shadrach was bloodied and curled into a fetal position covering his face.

"Get up, boy!" Roscoe yelled. Shadrach got to his feet with the help of Gabriel.

"Now get back to work. I'd kill you right off but we need the help right now moving this ore. Got some new orders to fill. But I can tell your day's coming and I'm looking forward to it," Roscoe said, with a serrated edge in his voice. Gabriel steadied Shadrach as he stumbled wearily toward the section of the mine in which they worked as a team.

"Ya take it easy. I'll do da liftin'," Gabriel said quietly. "And tonight we gotsta clean ya up." Shadrach lifted his pick-axe and swung it at the stone. Blood trickled down his back. He felt the burning of the open wounds as his mind cleared. It brought back his memories of being on the plantation tied to a whipping post. His anger was palpable and he started to swing the pick-axe with an unrestrained fury.

"Slow down. Dis ain't no contest," Gabriel cautioned, but Shadrach continued to push himself out of anger, while periodically turning a resentful eye on Roscoe.

That night, after their work ended, Rat and Skinny carefully washed the cuts on Shadrach's back and arms as best they could with their drinking water. The blood was caked on in spots and covered with the red dust which was endemic to the mine. Shadrach's body tensed up on occasion as the water burned in the cuts.

"Dis water ain't da cleanest but it gonna have to do," Skinny said, as he poured some more on Shadrach's back.

"Ain't nothin' clean 'round here, dat's for sure," Rat replied.

"Wish I had me sometin' to make a betta poultice wit' other den dis here mud. I need some charcoal," Skinny said, as he worked the mud he had moistened in his hand and placed it gently on certain spots on Shadrach's back. Shadrach remained quiet to the tenderness shown him as they did their best to clean and tend to his wounds.

"Hope dis make it betta," Skinny said, as Toussaint stepped over to see if he could assist. He lowered himself onto the ground next to Skinny. His ribs were still bruised and painful from Roscoe hitting them with the rifle butt. Roscoe had also continued to single Toussaint out each day for a whipping.

"One day. One day," Shadrach finally said through a clenched jaw.

"Ya best gives up all dat anger. Ain't gonna do no good 'cept maybe get ya killed. See a little man like me know betta, can't afford no anger," Skinny offered, moistening some more mud which he rolled around in his hands and spit in before applying it to other cuts on Shadrach's back.

"Skinny, what dey is doin' to us ain't right and I ain't never been one to lay down when wrong bein' done. Slavery be outlawed yet here we is as slaves again. Dat's wrong," Shadrach said.

"No question ya right. But it gonna be a long road to real freedom. We most likely won't be da ones dat see it, but maybe one day others like us be treated more equal. Maybe in da future t'ings be better. Maybe not. Can't worry 'bout dat now. Just gotta survive in dis here place till sometin' change," Skinny replied.

"Dere is more to livin' den just survivin'," Shadrach said.

"Dat's right, but when da only utta choice be dyin', I'll take survivin'," Skinny said.

"There are worst things than death," Toussaint offered. "It is better to live free than to live prostrate and crawling under the thumb of another."

"Ya keep talkin' back to dat Roscoe and he gonna kill ya," Skinny said to Toussaint.

CHAPTER 44.

Reverend walked into his in laws' house from a trip to town and Theresa greeted him with a kiss on the cheek which he did not reciprocate. That was unusual. He was somber, withdrawn, and distracted as he sat down at the kitchen table. Theresa noticed it but she did not immediately ask him what was going on.

"What will you preach on this week? Have you decided?" she asked, as she returned to the kitchen sink and rinsed off some dishes in a pan of water. Reverend didn't respond, but simply stared in front of him as if his eyes were searching for the outline of something that he could not see clearly. He then set his elbows on the table, closed his eyes, and rested his head wearily into his hands.

There had been times since he arrived home when he seemed lost in war related memories, scarred memories, and would, without notice, turn melancholy. Sometimes it lasted for a few hours, other times for a day or more. Theresa thought, as she looked at him, that maybe this was another one of those times. She waited to see if his mood would change or if he would open up about what was weighing on him. He didn't, but just remained seated at the table looking forlorn and preoccupied.

"What's wrong?" she finally asked, setting down a dish and moving to sit with him at the kitchen table. Reverend reached into his coat pocket and pulled out a telegram.

As of 1868 Samuel Morse's electrical telegraph, which was developed in the 1830s and 1840s, was still the best means of long distance communication in the United States. It used electric currents to send coded pulses which could be translated by the recipient and by 1866 the first transatlantic telegraph line had been laid allowing communications between the United States and London.

Reverend handed the telegram to Theresa without explanation. She unfolded it and read it out loud:

```
Shadrach needs help. In trouble. Arrested in Elyton,
Alabama, and enslaved in mine. Against his will. Debt
peonage. In real danger. His sister Cecilia asked that
I send to ask for help.
```

The telegram was signed and sent by "Mr. Blanchfield at the Walker Plantation." Theresa put the paper down on the table and shoved it to the side, away from her and Reverend, as if this would put some distance between the request it contained and Reverend.

"I'm so sorry, honey. I know that he's your friend," Theresa managed to say.

"I'll have to let Dalton and Midnight know," Reverend said, in a monotone voice that was stripped of any emotion. Theresa could feel him pulling away from her, protecting, or shutting down, some vital part of himself. At that moment her intuition suddenly told her that he was going to leave to help his friend.

"What about the church? What about your ministry?" Theresa immediately pleaded, trying in her own way to discourage him. Reverend stood up and walked around the kitchen, with his hands in his pockets, as Theresa watched him and began to bite her fingernails.

"I did not ask for this, but what type of man would I be if I turned away from a friend? Christians need to be worried about their conduct in this life as much, if not more, as the next one. I'm darn tired of those who only look to the next life and use that as an excuse to disregard their duties in this one," he said, turning to look at her and, perhaps, thinking of the attitude so often expressed by his father.

Theresa began to weep. Reverend lifted her off her chair and embraced her.

"I'm sorry. Please understand, but I must try to do something. I couldn't live with myself if I just turned away. We fought a war to end this," he said to her.

"I know this is who you are. I know that. That's the man I fell in love with, but I'm scared for you and us, for losing what we have just started here," she replied through her tears.

"I guess sometimes we have to go back before we can go forward," Reverend said.

Later that day Reverend told his in-laws. Mrs. Hymel began to cry.

"I mean you haven't been home that long. Are you sure you must do this? What about your other friends? Can they handle it?" Mrs. Hymel asked.

"I'm sure. This is my responsibility," Reverend replied.

"How is it your responsibility?" Mrs. Hymel asked, pushing back as best she could.

"I think we each have a responsibility to act when we see wrong being done. As it is written in Peter, 'each one should use whatever gift he has received to serve others,'" Reverend replied in a rote manner citing the biblical verse. Mrs. Hymel thought about what he said but stepped away without responding further.

The next day Reverend sent a telegram to Dalton in Union City, Missouri, and to Midnight, in care of Father Sprecht, in Columbus, Ohio. Two days later he received a telegram back from Midnight saying he would meet Reverend in Louisville near the army barracks where they had all been discharged. Dalton wrote back indicating that he was a deputy sheriff dealing with a possible miners' strike in Missouri and couldn't get away. Reverend showed both telegrams to Theresa.

"Dalton is not going, why must you?" she said, and when he reiterated that he was going anyway she left him to go cry in their bedroom. Mr. Hymel was sitting with Reverend at the kitchen table as Theresa left.

"Let's take a walk," Mr. Hymel said. The two men left the house to walk the neighborhood. Mr. Hymel was calm, businesslike, explaining that he would continue to watch over Theresa while Reverend was gone.

"But I have to say this to you," Mr. Hymel continued. "I don't know what you went through in the war with your friends. I can only imagine the bonds that develop. However, at some point your priority has to be Theresa and your life together. She waited for you for a long time and now you want her to wait for you again. Perhaps this is something you must do, at least this time, but again, at some point she must become your priority," Mr. Hymel said. Reverend knew this to be true.

"Of course, you are right. I appreciate your counsel and I will keep it in mind while traveling," Reverend finally said. He then excused himself so that he could go speak to Pastor Ellis whom he found at the church.

"What do you think you can do?" Pastor Ellis asked Reverend, after Reverend explained the situation. "You don't know what you are walking into down there."

"I don't know, but I have to try. I have to try," Reverend said, his voice tinged, for the first time, with a dull uncertainty and trailing off at the end.

"What about Theresa? This disrupts the life you were creating," Pastor Ellis said.

"Am I wrong to leave her now? I don't know. I just know in my heart of hearts that I can't abandon Shadrach. He is the one that needs my help now. Sometimes the right decisions are the hardest ones to make, especially when it affects others that you care about," Reverend replied.

"I guess the war ain't really over," Pastor Ellis said, sounding despondent.

"And it won't be over 100 years from now unless we can treat every person, black and white, as a child of God and stop abusing them," Reverend said.

"Reverend, I hate to preach to you on this but this is not about the difficulties of preparing the right words to one of your sermons. This sounds more like being thrown into the lions' den. We've heard horrible stories about the treatment of freed slaves and their supporters in the Reconstruction South," Pastor Ellis said.

"I was down there during Reconstruction. I'm not naive. Are you telling me, Pastor, that you would not be going down there for a friend in trouble?" Reverend asked. Pastor Ellis hung his head slightly and looked at the ground.

"No. I can't say that. I can't. But if you are going shouldn't you take a gun with you? I can ask around if you wish to get one," Pastor Ellis then said, lifting his head and placing a reassuring hand on Reverend's shoulder. Reverend smiled a sad smile.

"No guns. It will only provoke more violence. I'm done with killing and as far as being thrown in the lions' den, remember with the strength of his conviction in the Lord, Daniel survived unscathed in the lions' den," Reverend replied.

Pastor Ellis then reached into his pocket and gave Reverend a wad of bills. It was $30.

"Here, you may need this. It's all I have on me," Pastor Ellis said. Reverend thanked him and after shaking his hand began a slow walk back to his in-laws house to pack for the trip.

The following morning he advised his disbelieving parents and then said goodbye to Theresa and her parents. He brought his gear to the train station and, with a heaviness etched on his brow, waited alone to board the train for Louisville, Kentucky.

CHAPTER 45.

Word quickly spread among St. Mary's parishioners about Midnight heading down South to try to help a friend who was in serious trouble. Father Sprecht took up a small collection from some congregation members and gave it to Midnight as traveling money.

"I don't know all the details yet. He was headed down to Alabama to look for his family members. Seems that he was picked up by some sheriff and is being forced to work in the mines," Midnight told Father Sprecht.

"Emmet, this sounds like it could be very dangerous," Father Sprecht said. "I have a question for you. From what you've told me you weren't raised Catholic."

"No. Really wasn't much formal religion where I was raised, just some folks that knew a little of the Bible and every so often a white preacher would come by and say a few things," Midnight said. "The slave owners always seemed torn about how much religion we could be exposed to. Guess they thought it might rile us up."

When the slave trade first began the religious practices of the African slaves ran the gamut from animism, to polytheism, to Islam, and to Christianity. Although some attempts were made by missionaries to bring Christianity to slaves once they were in the United States, the effort met with mixed results. There was opposition from many slave owners who feared groups of slaves gathering together and planning a revolt. Other problems, at least as slave owners saw it, involved slaves wishing to retain or incorporate practices that had been handed down from Africa into the religious services. This led to, what came to be known as, 'Hush Harbor Meetings.' Slaves would meet secretly at pre-determined locations for religious services that combined African traditions with Christianity, a syncretism which the slave owners opposed. It is believed that the meetings are where spirituals, songs of hope and hardship, first began.

"Have you ever been baptized?" Father Sprecht then asked.

"Seem to recall Momma saying a traveling preacher might have done so in a stream when I was a baby but, of course, I don't recall it," Midnight said.

"Since we don't know the details, and whether he said the right things, I'd like to ask your permission to baptize you and then hear your confession before you leave," Father Sprecht said. "That is the Catholic Church's way of putting you in the best possible graces of the Lord."

Midnight agreed and Father Sprecht quickly performed a baptism ceremony in the church declaring that "I baptize you in the name of the Father and the Son and the Holy Spirit." Midnight then kneeled in the confessional and, with a little prodding from Father Sprecht, talked about the men he knew that he had killed in the war.

"It's strange. As I sit here with you I can recall a little something, an image or moment in my mind, about each one of them. I guess, sadly, I'll always have those memories. Maybe that's how they live on," Midnight said. Father Sprecht listened, absolved him of his sins and told him what to recite as his penance.

Several people, regular church goers, who Midnight had gotten to know, stopped by the church when they heard the news to wish Midnight well. He was genuinely touched by their kindness.

"You are part of the St. Mary family," one church member told him, while shaking his hand.

The smithy, a hulking Irish immigrant and member of the church, gave him a used but serviceable revolver, ammunition, and an old gun-belt which Midnight put on and thanked him for.

"It's still a good gun. I've kept it clean and oiled. Hopefully you won't need to use it, but you never know. Better to be prepared," the smithy told him.

"I'll bring it back," Midnight told him, as he buckled on the gunbelt.

"No need. It's yours. In this day and time a man should have a good gun. Go with the blessings of Saint Brigid of Kildare," the smithy replied in his thick Irish brogue.

Midnight thought about going to see Emmalene before he left, but didn't have the energy for the put down which he expected from her. Instead, he asked Father Sprecht to give her his best wishes.

After saying his final goodbyes to those at the church, who came to see him off, he and Father Sprecht walked to the train depot where he could catch the afternoon train toward Louisville to meet up with Reverend. Midnight had his saddle, bedroll, and satchel bag with him. He set these down on the station landing.

"It has been a pleasure to get to know you, but I must tell you I'm concerned for you," Father Sprecht said.

"Thanks for your help and teaching me to read better. It has opened up a new world to me. And I'll be alright. You know, I survived the plantation and the war. I'll be back as soon as I can. I promise," Midnight said.

"Your job will be here for you when you return," Father Sprecht replied. Father Sprecht told Midnight he would pray for him and then reached into the pocket of his cassock.

"Emmet, I have something for you in that regard," he said. He handed Midnight a bible.

"This way you can keep up with your reading," Father Sprecht said and then hugged Midnight.

"I can't say I ever been given a present this nice before. First, the gun from the smithy and now this. A gun and a bible, says something about the world we live in. Might be my best presents ever," Midnight said.

Father Sprecht released his hold on Midnight. As he did so someone grabbed Midnight's arm from behind and Midnight turned his head and saw Emmalene.

"I'll leave you two now," Father Sprecht said, nodding to Emmalene as he began to walk away.

"Thank you for this, Father," Midnight said, raising the Bible in his hand toward Father Sprecht.

"And you weren't going to come tell me goodbye?" Emmalene asked, her lips squeezed together suggesting her disapproval. Midnight didn't know what to say. Every time he tried to get close to her she had corrected him.

"I have to go do this. I have a friend who needs me," he finally said, ignoring her question as the conductor indicated that it was time to board the train.

"That was a real nice reading you did from the Gospel of Mark that day in church, very proper," Emmalene said, placing her hand gently on his chest. "And I think your full beard looks good on you," she said, playfully running her fingers through his beard.

"Thanks," Midnight replied, suddenly uncomfortable with her attention.

"I heard why you are leaving. And going to help a friend who is in trouble says a lot about who you are in here," Emmalene said, tapping her finger on his chest by his heart.

Midnight leaned down, picked up his saddle and satchel bag, and then, without responding, started to step away to board the train. Emmalene grabbed his hand and pulled him back to her and kissed him on the cheek.

"You better come back to me, you hear. Don't you try to be a hero," she said, releasing his hand so that he could hop on the train which had started to move.

CHAPTER 46.

Sheriff Wilson and Dalton were worried. It seemed that more and more people were pouring into Union City. There were out-of-state men, members of the International Workingmen's Association, who, informed of the potential strike, had come to support the miners. There were several more gun hands brought in by the mine owners, men with reputations and others seeking to create one. Dalton and the sheriff patrolled the streets breaking up fights or talking men out of fighting. It was tiring and there seemed to be no end in sight.

The International Workingmen's Association was formed in 1864 to support the rights of workers. It eventually evolved in the United States into the Workingmen's Party. In 1878 it gained 5 seats in the Kentucky state legislature before disbanding and changing its name to the Socialist Labor Party.

The influx of miners, and the expanding miner encampment that was growing outside of town, increased gambling and business for the saloons, dance halls, and brothels. More alcohol and more peer pressure did not, however, calm the tempers that were flaring among the miners over their work conditions. Sheriff Wilson and Dalton got little sleep trying to keep up with the demands of the job. Indeed they weren't successful in keeping complete order as fights among drunken miners periodically broke out. They merely managed to avoid an all out war, but the local paper continued to trumpet the lawlessness in the town and the influx of people as a "reign of terror."

Hawkins had been released from jail by Circuit Judge Wagner, after a brief hearing, for lack of evidence that he had paid or hired the men to kill the sheriff. He and the other mine owners then doubled their efforts to put together a small army of men good with a gun whose presence, walking the streets, interjecting themselves into miners' meetings, or hanging out at the Miners' Kitchen, would intimidate the miners into not striking. The gunmen they were bringing in did not immediately start any gunfights. But Sheriff Wilson and Dalton felt it was just a matter of time before a violent outbreak between the two sides occurred. If the miners went forward with a strike it seemed certain that there would be an all out war between the miners and the men retained by the mine owners.

Despite his release by the circuit judge rumors continued to circulate around town, and in the bars, about a bounty of $50 being put on Sheriff Wilson's head by Hawkins or by the other mine owners. It weighed heavily on Sheriff Wilson, although he pretended otherwise, and was just one more stressor which he and Dalton had to deal with. Dalton saw its daily effects on the sheriff, a dark storm cloud that hung over him, and decided it was time to try to derail it. So he went alone one morning, without Sheriff Wilson's knowledge, to the Hawkins Hotel and walked past the stares and posturing of several of the mine owners' hired gunmen into Hawkins office unannounced.

"Is there something I can do for you, Deputy? I don't recall agreeing to meet with you," Hawkins asked, seated behind his desk when Dalton walked in.

"Nothing you can do for me. I'm just here to deliver a message to whomever is offering $50 to kill the sheriff," Dalton said.

"I've told you I don't know anything about that and the judge has cleared me. Now if you don't mind I have business to attend to," Hawkins said.

"Nevertheless here is my message. If Sheriff Wilson dies you better have someone kill me as well because minutes after he dies I'm coming for you and I'm going to kill you and anyone who tries to stop me," Dalton said.

"That sounds like a threat," Hawkins said.

"Not a threat. A promise," Dalton replied.

He stood for a moment to watch Hawkins' reaction. Hawkins pinched his lips together as if he had bitten into something sour. There was little doubt in his mind that Dalton meant what he said.

"I could call in some of my men right now and you wouldn't get out of here alive," Hawkins finally said, trying to intimidate Dalton.

"You could and you'd be dead before they got through the door," Dalton replied, placing his hand on his dragoon. Hawkins cleared his throat.

"Is there anything else?" Hawkins asked, trying to hide his nervousness. Dalton didn't respond, but turned and left the office.

Sheriff Wilson lobbied the town council at an emergency meeting that evening to let him hire more deputies, but the mine owners on the council defeated every effort, fearful that an increase in deputies could be used against them in the coming conflict.

"You are tying my hands and increasing the dangers to everyone who lives here," Sheriff Wilson told the council.

"If you can't handle it, Sheriff, just tell us and we'll find someone else who can," Mr. Walsh said.

"Perhaps if you had been more cooperative with the mine owners at the outset we might agree, but since you haven't, we've provided our own protection," Hawkins responded at the meeting, eyeing Dalton as he spoke. Hawkins and Walsh argued again, unsuccessfully, to have Sheriff Wilson removed but the power of appointment and retention was with the mayor who would not agree to it.

"I'm not letting you run this town, not while I'm mayor," Mayor Adams said to Hawkins, in rejecting the request to remove Sheriff Wilson.

"I don't know what you are talking about, Mayor. We are business-men who are simply trying to protect the town's economy, of which we are a major part," Hawkins replied.

"I hope you don't expect to be re-elected," Mr. Gloop angrily interjected.

"Thankfully the voters decide on that, not you, but win or lose my conscience will be clear," Mayor Adams replied to Mr. Gloop as the meeting came to an end. Sheriff Wilson and Dalton left the meeting together still trying to figure out what to do.

And now Dalton had another problem, one that he had never expected and that sorely tested him: the telegram from Reverend telling him Shadrach was in trouble and needed help. He showed the telegram to Sheriff Wilson when they returned to the sheriff's office.

"Friend of yours?" Sheriff Wilson asked.

"Good friend. Excellent soldier. Probably the toughest yet kindest man I have ever had the privilege of knowing," Dalton said and then explained who Shadrach was.

"Sounds like he is in real trouble," the sheriff said.

"Yeah. But I can't leave you at a time like this, miners' strike, gunmen in town, and a bounty on your head. I sent a telegram saying I'm tied up," Dalton said.

"I appreciate you staying. I need you here," Sheriff Wilson replied.

CHAPTER 47.

Shadrach and Gabriel were getting concerned. They continually glanced over at Rat and whispered words of encouragement. Rat didn't look good. He was moving too slow, stumbling, perhaps dehydrated, and having trouble keeping up with Skinny who was doing his best to cover for him in order to avoid the wrath of Roscoe. They had seen this before, when a man's spirit, loaded down in despair, the loose ends of his life frayed beyond repair and his body poisoned by working in the mine, was gradually defeated and unable to continue. In the middle of the work day, when it was the hottest in the mine, Rat finally gave up and just sat down.

"No more," he said weakly, his voice barely audible.

"Ya got to get back up," Skinny said, trying to lift Rat back up on his feet and looking around to see if the guards had noticed.

"Ya can do it," Gabriel, offered supportively. But Rat just sat there struggling to catch his breath, wheezing and coughing, caked from head to toe in red dust. Roscoe walked menacingly towards Rat and as he stood over him he slowly unwound his whip.

"Get up!" Roscoe yelled, looking down on Rat who, with his legs stretched out in front of him and his shoulders hunched forward, suddenly seemed childlike and innocent.

"Leave the man alone. Can't you see he is suffering!" Toussaint yelled at Roscoe. Roscoe quickly cracked the whip against Toussaint, something he had been doing everyday in an attempt to break or demoralize Toussaint. When Toussaint covered up Roscoe dropped the whip and attacked Toussaint, punching him repeatedly until Toussaint, unable to defend himself, was laying on the ground. Roscoe then picked up the whip and turned his attention back to Rat as Toussaint struggled to get to his feet.

"He be alright, Mr. Roscoe. It be a hot one today. Just give him a minute," Skinny said about Rat, as the others working in the mine, with all too familiar pained expressions, looked on. Skinny tried again, unsuccessfully, to lift Rat by the arm to get him to stand. Rat remained seated, his eyes momentarily glossed over and his breathing becoming more labored.

Shadrach and Gabriel had stopped working. The rest of the work crew had also stopped, waiting for the inevitable. All except Levi who continued to work as if he was oblivious to the scene about to be acted out by Roscoe.

The whip from Roscoe came down hard on Rat. Skinny instinctively moved as far away from Rat as the chain binding their legs together would allow. The whip came down again. Rat sat there, bloodied, without resisting or covering up. His eyes flinched each time the whip connected with his flesh, but otherwise it seemed as if the rest of his body was impervious to the pain.

"I'm comin'," Rat said quietly, reaching out one hand toward a vision of someone. This seemed to infuriate Roscoe.

"You ain't goin' nowhere, except to hell!" Roscoe yelled, bringing the tip of the whip down on Rat's head.

Shadrach started to move towards Roscoe, but Gabriel and another prisoner grabbed him and held him tight, restraining him. One of the guards stood in front of Shadrach and pointed his rifle at him. The whip came down again, and again, and yet again, tearing more flesh each time. Rat finally fell over from his seated position. He was unconscious. Despite this fact the whip came down several more times. Skinny then moved to cover Rat's body with his own, hoping to discourage Roscoe and shield Rat's lifeless body from any further blows.

Roscoe wound up the whip as he looked disdainfully at Skinny. Some of the other guards circled closer to Roscoe, perhaps expecting trouble from the other prisoners in the mine. They each lowered and pointed their rifles towards the men.

"Get back to work!" Roscoe yelled.

The prisoners moved slowly, traumatized by what they had witnessed; one more numbing reminder that they were enslaved, that they were being regarded by the guards, and by the rest of the world for all they knew, as less than human. They picked up their shovels and axes and bent their aching backs to the work. Skinny turned Rat over on his back. He wasn't breathing.

"He dead," Skinny said quietly.

"Get him out of here," Roscoe said to Skinny. Skinny stood and tried to lift Rat up, but he wasn't strong enough and dropped his limp body. Roscoe uncoiled his whip.

"I said lift him up!" Roscoe yelled, bringing the whip down on Skinny who had Rat's blood on his chest and the upper part of his torn trousers from the attempt to lift him. The other men in the mine started to slow down again unsure of what to do in response.

And then something odd and unexpected happened. Levi stepped between Roscoe and Skinny. Roscoe took an uneasy step back. Levi lifted Rat up and with Skinny hobbling beside him carried Rat to the mine opening and set him down outside. Levi then returned to work.

Skinny sat next to Rat's body, shackled to his friend. He tried to wipe the blood off of Rat's face and talked to him as he did so.

"Look Rat, da sun be up. You picked a mighty nice day to go," Skinny said, squinting as he glanced up at the clear blue sky.

When he had cleaned Rat's face with his hand as best he could, he tried to recall a prayer to say. The only thing that came to him at the moment was the "Our Father" that he had heard said during his days working on the plantation. He didn't recall the entire prayer, but recalled the white folks prayed it often. He spoke silently the parts that he remembered over Rat's body.

"Ya needs betta words to be spoken ova ya. Don't know why God be allowin' dis to happen," Skinny mumbled, as tears formed in his eyes.

One of the guards finally got a hammer and chisel and took the leg irons off Rat freeing Skinny who took one last look at Rat and then was shoved by the guard back into the mine to return to work.

That night, at the end of the work day, Skinny scrubbed frantically at his skin trying to get all of Rat's dried blood off of him. Gabriel and Shadrach poured some of their drinking water on Skinny's arms to help him clean up. Levi walked over and gave them a cup of his drinking water to use. Skinny thanked him. Levi nodded, lightly touching Skinny on the head, and then left to return to the spot on the mine floor where he slept alone each night.

"Dat ol' Rat, he was a nice man. Wish I'd knowd him b'fore da mine," Gabriel offered, as he rinsed Skinny's arm with Levi's water.

"No one ought to have to die dis way," Skinny said.

"Too many of us is dyin' here for no reason. It be wrong and it need to change," Shadrach replied.

Toussaint lay in pain by himself, away from the other men, his breathing punctured by small cries. Shadrach checked on him but Toussaint waved him off.

"Roscoe gonna kill Toussaint. He can't stand the thought of him havin' been a free man," Shadrach said to Gabriel.

"Specially one dat stand up to him," Gabriel replied.

CHAPTER 48.

Midnight arrived by train in Louisville first. The next day, in the mid-afternoon, Reverend arrived. They met in front of the barracks with a handshake. Perhaps tired from their travel, or weighed down by the unexpected disruption of their lives, there was not much said between them initially. They set out to purchase horses and supplies as there were no rail lines running to or near Elyton.

The expansion of the railroad system exploded after the Civil War with an estimated 35,000 miles of track laid between 1865 and 1873, though most existing tracks going anywhere South were still damaged from the war or were incomplete. Indeed as of 1867, two years after the war ended, the entire state of Alabama had only 851 miles of railroad track. The nationwide expansion was propelled by Federal Land Grants in excess of 150 million acres to railroad companies. The expansion became one more element of the nationalization of commerce and created countless opportunities for corruption and bribery of politicians in southern and northern governments.

One of the more notorious examples was the 1872 Credit Mobilier Scandal. It was one of many scandals during the Grant administration, including the Whiskey Ring scandal and Black Friday. Credit Mobilier entered a contract to build the eastern part of the Union Pacific Railroad. Stock in Credit Mobilier was secretly given to a dozen or so Congressmen at below market value to help facilitate the venture and overcome any obstacles for getting the necessary land grants. In submitting its bills for the work Credit Mobilier double billed and money flowed back to those congressmen.

The railroads would eventually be on the frontlines in the enforcement of the evolving Jim Crow laws which segregated riders, on some railroads, by race. It would culminate in the adoption of the "separate but equal" doctrine endorsed by the United States Supreme Court in the 1896 case of *Plessy v Ferguson*, which upheld Louisiana's Separate Car Act. The separate but equal doctrine, which was then applied to other areas, such as public accommodations and educational facilities, would not be overturned by the Supreme Court until 1954 in the case of *Brown v Board of Education*.

Once all their supplies were purchased Midnight saddled the horses and packed their saddle bags. Reverend did his best to figure out from a map at the barracks where Elyton was and the quickest route to get there.

Midnight noticed that Reverend did not have a gun but he didn't raise the issue with him. The men saddled up, rode at a hard gallop for an hour and finally slowed the horses to a walk and began to talk. Midnight told Reverend about learning to read, about his reading the Gospel in the church, and his job duties with Father Sprecht. Reverend, when it was his turn, updated Midnight on his marriage and his recent preaching at First Church. Then they discussed the details of the telegram Reverend had received from Mr. Blanchfield.

"Reverend, what is this thing called debt peonage?" Midnight asked, rolling the word peonage around as he spoke.

"As best I understand it they arrest someone on false charges, like vagrancy or something similar under the Black Codes, so a local man can pay any fine. The person arrested has to work for the man until the debt is paid off. In Shadrach's case, work in a mine. But it's really a scam, just a way to get around the fact that slavery was outlawed," Reverend said.

"Then why did we fight the war and have all those soldiers die if they can still make people slaves?" Midnight asked, as they slowed their horses further to look for a possible place to camp for the night. A large oak tree a few yards off the trail seemed to present the perfect canopy.

"Well, remember the war started to preserve the Union. It was only later that slavery became the issue, though it was always foremost in my mind and in the mind of abolitionists. But I guess I'm learning that the evil behind slavery doesn't die that easily," Reverend replied, haltering his horse toward the oak tree with Midnight following.

"Why are people evil? Were some people created that way or do they learn it after they are born?" Midnight asked, as the men dismounted at the site they had chosen for their camp. Reverend did not immediately reply.

Reverend and Midnight tied their horses off, removed their saddles, saddle bags, and blankets and lugged these close to the spot that they had selected for the evening fire. They spread their bed rolls out as the wind picked up.

"It's starting to get dark. Looks like it will be a clear night and colder. We better get some firewood," Midnight said.

Both men began walking the perimeter and beyond picking up sticks and branches. Midnight retrieved a small hand axe from his saddle bag to chop up the branches from a dead tree he found as Reverend dragged several large tree limbs under the oak tree to be cut up later.

"Midnight, I wasn't ignoring your question. That may be the toughest of all questions for Christians to answer. What causes evil? Is it the devil? Is it original sin? Is it man's exercise of his free will?" Reverend finally replied, which prompted Midnight, who had started to walk with his axe toward the dead tree, to stop.

"What does the good book have to say about it?" Midnight asked, and then he pulled out the Bible that Father Sprecht had given him.

"Let's get the fire going, eat, and then talk about it some more," Reverend replied.

They picked up some more tree limbs, cut up some dead branches, and then settled in. After awhile Midnight broke up some kindling and got the fire started while Reverend prepared a pot of coffee.

"Midnight, the idea of evil has confounded thinking Christians for many years. There is no easy answer. Some people think it all began in the Garden of Eden when Adam and Eve ate the apple they were not supposed to eat. The idea that this is the original sin passed on to all of us," Reverend said.

"Reverend, I read about that in Genesis, the apple eating in the garden I mean. But, if you don't mind me asking, why would that be passed on to folks that had nothing to do with the disobeying? I mean no one around today was there at the garden and it seems to me that if we are to be judged it ought to be for our own actions, not for something someone else did before we were born," Midnight said.

"Good question. And I can't really answer it. It certainly seems unfair. But that's not the only theory about where evil comes from," Reverend replied.

"Are we born evil or good? I mean I have known some pretty evil folks and others, like my Momma, that never hurt no one despite what was being done to her," Midnight said.

"I can only give you my thinking on it. And it is always evolving. And let me make that point first. There are no easy or permanent answers. Our experiences may alter our thinking, at least if we are willing to reflect on things," Reverend said.

"So what is your idea on evil?" Midnight asked, as he stretched out his legs to warm them by the fire and then poured them both a cup of coffee.

"I think that we are all born good or at least with the ability to be good. It makes no sense to me that someone would be born evil, 'cause that would be evil that God would be responsible for alone. And like you the original sin idea no longer makes any sense to me," Reverend said, before sipping from his cup of coffee. "So the next step in my thinking is based on Jesus' command to love one another, including your enemies. To me that means we are supposed to do our best to put others over ourselves, their interests over our interests. So evil to me arises when an otherwise good person, a person born good, puts their own interest over those of others in a situation where they know doing so will harm them. But I admit I'm still thinking it through and there could be other factors about us, or about our biology, that science just hasn't figured out yet," Reverend said. Midnight thought about this for a few minutes.

"Well, if what you say is true, that it's about putting ourselves first, then we are all evil on occasion," he managed to say.

"In degrees, I guess that's true. No one of us is perfect. But we should try to remember to put others first. I think that is inherent in Jesus' command to love one another," Reverend said.

"You think that's what the slave owners did, put their own interests over others, over those they enslaved? Or what this mine owner that has

Shadrach is doing?" Midnight asked.

"I do. Clearly that's the case. They put their economic interests first," Reverend answered promptly.

"What is the punishment for such evil? Don't seem like it's much to me if people are still doing it," Midnight said, before drinking some of his coffee.

"I have to believe the punishment is yet to come. I have to believe that," Reverend replied.

"You mean in the hereafter?" Midnight asked.

"Yes, and in this life as well. The seeds of evil deeds sometimes lay fallow for awhile, but I'm convinced these deeds sooner or later burden a man, at least if he has a conscience. And it has other effects, maybe even ones that are not visible to the rest of us. As it says in Proverbs, 'For the evil man has no future; the lamp of the wicked will be extinguished,'" Reverend replied.

"I wonder about that, if the overseers or the plantation owners that bought and sold us ever regretted what they did," Midnight replied.

"If they don't, if they don't ask for forgiveness, there is always punishment in hell," Reverend said.

"Father Sprecht taught me a bit more about that. I'm not sure what I think about that yet. Heaven and hell. Seems like heaven is just an idea to make people accept their suffering in this life by looking to the next. Reminds me of the hopeful spirituals some people would sing in the fields or at the Hush Harbor meetings. Got to study on it a bit more. And I don't rightly know yet that I believe the stuff about people spending forever in hell. Seems like there is enough hell on earth for many people," Midnight said.

CHAPTER 49.

"**S**heriff, it's happening tomorrow. Nuncie Spizale and the others were in here earlier talking," Tony, the bartender, whispered to Sheriff Wilson.

Sheriff Wilson and Dalton were standing at one end of the jam-packed bar watching the crowd and looking for any spark that might start a conflagration. The bar was filled with miners, many of whom Dalton and the sheriff knew, but there were some new faces among them who had recently arrived in town. The sheriff nodded his head in understanding. The miners' strike, Tony was telling him, would happen tomorrow.

Dalton and Sheriff Wilson left the bar about twenty minutes later and stood outside to discuss their options. Two men against all the miners and the gunmen that the mine owners had hired.

"If one side doesn't kill us the other side will. And the mine owners are going to unleash the gun hands they brought in. They've been holding back but that will end 'cause they ain't gonna just sit by and let the strike happen," Sheriff Wilson said. As they started to walk back to the jail they noticed an overflow group of miners standing outside the Miners' Kitchen in a semi-circle and other miners walking up to join them.

"Let's go check this out," Dalton said.

"Yeah, if they're planning something that may be where it will come together," Sheriff Wilson replied.

As they approached they saw more clearly that the miners were gathered around one man, listening to him talk. It was Mack, the owner of the Miners' Kitchen.

"They are going to provoke you. Don't fall for it. Walk away. None of you are gun hands and many of you have wives and kids. Getting yourself killed ain't going to help anything. We've got to make them negotiate on your points," Mack said, as Sheriff Wilson and Dalton made their way through the crowd of miners.

"Mack is right. If there is any gunplay let Dalton and I handle it," Sheriff Wilson said, as he stepped up next to Mack.

"Some of us can handle guns," one of the miners said in response, and several other miners echoed their agreement.

"You're no match for these professional gunmen," Sheriff Wilson said, to try to dissuade the crowd.

"But there's more of us than there are of them," one miner said.

"Yeah, and I'm not a backing down from a no one," Nuncie Spizale said, in his Sicilian accent, to the crowd's approval.

"How many of you fought in the war?" Dalton then asked the crowd, as he moved to stand next to Mack and the sheriff. More than three quarters of the men raised their hands.

"I'm going to say this again, do not try to draw against these professional gunmen unless you have a great desire to be put in a pine box," Sheriff Wilson said.

"I can shoot pretty good," a miner replied.

"Me too," another miner replied, as the crowd again murmured their support.

"We ain't afraid of 'em," still another miner said.

"I have an idea," Dalton said to Mack and the sheriff.

"I'm not making any headway with them. You try," the sheriff said quietly to Dalton.

"I want to speak to the former soldiers. Spizale you stay. The rest of you men go home for now. If we decide on anything we'll get word to you through Mack," Dalton then said.

Once the other miners who were not in the war had dispersed Dalton asked the remaining men about their military training. It turned out that three of the men had been snipers and part of the regular US Army. Some had been drafted. Others had been in one or more of the 1,700 volunteer units from northern and western states and territories and had received rudimentary arms training offered by the Union Army. Several former Confederate soldiers, who were miners, had no such training but said they grew up using guns. All of them had been in battlefield engagements. Although none could compete one on one in a gunfight with the mine owners' gunmen, despite what a few of them claimed, they all had significant experience handling a rifle or a revolver.

"Sheriff, I know the Town Council won't let you hire any other deputies, but you can always swear in a posse. Right? I wonder if we can swear in these men, kind of like a posse, to create a temporary militia to guard miners' property and guard the miners' encampment during the strike?" Dalton asked.

"And what if these miners get out of hand after I swear them in? We'll have two armed camps fighting each other," Sheriff Wilson added.

"We may have that anyway," Dalton said. He had a plan which he began to set out while the sheriff, Mack, and the miners listened. The men would not seek out anyone to fight but would stand in groups to guard property and persons. "Certainly you have the power to swear them in to do that," Dalton said.

"Go on. I'm listening," Sheriff Wilson said.

"When you are dealing with a bully sometimes it's best to throw the first punch," Dalton said.

As Dalton explained it the idea was to change the dynamic away from the mine owners believing that they have all the firepower with the hired guns, that the miners would be too intimidated and too disorganized to fight back. Dalton and the sheriff could focus on any gun hands who got out of line and maybe if the gunmen saw the number of armed miners guarding property, or guarding the encampment, their calculus might change about risking their lives.

"Look, we'll assign a group of men to each property in town owned by a miner, for example here at the Miners' Kitchen and at the black-smith shop, and then have all the other miners stay in their encampment outside of town, which other posse members will be set up to guard," Dalton said.

"Stay in the encampment?" a miner asked.

"Right, don't come into town until the strike is over," Dalton replied. "You can't get in trouble or coaxed into a fight if you stay together out there," Dalton concluded.

"Might be hard to convince everyone to stay out there and not come into town, but it's worth a try," Mack interjected.

"I like a dis plan. I say we do as a you say," Nuncie Spizale said loudly to those assembled.

"The key is to be seen. So those guarding the Miners' Kitchen, the blacksmith shop, or the encampment, sit outside with your guns. Let the mine owners and their gunmen see you. And another thing. If you still have your army uniforms, Union or Confederacy, wear them. That will let the gunmen know you were in the war and know how to use a gun," Dalton said

"Yeah, maybe they won't want to fire on former soldiers," one of the miners suggested.

"I'm up for it," one of the miners wearing a Confederate soldier's cap said.

"I'll be right there with you, Johnny Reb," the miner standing next to him replied.

The sheriff shook his head but reluctantly agreed. There were about 35 miners who would make up the posse. Sheriff Wilson swore them in. He made them promise to uphold the law as he gave it to them. Mack helped select those who would stand guard at each location. They were warned by Sheriff Wilson not to start any fights but to return fire only if fired upon.

"Damnest posse I've ever seen," he said to Dalton, as they walked back to the jail with the posse following them. Most of the men had their own guns. For a few others Sheriff Wilson would pass out rifles and ammunition.

CHAPTER 50.

Reverend and Midnight continued on their journey south. They had spent their first night under the spreading oak tree, outside of Elizabethtown, Kentucky, but over the next few days they passed through the rural towns of Sonora, Bacon Creek, and Cave City. These were small towns that had not been strategic to the war in any way, but had, nevertheless, seen both armies trample through or engage in firefights in and around them. Bacon Creek, which later was renamed Bonnieville, saw the Confederates, under General John Hunt Morgan, purposely destroy their only bridge over the creek in a fight with the 2nd Michigan Volunteer Cavalry Regiment. It had been rebuilt by the town several times, only to see it destroyed each time during the course of the war.

As they passed through these small settlements they saw the ruins of war. Buildings stood charred and burned, bridges still teetered in disrepair, fences remained torn down, and populations had been left destitute. Reverend realized that he was seeing the towns and the destruction that remained from the war differently from how he saw it as a soldier.

These were not enemy positions, bridgeheads, or extraction points, but impoverished areas with poor folks, mostly white, who had been caught in the middle of a war that they didn't want and had often been abused by both sides. They were trying to survive and put their lives back together. Many of them were angry, an unfocused anger at anything or anyone outside of their small and insular world.

Reverend and Midnight camped at night outside of these towns not knowing how locals would react to them. At some point, however, they made their way into Franklin, Tennessee, where they had to buy more supplies. Franklin had been the site of Lt. General John Bell Hood's futile attack on Union forces led by Major General John Schofield in late 1864. Hood's forces suffered significant casualties eventually withdrawing to be decimated at the Battle of Nashville. Further, in 1867, unbeknownst to Reverend and Midnight, there had been rioting in Franklin, that resulted in the purposeful killing of 25-30 black citizens.

They stopped at Grafton's Mercantile where the locals there were talking openly, and it seemed to Reverend and Midnight somewhat proudly, about a recent Klan shooting and lynching of a Jewish man, Samuel Bierfield, and the murder of, Lawrence Bowman, his black clerk. The lynching occurred several months prior in August, 1868. It was unclear to Reverend and Midnight what the men had allegedly done but there had apparently been no trial and nothing they heard to justify the lynching, just the Klan exacting its misguided revenge. In the coming years Franklin, which was named after Benjamin Franklin, would see many more lynching's of black men as the Klan tried to intimidate black citizens from voting or from exercising their newly acquired rights as citizens. Reverend and Midnight quickly left town after picking up the supplies which they needed.

"They lynched a white man too? What's that about?" Midnight asked, surprised, as they rode out.

"A Jewish man. They seem to be killing blindly and hating anyone who they consider different, with no attempt to understand," Reverend said.

"Don't make sense, hating people like that," Midnight said.

"Midnight, I might be wrong but they are motivated by fear, by their own insecurities. They need to feel superior. Hatred arises from insecurity after passing through fear. Just an explanation, not a justification," Reverend replied.

"Seems like they need to have an enemy in order to try to feel good about themselves. I know times are hard but they don't get any better by putting the blame elsewhere. Sometimes you got to look at yourself and change yourself. Better yourself as they say. That's what they want us former slaves to do," Midnight replied.

"Probably right. There is a long history of people doing that, projecting their dissatisfaction with themselves or their life onto others," Reverend said. They discussed it further and, fearful of what they had witnessed, decided to put some distance between the town and where they would be setting up camp.

When they finally stopped for the night Reverend got a fire going while Midnight tended to the horses. Reverend had just put a pot of coffee on the fire when they heard movement in the woods. Midnight drew his pistol.

"Who's out there?" Reverend said, as he and Midnight stood by the fire. A lone man, a black man, stepped out of the darkness into the glow of the fire light.

"Gentlemen, I didn't mean to frighten. I saw your fire and was hoping that you would allow me to warm myself by it. It is rather cold out tonight," the man said. Although his clothes were dirty it was clear by his demeanor, and his manner of speech, that he was an educated man.

"Please join us," Midnight said, holstering his gun.

The man stepped up and warmed his hands by the fire. He introduced himself as James Dallas Burrus. He told Midnight and Reverend that he had been enrolled at Fisk University, originally founded as Fisk Free Colored School, in Nashville, but was recently run off by the Klan.

"I'm lucky to have escaped. They caught some of my friends. Hung two of them," he said, sounding fatalistic.

The Fisk Free Colored School had been founded by the American Missionary Association in 1866 and changed its name to Fisk University in 1867. It was set up after the Civil War to educate freedmen in and around Nashville. It was originally affiliated with the United Church of Christ and was meant to provide training for black teachers but eventually became a college for higher education. W.E.B. Du Bois was among its many graduates.

Several other historically black colleges were set up after the Civil War and were founded by churches or missionary societies. These included Shaw University (1865), Howard University (1867), Talladega College (1867), Morehouse College (1867), and Hampton University (1868).

"They burned down the little place where we were all staying. It wasn't much but it was a roof over our heads," Mr. Burrus said.

"Were you a slave?" Midnight asked.

"Yes. I was in Murfreesboro, Tennessee. Then my master, Colonel James Tappan, took me and my siblings with him as his servants during his time serving in the Confederate Army. We were with him in Texas when the war ended. After that I made my way to Nashville," Mr. Burrus said.

It was not uncommon for army officers with slaves to bring them along as their servants during and before the war. For example, Jefferson Davis, a West Point graduate and future president of the Confederacy, brought his slave, James Pemberton, with him on all his military assignments when he was a lieutenant in the United States Army.

"What were you teaching at that school?" Midnight asked.

"I wasn't teaching. I was being trained to be a teacher in mathematics, but some white folks are not happy that schools have been set up for freedmen to become teachers. I guess they want to keep us as slaves, ignorant, and reliant on them," Mr. Burrus replied.

"Slavery bound us, but I think it also bound the masters some kind of way as well, corrupted their character. Not sure I completely understand all aspects of it yet," Midnight said.

"That's very true. We weren't the only victims of slavery. It ain't the same in no way with our enslavement and what was done to us. You can't compare it, but slave owners were deformed by it too, self-abased morally and economically. They embraced morally incoherent positions. We were mere property or chattel when they abused us or when we sought citizen's rights, but we were persons if we committed a crime who could be prosecuted as such," Mr. Burrus said.

"It will stain this nation for a long time. It is, as Edward Beecher said, an 'organic sin' that has infected the nation," Reverend offered.

"But in the South, as much as some will not want to admit it, after nearly 250 years of slavery, we are part of each other's world. There would be no white southern culture without us. We influenced each other, white and black, slave and free, in countless ways. For example, here is a minor thing, but think of the African words that they now use that are part of the South's lexicon, words like tote, yam, banjo, and okra," Mr. Burrus replied.

"I guess that's right," Midnight replied. "Always thought of them affecting us. Never thought about it the other way around. So let me ask you. Seems like you have thought about these things. How do you think things are going to work out for the country with the war over and all? I mean, how are we going to overcome the past?" Reverend leaned forward when Midnight finished asking his question, to be sure he heard Mr. Burrus' answer.

"It's impossible to fix the past. Some folks will try to rewrite it or sanitize it, others will try to glorify it and still others will pretend to forget it. But the best we can do; what I think we must do as a nation and as individuals, is to try to understand it," Mr. Burrus replied.

"Amen," Reverend said.

"Father Sprecht mentioned folks were rewriting it already," Midnight said.

Reverend offered Mr. Burrus some coffee and then they sat down and shared their meal with him.

"Seems like you are headed in the wrong direction if you are running from the Klan. Ought to be going to the North don't you think?" Midnight said, as they finished eating.

"I'm not running away. This is just a momentary set back. First chance I get I'm going back. I can't give up on my dream of being a teacher," Mr. Burrus said.

"Might be safer to go elsewhere," Reverend said.

"No, as Shakespeare wrote in *Hamlet*, I'd 'rather bear those ills we had, than to fly to others, that we know not of,'" Mr. Burrus said proudly.

"I like that thought. I just learned to read proper, myself. I had a good teacher," Midnight said.

"Teaching is an honorable profession. You leave a legacy through your students," Reverend advised.

"I agree. There is another line in Shakespeare, in *Henry the Eighth*, that I like to think of: 'And when I am forgotten, as I shall be, and asleep in dull cold marble, where no mention of me must be heard, say, I taught thee,'" Mr. Burrus recited, his face aglow with the thought.

"I'm going to have to read some of that fella, Shakespeare, some day. Seems like he is relevant for lots of things," Midnight said.

The men continued to talk and eventually fell asleep around the warmth of the fire. When Reverend and Midnight awoke in the early light of the morning, Mr. Burrus was gone.

James Dallas Burrus was one of the first graduates of Fisk University. He then attended Dartmouth College and in 1879 received his Masters Degree in mathematics. He was the first African American to receive a Masters Degree in the United States. He then returned to Fisk University as its first Professor of Mathematics.

"I sure hope he stays safe and gets to teach one day. He was one smart man. I could talk to him all day," Midnight said as he and Reverend were breaking camp to leave.

"To put his life at risk to do so, to educate others, not many people would do that and he seemed to have a natural gift for teaching," Reverend replied.

CHAPTER 51.

Hawkins and Walsh stormed into the jail shortly after lunch time to confront Sheriff Wilson.

"This morning the miners all walked out of the mines and off the job on a strike," Mr. Walsh said to the sheriff as soon as they entered the jail.

"So I heard," Sheriff Wilson said, casually pouring himself a cup of cowboy coffee.

"And what do you think you are doing?" Hawkins demanded of the sheriff.

"Excuse me? I'm pouring myself a cup of coffee. What's your problem?" Sheriff Wilson replied, though he had a pretty good idea as to what Hawkins was referring.

"You know damn well what I'm talking about. There are miners wearing their military uniforms with rifles sitting outside the Miners' Kitchen and the blacksmith shop and I'm told there's more than a dozen guarding their encampments outside of town. Most of the miners are off the streets holed up in those encampments. The shops in town are all empty. There's no business. And I know this is your doing," Hawkins fumed.

"Oh, that! That's my posse. I swore them in to guard property and people. Perfectly legal, as you like to say when you hire gunmen," Sheriff Wilson replied, having warmed to the idea and enjoying his ability to call the miners his 'posse' in front of Hawkins.

"Posse? This ain't funny," Mr. Walsh said.

"Are you crazy arming the miners?" Hawkins asked, his voice again rising in anger.

"About as crazy as you mine owners are for bringing in a bunch of gunmen. Did you think I was going to let you gun down the miners to break the strike, or so you could take over the town?" Sheriff Wilson said.

"If this thing explodes it will be all your fault and, Mayor Adams be damned, I'll have your head over it!" Hawkins yelled, losing his composure and pointing his finger at the sheriff.

"I've had just about enough from you. You're arrogant and you're greedy. You've been trying to get me out of the way for awhile, but you can't seem to find anyone worth the $50 gold pieces you pay to do the job. Can you? And you ain't man enough to try me yourself," Sheriff Wilson said, his own voice rising as he stepped up face to face with Hawkins, who took an awkward step backwards.

"You can't threaten me. I'll have you fired yet," Hawkins said, though his voice sounded weak.

"The other business owners in town are already complaining. There is nobody in their shops. This is going to hurt every business," Mr. Walsh said, more conciliatory and hoping to defuse the confrontation.

"All the more reason for you to negotiate with the miners," Sheriff Wilson replied.

"Negotiate, my ass. No way," Hawkins said.

Dalton came into the jail behind the mine owners as Sheriff Wilson remained standing directly in front of Hawkins.

"Any news?" Sheriff Wilson asked, looking at Dalton and stepping away from Hawkins.

"Yep. Two of Hawkins' men, LeBlanc and Hardy, are leaving town. Just spoke to them. They just saddled up and I watched them ride out," Dalton replied.

"What? What did you do to my men?" Hawkins asked, still agitated but confused by what Dalton said.

"Nothing. I think they decided that you lied to them about the miners not being armed. They seemed to think that the odds were no longer in their favor and there were easier pickings elsewhere. Hardy said to tell you thanks for the cash advance, but he won't be returning it," Dalton replied. Hawkins was so angry his face turned a burnt crimson.

"This is an outrage!" Mr. Walsh replied.

"I agree. You will pay for this," Hawkins said. Dalton laughed in response, which seemed to only infuriate Hawkins more.

"Hawkins get off your high horse and go talk with the miners' representatives. Their demands aren't unreasonable. Work something out," Sheriff Wilson said, picking up his coffee cup, taking a few sips and then buckling on his gunbelt as Hawkins, Walsh, and Dalton silently watched. He loaded his revolver and headed toward the door to leave.

"Where are you going? We're not done talking to you," Hawkins demanded.

"Maybe not, but I'm done listening to you. Dalton and I are going to encourage a few more of your men to leave," Sheriff Wilson said, before stepping past Hawkins and Walsh so that he and Dalton could exit the jail.

"So far your plan for a posse seems to be working. Just need to get the miners and mine owners together to work something out before this unravels or someone does something stupid," Sheriff Wilson said, as he and Dalton walked down the middle of the street.

"Stupid is always a possibility," Dalton replied.

CHAPTER 52.

Reverend and Midnight passed through Decatur, Alabama, where the Battle of Decatur had occurred in October 1864. Approximately 4,000 Union troops stopped the ragged Army of Tennessee from crossing the Tennessee River. Thereafter the Union Army occupied the town and before departing destroyed most of the buildings. Many of the buildings in Decatur still remained damaged and in disrepair.

They spent the night by the town of Priceville. The next morning they finally arrived at Elyton and sat astride their horses at the edge of town. Both were tired, pensive, and trail worn. Neither was in a particularly good mood.

"What are we going to do first?" Midnight asked, nervous about being back down this far in the rural South. Reverend was nervous as well. Their tour through small southern towns damaged by the war, and their few interactions with local citizens, had increased their anxiety.

"I'd love to get a good meal if there is one to be had, but I think it's best to go see the sheriff first. See what we can find out. I don't want

Shadrach to be detained any longer than necessary. We get him and then get out of here as quickly as we can," Reverend replied.

"Might be best if I wait outside the sheriff's office," Midnight said, knowing southern sentiments better than Reverend.

"Nonsense. You come in with me," Reverend replied, spurring his horse forward with Midnight following.

The two men rode up to the jail, got off their horses, stepped onto the porch, and then into the jail and Sheriff Maddox's office. Midnight was wearing the gun and gunbelt that he was given by the smithy in Columbus. Reverend had on a long black coat, black pants, and a black shirt. He also wore a cleric's white collar which he had put on immediately prior to getting to town. The sheriff was seated behind his desk half asleep. He was alone and did not initially look up when Reverend and Midnight walked in.

"Sheriff, my name is Reverend Harrison. I wonder if you could help me with something?" Reverend said. Midnight stood behind Reverend as they had entered, but as Reverend spoke he stepped up next to him in full view of the sheriff.

"Is this your boy?" the sheriff said sleepily to Reverend while pointing a lazy finger at Midnight. Reverend was taken aback by the comment but before he could respond Midnight spoke up.

"Yessa, Mr. Sheriff. I be on da trip to hep's da Rev'ren," Midnight said, in a purposely exaggerated pantomime.

"Why does he have a gun?" the sheriff then asked Reverend.

"To shoot dem squirrels and rabbits and such for us to be eatin'," Midnight replied.

"Sheriff, I'm looking for a young man named Shadrach that I understand was arrested a while back. He was sent over to a local mine to work, I believe," Reverend said.

"What's so special 'bout that boy? You're the second person who asked about him in the last month. Had that damn carpetbagger Blanchfield in here asking as well," the sheriff replied, annoyed and continuing to stare at Midnight.

"He be my relative and we told his family we—I mean da Rev'ren— would look for him, check on him, ya see," Midnight said, continuing his submissive pantomime. The sheriff stood up.

"I'm not speaking to your boy," the sheriff said to Reverend.

"He's not a boy. He's a grown man, a former Union soldier as am I, and you will speak to him and to me whether you like it or not," Reverend said forcefully, which clearly offended the sheriff. "What do I need to do to get Shadrach's freedom?" Reverend then asked.

"Nothing. He is the property of Mr. Talbot now. He couldn't pay the fine I imposed on him and Mr. Talbot generously paid it," the sheriff replied, seemingly happy to be able to say so and sitting back down.

"Nobody is another's property, Sheriff. And saying it don't make it so. You lost that argument in the war, I remind you. And the Thirteenth Amendment outlawed slavery that's against the law," Reverend replied. The sheriff chewed on something, perhaps a bit of chewing tobacco in his cheek. He didn't immediately respond.

"You a preacher or a lawyer? You might want to check the Thirteenth Amendment as it allows for slavery as a form of punishment for a crime. Besides, Alabama put a condition on its forced adoption of the Thirteenth Amendment. So I can do as I please," Sheriff Maddox finally said, trying to show that he knew the law as well.

Alabama and several other southern states approved the Thirteenth Amendment outlawing slavery in order to be readmitted to the Union, but only after putting conditions on the approval to try to blunt the effect. In Alabama that condition was that the amendment "does not confer upon Congress the power to legislate upon the political status of freedmen in this state."

"I know the amendments. That punishment requires a trial and a conviction. Was there a trial?" Reverend asked. The sheriff chewed on something again and simply stared back without answering.

"What was he charged with?" Reverend repeated as the sheriff still did not reply. "And he is a citizen of the United States just like you and me, with the same rights. He is entitled to a trial," Reverend said, his voice rising in rebuke.

"That ain't the case. Never will be in this town, not as long as I'm breathing. He ain't got no special rights," the sheriff finally said.

"The 14th Amendment was ratified, even by Alabama, granting all men born here, regardless of their race, citizenship," Reverend said, in a fruitless attempt to reason with the sheriff.

"Such laws are meaningless down here. I will maintain order as I see fit. The slave master may be gone 'cause of the war, but good southern government will be the master of the slaves now. Ain't nothing gonna change that. And in Elyton, I'm the government. Now get your asses out of my office before I arrest you both," the sheriff replied.

Midnight stepped further away from Reverend and put his hand on his gun.

"You want to try to arrest me? You go right ahead," Midnight challenged, dropping his pantomime.

"Niggers ain't to have guns in this town," Sheriff Maddox managed to say, his eyes blinking nervously as he spoke.

"This nigger has one. You want to take it from me?" Midnight quickly replied, as he continued to stare down the sheriff.

"Let's go. We'll get no satisfaction here," Reverend then said to

Midnight, realizing the futility of further discussions. Midnight paused. He finally turned to leave with Reverend.

"You two better be careful. We ain't too partial to your kind down here and don't think that collar you are wearing Reverend, if you are in fact a Reverend, is going to matter to me or mine. We'll do what we need to do to protect our way of living," the sheriff threatened, as he leaned back in his chair.

"Sheriff, as it is written in the Bible, 'For they sow the wind and they shall reap the whirlwind,'" Reverend said, facing the sheriff.

Midnight then stepped up to the sheriff's desk and, placing both his hands on the desk, leaned toward him. With his face inches away from the sheriff's face, displaying a reciprocal contempt, he delivered his own message.

"And Sheriff, just so you and your kind know, I don't use this gun to shoot squirrels and rabbits. I know how to use it. I killed my share of your kind in the war and I'll do what I need to do to protect us. Won't lose a minute of sleep over killing someone like you," Midnight said with emphasis, eye to eye with the sheriff who gritted his teeth and swallowed hard. After a few seconds Midnight straightened back up and again placed his hand on the butt of the gun. "Just try me," Midnight said. Midnight and Reverend stood as the sheriff looked away nervously and did nothing.

"Didn't think you would. Probably need to turn my back for you to find your courage," Midnight then said. The sheriff finally looked back at Midnight, his neck reddened, but he stayed seated. Reverend and Midnight then backed out of the sheriff's office.

"Now what?" Reverend said, as they stood on the porch in front of the sheriff's office.

"That sheriff ain't going to take kindly to us talking to him like we did. He's gonna do something first chance he gets when the odds are more to his liking," Midnight said.

"We can't harm him," Reverend said, deflecting the implied threat in Midnight's comment to go back in and do something to the sheriff.

"What about the fellow that sent the telegram, Blanchfield. Maybe we can go see him?" Midnight asked.

"Need to get someone to tell us where he lives," Reverend said, but as he spoke he had an unusual feeling. He became lightheaded, his chest felt heavy and his breathing was momentarily labored. He bent over and put his hands on his knees. It felt like mild suffocation from the oppression and hostility he had just witnessed.

"You alright, Reverend?" Midnight asked.

"Yeah, just give me a moment to collect myself," Reverend replied.

Reverend stood up straight and they walked together towards Murphy's dry goods store to see if Reverend could get directions to Mr. Blanchfield's place. Reverend went into the store while Midnight waited outside and kept his eyes focused on the jail to see if the sheriff would follow, but he didn't.

Reverend emerged a minute later with directions.

CHAPTER 53.

Things remained tense in Union City. The miners who the sheriff had sworn in as his posse by and large followed his orders and sat outside select properties, like the Miners' Kitchen, armed and ready to protect it. Other posse members were posted at the miners' encampment frustrating any attempt by the mine owners remaining gunmen to intimidate them.

There were a few hiccups in the plan. Many miners resented being told not to go to town and to stay in the encampment. Several came in to go to the Miners' Kitchen, but Mack encouraged them to immediately return to their encampment. A few sneaked into town to empty saloons to drink where, outnumbered, they were beaten badly by the mine owners' gun hands.

Nuncie Spizale emerged as a leader in that regard, constantly patrolling the encampment and encouraging miners to be patient. The unofficial quarantine had the effect of galvanizing local business owners, not involved in mine ownership, to support a quick resolution of the strike. Without miners in town purchasing dry goods, getting haircuts, buying liquor, or visiting brothels, the local businesses began to suffer financially.

In one of the more humorous results of the quarantine the owner of one of the local brothels rented a large carriage and driver to take her and a half dozen women out to the miners' encampment hoping to ply their trade there. Unfortunately they did not reckon with the miners' wives who were at the encampment and were soon run off by the wives who chased them away wielding brooms and skillets.

Local business owners met with Mack, the miners' representative, and began trying to negotiate, as a go-between, with the mine owners. The miners' initial demands included a regular set of work hours, no deductions from pay for broken tools, shoring up the interior of some of the more dangerous mines, and a $5 per month increase in pay. Mr. Hawkins was resistant to all of the demands, but the less affluent mine owners indicated that they were willing to listen and negotiate which caused fissures to develop within the mine owners' organization.

"We need to get more gunmen to replace those that left and take on this damn posse. That's the only way to show these miners and the sheriff. If there is enough violence the miners will fold, we'll break the strike, and they'll return to work. Trust me," Hawkins told Mr. Walsh and Mr. Gloop.

"Any idea where to get more men or what it will cost?" Mr. Walsh asked.

"I'm looking into it," Hawkins replied.

"Look, I disagree with you both. I ain't paying for any more men. It hasn't worked. You'd need an army of them to counter the armed miners. The town will get shot up and innocent people hurt. You won't like this but I think we should start talking to the miners. The other business owners are blaming us for this mess," Mr. Gloop replied.

"So they are getting to you?" Hawkins asked.

"We all need to make money and this is hurting that," Mr. Gloop replied.

Eventually business owners confronted with a strike by workers, which became more common toward the end of the century, would hire the Pinkerton National Detective Agency to forcefully break up the strike. Allan Pinkerton had been the head of the Union Intelligence Service during the initial phase of the Civil War. He had also held the position of Chief of the Secret Service before opening his detective agency. Pinkerton's men were used as muscle by businesses in the Homestead strike (1892), the Pullman strike (1894), and during the Colorado labor wars (1903).

CHAPTER 54

"**S**end word to Talbot that there's a fellow claiming to be a preacher looking for that Shadrach boy and if there is any trouble at the mine from him to let me know," Sheriff Maddox said, later that day, to his part time deputy, Rusty. "I'm going to ask around to see if anyone knows where they went, but I'm guessing they will head to the mine," Sheriff Maddox concluded.

Rusty nodded and headed off to the mine to relay the message. Upon arriving there he dismounted and went to the large house on a slight hill, where Mr. Talbot lived, which overlooked the mine.

"What does the sheriff expect them to do?" Mr. Talbot asked Rusty, after he explained what Sheriff Maddox had told him.

"He doesn't know. Just wanted to let you know that they were asking about that Shadrach fellow. And he said to tell you that if the preacher or the fellow with him shows up at the mine, do what you please with them. He don't need to know about it unless there's trouble," Rusty said.

"Why don't the sheriff arrest them?" Mr. Talbot asked.

"He's not sure where they went after they left his office. He's gonna ask around. Might know something when I get back to town later tonight. Got to go over to Trussville first before it gets too dark," Rusty said.

"Why didn't he just arrest them when they came to the jail?" Mr. Talbot asked.

"Said one of the fellows was a gunslinger and dangerous. The nigger fellow that's with the preacher," Rusty said.

Several miles away, in the late afternoon, Reverend and Midnight were seated on the porch at the Walker plantation speaking with Mr. Blanchfield. Cecilia stood by listening.

"I don't want to discourage you, but you two are asking for trouble. There is no way Talbot will let your friend go. As I'm learning these are not people you can reason with," Blanchfield said.

"Mr. Blanchfield, he's our friend. We were all Union soldiers together and we have to do something. Our cause is good, our hearts are pure, and my belief is that the Lord will protect us. Even Napoleon admitted that 'the sword is always defeated by the spirit,'" Reverend said.

"No offense, Reverend, but moral suasion will not work. As Henry Beecher noted it would be like reading 'the Bible to Buffaloes,'" Mr. Blanchfield said. "I hate to imagine the conditions there. I've learned it's an open secret in town the way the sheriff and Talbot operate. The Union Army destroyed those mines and furnaces toward the end of the war, but a mining company has recently opened one back up. I'm guessing it's the one Talbot operates and is where your friend is. But it pains me that this is happening, especially to a former Union soldier," Mr. Blanchfield concluded, clearly wishing to help but feeling conflicted. The men spoke for awhile longer and Reverend explained the conversation that they had with the sheriff.

"If you got directions at the dry goods store on how to get here it won't be long before the sheriff talks to Walt, the owner, and knows you were headed this way. It's getting late but I'll expect him with his deputy or some of the Klan boys that he can round up," Mr. Blanchfield said. Mr. Blanchfield reluctantly told them they could camp on the grounds of the plantation away from the house, but they needed to be gone in the morning in case the sheriff came looking for them.

"I have to live here and, as it is, the sheriff and others don't want me here. They tried to burn down my new bunkhouse and almost succeeded. It's just a matter of time before they try something else. If they found out I helped you I don't know what they would do," Mr. Blanchfield said. Reverend and Midnight thanked him for his hospitality and for taking the risk of sending them a telegram to tell them about Shadrach's situation.

"I'm not sorry about sending the telegram. Something needs to be done. I've been trying to think of what to do, but I'm just one man," Mr. Blanchfield said. "I'll arm my men here in case the sheriff shows up tonight or tomorrow looking for you two. Didn't want to, but I'll have to do so now."

"It looks like you have started rebuilding the bunkhouse," Reverend said, looking at the men who were working to put up rafters on the new roof.

"Yes. I was able to get the lumber, but we are just getting started on the rebuild. We've been delayed by the weather, other work, and waiting for the inside to dry out completely," Mr. Blanchfield said. "My workers have had to sleep outside." Midnight stood and unbuckled his gunbelt, setting it on the porch.

"We'd like to help, if that's alright," Midnight said to Mr. Blanchfield.

"It's the least we can do," Reverend added.

Mr. Blanchfield thanked them for the offer and in short order Midnight, Reverend, and Mr. Blanchfield were passing roof rafters and wooden shingles and other boards to the men on the roof in the gloaming of the evening.

Once the sun went down most of the roof was finished. When the work stopped Reverend and Midnight spread their bedrolls out in a hidden area behind some trees and, with Mr. Blanchfield's permission, started a small campfire. That evening Cecilia brought them some food from the kitchen.

"Mr. Blanchfield said to bring ya dis here food," she said.

Midnight asked her to stay and the three of them sat around the small campfire talking. Cecilia wanted to know any and everything about her brother's time in the Army that they could tell her. Despite the circumstances of the moment she laughed at several of the funnier stories they told her about him.

"We hadn't seen much of each other since he was sold when we was youngstas, though I heard when he run away. Doze type of t'ings always traveled thru da grapevine," she said. "Well, I best be gittin' back to da house," she said after awhile. She embraced Midnight and hesitantly Reverend and, as they stood and watched, she walked off into the darkness toward the big house.

"Families ripped apart in the name of so called property rights. It was immoral," Reverend said as they sat back down. "Midnight, you've never spoke in much detail about your own family. Do you know where they are?"

"Sure don't," Midnight replied.

Midnight then told Reverend the little bit he knew, a child's recollection of his mother and sisters being sold, of working long days and growing into a man alone in the cotton fields, and of other adults he met that were sold.

"I believe I might have an older brother but I can't be sure. Seems he was sold before I had much of a recollection of things. Momma never talked much about those that were taken from us. Too painful for her I reckon," Midnight said.

"Do you know where your family is originally from?" Reverend asked.

"Well, I recall Momma mentioning a place in Africa called, Angola, where my father's family was from. Momma's folks were born in Nigeria. She said her great grandfather was a tribal leader there, but I was born in Louisiana at the Belle Grove plantation. I don't really know nothing about Africa or my family history," Midnight replied.

The best estimates are that the largest number of slaves brought to the United States, about 26%, came from Angola. Approximately 17% of the slaves came from Nigeria.

"So you knew your father?" Reverend asked.

"Not really. He was sold when I was a toddler. Only know what my Momma told me about him. They weren't married. Don't know if she chose him or if the master chose him for her. She never said."

Although some informal slave marriages occurred and were 'officiated' by plantation owners or, on occasion, by a minister, slave marriages were not legally recognized in slave states. Some pro-slavery advocates like Henry Hughes and George Fitzhugh argued in favor of recognizing such marriages to no avail. Indeed since slaves were considered as chattel there was legislation and jurisprudence in southern states prohibiting marriage between slaves. This prohibition allowed for the easy break up of families at the sole discretion of the slave owner.

"Family is so important. It is part of who we are. Think of the generational stories passed on by parents, by grandparents, that make up a family's narrative and provide comfort to each generation. What happens when one is deprived of that history, deprived of the knowledge of your beginnings, of part of your identity? The roots of the African family tree were tore up with slavery, orphaning generations," Reverend said, wondering out loud.

"Reverend, it seems odd to me but being back here in the South, and having learned to read, I been thinking about something. I'd like to know what my real family name might be and how I might find out. It's a simple thing but maybe a first step to learning more about my history and overcoming the fact that slave owners shaped our identities down to even choosing our names," Midnight said, as they sat around the small campfire.

"I don't understand," Reverend said.

"Well, my slave master's last name was Lemoine so I was named Emmet Lemoine. That's how most of us was named and having your master's last name was a kind of protection from harm by other whites, 'cause they would know who owned you. But neither Emmet or Lemoine are African names. I wonder about my family and what my family names were in Africa, in those places Momma called Nigeria and Angola. Not sure why it seems so important now, but it sure would be good to know. Might be part of knowing more about my own identity, as you said, or reclaiming it," Midnight explained.

Reverend stretched out on his bedroll. The sound of wood cracking as flames bit into it provided the background music in an otherwise clear and cold night. He thought about what Midnight had said and realized fully, perhaps for the first time, that slavery had deprived slaves of the supporting familial mythology created by and for all cultures and families. As he looked up wide-eyed at the starlit sky he searched for answers to questions that he had never imagined he would have to ask himself.

CHAPTER 55.

The next morning Midnight and Reverend rose in the dark, planning to set off for the mine. Although neither said so there was an uneasiness that sat between them. They had no idea exactly what they were riding into and the righteousness of their cause seemed to be their only weapon.

Cecilia had risen early to give them some biscuits to take but they chose to eat these around the smoldering campfire and spend a little more time with her before leaving. After telling her goodbye, and putting out the remnants of the campfire, they saddled up and left at first light.

"How we going to do this? You got a plan?" Midnight asked Reverend, as they began to ride off with their horses starting to break into a trot. Reverend didn't have a plan, though he had tried the entire trip to think of one. What was being done seemed so wrong and criminal to him that he felt it would be obvious even to the mine owner.

"I'm going to talk directly to the mine owner," Reverend replied.

"Reverend, I trust you and all but there ain't no way you're going to convince that man to let Shadrach go free. I think Mr. Blanchfield is right. People that would do this type of thing can't be reasoned with," Midnight replied.

"Midnight, we must try to persuade him of his error. It's up to you and me. I simply must convince him to let Shadrach go," Reverend said.

"So what are you going to tell the mine owner?" Midnight finally asked.

"I'm going to assume he is a Christian man. I'm going to start by appealing to him as a Christian," Reverend replied, in as certain a tone as he could muster. Midnight was clearly doubtful about such an approach.

"That ain't going to work. All those plantation owners that bought, beat, and sold slaves like Shadrach and me claimed to be Christians and it didn't stop them. You know they even used the Bible to justify it like Father Sprecht said," Midnight said. Reverend wasn't naive, he understood the dilemma.

"You got a better plan?" Reverend asked, knowing full well that he might be dealing with the devil. Midnight didn't.

"No, but maybe you should go meet him alone. Let me hang back in case you get in trouble. You saw how that sheriff reacted to me being with you and having a gun. The fellow running the mine would prob-ably be the same," Midnight said. Reverend thought about what he said.

"OK. We'll set up a camp site a ways off from the mine, and that way I'll know where to find you after I meet with the mine owner," Reverend said.

After riding for about an hour the men stopped by a clearing in the forest and decided this would be a good place to set up camp.

Not long after Midnight and Reverend left the Walker plantation Sheriff Maddox, his deputy, Rusty, and two other men from town that sometimes worked as deputies, rode up. Mr. Blanchfield had seen them approaching at a distance and quickly alerted his workers before standing on the porch, waiting, with a shotgun in his hand.

"Blanchfield, looking for a fellow that says he's a preacher and a gunslinger that's with him. Walt at the dry goods store told me this morning that the preacher asked for directions to your place," Sheriff Maddox said, once he halted his horse in front of Mr. Blanchfield. Rusty sat on his own horse next to the sheriff with the other two men behind them.

"They're not here," Mr. Blanchfield replied.

"You certain about that?" Sheriff Maddox said.

"I told you they are not here," Mr. Blanchfield said.

"Not sure I believe you. So I think I'll just have a look around," Sheriff Maddox said, starting to dismount.

"You've got a lot of nerve coming here," Mr. Blanchfield said, raising his shotgun and pointing it directly at the sheriff. He was tired of the ongoing harassment and finally decided to push back. "You sure you didn't come by to check on the bunkhouse you tried to burn down?"

"Don't get smart with me, Yankee. There's four of us and no one will care if you happen to turn up dead. I'm the law around here," Sheriff Maddox said, settling back in his saddle for the moment and putting his hand on his pistol.

"Is that a fact?" Mr. Blanchfield interrupted, lowering the shotgun slightly and pointing toward the bunkhouse with his free hand. The sheriff, Rusty, and the other men turned in their saddles and saw one of the workers standing on the side of the bunkhouse with a rifle aimed at the sheriff. Another worker stepped out from the other side of the bunkhouse with a rifle pointed at Rusty.

"And they're not alone," Mr. Blanchfield said. Mr. Blanchfield then directed the sheriff to each side of the porch where another man and two women, kitchen staff, also appeared out in the open with rifles pointed at the sheriff and at Rusty. "Still want to try your luck?" Mr. Blanchfield asked, raising his shotgun and pointing it again at the sheriff who backed his horse up slightly. He glanced back at the workers with the rifles and then back at Mr. Blanchfield.

"I'm leavin', Sheriff. See you back in town," Rusty said, anxiously spurring his horse and galloping off. The other two men quickly followed him.

"Seems like your deputies are smarter than you," Mr. Blanchfield said, smiling widely.

"This ain't over between us. Don't think I'll forget this," Sheriff Maddox said.

"I don't expect you will and neither will I. Now get off my property. If you come back again I won't be talking, I'll be shooting. And the same goes for your Klan buddies," Mr. Blanchfield said, as the workers moved several steps toward the sheriff with their rifles still pointing at him.

The sheriff then haltered his horse and left at a leisurely pace, as if to prove that he was not intimidated.

Mr. Blanchfield called his workers together.

"Rory, I mean Seydou, you and the other men keep those rifles handy. I expect he'll be back at some point and he probably won't be alone. I'm afraid you will all be targets now because of this," Mr. Blanchfield told them.

"Don't worry. We be ready if he comes back," one of the men said.

"If I gots to die by a white man, it best be when I can finally defend myself," Seydou said.

CHAPTER 56.

"Midnight, you stay here and hopefully I'll be back soon. The mine can't be too far from here," Reverend said, as he got back up on his horse to leave their temporary campsite in the woods.

"Be careful," Midnight said. Reverend nodded his head in response and set off.

Midnight walked the perimeter of the campsite but he had no intention of sitting and waiting. In short order he mounted his horse and began to follow Reverend at a distance and out of sight. He was worried and wanted to be able to watch Reverend as he approached the mine.

Midnight continued to stay off the road leading to the mine and to ride through the woods parallel to it. At some point, however, the forest opened up to a flat empty plain. The few trees surrounding the mine had been cleared or were dead, seemingly killed by the toxins released in the mining process or by the nearby furnace that was once again operational. Midnight stopped at the edge of the forest, concealed, and dismounted. The mine was about 60-70 yards away. The road Midnight had paralleled went directly to the mine and he could see Reverend getting off his horse in between the mine opening and the house which sat on a hill opposite the mine.

Midnight watched as a man with a rifle approached Reverend, they exchanged words, and then the man walked with Reverend toward the house. He saw another man step out onto the porch of the house.

"Mr. Talbot, my name is Reverend Harrison. I understand that you have a friend of mine here, Shadrach, and I'd like to get his release," Reverend said, as firmly as he could to Talbot, who stood above him on the porch at his house with his hand in his coat pocket. The guard who had escorted Reverend remained standing nearby.

"I heard from the sheriff that you might be coming, Reverend, but I bought and paid for your friend by paying his fine. He didn't have the money so he has to work it off for me," Talbot replied.

"Mr. Talbot, if I may as a man of the cloth ask, aren't you worried about your salvation in the hereafter, doing what you are doing to these innocent men?" Reverend said. Talbot laughed.

"No. Why should I be?" Talbot asked, making it clear by his tone that he was amused by the question.

"You know that you are enslaving men against their will. These men have committed no real crimes. As I understand it, there have been no real trials. It is simply immoral and unless you change things it will forever darken your soul before God almighty. As it is written in Psalms: 'His mischief shall return upon his head and his violent dealings shall come down on his pate.' You certainly want to avoid that," Reverend said, in his best sermon voice.

"I'll worry about my own soul, but Reverend, enslaving men is part of the natural order. It's sanctioned in the Bible, in Leviticus, in Exodus, and in the Epistles, where men like your friend were sold into slavery for various reasons, including not paying their debts. You should know that if you are a minister," Talbot replied. Reverend felt a surge of anger but maintained his composure.

"That is not the spirit of the Bible. That is not the Christian spirit of love and forgiveness. You should take to heart the words of Philippians wherein it is written that 'in your relationships with one another, have the same mindset as Christ Jesus,'" Reverend replied.

"Why, Reverend, those are the words in the Bible, the actual words, that sanction slavery," Talbot said, seeming to enjoy his theological debate with Reverend.

"Will you pray with me, ask for forgiveness, or allow me to pray for your soul in light of what you are doing here? The Bible is clear, 'Everyone who calls on the name of the Lord will be saved,'" Reverend said, trying another gambit.

"No. I don't need your prayers or for you to call on the Lord. I'm fine with my God," Talbot said becoming impatient.

"One cannot have knowledge of God, or be a godly man, except through love and this, what you have done here in this mine and to these men," Reverend said, gesturing toward the mine, "is not love." Talbot shook his head.

"A preacher. All you preachers are useless in the real world. Just talk, talk, talk," Talbot replied.

"What will happen if what you and the sheriff are doing becomes public? If you are not worried about your soul, aren't you worried about your reputation as a businessman or about the possibility of being charged with crimes for this? It is clearly illegal," Reverend said, trying one more approach.

"Now that sounds like a threat. But let me answer your question.

No one will care what happens here. Not now and not in my lifetime. It's all perfectly legal," Talbot replied.

"I see you are not to be convinced, so instead I offer to reimburse you the fine you have paid for Shadrach so that he can be released. How much was it?" Reverend asked, naively reaching into his coat pocket and pulling out his wallet. Talbot laughed again.

"You insult me, pretending to know the will of God, to pray for my soul, threatening me, and then offering to repay me. I'm a business man and now what I see is that I can get one more worker in the mine at no cost," Talbot said. He then spoke to the guard. "Put the good Reverend in the mine to work, shackle him to his so called friend and relieve him of his money."

Midnight had stood watching from the edge of the woods. He saw the guard grab Reverend's arm and Reverend pull away. Then he saw the guard strike Reverend with the rifle butt to his stomach as Reverend tried to shield himself from the blow. Reverend bent over and then fell to his knees. The guard shoved Reverend to the ground and took the wallet from Reverend's hand and tossed it up to Talbot. He reached into each of Reverend's pockets and in one coat pocket found the photo of the Confederate soldier's wife and child that Reverend always carried. He looked at it and then handed it to Talbot.

"Looks like he's got a wife and kid," the guard said, thinking this was a photo of Reverend's family.

"So what?" Talbot replied, tearing the picture into pieces and tossing it onto the ground. "Once you get him shackled send word to the sheriff that the preacher is here but not that other fellow, the gunslinger," Talbot said. The guard nodded in understanding and then grabbed Reverend by the arm and lifted him back up. Reverend stumbled toward the mine entrance with the guard following and pushing his rifle in Reverend's back whenever he slowed down.

Midnight thought about riding in to try to save Reverend, but resisted the urge, knowing he would just be shot down if he did. He stayed in the woods for another hour watching to see if Reverend came out of the mine. He didn't. Midnight got on his horse, still unsure what to do. He rode back to the temporary campsite and stayed there a while longer in case, miraculously, Reverend showed up but he did not.

Then Midnight decided to ride back toward the Walker plantation to see Mr. Blanchfield and Cecilia. It was his only option as he didn't know anyone else. He needed to talk with someone about what to do and he needed someone to help him. Mr. Blanchfield was a former Union officer and had some men working for him, maybe he could help or come up with a plan. Maybe Mr. Blanchfield knew someone else who could help him. And Midnight had his own ideas on what to do. He just hoped that he could convince Mr. Blanchfield to help him.

CHAPTER 57.

The guard following Reverend into the mine pushed Reverend to the ground at the feet of Shadrach and Gabriel.

"Brought you someone," the guard said, as Roscoe walked over. "This is that preacher we heard about. Talbot said chain him to this one and put him to work," the guard said to Roscoe as he pointed at Shadrach.

"My pleasure. We ain't had a white man work in the mine before. A preacher's gonna be soft like those Union soldiers at Andersonville, likely won't last long before he's buried with the rest out there," Roscoe said, taunting Reverend.

Shadrach and Gabriel lifted Reverend up off the ground. One of the guards came over with a chisel and hammer and put leg irons on Reverend and then removed the chains binding Gabriel to Shadrach. He attached these to Reverend so that he was bound to Shadrach as the other prisoners looked on curiously.

"Now get to work!" Roscoe yelled.

Reverend was dazed. It might have been from being hit with the rifle butt or it might have been a result of where he now found himself. Shadrach handed Reverend a pick axe.

"We talk tonight," Shadrach said quietly. "Ya gotta work to avoid da whip." Reverend coughed from the dust and then began slowly to swing the pick axe at the rock where Shadrach directed him.

Later that night, at the end of another 18 hour day, work was halted. Reverend's hands were blistered and he had developed a recurrent cough. He sat with Shadrach and the other men, tried to drink some discolored water, and leaned against a rock wall exhausted. His ribs were bruised from where the guard had hit him with the rifle butt, making any movement painful. He quietly told Shadrach that Midnight had come down with him after they received a telegram from Mr. Blanchfield, but he had left Midnight at a campsite in the woods.

"Mr. Blanchfield wrote ya?" Shadrach asked.

"Sent a telegram at your sister's request. I'm guessing Midnight will go back to see him," Reverend replied.

"Best dat Midnight not come here. Dey just put him in da mine too," Shadrach replied. "What 'bout Dalton?"

"No. He's tied up in Missouri as a deputy," Reverend said, wheezing as he spoke.

"What's Midnight gonna do now?" Shadrach asked.

"I have no idea, but he can't do much by himself. We need to figure out what we can do on our own," Reverend replied.

"Dat gonna be hard. No easy way outta here. Been thinkin' on it. We ain't got us no weapons, other den da shovels and pick axes, and da guards are always here, even be here at night outside. If we could get one of da rifles we might have a chance," Shadrach said.

"We'll have to think of something," Reverend said.

The men in the mine, tired as they were, began to crowd around

Shadrach and Reverend, wanting to hear Reverend's story. What was a white man, a preacher no less, doing here? Shadrach told the men the story of their time together in the Union Army. They asked various questions which Shadrach answered as Reverend continued to lean against a rock wall next to him.

"He really be a preacher man? Serious like?" Skinny asked.

"Yes," Reverend replied, regaining his voice through the coughing spells from the inhaled dust.

This seemed hard for some of the men to believe. Others clearly admired that Reverend had come to try to help his friend. But Skinny had a different perspective and, after thinking about it and listening to the men questioning Shadrach, he had an unusual request.

"Reverend, I know dat it ain't no church in dis here mine, but could ya maybe say mass sometimes or tell us some stories from da good book? I ain't neva learn to read and can't say I is a religious man, but I be wantin' to know more and it might be a liftin' up t'ing if ya could since dis is likely where we is all gonna die," Skinny said. Several men murmured their approval. Reverend almost cried at the request.

"Yes. We'll make do in the evenings after work," Reverend said. The men shook their heads and a few said 'amen,' momentarily excited by the possibility of this break in the harsh monotony of their days.

Shadrach then did his best to introduce Reverend to all of the men gathered around, calling each by name. Levi sat off alone, by himself, so Shadrach pointed at him for Reverend. Although he did not participate Levi seemed to listen to everything they said.

"I'll do my best to remember each of your names," Reverend replied.

"I hep ya if ya forget," Skinny volunteered.

For the next few weeks after each day of back-breaking work, Reverend stood in front of the men who would sit before him in a semi-circle and told them stories of the Bible, of the creation in Genesis, of the great flood, or of David and Goliath. He recited the Ten Commandments, told them many sayings of Jesus and the story of Barabbas. The men would periodically say 'amen' or 'hallelujah.' They asked if they could sing a hymn or spiritual and Reverend readily agreed. Even Levi gradually moved from the outside of the semi-circle into the center of the group, next to the other men, to hear the stories, shaking his head in acknowledgment of a story on occasion, though he remained quiet throughout.

And then, in lieu of a homily, Reverend decided to ask a different man each night to tell the others about himself. In their telling Reverend said they could talk about anything. Some men were nervous and struggled to articulate their thoughts, others found their natural born comedic selves and told funny stories making the others laugh. Some men told sad stories of their families separated, of brothers or sisters sold, or stories passed down about relatives in Africa. Through this process Reverend hoped that each man, physically imprisoned though they were, could rediscover and be reminded of their humanity which was being stolen from them by their imprisonment in the mine.

On this particular night, several weeks after he was placed in the mine, Reverend asked Toussaint, who was sporting a black eye and a swollen lip from another recent beating by Roscoe, to speak. Toussaint stood up slowly, his body wracked by pain from the ongoing physical abuse.

"My name is Toussaint," he said before pausing to catch his breath. "A strange name to many of you, but a famous name. I am named after Toussaint L'Ouverture."

"Neva heard dat name," Skinny interrupted.

"My parents, had both been slaves in Kentucky but were set free when their master died. They gave me this name to indicate that I was born free. You see Toussaint L'Ouverture was also born a slave."

"Den how his name mean free?" Skinny asked.

"He was a slave who led the only successful slave rebellion in the world. He organized other slaves in Saint Domingue, now called the Republic of Haiti, and defeated the white plantation owners, the Spanish, the British, and eventually the French."

"Dat mustta been lots of fightin'," Skinny said.

"It took nearly ten years and he had died before it was final but because of him all the slaves remained free and Haiti became an independent nation. After the defeat of the French, Napoleon chose to remove French troops from the new world and as a result he sold the area known as Louisiana to the United States. Toussaint L' Ouverture, a former slave, was the man that set it all in motion," Toussaint said as the men listened closely.

"He seem like a free man dat wanted freedom for all," Skinny added.

"It is ironic but he died in prison. His followers continued the fight and succeeded," Toussaint said.

"So he was a slave, den free, den in a prison like us in dis mine," Skinny said summarizing.

"I was down here looking for family members who had been enslaved. I was seized by the sheriff and put in this mine. It is difficult to lose one's freedom once you have had it. It's a taste in your mouth, like the kiss of a favorite lover, that doesn't leave you," Toussaint said.

"Hopefully you will be free again one day," Reverend replied trying to be encouraging.

"I've been thinking about it, about freedom and what it means, what it has meant to me, and I think you are right, I will be free again," Toussaint said, and then he sat down without elaborating. Shadrach looked quickly at Gabriel.

"We needs to talk wit him when we gets da chance. Sound like maybe he know sometin' 'bout escaping," Shadrach said quietly to Gabriel.

The men, tired from the workday but uplifted from the service, all laid down after the singing of a song to try to get some sleep. All except Toussaint who stayed awake, pacing back and forth, until everyone else was asleep.

The next morning as the men stirred to begin the work day they were greeted by a gruesome sight. Hanging from one of the rafters in the middle of the mine was Toussaint's lifeless body.

Reverend and Shadrach immediately approached Toussaint's body as the other men looked on. Shadrach lifted Toussaint's body, while Reverend pushed a cart next to the body to stand on so that he could untie the rope around Toussaint's neck. As Reverend stepped onto the cart Roscoe struck Shadrach with his whip forcing him to let go of Toussaint's body.

"Leave him!" Roscoe demanded.

"He needs a proper burial," Reverend replied.

"He'll be buried when I say so and not before. Now start work!" Roscoe bellowed flinging the whip at Reverend forcing him to retreat from the cart. The men who were gathered around moved slowly, looking disdainfully at Roscoe, and retrieved their tools to begin work.

CHAPTER 58.

Toussaint's death hit the men hard. Some wondered if it was Roscoe that had actually killed him. Roscoe left Toussaint's body hanging from the rafter for 2 days. Finally he instructed Reverend and Shadrach to take the body down and bring it outside to the common grave site to be buried.

Shadrach and Gabriel continued to try to come up with a way to escape and discussed it with several other men. But not everyone was in agreement. Some of the men were simply resigned to their fate and refused to participate.

"If we rush dem we got a chance," Shadrach said to a group of the men.

"Dey gonna kill most of us if we do and I ain't wantin' to die," one of the men said to the agreement of several others, frustrating Shadrach's attempt to organize the men.

Several nights later, as the men sat around talking after his service, Reverend had an idea, but it wasn't a plan of escape.

"Let's try something. I know this will be hard. No matter what they do or say, don't give the guards an excuse to whip you," Reverend said to the men.

"Reverend, dey whip us for no reason, 'specially dat Roscoe. Don't matter what we do, ya seen dat," Skinny replied.

"They whip you because they are scared of you. They are fearful and they've been raised to think you are less than human. Lets prove to them that you are men," Reverend said.

"Why should I has to prove dat? No one else got to prove dey is men," Gabriel asked, properly defensive at Reverend's suggestion, as several men spoke up in agreement.

"Rev'ren, we been told dat we ain't men for a long time. Dat we is inferior. Dat we is lazy. Dat we needs to be more like da whites. Some prob'ly believe dat. Not me. It be hard 'nuff to be a negro dese days to has to also try to be white and it wouldn't make no difference no how in how we is treated," Skinny said, again to the approval of several others.

"I know. You shouldn't have to prove anything. You are all men. I know that. Believe me I know that. But let's see how they react if we don't resist. Remember Jesus said 'resist not evil,' that we turn the other cheek when we are subjected to evil. And imprisonment in this mine is an immense evil. Let's see how they react if we treat them as men. I've got to believe we can reach their humanity and that they can be made to see your humanity," Reverend replied. The men around him seemed to disagree with this idea.

"How is we gonna do dat? We ain't suppose to even look dem in da eye. And Rev'ren, no offense an all, but I 'member da story. Jesus was killed for turnin' da utta cheek," Gabriel said. Again the men grumbled their disapproval of Reverend's plan.

"Look, let's start simple with just saying 'good morning' to them," Reverend said. The men remained unconvinced.

"Ya agreein' wit' dis?" Skinny asked Shadrach, loud enough for the others to hear.

"It be really hard for me, especially wit' dat Roscoe, but I say let's give it a try. We got nothin' to lose. Maybe it help some, 'cause we got to figure how to get outta here," Shadrach said.

"Well, I'll try, but I'm doubtful," Gabriel then said.

"Me too. Don't t'ink it gonna work," Skinny added.

And so it began. The men began working at a faster pace than before, as if, strange as it seemed to the guards, they were a team and took pride in their work. They even cheered each other on occasion when someone found a large ore deposit.

Reverend said, "good morning" each day at the beginning of their shift to the guards. When the work day was done, tired though he was, Reverend would wish the guards a "good night."

Slowly, some of the other prisoners, watching the guards' reactions to Reverend, began to follow his lead, greeting the guards in the morning, or laughing together while working. They would speak to the guards even if the guards didn't respond, saying things like "it sure is a hot one today," or "ya lookin' tired, hope ya get some rest tonight." It gradually became a bit of a game for the prisoners and clearly, at the outset, puzzled the guards.

Reverend, while he worked, also began asking the guards about their families, or whether they were in the war, and if so, where. The guards resisted responding, at least when Roscoe was around. But, when he wasn't nearby, a few of them answered some of the Reverend's questions.

"And you, Reverend, do you have family?" one of the guards, named Martin, asked him as the work shift ended.

"Yes, a wife outside of Boston," Reverend replied.

"Are you really a preacher?" the guard named Collins asked.

"Yes. Was starting a ministry in Boston when I got word about my friend Shadrach being here," Reverend replied.

"Were you in the war?" Martin asked Reverend.

"Yes, but mostly I tended to people's wounds," Reverend replied.

"He patched up da soldiers on both da sides, Confederate and Union. I know 'cause I was wit' 'em," Shadrach chimed in.

"Didn't know you was in the Union Army. I was in the Confederate Army, 2nd Infantry Regiment, Alabama infantry. We were called the Magnolia Regiment, disbanded in '62 and then I bounced around in different companies," Collins said to Shadrach as Martin stood by listening.

"I heard 'bout dat Magnolia Regiment," Shadrach replied.

"Still don't know what I think about that war. Lost both of my brothers in it. One of them died imprisoned at Elmira. Don't know how he died. Was angry 'bout it for a while, but I don't hold it against no one anymore. Not sure why," Collins answered.

Elmira Prison was originally a barracks for Union troops but was converted, in part, into a prison for Confederate troops in 1864. Early in the war the Union and the Confederacy routinely exchanged prisoners but by May 1863 that practice was ended by President Lincoln because the South refused to return captured black soldiers. The prisoner exchange resumed in early 1865 once the South agreed to exchange black and white prisoners. At its peak Elmira held in excess of 12,000 prisoners, though its capacity was for much less. Approximately 2,970 of its prisoners died. The deaths were for various reasons including disease and poor medical care. The dead were buried nearby in what is now Woodlawn National Cemetery.

"We was both just soldiers, doin' what we was told. Can't hold dat against each utta," Shadrach replied.

"My family was just getting by when the war started. Had a small farm in North Alabama. We never owned no slaves, never thought much of those that did. That was the case for most of the guys in my regiment," Collins said.

"We didn't have slaves either," Martin added before leaving to go to the front of the mine.

It is estimated that of the approximately 5.5 million whites who lived in the Confederate states at the start of the war, only a small percentage were slave owners. Among slave owners about 8,000 were significant slaveholders owning nearly 3 million of the 3.5 million slaves in the South. Most whites in the Confederacy were poor, with little education, who either lived in the mountains or in the lowlands. By one estimate only about 25% of the poorer whites were literate.

"Toward the end of the war we heard that Congress, the Confederate Congress, had approved using slaves as soldiers, the same slaves we were always told we were better than. It was just confusing," Collins added, before scratching at his forehead.

As the military tide turned against the South and it dealt with desertions and manpower shortages, the Confederate Congress, in March, 1865, approved a law allowing for slave soldiers. Only two companies were formed prior to Lee's surrender in April, 1865. The prospect of using slave soldiers to defend the Confederacy prompted Howell Cobb, a southern Democrat and former member of the Provisional Confederate Congress, to remark that, "If slaves make good soldiers our whole theory of slavery is wrong."

"If I might ask, since you didn't own slaves, why did you fight?" Reverend asked.

"Reverend, it might be hard to understand but in the South honor is an important thing. It woulda shamed my family if my brothers and I hadn't fought. So, I guess that was a big reason, though I admit I thought about quitting more than once, especially after the 2nd disbanded," Collins replied.

In fact as desertions and avoidance of service plagued the Confederacy in the latter part of the war, Jefferson Davis was quoted as saying that those who didn't fight, "deserted their duty to their families, to their country, and to their God."

"That's a heavy price for you and your family to have paid, losing two brothers," Reverend said, as the men set down their tools for the night.

"Never got either of my brothers' bodies back. My Maw, she never recovered from it. Lost her last year," Collins said.

"I'm sorry to hear 'bout dat. My Momma died durin' da war. I had come down to find her but just learned dat she died b'fore da sheriff arrested me," Shadrach replied.

"From the little I know it seems like most men that fought for the Confederacy were fighting to preserve a system, the plantation and slavery system, that they weren't a part of," Reverend offered.

"I guess that's true. We talked about that in the regiment sometimes, that we were fightin' for the plantation owners that looked down on us," Collins replied.

"We has dat in common, us two, 'bout da plantation owners lookin' down like ya say," Shadrach said. Collins forced a smile in response.

This new approach by the prisoners went on for a week or two until Roscoe figured it out. One day Skinny had a coughing spell, not uncommon among the men in the mine. Collins, who seemed most affected by Reverend and the prisoners' kindness and conversation, fetched a cup of clean water from the guards' covered water bucket for Skinny to drink to calm the cough.

"Thank ya," Skinny said, as the other prisoners watched, surprised by the gesture.

"No problem," Collins replied.

"What's going on here?" Roscoe bellowed when he walked up, seeing Collins standing there and Skinny drinking from the cup.

"He was coughing, so," Collins began to say.

"Give me the damn cup," Roscoe interrupted, grabbing it out of Skinny's hand and pouring the water on the ground. "Stop talking with the prisoners and get back to work," Roscoe barked at Collins. "I'll teach you a lesson," Roscoe then said to Skinny.

Roscoe unfurled his whip to use on Skinny who had backed up against a wall in anticipation of being whipped.

"It ain't his fault," Collins said. Roscoe shoved Collins out of the way and turned back to face Skinny. However, before Roscoe could use the whip Levi, holding a large boulder, stepped in between Roscoe and Skinny blocking him from being able to use the whip. Levi stood there, without speaking, and stared at Roscoe while Collins and the prisoners watched. Roscoe slowly coiled the whip back up and, muttering to himself, walked away. Levi turned and looked at Skinny, nodded his head slightly, and then walked off to drop the boulder into a mine cart.

The next day Collins didn't show up for work. He never returned.

CHAPTER 59.

Roscoe was becoming increasingly angry. He felt that something wasn't right. The men imprisoned in the mine didn't seem to fear him anymore. When he yelled, they would now respond politely, "Yes, sir," with a smile. The harder he drove them it seemed the less that they complained. And there was something else he couldn't figure out; the men laughed with each other on occasion while working. He was convinced that they were laughing at him.

Roscoe was used to being feared, was used to men being scared of him and, through his brutality, breaking their will. It all went back to what he thought he had learned at Andersonville and something was wrong. He thought he knew the reason for the change in their attitudes and went to talk to Talbot about it.

"I'm telling you Mr. Talbot, it's that preacher. I don't know what he's telling them at night after their shift, but it's him. He has somehow given them hope and I don't know how but I think he's the reason that Collins left," Roscoe said. Several other guards stood uneasily next to Roscoe at the end of their work shift as he spoke to Talbot.

"Collins was just being friendly. The man was choking," the guard named Martin replied, in defense of Collins giving Skinny the cup of water.

"Shut up!" Roscoe responded.

"If they're working hard does it matter? The preacher's probably promised them a wonderful time in the hereafter. That's a good thing, right? Keeps them compliant," Talbot said.

"Yeah, why does it matter? And that preacher said he's got a wife in Boston. Don't seem right keeping a white man like him here," Martin said.

"I told you to shut up," Roscoe said, taking a menacing step toward Martin. "Mr. Talbot," Roscoe said, turning back to face Talbot, "I think the preacher has raised their hopes that they will be rescued or escape and set free in this life. They might be planning something. Why else would they be laughing?" Talbot looked at Martin and thought about Collins leaving.

"Well, I can't have him affecting the guards. What do you want to do?" Talbot then asked.

"I think we need to make an example of the preacher and the other one, Shadrach, the troublemaker. You know cut them down to size and break their spirit. Ain't no one gonna follow them if they are broken. And I can break 'em," Roscoe said. Martin frowned at Roscoe's comment as Talbot watched his reaction.

"Alright, if you think so. Handle it tomorrow," Talbot said.

Inside the mine the men were once more gathered around Reverend after their work day. He had been calling their nightly meetings the Morning Glory Church. Each night he would recite as best he could the Bible verses and stories he had committed to memory.

On this particular night Reverend was asked by one of the men to tell the story of Moses and the Pharaoh, as set forth in the Book of Exodus.

He told them how Moses, obeying God, went to Pharaoh and on behalf of God said: "Let my people go," referring to the children of Israel who were slaves to the Egyptians. Pharaoh replied:

Who is the Lord that I should obey his voice to let Israel go? I know not of this Lord, neither will I let Israel go.

"Dat sound like a big mistake by dat Pharaoh fella. I'm bettin' Moses gonna win," Skinny immediately opined, to the agreement of the others who listened attentively.

"Wish we had us a Moses. Instead we got us a Pharaoh in President Johnson. Glad he be leavin'," Gabriel chimed in.

Reverend then walked the prisoners through each of the plagues that God descended on Egypt because Pharaoh would not comply. The plague of the frogs, which the prisoners found amusing. The plague that killed all the cattle of Egypt. But still the Pharaoh would not let the Israelites go because, Reverend then told them, the Lord had hardened his heart not to do so. This confused and surprised some of the prisoners.

"Why would da Lord have Moses try to get da Pharaoh to let da Israelites go but make it so he wouldn't do it?" one of them asked. Reverend said it was a conundrum, but reminded the men that the ways of God are often a mystery to us.

"Perhaps Pharaoh still had free will to decide. We just don't know," Reverend mused.

"Don't seem right to me," one of the men said.

"Maybe dat's what happen to dat Roscoe. He harden Roscoe's heart too," another man suggested, to the immediate disagreement of the others.

"No, he be makin' his own decisions and he just evil," another replied.

"Yeah, he brag 'bout starvin' doze soldiers at Andersonville. And look what he was doin' to Toussaint. Dat's evil," still another said.

Reverend then told them of the plague of boils which was upon all of Egypt and the hail storm and "fire that ran along the ground." And then he told them of the plague of locusts and the men shivered with the thought. And the final plague of killing all the first born in Egypt. Again men asked, what did these children do to deserve this?

"Why kill innocent chil'ren, 'specially if God already made it so dis Pharaoh wouldn't agree? Da chil'ren hadn't done nothin' to deserve it," someone said.

"Dat sound kinda like when dey sold da chil'ren at da slave auction. I was one of 'em," Skinny suggested, thinking of his own experience.

"Me too," another man said.

In each of these plagues, Reverend told the men that Pharaoh, his servants, and the Egyptians suffered, but not the Israelites. The men asked more questions and Reverend did his best to answer each.

Reverend concluded with the story of the escape by the Israelites when Pharaoh finally consented to their release. At word of the Israelites escaping their captors and crossing the Red Sea a smattering of applause arose from the prisoners.

"It be 'bout time as dere weren't no utta plagues left," Skinny said.

"For those of you that grew up hearing ministers and others claim that you were meant to be slaves because all slaves were supposedly descendants of Ham, Noah's son,—the so called 'curse theory,'" Reverend said.

"I recollect dat," Gabriel interjected as others indicated that they had heard it.

"Well, the Israelites, who believed they were the chosen people, who were led by Moses, were slaves and they were not black like you or considered descendants of Ham," Reverend said.

"Dat's good to know," Skinny replied.

"We is like da Israelites. It was wrong to make dem slaves like it be wrong to do it to us," another man said.

"It be wrong to make anyone a slave," Shadrach replied.

Reverend then requested that someone sing a song to end the service. Gabriel, who had sung at Hush Harbor meetings as a slave, volunteered to sing.

"Since we talked 'bout Moses and da Pharaoh I thought I'd sing dis one," he said. Gabriel stood and lifted his voice in a strong baritone and sang:

> *When Israel was in Egypt's land*
> *Let my people go.*
> *Oppressed so hard dey could not stand*
> *Let my people go.*

Several of the men joined in the chorus singing:

> *Go down Moses*
> *Way down in Egypt's land*
> *Tell old Pharaoh*
> *Let my people go.*

When Gabriel finished the song the men clapped.

Reverend then turned to his practice of asking someone to speak and surprised everyone by asking Levi, who was seated up front and had been listening carefully to the Exodus story, to speak about himself. Levi stood slowly, towering over the men next to him, and looked around nervously. Skinny, who was seated next to him, prodded him with a joke. Levi's eyes darted anxiously back and forth to the men around him. Reverend walked over and put a reassuring hand on Levi's broad shoulders and, looking up at him, asked him again to speak.

"There is nothing to be afraid of, Levi, just tell us about yourself," Reverend said.

Levi looked down at him and Reverend saw that he was frightened. He shook his head frantically to indicate he would not speak. Reverend tried to reassure him. Tears formed in Levi's eyes and then rolled down his cheeks and down his neck. His body suddenly heaved and his head leaned forward as he began to cry. He opened his mouth, gasping a bit for air, but without making much of a sound. At that moment Reverend noticed something. He was startled by it. Reverend embraced him. The men around them didn't know what to make of the big man weeping.

"Levi, look at me. Do I understand correctly that you cannot speak?" Reverend asked, stepping back and gently placing his hand on Levi's chest as Levi lifted his head up. Levi shook his head to indicate that he could not and opened his mouth to reveal that his tongue had been partially cut out. He then made a cutting motion with his hand across his throat to indicate a cutting before looking around at the other men, embarrassed, to see their reaction. Men mumbled and stared, surprised by the revelation but understanding immediately what this meant.

Slave masters used two cruel methods to try to silence a slave that they feared might lead an insurrection. There was a device called an iron bit that was placed on a slave's head, similar to the bit used on a horse, that gagged the slave and made it difficult, if not impossible, for the slave to speak. In addition, on less frequent occasions, a recalcitrant slave, usually after an iron bit had failed, could have all or part of his tongue cut out. The slave master would not want to lose the slave as a worker, so a doctor was used to cut the tongue out so that the slave would not die. The men wondered how this had happened to Levi and why they had never realized it before. But it was clear. It meant that Levi's owner feared he would lead a rebellion.

"I woulda followed him," Gabriel said, as Shadrach shook his head in agreement.

"Maybe now we see if he wants to work wit us to get outta here," Shadrach said.

The most well known slave rebellion in the South was led by Nat Turner in 1831 in which over 50 whites were killed. There were, however, others that occurred or were planned, including the Stono Rebellion in 1739 that occurred in the original 13 colonies, the New York City Conspiracy of 1741, Gabriel's Conspiracy of 1800, the German Coast Uprising of 1811, and the Vessey Conspiracy of 1822. The leaders of these rebellions were often deeply religious men who relied on scripture to support their attempts to throw off the yoke of slavery.

"Well, since he can't do it, I'm gonna tell Levi's story," Skinny suddenly announced, standing up next to Levi.

Levi looked at Skinny who guided him with his hand to sit back down. The men who had stood when Levi had started to cry, sat and quieted. Reverend looked at Skinny uncertain as to what Skinny intended to do.

"Gents, Levi, now I'm askin' ya, ain't he da strongest man ya is ever seen?" Skinny began in a ministerial tone offering a call and seeking a response. Several men said "yeah."

"When he was a boy did ya know dat Levi was so strong he cut down trees in da forest wit' just the swipe of his big ol' hand," Skinny said, holding his hand like a knife edge, prompting a small smile from Levi, between his tears, and from Reverend. "Ain't ya heard 'bout dat?" Several more men said "yeah."

"And when Levi was a sailor on one of dem big ships in da sea, when da other mens caught a fish too big to bring in to da ship, one of dem whale like fish, Levi hauled it up all by his se'f. Ain't you heard 'bout dat?" Skinny said.

"Yeah!" and "I did!" men yelled out, as they understood what Skinny was doing. Reverend sat down to listen. Skinny had everyone's attention.

"Once when da massa's mule couldn't pull da wagon all loaded wit' all da massa's fat womens out of da mud ol' Levi did it easy like. Now I know ya heard 'bout dat," Skinny said. The men almost in unison said "yeah!" as Levi continued to smile widely at the telling of the stories. Tears reformed in Levi's eyes but these were tears of joy, tears of acceptance.

"When dat overseer at da ol' plantation tried to whup Levi, he took da whip in his hands and pulled till he tore it in pieces. I know ya heard 'bout dat!" Skinny said loudly. The men cheered in response.

Skinny then spun a humorous tale of how Levi, without speaking, had routinely outsmarted the guards. In Skinny's telling Levi was really the one in charge of the mine and every day he made those old guards look like fools: "big ol' fools" Skinny said. The men laughed and clapped.

"He could leave if he wanted, but he makin' too much money," Skinny said to the men's collective laughter.

"But now, I has to say it. I has to be truthful. Levi ain't da most hansomemest man in here? Cause dat...be me," Skinny said, pointing a finger to his chest to a chorus of boos and more laughter.

Roscoe and the other men guarding the mine opening were perplexed by the laughter they heard coming from the men inside the mine.

"I'll teach them all a lesson tomorrow. They won't be laughing when I'm done with them," Roscoe muttered, walking away from the other guards toward Talbot's house.

CHAPTER 60.

The next day two of the guards, at Roscoe's direction, hauled Shadrach and Reverend out of the mine. They unchained the men from each other, though shackles remained on their legs. Shadrach's hands were tied to the crossbar above his head on the whipping post, which was outside the entrance to the mine. Roscoe ripped off the remains of Shadrach's tattered shirt to expose all of his back, revealing some healed scarring. Roscoe then uncorked his whip. Reverend was tied to another post nearby with his hands behind his back, but in a position where he was facing Shadrach.

"Wait!" Talbot, who was standing nearby, yelled. He walked over to Roscoe and the guards who had tied Shadrach to the cross bar. "Get the others out here. I want them to see this and get the message that this is what is in store for them if they listen to the preacher or try to escape." The guards then went into the mine and the men in the mine slowly ambled out, covered by red dust, some temporarily blinded by the sunlight, and bound together by the chains on their leg irons.

"If any of you think you are getting out of here or that this preacher is going to save you, think again. I don't care what happens to you in the next life, but in this life you belong to me and you better get straight with that," Talbot said, walking back and forth in front of the men as he spoke. The guards encircled them and held their rifles trained on the men.

"This is not human. Think of your souls before you do this. He is a man!" Reverend said, so all could hear him. The prisoners voiced their approval of Reverend's comments making the guards nervous.

"Shut him up," Talbot said.

One of the guards grabbed a soiled rag covered in dust off the ground. Talbot took it from him and walked over and shoved the rag into Reverend's mouth to quiet him.

"Don't worry, Reverend, there'll be plenty of whip left for you when I'm finished with this one," Roscoe said. He then reared back and flung the whip striking Shadrach in the back. Shadrach's body recoiled but he didn't scream as all those present watched. Roscoe reared back again and the tip of the whip hit breaking the skin on Shadrach's back. Roscoe stopped and, laughing, dipped the tip of the whip into some sand. Several prisoners looked away from Shadrach so as to not see the next lashing.

"Mr. Talbot, there are two riders coming...from the east," one of the guards called out, pointing in the direction of the riders. Talbot and the others shielded their eyes and looked into the mid-morning sun and saw the outline of a rider wearing a tan duster, with his cowboy hat tilted back, approaching. The other rider was without a hat and his hands were tied up, his horse being led forward by the first rider.

"Hold on Roscoe," Talbot said. "Keep your rifles on the men in case this is some kind of trick and Martin, you put a rifle on that lead rider," Talbot told the guards, who obliged.

Martin did as instructed. Roscoe slowly wound up the whip and held it tight, but remained in the same place ready to unfurl it again, as he watched the riders approach. The prisoners also looked in the direction of the two riders.

"It's a white man. Looks like he's got a prisoner with him. A nigger," Roscoe said, looking to the east. Martin lowered his rifle that had been aimed at the lead white rider.

The riders came closer and when they got within a few feet of Talbot the white rider dismounted while the black rider remained tied up on his horse.

"Sorry, looks like I'm interrupting some fun," the rider said, as he looked around. "Sheriff Maddox told me to bring this fellow to you. His name is Emmet, if that matters. Caught him outside of town before he could cause any trouble. Said he was friends with some preacher that you would know about," the white rider said.

"Glad you caught him. Who are you?" Talbot asked, offering his hand for a handshake as the white rider stepped up next to him. Roscoe unfurled the whip getting ready to strike Shadrach with it again.

"I'm a bounty hunter. Was passin' through town when I heard about this fellow," the white rider said, extending his hand to shake Talbot's, and then in a cat quick move he pulled out his dragoon with his other hand and pointed it at Talbot's head. Talbot raised his hands in the air.

"Don't know what this is about but there ain't no reason for this. What goes on here is none of your business," Talbot said, as his guards watched closely.

The rider, Dalton, pressed the barrel of the gun against Talbot's temple. Midnight got off his horse and dropped the ropes that he had held to make it appear as if his hands were tied up.

"Drop your rifles and unbuckle your gunbelts boys unless you want to be minus one boss," Dalton said.

"I can pick him off from here, boss," one of the guards said, lifting his rifle to point at Dalton. Reverend tried to speak but couldn't. Shadrach glanced over at Dalton and smiled weakly.

"Go ahead. Try me. Your boss will be dead before you shoot," Dalton said, as he cocked the gun and pushed it harder against Talbot's temple.

"Don't shoot. Do as he says!" Talbot yelled. The guards, including Roscoe, dropped their rifles and reluctantly unbuckled their gunbelts letting these fall to the ground.

"Pick up their guns," Dalton said, and several of the prisoners from the mine began to do so. Midnight walked over to the whipping post and untied Shadrach. Once he was done he then untied Reverend.

"Tie up the guards," Midnight said.

The prisoners, still chained together, took the ropes used on Shadrach and Reverend and immediately tied up two of the guards. They grabbed other ropes in the mine and roughly pushing the remaining guards onto their stomachs on the ground tied their hands behind their backs and then tied the ropes around their ankles, leaving the guards laying uncomfortably arched on their stomachs. Roscoe was shoved to the ground by the prisoners. He was kneeling, still looking mean, waiting his turn to be tied up when Shadrach spoke up.

"Not him. Not yet. I got me some business wit' him," Shadrach said, pointing at Roscoe and speaking to the other prisoners. The prisoners dropped the ropes they were going to use on Roscoe.

"Are you thinking what I'm thinking?" Dalton said to Shadrach.

"Exactly," Shadrach said, while Roscoe remained on his knees.

Midnight found the hammers and chisels and, after removing the leg irons from Reverend and Shadrach, began to remove the leg irons off some of the prisoners. Shadrach stomped his feet as if to assure his blood was circulating. He threw a few shadow punches to loosen up. Reverend used another hammer and chisel to remove leg irons off other prisoners.

"You'll never get away with this. Sheriff Maddox will hunt you down and have you arrested. You'll end up working in this mine if they don't hang you first," Talbot said. Midnight, who was still helping to remove leg irons, glanced up at Dalton who still had his gun pointed at Talbot.

"You want to tell him?" Midnight said.

"Unless the sheriff can rise from the dead that ain't gonna happen," Dalton said to Talbot's obvious shock.

Dalton pushed Talbot toward the prisoners who were removing leg irons.

"Tie this one up as well," Dalton said.

Midnight picked up some rope and took Talbot by the arm leading him to the post where Reverend had been tied up. He tied him to the post facing toward Roscoe. When the leg irons were off all the prisoners, Dalton asked that they form a circle around Roscoe, who was still kneeling on the ground. Shadrach stepped into the middle of the circle, facing Roscoe. Dalton holstered his gun and stood next to Roscoe.

"Get up," Dalton said to Roscoe, who stood up warily looking around at the freed prisoners surrounding him, several of whom were now holding the guards' rifles. "Gentlemen, we are going to have a bare knuckles boxing match. Since we don't have a proper ring we are going to do like we did in the army. Form the ring by encircling the two men," Dalton said. Roscoe laughed awkwardly as he looked at Shadrach and realized what was about to happen.

"A boxing match? I'll kill that black bastard. Ain't no one ever beat me in a fist fight," Roscoe said.

"I ain't Toussaint. I be fightin' back," Shadrach immediately replied staring hard at Roscoe.

"Your problem big man is you talk too much. Let's see how

much you're talking in a few minutes," Midnight said to Roscoe with a chuckle.

"You ready, Shadrach?" Dalton asked. Shadrach nodded his head as the men in the circle began to get boisterous at the prospect of the fight and the possibility of Shadrach getting some long delayed revenge on their behalf against Roscoe.

"But he too big to fight," one of the prisoners said about Roscoe. A couple of other prisoners rumbled their concern.

"No one's too big for Shadrach. He's been punching above his weight his entire life," Dalton interrupted, which caused Shadrach to smile at the comment.

"Yeah, let's see how tough he be wit' out dat whip," Gabriel said in response.

Shadrach, still bleeding on his back from the whip, approached Roscoe with his arms raised. The difference in their height and weight was significant. Roscoe outweighed Shadrach by about 50 pounds and was several inches taller, but despite his imprisonment Shadrach's body still looked sculpted and solid.

"Anytime ya ready," Shadrach said.

Roscoe swung a looping right hand that caught Shadrach on the side of the head knocking him sideways but not down. He approached Shadrach again, carelessly, thinking this would be over quickly. Before Roscoe could throw another punch Shadrach put his head close to Roscoe's chest, eliminating the reach advantage of the bigger man, and began to hit him with a series of rock-hard lefts and rights into his mid-section. He almost doubled Roscoe over with a well placed kidney punch. The circle of men, perhaps realizing the advantage to Shadrach of keeping the men together, closed up around the two fighters.

"Chop him down!" Midnight yelled.

Roscoe kept swinging, glancing blows to Shadrach's head and shoulders, but Shadrach stayed too close for him to generate any power or do any damage. Shadrach kept pummeling the big man's body with hard kidney, stomach, and rib shots..10..15..20..25 times. Roscoe tried to push Shadrach off him to keep him at a distance and use his longer reach, to no avail. When Roscoe finally got Shadrach off of him momentarily the prisoners in the circle pushed him back towards Shadrach who continued his assault on Roscoe's middle. He would periodically land hard shots to Roscoe's head but his main focus was on Roscoe's midsection. Blood began to spill from Roscoe's nose and mouth as Shadrach busted up his insides. A grimace etched across Roscoe's face every time Shadrach landed a punch. As the fight continued Roscoe was having trouble holding up his hands to protect himself and trouble breathing because of the accumulation of body blows. The prisoners were screaming and cheering Shadrach on.

"Hit 'em! Hit 'em!" Skinny screamed out jumping up and down standing next to Levi as Shadrach landed another right to Roscoe's left eye which was nearly closed shut from swelling.

And then it happened. Shadrach connected with a left to the side of Roscoe's head and before Roscoe could recover his balance Shadrach dipped his right shoulder and in a blur of motion he landed a powerful right uppercut on Roscoe's chin snapping his head backwards. Then he landed a second uppercut as Roscoe's arms were falling lifeless to his side. Roscoe's eyes rolled back, his knees buckled, and he fell forward like newly cut timber onto the ground. The prisoners in the circle swarmed, hollered, and after a few well placed kicks, tied him up.

And suddenly they grew quiet. Levi had stepped up next to where Roscoe fell, stood over his body, and pushed back a few of the men who were kicking Roscoe. He looked around at them. No one was sure what he was going to do. He had picked up Roscoe's whip and held it by the handle as he continued to look at the men who moved uneasily back from him.

Reverend stepped up next to him, but Levi gently pushed him away. Levi stared at the whip in his hand. He then pointed at Skinny, as the men watched uneasy, and tried to speak but only a slight indecipherable moan came out of his mouth. He began to pull against the middle of the whip with one hand while holding the handle of the whip with his other hand. In a remarkable show of strength he pulled the handle off the whip. Then he wrapped the tip of the whip around his left hand and held the leather leading to it in his right hand. The muscles in his arms bulged, the veins in his neck became more prominent, and with his teeth clenched he pulled until the dried leather popped. He dropped the pieces of the whip onto the ground and raised his hands in the air as the men cheered.

"I told ya! I told ya he could do it!" Skinny yelled to the men as he stepped up next to Levi.

"Let's blow da mine," Shadrach then said, when the men's excitement with Levi was dying down.

"I know where's da dynamite," one of the prisoners said. He returned with a handful of dynamite sticks a few moments later. In short order two men ran the dynamite into the interior of the mine and placed sticks next to support beams.

"Skinny, ya says ya is fast. Run in and light da fuses," Shadrach said.

"I is not only good lookin' but I is also fast. Has to be wit' all da womens dat be chasin' afta me," Skinny said. And then, as he started toward the mine with a burning stick in hand, he turned and yelled back to the men: "Dis be for Rat and Toussaint!"

Skinny ran into the back of the mine lighting each fuse on the way out and then running up near the house where the rest of the men had gathered, leaving the guards and Mr. Talbot tied up in front of the entrance. A few moments later the first charge, deepest in the mine, exploded followed by two more explosions completely sealing the entrance to the mine sending debris and dust out of the mine which covered the guards and Talbot.

"They won't be using this place for a good while," Midnight said.

"Is there anyone in the house?" Dalton asked Talbot.

"Leave my home alone!" Talbot yelled.

"Burn it!" Dalton said, and in no time the men had lit brush and loose timbers to set the porch and roof ablaze.

"You will pay for this! You will pay for your crimes!" Talbot yelled as Reverend walked up to him.

"Mr. Talbot, as it is written in James, so it seems to be with you and your mouth; 'it is restless evil, full of deadly poison.' As a minister I do not believe in violence, but I have nothing against shutting up a sinner," Reverend said and then proceeded to pick up the soiled rag that had been in his mouth and put it into Talbot's mouth. He then went through Talbot's pockets and found over $1,000 in greenbacks and gold coins. He took back the monies Talbot stole from him, as the men stood around watching the house burn. He handed the rest of the money to Skinny to hand out to the men.

"Thanks, Reverend. I has to say I ain't never met a white man like ya," Skinny said. "Ya is a truest friend a man could have and I'm proudest to say I knowed ya. Wish dere be more like ya. Ya be safe goin' back to dat Boston. I think maybe Levi and I we gonna go to da North. We gonna be a good team workin' together. I be da brains and he be da muscles," Skinny said, as Levi stepped up next to Skinny and shook Reverend's hand.

"You both take care of yourselves as well. Go with my blessings," Reverend said.

"Men, split up. Don't stay together. Less chance of gettin' ya se'f caught," Shadrach told the assembled group. "Gabriel, ya be a'right wit dat leg?" Shadrach asked.

"I will. It be a long walk but I knows where I be goin,'" Gabriel answered.

Midnight had retrieved his horse and Dalton's and two more with saddles for Shadrach and Reverend from the nearby barn before it was also set afire.

"Might as well add horse stealing to our charges," Midnight joked. The four men mounted up as a final cheer went up from the men at the mine.

"We gots to get my sister," Shadrach said.

"She is over in the woods. We brought her with us," Midnight said.

CHAPTER 61.

Cecilia was waiting at the edge of the woods. As the men approached on horseback Cecilia emerged from the woods running towards them with a make-shift knapsack on her back. The knapsack had food, Midnight's gun, gunbelt, and another pistol that Mr. Blanchfield had given her. Dalton was in front so he slowed his horse and reached out his arm for Cecilia to grab. She did and in one fluid move he flung her up on his horse behind him. She wrapped her arms around his waist as Shadrach, Midnight, and Reverend approached.

"Let's put some distance between us and the mine," Midnight said, as they looked back toward the burning house. "That fire is going to draw some attention." The other men who had been enslaved in the mine were scattering, some running into the mountains and others headed in the opposite direction from the town.

"Agreed," Dalton replied and they started the horses at a gallop headed to the North.

After several hours of riding, slowing occasionally, on and off the main roads, they decided to stop and eat by a small lake. They had not spoken much as they rode fast and hard to get away from the mine. As soon as he dismounted Shadrach stepped over to help Cecilia get off Dalton's horse. They embraced.

Reverend, Midnight, and Dalton unsaddled the horses while Cecilia turned her attention to cleaning the wound on Shadrach's back. She had brought some men's work clothes which Mr. Blanchfield had given her and, after cleaning off in the lake, Shadrach put these on. Reverend also disrobed and bathed to get the red dust off him. Cecilia did her best to beat the dust off Reverend's clothes which were torn in several places.

Gradually the four men and Cecilia sat down to eat. Cecilia had some biscuits which she removed from her knapsack and Dalton had some jerky which they all shared. A canteen of water was passed around.

"I didn't think you were coming," Reverend said to Dalton.

"I got a second message from Midnight after they put you in the mine, sent by Mr. Blanchfield, right after the miners' strike in Union City had ended. Took the train as far as I could, bought a horse in Louisville, and damn near killed it getting here the rest of the way," Dalton replied.

"Did I hear ya right, ya'll killed Sheriff Maddox?" Shadrach asked. Midnight and Dalton immediately started laughing.

"What's so funny?" Reverend asked.

"He's not dead," Dalton said.

"He might wish it were so," Midnight said, again laughing.

"I figured we needed to be sure he was unavailable to come after us or to lead a posse when Midnight and I came to the mine and when we left, if we freed you two. So, after meeting with Midnight and Blanchfield at Blanchfield's place and coming up with a plan, I rode into town, stopped at the dry goods store and bought some jerky and a large bottle of castor oil. I then went over to the jail. It was actually Blanchfield's idea to use the castor oil on the sheriff. He said he had read about it being done in other countries. He seemed to get a real kick out of suggesting it, like he had been thinking about getting back at the sheriff for some time," Dalton said.

"He made the sheriff drink the whole bottle," Midnight said, as they all began to laugh.

"Oh, my! Dat's a strong laxative," Cecilia said.

"How did you manage that?" Reverend finally asked.

"Let's say he had to be convinced," Dalton said pulling his dragoon out. "I made him strip to his underwear. After he drank the castor oil I tied him up and gagged him. I left him locked in one of his cells and then took the cell keys, along with his clothes, and dropped them in the woods as we were headed to the mine."

"Dat gonna be one messy cell," Shadrach said.

"And a messy sheriff," Midnight said laughing as he spoke.

"Lordy, ya boys a like chil'ren," Cecilia said, as all four of the men laughed.

Castor oil was often used in the mid-1800s as punishment by the British in India and by the Belgians in their brutal colonization of the Congo. It was later used extensively in Italy by Mussolini's Black shirts against his political opponents.

"I sure hope dat Mr. Blanchfield be alright. He a good man," Shadrach said.

"I think he will be. He told us he was considering running for Congress," Midnight replied.

"Wouldn't dat be sometin' if we knowed a man dat be in da Congress," Cecilia said.

After eating the biscuits and jerky they saddled their horses and rode again at a gallop until it was dark.

"Decatur ought to be da next city," Shadrach said.

"We covered a good distance, I guess," Midnight replied. They set up camp and felt comfortable enough to start a fire and sleep for the night.

CHAPTER 62.

The following day they rode fast on their way toward Chattanooga, passing through many of the small towns and settlements that they had each passed through on their way to Elyton. They began to slow down, take their time, and relax, feeling that they had put enough distance between themselves and Elyton. Each night on the trail they sat around a campfire talking and catching up. Reverend had them all laughing with his story of Midnight trying to flirt with Emmalene. They sat somber as Dalton told of the gunfights with Batiste and Annala. Midnight told them about learning how to read from the Bible and learning about the women's rights movement. It was the conversation of friends who had simply paused for awhile and picked up where they left off that day when they were all discharged from the army. Dalton confided that he was having recurring nightmares about Petersburg and other battles. Reverend talked about his dreams of the wounded men who died while he had tended to them.

"I think I need to get away for awhile, away from people. Settle in somewhere in the woods. Maybe I need to step away from using my gun and from things that might bring the memories back," Dalton said, revealing to his friends the weight of his war experiences.

"Probably a good idea. The wilderness might be a good place for reflection," Reverend replied.

The group noticed that each time Dalton spoke of his nightmares it was Cecilia who seemed to soothe him. Often when the others had bedded down for the night Dalton and Cecilia stayed up talking next to the fire. There was a growing intimacy between them but neither Dalton or Cecilia was sure what to do about it.

Laws barring interracial marriage had existed for many years in many states but the term 'miscegenation' was first used during the Civil War to stoke fear and try to discredit the abolitionists with the claim that they were promoting interracial marriage. The laws that were passed by the states generally prohibited mixed race marriages, cohabitation, and/or sexual relations between the races. Such laws were originally upheld by the Supreme Court in the 1883 decision of *Pace v. Alabama*. It was not until the case of *Loving v. Virginia* in 1967 that the Supreme Court reversed itself and held that such laws were unconstitutional as a violation of the Equal Protection Clause of the Fourteenth Amendment.

"What were you doing in that town, Elyton?" Dalton finally asked one evening, after the others had gone to sleep. Cecilia pursed her lips together and looked away from him. A single tear rolled down her cheek. "Sorry, I mean you don't have to answer," Dalton said, concerned that he had overstepped his bounds.

"No, I need to be honest. Da man dat bought me durin' da war kept me dere to do favors for him and other white men. I couldn't get away. He bought all da women dat was dere," she said, her voice breaking with a few more tears shed as she turned back to him. Dalton replayed in his mind several times what she had said before responding. He had heard about such things and could see the repressed trauma in her eyes.

"I guess we all have things in our lives we need to forget, or get past," Dalton finally said. Cecilia nodded her head. "And remember, I think this is important to remember, what that saloon owner and those other men did was not your fault," he said. Cecilia smiled through her tears at his kind words.

"It's gonna take time to try to forget, if I ever can. Might be hard to do like doze battle memories ya have. I rather be thinkin' 'bout da future now dat I'm free of it. What 'bout you?" Cecilia asked.

"Me, I'll be alright. I just been having too many dreams about the war and it has me thinking about what I did," Dalton said.

"Ya said dat, but 'bout what in particular?" Cecilia asked. "I'd like to know more if ya don't mind talkin' 'bout it."

"I killed a lot of people in the war. Maybe some deserved it, maybe others didn't. At the time I didn't think too much about it. It was just what we had to do as soldiers. Killed some up close and others at a distance off as a sniper. And I've killed some men since the war. It never bothered me before, but the dreams of reliving Petersburg and a few other battles we were in are difficult. Wakes me up sometimes. I hope it don't continue. Not sure what to do about it," Dalton said, pinching his lips together once he spoke.

"Sounds like ya got lots of courage to have done doze things," Cecilia said to try to be supportive.

"Courage comes easy when it wraps itself in what other people need. At least for me. Now I need to find my own," Dalton replied.

"Dat's interestin'. Sometimes da battles we fights wit' ourselves, wit' what dey call our conscience, are da toughest ones to win. At least dat be true for me," Cecilia said.

"Yeah, I guess. You know we tell ourselves there are things we won't do, things we were taught were wrong, and then, especially in war, we do 'em. How do we explain that?" Dalton managed to say.

"Maybe talkin' 'bout it would help. Maybe ya also needs to get away from da killin' and let someone take care of ya and den try to live different so ya ain't always reminded of it. Momma used to say when things on da plantation was hard on us 'don't let da past be da future.' Maybe you just needs to look forward 'cause den da past ain't on ya heavy so much," Cecilia said, looking at Dalton with the simmering fire reflected on her face.

"Sounds like your mom was a smart one. I barely knew mine. She died of the fever when I was young," Dalton confided.

"How old was ya?" Cecilia asked.

"Nine. My old man died about two years later in a gunfight. I was on my own after that," Dalton said before pausing. "Ain't never really learned how to be in a relationship," Dalton confided more quietly. Cecilia reached out and touched his hand. Dalton seemed to blush in response.

"Momma got shot durin' da war defendin' Mr. Walker's house. Guess she thought it was her own. I wasn't dere to help as Mr. Monroe had already bought me from Mr. Walker. Ain't never known my father. Momma never spoke of him. People say he might a been a white man," Cecilia explained.

It was not uncommon for former slaves not to know who their fathers were, especially if he was white. For example, neither Frederick Douglass or Booker T. Washington knew for certain who his father was.

"Looks like other than Shadrach, neither one of us have any family," Dalton replied.

"Yeah, dat seem true. Well, we talk 'bout it more later, but ya needs ya rest now," Cecilia said.

"Taking care of me already," Dalton said and they both smiled.

CHAPTER 63.

A week and a half later they arrived in Louisville, Kentucky.

"Back where we started," Reverend said, as he dismounted near the middle of town in front of a diner. Dalton stayed on his horse with Cecilia seated behind him, her arms wrapped loosely around his waist. Midnight got off his horse as well to go into the diner with Reverend, but Shadrach stayed on his horse.

"Midnight, Reverend, I been talking with Cecilia and Shadrach and we are going to head up to the Montana territory, into the mountains," Dalton said.

"Goin' somewhere, I hope, where dere ain't so much hate, no burden of da past on us, and we can live free," Shadrach replied. Reverend and Midnight stepped up next to Dalton and Shadrach's horses and shook hands with each man.

"I'm headed back to Columbus," Midnight replied, stepping back from Shadrach's horse. "Back to Father Sprecht and the church."

"And to Emmalene?" Reverend asked.

"If she'll have me," Midnight said.

"If? Ya has to make it happen," Shadrach said, with a light-hearted laugh.

"I'm back to Boston and Theresa. You know where to reach me," Reverend said.

"No long goodbyes this time," Dalton replied, again uneasy with the emotion of departing, as he tipped his hat to each of them and turned his horse to leave.

"Stay out of trouble, my brothers," Reverend said to Dalton and Shadrach.

"It does seem to follow us," Dalton replied.

"I be keepin' dem both outta trouble," Cecilia said, over her shoulder.

"Dat might be a full time job," Shadrach joked.

"Dalton, before you leave, I've got a present for you. Don't think Father Sprecht would mind," Midnight said. Dalton reined his horse back in and stopped as Midnight stepped up next to him. He pulled the Bible from his pocket and handed it to Dalton who gave it to Cecilia to hold for him.

"Thanks," Dalton said.

"It kept me safe. Maybe it will do the same for you and help keep them dreams away," Midnight replied, stepping back from Dalton's horse.

"And you should study it," Reverend said, as he and Midnight watched Dalton and Shadrach turn their horses to start to ride off.

"Damn, Reverend. Always preaching!" Dalton yelled, waving his hand before his horse broke into a trot.

"Invite us to da wedding!" Shadrach yelled back to Midnight.

Reverend and Midnight watched until the others were almost out of sight.

"Midnight, let's get something to eat. I need to talk to you about how you are going to deal with Emmalene," Reverend said, placing his hand on Midnight's shoulder.

"Reverend, trust me I need all the help I can get," Midnight replied, as they walked into the diner.

A BRIEF BIBLIOGRAPHY

To read more about the practice of debt peonage or the leasing of convicts in the South, after the Civil War and until the 1940s, pick up *Slavery By Another Name*, by Douglas Blackmon and/or *Worse Than Slavery*, by David M. Oshinsky. For more information about the development of the for profit prison system and its use by southern states pick up *American Prison*, by Shane Bauer and/or *Slavery and the Penal System*, by Thorsten Sellin. To read about slavery before the Civil War see *The War Before The War*, by Andrew Delbanco. To read an analysis of the Civil War from a theological perspective read *The Civil War as a Theological Crisis*, by Mark A. Noll. To read about the role of whiskey in war, including the Civil War, pick up *Bourbon and Bullets: True Stories of Whiskey and Military Service*, by John C. Tramazzo. For additional information about state sponsored churches in the 1700s and early 1800s see *Church and State in America, The First Two Centuries*, by James H. Hutson. For a fascinating and detailed overview of the world inhabited by slaves see *Roll, Jordan, Roll*, by Eugene D. Genovese. For an interesting overview of the limits of slave marriages see, "The

History of Slave Marriages in the United States," 39 J. Marshall L. Rev. 299 (2006) by Darlene C. Goring. For an overview of abuses by Union troops in the South read *War Crimes Against Southern Civilians*, by Walter Brian Cisco. To read about slave revolts pick up *American Negro Slave Revolts*, by Herbert Aptheker. To read about John Brown's life and his attempt to start a revolt, see W.E.B. DuBois biography entitled, *John Brown*. For significant information about the Reconstruction period read *Reconstruction, America's Unfinished Revolution, 1863-1877*, by Eric Foner, *Black Reconstruction in America*, by W.E.B. Du Bois and *Reconstruction, a Concise History*, by Allen C. Guelzo. For more information about the successful slave rebellion in Haiti read *The Black Jacobins*, by C.L.R. James. To read about the towns set up by former slaves in the Oklahoma territory check out "The All Black Towns in Oklahoma" by Hannibal B. Johnson at www.hannibalbjohnson.com. For an excellent biography of Andrew Johnson and his motivations for opposing Reconstruction see *Andrew Johnson, a Biography*, by Hans L. Trefousse. Similarly, for an overview of Jefferson Davis' life and his arguments for secession, see *Jefferson Davis, American*, by William J. Cooper Jr. For information about the 1877 Compromise which ended Reconstruction and resulted in Rutherford B. Hayes becoming president, see *Reunion and Reaction, The Compromise of 1877 and the End of Reconstruction*, by C. Vann Woodward or *Fraud of the Century*, by Roy Morris Jr. For information on words and language from Africa that slaves brought to America, see *Travels in the Confederation*, by Johann David Schoepff. Finally for more information on black soldiers who served in integrated units for the Union read, *The Forgotten Black Soldiers in White Regiments During the Civil War*, by Juanita D. Moss.

DISCUSSION QUESTIONS

What effects, if any, do you think the forceful breakup of slave families had upon the African American family structure going forward?

Why do you think southern states passed anti-literacy laws making it a crime to educate slaves?

What long term effects did the Civil War and Reconstruction create for the relationship between state governments and the federal government? Were these positive or negative?

What do you think about southern governments leasing convicts to private companies in order to raise revenue for the states?

What do you think about ministers using excerpts from the Bible to support slavery?

What effects did the existence of slavery have upon the slave owners?

To what extent is southern culture, even today, rooted in the historical relationship between the slaves and the slave masters?

How does the history contained in this book compare with the history you were taught in school about slavery and Reconstruction?

ALSO BY MICHAEL T. TUSA JR.

"...A soul-searching quest reminiscent of the great twentieth-century existentialist narratives." —Gary Gautier, Ph.D., author of *Hippies*, *Mr. Robert's Bones*, and *Year of the Butterfly*

A Second Chance at

Dancing

A MEMOIR OF SORTS

Michael T. Tusa, Jr.

Author of *Advancing On Chaos*

CHASING
CHARLES
BUKOWSKI

MICHAEL T. TUSA, JR.

Made in the USA
Las Vegas, NV
04 June 2023

72936197R00215